MW01703115

Hanson Mitchell is the author of a series of books collected together as *The Scratch Flat Chronicles* that focus on a single square mile of agricultural land in eastern Massachusetts.

He is also the author of *Looking for Mr. Gilbert*, the story of his discovery of the lost glass plate negatives of the first African-American landscape photographer. It was while he was researching that book that he uncovered the story of Marcus Aurelius.

He also happens to be the descendant of one of the players in this book.

For Clayton and Lelia

Hanson Mitchell

The Sweet Revenge of Marcus Aurelius

Based on the True Story of a Slave Who Sold his Master

Austin Macauley Publishers™
London • Cambridge • New York • Sharjah

Ordering Information
Quantity sales: Special discounts are available on quantity purchases by corporations, associations, and others. For details, contact the publisher at the address below.

Publisher's Cataloging-in-Publication data
Mitchell, Hanson
The Sweet Revenge of Marcus Aurelius

ISBN 9781647506278 (Paperback)
ISBN 9781647506285 (ePub e-book)

Library of Congress Control Number: 2024902474

www.austinmacauley.com/us

First Published 2024
Austin Macauley Publishers LLC
40 Wall Street, 33rd Floor, Suite 3302
New York, NY 10005
USA

mail-usa@austinmacauley.com
+1 (646) 5125767

First and foremost I would like to thank Susan Harvey for our long conversations on the Atlantic slave trade, plantation life, and the French and American abolition movement. Also, Sheridan Harvey at the Library of Congress, as well as the staff at the Virginia Historical Society, the research team at Oatlands Plantation, and the staff members at the James River plantations, Berkeley and Shirley Plantation. In New Orleans, thanks to the people at the Whitney Plantation and the staff at the Historic New Orleans Collection and the New Orleans Historical Society. For information on Gulf of Mexico shipping lanes, thanks to Tony Higgins, and also W.H Bunting, for information on 19th century passenger vessels, as well as Mary Decher for her information on 19th century carriages and horse breeds. Those are only a few of the various contacts in Richmond and Leesburg, Virginia, Paris, France, as well as the street guides, carriage drivers, street musicians, and gossip mongers of the New Orleans French Quarter.

Table of Contents

His story, probably growing with age, has beguiled many a lonely hour.
Enaes Africanus, 1872

He was born with the gift of laughter and a sense that the world was mad.
Rafael Sabatini

The horror! The horror!
Joseph Conrad

Notices

1845 Reward: $50 Fled Mayfield Plantation on June 7th:
Marcus Aurelius. Light-complexioned. Six feet. Last seen wearing tattered cutaway and field trousers.
Subscriber H. Johnston

1846 Reward: $75 Fled: Mayfield Plantation: Marcus Aurelius.
September 3 or 4.
May be in the region around Mary Plantation, Charles City.
Tall, light-skinned with distinctive green eyes.
Believed to be carrying a forged pass.
May feign ignorance of the English language.
Subscriber: Horace Johnston

1847 September Reward: $90 Escaped from Mayfield Plantation, Charles City: Marcus Aurelius. Light-skinned. Tall.
Wearing upon escape his master's red waistcoat and striped flannel trousers.
This man is skilled at disguises, including that of a supposed French nobleman.
Can be identified by his distinctive green eyes.
Caution: May be armed with a Navy cutlass and two pistols.
Horace Johnston Mayfield 1854 New Orleans

Wanted: Dead or Alive Generous Reward:
Two hundred dollars if captured alive. One hundred dollars, dead.
For the return of Marcus Aurelius, my valet.
Escaped New Orleans on 3 September.
Attention:
This man is armed and may be dressed in a blue waistcoat cutaway and calfskin riding boots.
Tall, light-skinned, Virginia-born Negro with distinctive green eyes.
This man is haughty and dangerous.
Fluent in French and Spanish and is a notorious impostor.
May claim to be a French nobleman visiting America.
Carries an expensive Coulax dueling sword.
May also be in possession of identity papers in the name of subscriber.

Caution:

Do not attempt to apprehend this man unless armed. Report sightings to local militia James Hubbard, Esq.

New Orleans:

HISTORICAL NOTE

According to the records, it should be added that there was nothing in the flyers, bulletins, bills, broadsides, newspaper ads, and posters that followed this man's various escapes about the fact that Marcus Aurelius was read deeply in both French and English. That he was also fluent in Spanish and the Creole dialect. Was a skilled duelist, a violinist in the devil's style, and an unusually handsome man to boot, with high cheekbones, slightly almond-shaped green eyes, a straight nose and a square chin. It was his hair and his cocoa-colored skin that gave him away, and that alone meant very little in the mixed-race culture of New Orleans where he was last seen.

Notes in the slave rolls of the three plantations where he was held indicate that, along with his smooth talk and apparent good manners, Mac, aka Marcus Aurelius, was a scoundrel: He was an inveterate liar, a constant runaway, and a man skilled at trickery and disguises. Extant documents also make clear that he was comfortable with whites, especially Europeans, and he was affable, entertaining, and believed to be the lover of not a few women of French society—although that may be merely the gossip of those Americans in Paris who knew him.

Part One

The James River Bottomlands
First Big River to Cross

Put the case that in 1862, after many travels and travails, having secured a fine estate in the countryside near Rambouillet, France, Count Marc d'Aurèle (*soi-disant*) retired to compose his memoirs.

At the time, the good Count would content himself with walks through the countryside, evening musicales with his wife Tillisande, and periodic work on his letters. But in spite of his current circumstance, life for the Count was not always comfortable. For the first twenty-five years, Count Marc, formerly known as Mac or Marcus Aurelius, had been held in bondage in the United States of America as a slave.

Put the case further that on a fine May morning in 1865 in Rambouillet, Count Marc found himself beside a small tributary that ran down the east side of his holdings to the river Hay, where he settled on a dry bank to watch the misty spears of sun break through the lacework of the vernal trees. Trout were feeding in the clear waters of the stream that day; the lilies of the valley were all abloom around him, and above, in the green bower of the tree canopy, he could hear the songs of the cuckoo, blackbird, and thrush. But sitting there, musing on the pleasures of his current situation, his reverie was rudely interrupted by the thunder of horse hooves and the baying of hounds out on the Versailles highway.

These were merely the foxhounds of his neighbor and nothing to concern himself with. But what individual who has ever been held in bondage for any length of time can ever be truly free? What's past is present in certain hours of the night for such a people. And the baying, coming as it did in the midst of a pleasant daydream in which linear time was suspended, propelled the Count back into darker days along the James River bottomlands of Tidewater

Virginia, when, at age of nineteen, he had also heard the baying of pursuing hounds.

******

He was on his feet in an instant that morning and running before he was even fully awake. He snatched up his satchel of victuals and a stolen cutlass, charged into the brush and raced onward through the swampy tangle where he had hidden after a night of slow travel. Four days earlier Marcus Aurelius had executed a successful escape from Mayfield Plantation and he was now headed for freedom.

Or so he believed.

His course through the swamp that morning was checked by cypress knees and thickets of buttonbush and catbrier. But he knew where he was, and within a few minutes of hard running and tripping and barked shins, he came to a wide slow-running stream that he had passed the night before. Here he stopped in a sunny clearing to listen for the dogs and catch his breath. He could hear the slow approach of the hounds to the north, but they were still far off, and he sat down to rest before entering the water. Then, minutes later, he heard a closer bark.

He stood and heard another powerful bark followed by a loud snarl. A huge lion-brown dog broke from the brush and charged across the clearing at him.

Without forethought, Marcus snatched up his stolen cutlass, cocked it back over his right shoulder like a broad sword and waited.

Just as the dog leaped for his throat, he dodged to the right and brought the sword down across the dog's neck. It gave out a low, gurgled bark, and, propelled by the downward force of the cutlass strike, dropped to the ground, its legs quivering.

He knew this type of dog. It was one of the so-called slave hounds—vicious curs trained specifically to track people of African descent. They were kept in kennels and freed only to hunt escapees. Marcus had known about them since childhood. A dog of this sort had killed a boy on a nearby plantation when he was growing up.

Marcus stood in shock, staring down at the body of the dog. It had all happened so fast. It was unreal, an instinctive, primal interplay of man against beast. Slowly, he became aware of the approaching pack of the more distant hounds, and still dazed and shaking he gathered his things and waded into the water.

This was September, and the waters of the stream were sluggish and warm, and he kicked and splashed his way downstream, riding with the slow current and doing his best to keep his satchel of food dry and listening all the while for the yelp of the pursuing hounds.

Marcus Aurelius was not by any means a strong swimmer. In his time, slaveholders would not allow their charges to learn to swim for just the reason now evident. It made escape from dogs easier.

Behind him, he could still hear the confused baying of the hounds, some casting about to the northeast, upstream, some snuffling southward along the western bank.

Slowly, more confident now as the baying faded, he turned and floated with the current under the rose-colored morning sky and watched the network of leafed branches pass overhead.

Where all this would end he did not know. But the waters of the rivulet cooled the still raw welts of the whiplash etched into his back, and whatever lay ahead could hardly be worse than what he had left behind.

It was the final beating at the hands of the overseer that inspired this latest flight. The whip had only served to fix his determination to make a definitive run or die in the process. This was his last try, and he knew his fate if captured again.

Mayfield Plantation
Wade in the Water

According to the records, the slave known as Marcus Aurelius was perhaps the worst possible sort of individual to be held in bondage. He could read, he was single, he was strong, male, independent-minded, and in the parlance of the time, a 'rascal'—just the type that did not make an obedient house servant or field hand. Such types were haughty, inclined to disobey, and at some point would surely attempt escape.

Horace Johnston, the owner of Mayfield Plantation, had a workforce of eighty slaves, the majority of them trained by one means or another to be obedient and hardworking. Marcus Aurelius was not one of them. Not that he was disfigured by cropped ears or a cheek brand; quite the contrary: he was tall, with smooth light-colored skin, curious green eyes, and a handsome high forehead and sharp cheekbones. It was his hauteur that got him into trouble. He would not jump when commanded, was slow to obey, and, on occasion, would look a white person in the eye, something no slave was permitted to do—eyes must be lowered and hats removed while speaking to whites. Marcus would hold the glare just long enough and then, slowly, obey. He was thus marked. His type bore watching.

This September flight through the swamps was his fourth escape and, as did many would-be runaways, he knew the locations of safe houses along the Underground Railroad—most of them in his area lay to the north of the James River where Mayfield Plantation was located. He knew also that the patrollers would scour the northern route first and that the bulletins and escaped slave notices would be distributed during the week after he broke free and would be printed in the escaped slave ads in the local newspapers not long after that.

On the first night of this final flight, he had sculled out to mid-river in a stolen punt and proceeded downstream, letting the current carry him along, past swamps of walled cypress and the open sweep of the isolated plantation fields that ran down to the river bank. His intention was to head in the wrong direction, that is to say, southeast, away from the North Star, the benign guide for most escaped slaves fleeing northward.

Two nights after his escape, before first light, he clambered ashore, hid the punt in the shrubbery and sloshed through the swampy bottomland to a dry spot where he spent the day, alternately sleeping and eating. He had stolen a Navy cutlass and had been supplied with sweet potatoes and slabs of bacon by friendly kitchen help. He had also managed to copy a map of East Virginia, from Charles City down to Norfolk. His plan was to row downstream, stop above Norfolk, and then strike off inland and southward, an unlikely course for most local runaways.

By dawn on the third day, he calculated that he had gained thirty or so miles, which he determined to be a suitable site north-east of Norfolk. The next night, traveling by dead reckoning and the rudimentary map, he once more headed south, trekking through dank bottomlands and dark halls of cypress and oak. His intention was to reach the Great Dismal Swamp, southwest of Norfolk, a vast, dank wilderness that stretched from southern Virginia into North Carolina.

As early as the mid-18th century, the swamp housed a renegade population of escaped slaves known as maroons. Most of these people had fled from local plantations, but a few were newly arrived Africans who had bolted as soon as they landed and fled to the interior, and even without knowledge of the local plants and animals, nor any sense of the geography of the new land, had survived and made their way to the refuge. Even in the time of Marcus Aurelius, the 1840s, native Africans with no knowledge of English were living free in the swamp. The place was also a hideaway for a few white criminals, and also the remnants of the broken people of the local Native American tribes.

His idea was to find a settlement, shelter with the maroons for a few weeks or months, and then retrace his steps northward, after the patrollers had been called off. He would still be in danger from the regular militia-like patrols that worked the back roads on a regular basis, the so-called paddyrollers. But they were easy to hear on their approaches and easily avoided. Furthermore, Marcus had forged a pass for himself that he carried tucked into his shirt wrapped in a leathern wallet. He guarded it as carefully as a pilgrim would guard a sliver of the True Cross, although he hoped fervently that he would never have to use it.

****

Once out of hearing of the dogs, that September day, Marcus moved onto high ground, found a place in the sun, stripped, and sat there drying himself and his clothes. It was then mid-morning and he was hungry. Nothing unusual about that, he had been hungry for the last three days, portioning out his supplies, which were now almost finished.

Having consumed the last of his stolen foods, Marcus began to forage. In one section of the woods, he discovered a batch of groundnuts, which he consumed raw, also a stand of hog peanuts, which offered a mere handful or two of tiny pea-like root nodules, hardly worth digging out. He pushed on, haunted all the while by the thought of the baying of hounds, some imaginary, some perhaps real. He found more groundnuts and a batch of bitter greens, and finally, he scooped down and ate some soil, a supplement that his old seasoned-escapee friend, Jemma, had claimed would at least stave off hunger and even supply a few necessary minerals.

Marcus slept, walked, foraged, and lost track of days until finally, early one morning, he came upon an isolated house and farm with chickens. Marcus decided to commit his first crime (or at least his first crime away from the plantation). He had come upon the place before dawn, and he broke into the coop, stole two chickens and fled back to the borderlands before the aroused flock could wake the owners.

He had also learned from old Jemma the art of skinning and the use of a fire drill, in the absence of flint and steel. Using his new skills, after a great deal of effort he managed to get a fire going, and he singed the chicken, tore it open with his teeth, gutted it and, using a greenwood spit, managed to cook at least part of it. The meat sustained him for three more days, at which point he calculated that his final destination was near at hand.

Shockoe Bottom, Richmond, Virginia
The Slave Sale

Historical documents indicate that Marcus Aurelius was born in 1825 to Lucilla Bishop, a young woman enslaved on the Live Oak Hundred Plantation outside Norfolk, Virginia. His actual father was unknown, but inasmuch as the child was light-skinned and had distinctive green eyes, his father was undoubtedly white, or at least a Quadroon, a quarter-African. One earlier Virginia record suggests that his grandmother was a descendant of John Wayles, the father of Thomas Jefferson's wife, Martha. But that much is hearsay; it was perhaps struck from the histories set down by the post-war chroniclers.

The boy was called Mac; the name Marcus Aurelius was given to him later, when he was about seven years old. As far as any child knows, he was born free; he had to learn that he was enslaved. In his infancy, he was carried to the fields by his mother and set in the grass at the side of the cultivated land while she picked tobacco. On some plantations, hungry slave babies were left in the grass to wale until sundown when the workday ended. But his mother's master was not ruthless, nor was the overseer, and whenever the baby woke, Lucilla was allowed to leave the field and nurse him.

As soon as Marcus was able to walk, he was turned out to play, as were other children of the plantation, both white and black. These were the best years of his life, as it was for many underage slaves. He was too young to work, probably didn't even understand that he was Black, or for that matter actually 'owned' by someone—all that would come later, after he was seven.

In August, 1842, rumors began spreading around his plantation that the master was preparing to sell a group of slaves. At this time in Virginia, the tobacco croplands were wearing out. In 1808, the United States government had outlawed the sale of transported Africans, although the trade still went on illegally. With the profits from tobacco declining in Virginia, and new cotton lands and sugar plantations opening up in the Deep South, there was only one profitable crop left, and that was the sale of slaves. And Virginian-born slaves were, so it was believed, the best trained, the healthiest, and the best workers.

As it turned out, the rumors of a pending sale were true, and one morning the overseer rounded up all of the seventy-five plantation slaves. He and the master circulated among them and selected ten men and eight women. Lucilla, Mac's mother, was among them.

Lucilla grabbed the boy's wrist and pulled him along by her side, half hiding him in her skirts. There was an old live oak behind the summer kitchen and the selected slaves were told to sit there in the shade and rest. About an hour later, an angular man in a soiled linen suit and a slouch hat rode into the yard in a wagon, followed by three scruffy, armed white men on horseback. The three men were told to rest on the porch, while the man in the linen suit went into the house with the owner.

The morning stretched on. The men on the porch smoked. One came by and looked over the people seated under the oak. No one spoke. The other two wandered over and the three of them talked quietly, out of hearing. They kicked the dust, hitched up their pants; one of them spit. They pushed back their slouch hats. Smoked. Laughed at something, all the while glancing over at the collected slaves shaded under the live oak, some few looking back at white men under their brows, surreptitiously.

The cicadas were whining in the fields. The heat increased and the people under the oak could see shimmering heat waves in the distant fields. Time was a heavy elephant, pressing on them. They knew, all of them, what was coming. Some of these people had been sold before. Some grew up on the plantation and were not familiar with the auction block. But everyone, young and old, men and women, knew what was about to happen. They lived day and night with the threat of sale and the break-up of families, mothers and fathers from children, couples, friends, and allies.

After a while, the owner and the man in the linen suit came out and the overseer told everyone to get up and come over to the porch.

This was the dreaded hour.

Lucilla's hand tightened on the boy's wrist.

"What's happening?" Mac wanted to know.

"Hush," she said.

"But we going down the river, Mama?" he asked.

"Hush up," she said. Her hand tightened. He scrunched down behind her back, hiding his face in her skirts, as if to banish the reality.

They stood in a line strung along the front of the house while the buyer walked up and down. He grabbed a young man's chin and turned his head left to right, drew back his lips and checked his teeth. Down the line, checking the condition of his future purchases, until he came to Lucilla.

Mac was hard pressed now against her back legs, nearly invisible in her voluminous skirts.

"Do I see a little pickaninny hiding back there?" the buyer asked in a joking way. He reached around and dragged the boy around to Lucilla's side. "What's your name, little boy?" he asked.

"His name be Mac and he's my only little boy," Lucilla answered.

The buyer turned to Lucilla and grabbed her chin, turning it from side to side, checked her teeth, felt her breasts and hips. She was tall, well fed, and full.

Good stock.

Of the eighteen people lined up, twelve were told to step forward. Lucilla was among them, and she pulled Mac out with her.

"He didn't say nothing about that little boy," the plantation overseer said to her.

"He's my only little boy," Lucilla said.

"We know that."

"Well, I ain't going without him," Lucilla said. She looked over at old Massa, who was standing to the side, his thumbs tucked into his waistcoat. He looked away when she fixed his eyes. No words; she just looked. He was not a bad master as slaveholders go. Sundays off. Big, weeklong Christmas holidays. Not a bad sort, and in fact reluctant to sell his people. But money was tight. Three bad years. He nodded back to Lucilla.

"It's all right," he said to the buyer, "take the boy."

That afternoon, the sale completed, the men were chained together ankle to ankle. The women, unchained, lined up behind them, and they set off on the Richmond road. The buyer rode ahead in a wagon; the three men with him drove the slaves, two behind the women, one at the head of the coffle of chained men. It was a three-day walk plus a barge ride.

The Richmond slave market was the biggest in the United States outside of New Orleans, also one of the most infamous. It was located in the Shockoe Bottom district along one of the canals and included a number of auction houses and slave pens where the enslaved people were held, sometimes for weeks. Lucilla and Mac were held for three days in one of the pens with a few others from their plantation and a number of strangers.

On the day of the auction, Lucilla was outfitted with a full osnaburg cotton dress and a white apron with a red ribbon at her throat and a red bandanna tied over her hair. The idea was to present her as a well-cared for woman, clean, competent, a fine house servant if needed, but also strong if she were to be sent to the fields. There was in fact no need to doctor Lucilla up; she was healthy and strong and well-fed.

Mac too was dressed for the sale. He never wore any clothes at all for the first few years of his life, and later he was dressed in a heavy cotton smock. Now, they dressed him in pants and a white cotton shirt.

The auction posters had been up for three weeks, and on the day of the sale, crowds began to gather. There were fifty people all told for sale that day, men and boys, women, some girls: 'bucks', 'wenches', 'pickaninnies', all advertised as healthy.

The bidding started at ten o'clock.

Mac and Lucilla and the others from her plantation were sitting in a wide room in back of the block, which in this case was a sort of stage. After an hour's wait, they were brought out together, Mac still clinging to his mother's skirt with his left hand, right hand in his mouth.

This was late September, and there was a white couple from a James River plantation visiting Richmond that day, Mr. and Mrs. Gabriel Maxwell from Greenwood Plantation. Willa Maxwell had a sister in Richmond and the three of them decided, on a whim, to attend the auction. They came a little late and stood around, watching the proceedings: the auctioneer, announcing each group, or individual, the potential buyers, poking and probing and squeezing and questioning the slaves about their past positions.

There was, on these dark occasions, a certain dynamic that went on between the buyer and the person who was to be sold. It was a complex, understated arrangement and required a certain skill on the part of both parties. The buyers knew exactly who and what they were looking for. But the slave, especially those who had been sold a few times, had developed an art of selecting potential buyers. This involved an ability to judge character, not only from looks, but by behavior, as well as a little sensitivity to unseen aspects of the character of the buyer. As best they could, slaves worked the buyer. They determined among the crowd who would be a good master and who would not.

It was easier to discourage a sale—a sneer, a glare, an ability to play the part of a stoop-shouldered weakling or a drooling fool. But it was also a dangerous game since the sellers too were watching, and any obvious misbehavior would be dealt with if a pending sale fell through because of the slave's antics. The chosen punishment in such cases was a severe beating with the 'paddle', a device fitted out with holes, applied to the bare buttocks. The paddle left no scars, unlike the whip, and therefore did not necessarily discourage future sales. A heavily scarred back was a sure sign of a rebellious slave.

In the case of the Maxwell family, Lucilla had spotted them, made her choice, and played her part well. She repeatedly looked at them with a faint familiar smile, or an expression of mercy—indicating without words, *please buy me*. There were some nasty types among the buyers that day, cruel-looking, narrow-eyed devils carrying mean-looking canes. There were also a few haughty, self-assured, well-fed white men in linen suits who stood by watching the sales. And then there were the pleasant types, innocents almost, with kindly eyes. The Maxwells were among this latter group, and they noticed Lucilla and her cute little boy—that is to say, Willa Maxwell spotted the cute little boy.

She leaned over when Lucilla was brought out, and said, "Gabriel, look at the cute little pickaninny up there, clinging to his mama's skirts."

And Gabriel Maxwell looked up at Lucilla and Lucilla looked back at Mr. Maxwell, and there was a certain inexplicable, unconscious and agreeable exchange.

The bidding started: $600 for Lucilla, $670, including the boy.

A man in the back row offered $600, no boy. Lucilla's hand tightened on Mac's wrist.

The auctioneer asked for more bids. No takers. Lucilla's heart began to hammer.

"$650, no boy," someone shouted.

Willa leaned over. "Gabriel, say something, you can't let that little boy go."

"$680 with the boy," Maxwell said.

"$680, do I hear more?" the auctioneer shouted.

A bidding war started. $900, $1000, $1500, $2000, and upward.

"Bid, Gabriel!" Mrs. Maxwell whispered. "Bid."

The prices rose.

"$2500," Maxwell called.

"$2500, then. Do I hear more?" the auctioneer said.

Silence. "This here is a fertile wench if ever they was one," the auctioneer shouted. "You look at her. Full bust, wide hips. You look at her healthy pickaninny."

Lucilla could barely breathe. She felt faint.

Silence.

Lucilla's world began to spin.

"This little boy, you look at him. A fine healthy field hand, in just a couple of years." [That would be age nine, old enough for a working slave child.] "Or a house boy," the auctioneer added.

Silence.

"I'm looking here at over $3,000 worth of chattel if you count that boy when he grows up. Maybe $3,500 or more. Do I hear a bid?"

Silence.

Lucilla's world beyond the stage was turning. She heard voices without meaning, saw a whirl of upturned white faces, smelled the pungent odor of cigar smoke and fresh-washed cotton.

"This boy here," the auctioneer said. "You look at him. You look at his mother. This boy here alone could bring in over two or three thousand someday. Worth at market price more'n that. You got forty years of work from that little pickaninny."

Silence.

"Do I not hear more?" he said.

Silence.

"Sold then: $2500."

This unplanned, almost accidental sale would change the life of the child who would become Marcus Aurelius.

Greenwood Plantation
Amanda Maxwell

Greenwood Plantation, which had been in the Maxwell family for three generations, sat on the northern banks of the James River not far from the town of Charles City and just upstream from two other plantations located to the east. The estate was set on a rise above the river, above a series of plantings of boxwood rooms and florid ornamental gardens and parterres, overseen by Willa Maxwell herself, aided of course, by a team of enslaved gardeners who tended the flowers and clipped the extensive boxwood hedges.

The house itself was a Federalist-styled two-story building of brick, with double sashed windows and a gable roof with a traditional pillared front porch facing the river and wide double doors at both the north and south side, arranged so as to catch the cooling river breezes. There was an extensive vegetable garden just west of the porch with a summer kitchen close to the main house, and slave quarters running off in a double row of substantially framed wooded one-room cabins and a rough dirt track running between them. The walls of the cabins were lined with sleeping benches with a stone or wattled fireplace and chimney at the back wall. As many as six or eight family members lived in each cabin, and some of them had little fenced gardens off to one side. There were, at the time, about one hundred slaves working the mix of tobacco and cotton fields, something of an experiment arranged by Gabriel Maxwell, who seemed to have had a good eye for economic trends.

The agricultural fields lay to the east of the big house, some 200 acres all told, and 200 more of pasture land, woods, and bottom land along the river and all of it surrounded by wooded, uncultivated borderlands.

The Maxwells had two children, an older boy, Robert, and a younger eleven-year-old girl named Amanda, who was something of an enigma to her parents. She was one of those natural-born troublemakers who from time to time appear for no apparent reason in otherwise normal, traditional families, as if a genetic throwback to some wilder, more primitive ancestor.

When she was a young girl, as did all the plantation children, she played in the yards with whites and slave children. But unlike other girls, who were fond of gossip and dressing up and playing with dolls, Amanda learned to throw stones at frogs in the ornamental ponds of the estate. She fought the boys with sticks and clods of mud and would periodically beat up her older more tamed brother. She sometimes used barnyard language, sometimes talked like one of the 'darkies', and she could spit farther than any of the boys on the plantation white or black alike. But she also had a taste for books and learned to read at an early age. Along with her bad behavior, her mother and father recognized in her a certain high-spirited intelligence and, hoping to tame her, hired a tutor who was versed in the classics.

When she was ten, the family spent the summer touring France, an event that would change Amanda for life. She loved the country, and by the time she turned eleven, she could read and speak a little French. Thinking it might civilize her, the family hired a French tutor, an American woman who had lived in Paris for a few years. Amanda was also studying Latin, and she was fond of theater, influenced by some incomprehensible (to her) Molière plays she had seen in Paris with her parents. She would sometimes write little dramas for the neighborhood children and force her brother to act out parts and made little Black children play the parts of servants.

And then, at the height of her theater career, she met Mac.

On his first afternoon at Greenwood, Mac was led into the big house by Amanda's mother, who was holding him by the hand. The little boy had curious green eyes for a Black child and said nothing when he was introduced to his new charge. Willa Maxwell announced that the child was a little birthday present for Amanda.

It was love at first sight. Of all the slave children who had come and gone in her years, Amanda had never seen such a cute little boy, and she went over and stooped to his level, and he, being who he was then and would become in the future, stood his ground and stared into her eyes, something adult slaves were not supposed to do. But Mac was untrained (and would remain so).

Willa Maxwell ordered the boy to say hello to Miss Amanda, which he did. He greeted her haltingly and she asked him if he would like to meet her dog, Miss Pixie, and he would, he said, and so they went around to the back door and out to the summer kitchen where Miss Pixie lay in a dog bed under a work table. Amanda introduced the two of them formally, and said "why don't you pat her?" and so Mac squatted down and patted her back and then lay his head on the dog's shoulder, the dog all the while looking up at Amanda as if to say—"Is this OK?"

Within the first few weeks, Amanda made a pet of the boy. She would walk him along the local lanes with her favorite parlor dogs, stopping often to look at blooming weeds and catch crickets and grasshoppers. She showed Mac crab spiders and jumping spiders. She invented games for him and trained him to take on roles in her little theater pieces.

One day, on one of their dog walks in the woodlands on the western edge of the plantation, she instructed Mac to break off a small straight branch from a tree. Then she went on and found another and instructed him to break that off as well. "Good, now we are armed," she said. "There are said to be highwaymen riding through here."

"What a highwaymen?" Mac asked.

She explained; and then said she would teach him to defend himself in case of attack. She took up her stick, turned sideways to a tree trunk. "There's a devil now," she shouted and executed a fine lunge at the trunk.

Mac watched, wide-eyed, while she acted out a duel against another tree, and then another.

"You see," she said. "Like that. If ever we encounter a highwayman on our walks, we must fight them off, you hear?"

"Yessum," he said, having absolutely no idea what she was talking about. But he liked the stick part.

She handed him the second stick and proceeded to teach him parries and lunges and defense measures that she had calculated from descriptions in her readings of Alexander Dumas.

Mac was a good student, and recognizing his natural coordination, on every dog walk they would practice dueling. And then, having completed a lesson, she would set the dogs to barking and then fight off imaginary intruders. Then she began to write short dramatic sketches in which she would be attacked by highwaymen, and Mac, now playing the role of a cavalier, would come upon the scene, toss her a sword, draw out his knife, and fight off the gang.

In one drama, the two of them were cornered by a cruel black-bearded pirate. In the course of the struggle, Amanda lost her sword. Mac, having learned the art of fighting by then, circled the attacking pirate and stabbed him in the back.

"Well done, good sir. Very well executed," she said.

Mac very much enjoyed these fights. He had nothing better to do in those long summer afternoons the year he was seven. And by the time winter came, the two of them moved their theater indoors to a big attic room. Her parents approved of her companionship with Mac. It kept her from engaging in actual fights with the plantation children, and even improved her behavior somewhat, since in her dramas, she often played the part of a distressed demoiselle with refined parlor habits.

The tutor allowed the illiterate young enslaved boy to sit in the corner during Amanda's French lessons. She, Amanda, was surprised to learn that he had been listening all along and not daydreaming, so as a joke, she encouraged him to say words in French. And then, since he seemed to catch on, she encouraged him to actually speak French. Then she began sharing her Latin lessons. And then, recognizing in the boy a natural interest in actually learning, she broke an established state law. It was illegal, according to Virginia law, to teach a slave to read.

She taught him anyway.

"But tell no one," she said. "Not even your mama. That way, we'll have a private language."

Amanda also began to share her violin lessons with him. The two of them would retreat to the attic where she could practice alone. But in fact, half the practices were carried out by Mac. Then she shared her dancing lessons with him, and began to tell him stories out of the old romantic novels, which only served to induce in the boy a sense of a wider world, a world filled with possibility.

Amanda's lessons became something of an obsession with her. She had been taught that Africans were closer to animals than to human beings, and the fact that this little African boy could learn so quickly confused her, and intellectually curious soul that she was, she began to look on her lessons as something of a social experiment, although she didn't think of it that way.

News of abolition was in the air in those years in the South, and after Amanda recognized that this particular Black boy was perhaps special, she began to understand what the Yankees were talking about. She was nearly twelve by then, and she saw her project as a secret act of rebellion against her parents, her stupid older brother, and also in particular, Mr. Pottle, the overseer, a man whom she despised for the ease with which he used the whip, even on young women. Especially on young women, it seemed to her.

But there was something more. She had loved Mac since the day they met. But the love was more like that which she shared with her parlor dog, Miss Pixie. She at first saw the education of Mac as a matter of teaching the boy tricks, like a dog albeit a smart dog. But as she aged she saw, perhaps unconsciously, that this person was a human being. Her love evolved into a form of parental love. She wept sometimes at night alone in her bed to think of the life her society would soon cast him into.

Because of his agility and obvious wit, by the time he was put to work, at age eight, Mac was posted as a houseboy and not a field hand. They renamed him 'Marcus Aurelius' because of his verbosity and apparent wisdom, dressed him in livery, and put him on as entertainment at the plantation soirées. He would dance and sing, fiddle, and play the fool. (The wise fool, by that time; he was learning even at that young age, the art of survival.)

Amanda taught him to recite passages from Horace and Virgil and passages from Molière and the *Chanson de Roland* in French. And on certain evenings, the small dark boy in his satin livery would stand in the middle of a circle of well-attired ladies and gentlemen and declaim passages in Latin to the great amusement of the assembled. The entertainments became the talk of the plantation circle and whenever there was a gathering Marcus Aurelius would be summoned to perform.

On one such occasion, there was a visiting Englishman in the group, a writer touring the plantations of the American South. Marcus Aurelius was called out.

On the east side of the parlor, there was a black marble fireplace with two bronze candelabras set on either side of the mantle and a portrait of the great grandmother of the family in the center, framed in gold leaf. A divan, two armchairs and an assortment of dining room chairs had been moved to the side walls of the room, and a blue woolen rug with a border of a floral pattern and been drawn out into the center of the room. It was here on this rug that Marcus Aurelius took his stance and prepared to deliver his lines. He placed his left hand on his chest and then flung his arm out to the audience as he declaimed his set pieces.

At one point in the recitation, the visiting Englishman chuckled privately, and later during a passage from Ovid, could not contain himself. He slapped his knee and burst into boisterous laughter.

The event was indeed absurd. An illiterate slave, their performing monkey, declaiming phrases in apparently good Latin was certainly amusing to the assembled but the visiting Englishman found it so amusing that he guffawed loudly, coughed and recovered only to laugh more, and when the performance was completed he applauded loudly, jumped to his feet and said "Well spoken, young man—very well pronounced if I dare say so myself. Bravo!"

What said Englishman heard, and the others had not perceived, was the fact that this young illiterate was ahead of the game. Amanda had gone through her Latin ponies and dictionaries and substituted words so that quotes such as Virgil's line: "What makes men indifferent to their wives is that they can see them whenever they please," come out in the words of Marcus as, "What makes men indifferent to their wives is the fact that they are fat, overfed sows…"

Or another invented quote, supposedly from Horace: "Oh sweet pig, Oh love of my life, I kiss thy drooling snout…"

Or, more pointedly, this: a direct, unchanged quote from Virgil, chosen by Amanda for this occasion:

"Withdraw yourself from vile bondage; come, say, I am free, I am free."

******

It was not long after that evening of Latin recitations that Gabriel Maxwell drew the boy into his library and sat him down on a hard-backed chair. He went to the bookshelves and selected a volume and returned to face the small figure who, given the solemn demeanor of his Massa, was feeling decidedly uneasy.

Maxwell addressed Marcus in a grave tone: Was he able to read, he asked. And the boy, quick-witted as ever, announced brightly, "Yessuh Marse, I sure can read, and write too."

And so, Maxwell handed him the book and said, "Read a few lines to me then."

Marcus took the book and, purposely holding it upside down, squinting at the page, running his finger along the lines, and stumbling on words, pronounced a few memorized lines from Horace and Virgil, in English.

The ruse may well have saved Amanda from more severe punishments because of her illegal reading lessons. It was also a prelude. The art of subterfuge, coupled with the lessons in the world of civilized white society served to set the course for the life Marcus Aurelius was about to embark upon.

The Great Dismal Swamp
Steal Away

After a week or so in his final flight from Mayfield Plantation, having struggled through the bottomlands and dry woods west of Norfolk, weakened and soiled and hungry, his rumpled map notwithstanding, Marcus Aurelius finally admitted to himself that he was thoroughly lost. He knew the swamp lay to the south but he couldn't establish whether he had wandered perhaps too far to the west or east and had missed his destination entirely. Inasmuch as his pass was still fresh and clean he decided to risk asking for directions.

He had crossed a road shortly before dawn, and he decided to go back and ask the next traveler where he was. It did not take long. Fifteen minutes or so after he reached the road he saw an older Black man coming along with a wagon full of hay, drawn by the sorriest looking nag he had ever seen. He hailed the driver and the wagon pulled over. Strangers, either white or black, were always suspect to runaway slaves. Any number of escapees had been turned in by fellow slaves, anxious to maintain good standing with their masters or in some cases collect the posted rewards.

But Marcus determined that this was a seemingly trustworthy old man, and he started to ask outright for directions, but before he could even get a word out the man turned the tables and asked him for directions. He said he had been wandering this section of Virginia for months, looking for a plantation in Groverville named Twelve Oaks. His master had asked him to deliver a silver wedding urn to a distant relative at the plantation and had given him explicit directions. But the old man had taken the wrong turn at the end of the long plantation drive and couldn't calculate where he was. He continued wandering, stopping to work on various plantations before venturing onward with new directions supplied by plantation owners.

"I just keep getting loster," he told Marcus.

Marcus apologized and explained that he was in a similar predicament, and couldn't help him, but asked if he had run across a very big swamp in his wanderings. The old man smiled knowingly. The Great Dismal Swamp was widely known among the enslaved people of Tidewater Virginia. Among other things, it was the first place Nat Turner fled to after the notorious killing spree that he had organized a few years earlier. There was even a little saying among the local enslaved people whenever the subject of a recent runaway came up—"Gone to the swamp, like Nat."

"You get in and don't tell me you run off," the old man said.

Marcus had not slept the night before, and a ride in a wagonload of hay seemed inviting, and would the old man mind if he slept under the hay for a few hours.

"Make no mind," the old man said. "Get on in."

Marcus climbed aboard, burrowed down in the hay and shortly thereafter fell into a deep sleep, notwithstanding the fact that sheltering in a hay wagon was not always the safest refuge. Patrollers would often dig into loads of hay when news of a recently escaped slave was announced locally. And as it turned out he was awakened after an hour or so by the sound of voices. He could not quite hear what was the talk was about but he could hear the nasal intonation of a white accent, followed by the softer, more rounded tones of the old man.

Marcus lay still, plotting, his heart battering at his ribcage, and he instinctively fumbled for the handle of his saber. He did have the forged pass and could risk an interview, and if the questioner was alone, he calculated that he could fight his way out. But even as he lay reviewing the possibilities, he felt the wagon begin to move again. It had not occurred to him that the old man, ever innocent and loyal, had stopped to ask someone directions.

He settled back into sleep, but felt something hard digging into his hip and reached around and fished it out. It was the silver wedding urn. This, too, invited possibilities. He could easily slip it into his sack and make off with it. But relaxed by the slow hoofbeats of the nag and the sway and creak of the wagon, he thought of the consequences. If the loyal old slave did in fact finally reach his destination and discover that the urn was missing, what would happen? The loyal old man would be suspect, perhaps even whipped.

Marcus Aurelius was no innocent. He was known on the two plantations where he had been enslaved as a skilled liar and fabricator, talking his way out of trouble whenever possible. He was also potentially violent, a thief of arms.

But, as later records would indicate, he was also a humane, helpful individual especially concerning the enslaved. He perished the thought of stealing the urn.

Just as he was drifting off again, the wagon stopped and the old man called out to him. The straight road had split into a wide fork.

"I'm turning right here," he said. "You'n get out here if you like, or carry on with me. But a white man back a ways told me they's a big plantation about five miles down this right road and I'm going there to ask and maybe stop for a spell."

Marcus, bleary-eyed, rose from the hay. Before him was a wall of trees, the sun lay directly overhead and he calculated that it was about midday. The right hand road turned eastward, and the left made a curve to the west, toward wilder land.

"I axed that white man about the big swamp," the old man said. "He say the big one lay down that a' way. He say don't go there though—too dangerous, snakes and gangs of wild maroons down that way."

Marcus thanked the old man and wished him luck on his quest and walked on down the road keeping his eyes and ears open for other travelers. By late afternoon, he could see ahead of him a veritable wall of gray trunked cypress stretching north and south as far as he could see. He calculated that this must be the swamp. He had no idea where to find the maroon community, but he skirted the wall looking for any possible evidence of a trail and then, on the outskirts of the swamp he saw a lone slave, cutting timber.

In those years, on the borders of the Dismal Swamp there were camps of semi-free Africans working as shingle cutters. Some of these people were rented out by plantation owners, some were freeborn and some were runaways who the local whites chose to ignore. The older man said he was a member of this community. Marcus studied him for a while, and since he seemed to be alone, with no overseer nearby, Marcus decided to risk asking him for directions.

The timber cutter turned out to be a sympathetic sort, or seemed to be. Marcus described his situation but the shingle-cutter had only a vague idea where a village might be located, although he explained that there were many individual escapees living in the interior who would sometimes come out to the camps to get food and supplies. But the maroon villages themselves were very well hidden, some lying like islands of high ground in the center of nearly impassable marshes. These had successfully endured for generations. There were people there who had never seen a white man, and years later, after the Civil War, there were those who never knew there had been a war and that they were now free.

The shingle-cutter warned Marcus, "There were paddyrollers all over the place that week." If Marcus intended to find the maroon colony, he'd best be on his way sooner than later. He thereupon gave Marcus directions—more or less—to a path of higher ground that would get him into the deeper swamp. He warned him to beware of the cottonmouth snakes and the feral hogs and wild so-called cattle beasts that roamed the swamp. Then as an afterthought, he told him to watch out for 'hants' and wild, spear-carrying African natives who also populated the interior, living free as hunters.

Marcus set out, following the directions given to him. He walked first along the south banks of a wide, brown-colored stream, its banks set with bossy, dark green water oaks, wreathed with muscadine grapevines. He followed the stream for a while, and then entered into a watery hallway of cypress checked all around with cypress knees.

Eventually, he settled on a hummock of high ground and rested for the next day and night, still lost in the dank gray trunks of cypress. The second dawn was dense with fog, with wraiths of mists rising from the hummocks and cypress knees. He was awakened that morning by a tinny rattle of bells, and, slowly, out of the mist a vision from spiritus mundi appeared, moving as if disembodied through the ground fog. It was the upright figure of an unclothed dark man, his face shadowed by a slouch hat with the brim turned down, arms elongated and hanging down, and gaunt. Around his shoulders and neck Marcus saw the source of the bells. The man wore an iron version of something that looked like an upside-down, skeletal lampshade, an iron spiked collar that rested on his shoulders, with bells at the end of the spikes.

The two of them stared at each other briefly in silence and then, still wordless, the vision slowly raised his right arm and pointed westward, away from the rising sun. The ground fog rolled back in, and as if floating backward, the form disappeared.

Marcus shivered with the encounter. He knew of this thing, he had heard tales of it in the fires of winter nights among the old men in the slave quarters. It was the Dismal Bondsman, the ghost of a runaway slave who had died of starvation long ago.

No sooner had the spirit faded than Marcus heard again or thought he heard—the distant yelps of pursuing hounds. This was still early dawn, and Marcus reasoned that the sound could be a pack of hounds and hunters just now returning from a night hunt. The presence of patrollers so early in the morning also seemed unlikely. But the sound of the barking grew louder.

And then on the heels of that thought, it occurred to him that the old shingle-cutter could be one of those slaves that side with their masters. Still unlikely, but Marcus collected his gear and once more began to scramble through the thickets heading westward, away from the barking.

His progress was slow. He was forced to leap from hammock to hammock in the wet places, and he stayed to the high ground whenever he could, waiting from time to time to listen for the dogs and get his breath and then set out again. After a mile or so, he slowed to listen; the yelping was more distant but still approaching, so he slogged on, sticking again to the high ground, until finally, exhausted and sweating and breathless, he burst into a clearing of higher ground. And there, in the middle of the clearing, stood the wildest congregation of human beings he had ever seen in his sheltered life.

The people were mostly African, but there was also among them a company of copper-skinned Chickahominy or Pamukey Indians, the local mostly decimated, tribes. The people were dressed in motley, some in formal wear, breeches and culottes stolen from their masters, some in shredded field wear and some, the Indians and a few Blacks, in leggings and skirts of deer skin. They were also armed, some with ancient flintlocks, a few with swords, and some with spears and bows and arrows.

They were as surprised to see young Marcus as he was to see them. They drew back their spears and pointed their guns at him, but he raised his hands and fell to his knees, and they put down the weapons and approached.

Was he a runaway, they wanted to know, were the dogs they could hear after him, and what was the name of the plantation he belonged to, and on and on with questions and requests for news from the outside world.

He told them what they wanted to know and then some, and explained he was hoping to lie low here in the swamp until the search for him was called off and how he had a bad master who was hot for revenge, and how he wanted, once the noise quieted down, to start north by one means or another.

The band of men drew apart and made a circle, obviously discussing the boy's fate. Then one of them came over, one of the Indians, and told him in broken English to go along with a small group of men, the others would stay.

But the dogs, Marcus wanted to know.

"We'll take care of the dogs," he said. "You get on."

Three younger Black men led Marcus to a stream, which they entered. They walked in the water for a few hundred yards or so and then climbed onto a muddy bank. Halfway up, the lead man jumped back, knocking into the troupe behind him. Then he stepped forward and with a swift downward blow of his machete, decapitated a cottonmouth, which he then eviscerated and put in a satchel slung over his shoulder.

The maroons, as Marcus later learned, were skilled hunter-gatherers; they would eat almost anything.

After another mile, still walking periodically in streams and marshes, they climbed to high ground and finally reached the settlement.

****

Marcus knew poverty, even though he personally never experienced it since he had been a houseboy for most of his young life. He knew the squalor of the slave quarters, the rough one-room cabins where whole families of field hands made their home. His own girlfriend back on the Mary Plantation lived in such a place. But he had never seen such a primitive collection of dwellings as those that he saw before him now.

They were mostly log cabins or lean-tos, ill-constructed, and there were also some structures made entirely of saplings, stuck into the ground, bent over and laced together with slender branches and vines and covered with bark. The settlement seemed to have modeled itself on an African village. The cabins and huts were set more or less in a circle, with fire pits just outside a single door, and various ancient worn-out tools and buckets and baskets scattered around the fire pits. Flocks of chickens and geese scratched and grazed in the bare soils near the cabins and there was a pack of unfriendly scrawny curs who charged out barking at the arrival of a stranger in their midst and were summarily kicked and chased off.

As soon as the group entered the clearing, people streamed out and gathered around Marcus, not unfriendly, but not entirely trusting him at that point. There were bands of naked children among them, and women dressed in soiled and tattered calicos, some in short aprons and leggings, and some few bare-breasted, wearing a short, deer hide skirt. Others were dressed in robe-like garments held up by a single shoulder strap and all manner of torn rags, and bonnets decorated with the feathers of owls and hawks and egret plumes.

As had the hunting party, this group fired questions at Marcus: What was his name? His plantation? How long had he been on the run? And then, an odd question for the sheltered, civilized sort such as Marcus—an older African man asked him what tribe was he from. These people spoke English, but their dialect was so laced with non-English words that Marcus had trouble understanding some of them, even though he was skilled with languages. He caught the Fon word for turtle—kudha—and phrases that were spoken by older, African-born slaves he had known when he was younger back on Greenwood Plantation. But these people seemed to have added a few words of their own, 'Pokaunah'—as he learned later—was their word for bear. And they smoked a combination of local herbs and tobacco that which they termed 'kinnikinick'.

While they were questioning him, an older heavyset woman came out of one of the huts. She was a big woman with dark African features, and was dressed in a full-length white cotton dress, cinched at the waist and a white headscarf.

She stood for a moment, looking at the group and then approached slowly, with a regal stride, as if she were on parade or a player in some formal ritual. This, he was given to understand by the others in the group, was Queen Nanda, a combination leader and medicine woman for the settlement.

She strode up to Marcus, drew him aside and inspected him as one would a potential slave purchase. She felt his arms and shoulders, turned his head from side to side and drew up an eyelid. What she saw, was a tall, skinny, light-skinned young man, with a straight nose and strange green eyes. He was barefoot, scratched and cut, his clothes were torn, and he had a decidedly scared and hungry look about him. She spoke to him in a strange language that sounded to Marcus like French, or a version of French, and she indicated by sign that he was to follow her to the hut.

Queen Nanda took Marcus to one of the sapling huts and gestured that he should sit on the ground by the front door. There was a big iron pot set on rocks over a smoldering fire, and the woman went into the hut and came out with a wooden spoon and a carved wooden trencher. She filled the plate with what she called succotash, a brown mushy stew of an unidentifiable combination of bits of meat and roots. She nodded, put her hand to her mouth, and instructured him to feed.

Marcus had not eaten anything but raw greens and roots and half-cooked chicken in the past ten days and was indifferent to the ingredients. He consumed so much stew—at her behest—that he began to feel sick.

Once he was finished, Nanda indicated that he should come into her lodge and he followed her into the shadowed darkness. The floor of the dwelling was covered with a matt of sweet-smelling grasses, and there was a surround of benches along the walls. She pointed to one of the benches and told him to lie down and rest. Which he would have done—he had had very little untroubled sleep in the course of his escape—but outside the door, he heard a ruckus of shouting and laughter and rhythmic hand clapping. Queen Nanda went out to see what was happening and he followed her.

He saw across the compound that the men he and the group had left behind were just entering the clearing. Over their shoulders, they were carrying the bodies of four dogs, three bloodhounds and a beagle. They brought them to the fire pit by one of the huts and set to skinning and gutting them.

Marcus, young gentleman of big house parlors that he was, found this profoundly disturbing. He was raised with house dogs and had a special fondness for Amanda's spaniel, Miss Pixie, who he almost considered his sister. He also liked the field dogs that slept around the plantation kitchen doors—dogs so lazy in the summer heat, the only way you could tell that they were alive was the fact that, without raising their heads or even opening their eyes, they would slap their tails in the dust when you passed. He liked them all. Dogs were indiscriminate as to color. Or most of them were.

Marcus was already feeling sick, and at the sight of these fellow travelers being gutted in the clearing, a wave of nausea passed over him. Then, as the wave subsided, it struck him that these dogs were not exactly his friends. Had they caught up with Marcus, they would have treed him as they would a raccoon or a bear. Either that, or torn him to shreds. Marcus had heard a story about this from one of the plantations near the Maxwells. Years earlier, the patroller's hounds had cornered a slave far ahead of his human pursuers and by the time the patrollers arrived, they had killed him. Not by any means what his master wanted. Slaves were very expensive.

Dogs were, in fact, the bane of the individual maroons who lived alone or in small family groups in the swamp. Slave hunters often patrolled the outskirts of the swamp and the nearby interior borderlands with packs of hounds. Some runaways fashioned a sort of dog spear, a scythe blade bound to a short straight handle. One good swipe could sever the forelegs of an attacking dog. Others had axes and hatchets with which to defend themselves. Even in the deep interior of the swamp the maroons lived ever watchful lives like a lost battalion living behind the lines, deep in enemy territory.

Queen Nanda returned from the butchering with her distribution of the butchered dog meat, and encouraged Marcus to go back to sleep, while she chopped the meat further and threw it into the stew.

The waves of nausea returned.

Marcus spent the rest of the day in troubled sleep. By nightfall, the old woman came back into the lodge, lay down on one of the benches and lit a pipe. The pungent odor of her smoke mixed with the scent of wood ash and bitter greenwood and in time Marcus fell asleep again.

This was a night of confused, brightly-colored dreams. Dogs, friendly and otherwise, appeared and disappeared. He saw dog fangs and snakes, and the Dismal Swamp ghost, and heard singing—long African call and response chants, and finally, toward dawn, standing in a sun-struck clearing in the surrounding dark cypress swamp, as if illuminated, he saw the figure of his first love, the enslaved girl Tilly Washburn of the Mary Plantation.

She was a small fifteen-year-old girl, standing with her palms turned up and her face to the sun, as if praying for freedom from some benign god. The forest around her was bright and glittering with moisture, the air was warm and sultry, and an indescribable peace settled over him.

He woke from the dream saddened and lonely but then was suddenly energized with hope. He felt that he would someday get himself and Tilly free.

Mary Plantation
Tilly Washburn

Serena, the cook at Henry Washburn's Mary Plantation on the James River, came to the big house after she was purchased along with her daughter, Tilly, a scrawny young girl with Bantu pigtails. When she turned seven, Tilly was put to work with her mother, doing such chores as a seven-year-old was capable of. She was, from her earliest years, a sassy young thing. She ran with the children of the plantation in a mixed gang of whites and Blacks catching frogs, jumping out of the hayloft, and teasing aggressive sows. She was the wildest of the bunch, and the most inventive, but she also often disobeyed her strict mother and got slapped around frequently.

Her father, who she barely remembered, was sold when she was about three or four, and he himself, according Tilly's mother, was something of a wild man. His ultimate sin, and the thing that got him sold down the river, was the fact that he broke free during one of his frequent beatings, snatched the whip from the overseer knocked him to the ground and began lashing him brutally and kicking him in the ribs. Then he threw down the whip and raced for the woods. He was caught the next day and sold a week later. Serena never saw him again.

Tilly first learned trickery in her mother's kitchen. Early on, she devised ways to skip work so that her mother wouldn't know and she could spend more time daydreaming—one of her favorite pastimes. Once she was put into service in the big house, she carried on with her white owners, Elizabeth Washburn, old Master Washburn and their two boys, Jefferson and Winslow—who were not much older than Tilly herself.

Tilly's cabin, where she lived with her mother, was a neat, solidly built structure with a shake roof and planked walls and a brick chimney. Along with her cooking, Serena was well known for her finely kept garden, which she maintained behind a stake fence on either side of the cabin door. Here she grew potatoes, peas, cabbages, and melons in such abundance that she was able to help supply the kitchen of the big house.

The earlier Washburn family, owners of the Mary Plantation, were fair-minded people who treated their 'servants' (as they termed them) humanely. Periodically over the history of the plantation certain family members had even freed their slaves in their wills. But the terms were broken in the next generation. The tradition of fair-mindedness slowly withered, and the current master, Henry Washburn had a mean streak which, thanks to the efforts of his wife, he managed to control—usually. He sometimes chose to take up the whip against a recalcitrant slave himself rather than leave the work to the plantation foreman, a somewhat too-sympathetic man named Calvin Billings.

Certain enslaved people on the plantation, aware of the rumored tolerant traditions of the earlier Mary Plantation, seethed at the very concept of being 'owned' and working without pay. Tilly was one of these. So was her mother, and secretly, in what must have been a metaphorical statement of freedom, Tilly's mother commonly supplied food to escaped slaves who chose not to flee to the density of swamps and the wilderness, but survived in the so-called borderlands, the wood lots and swamps between the cultivated plantations. Some escapees from the James River plantations had been living in hidden camps and caves and hollows for years, free, but ever wary of capture. They would return to Serena's garden and the gardens of other local plantations at night and were supplied with extra food set aside for them. Some local maroons even managed to kidnap their entire families and live free in such isolated hideaways.

Tilly was just the type to make such a break. She was one of those enslaved people who could be found on almost any plantation. She was a housemaid and kitchen servant, and she was good at her job; she sewed, she cooked when necessary, she tended to her chores and she was well-liked and well-treated by her mistress. But she brooded. Nobody in the big house knew she hated them all. She was *yes ma'am* this and *yes Mom* that, and 'I'll see to it right away' on the surface, and she was all the while thinking: *get me away, Lord, from this old white hag with her snaggly teeth.*

Never mind that the snaggle-toothed hag was in fact Tilly's greatest supporter, sometimes covering for her when she knew Tilly had misbehaved. Nonetheless, she believed she 'owned' Tilly.

Nobody owned Tilly.

Mayfield Plantation
Nights on the James River

Maxwell's plantation fell on hard times in 1839, the result of flooding and worn-out soil and the failure of three successive tobacco crops. Marcus was fourteen by that time, tall, fine-boned, agile and even though Amanda pleaded and cajoled and shed tears, her father sold Marcus as well as his mother and her two other siblings to a plantation owner named Johnston who lived a few miles to the east at Mayfield Plantation, on the James River.

On the night before the sale, Amanda met with Marcus under a live oak on the south side of the big house verandah. She just wanted to say goodbye privately, she said.

It was a slightly awkward meeting, formal almost, and very unlike their formerly playful exchanges. She began to explain, haltingly, that even though he didn't realize it, he had changed her views. The fact that he was such a fast learner, a fluent linguist, a skilled reader and writer had entirely altered her perspective on the institution of slavery. She was taught, as were all white children, that people of African descent had limited intellectual abilities, were better able to handle heat waves, were immune to mosquito bites, did not experience pain in the same way as whites did, and, furthermore, were lustful. The males bore watching.

"You've changed my whole life," she said quietly.

"But Manda," he said, using his private childhood nickname for her. "Manda, you changed my life. Weren't for you, I'd been sent to the fields when I was ten."

A silence fell.

"I know," Amanda said. "I know that, and I feel like in some ways, I hope at least, I will someday have helped to set you free. I hope you can get yourself out of this prison you are destined to live in. Any time in the future, whenever you can get away with it, write me. Write me in French and sign a different name so Papa won't know. And if you ever run away, which I do hope you will, and you need help, write. Please write. Please stay in touch."

Marcus shook his head, turned away, kicked at the ground, and when he looked up, his eyes were filled with tears. Amanda, seeing this, let out a deep sob. She longed to embrace him, but the ancient cords of her culture restrained her and she merely held out her hands. He reached out, gathered them up, drew them to his cheek, and let forth a loud sob. "Thank you. Thank you," he sobbed repeatedly. "Thank you, thank you."

Amanda turned and fled onto the verandah in tears.

Amanda stayed in touch with Marcus, clandestinely, over the next two years. But things went downhill after that. Amanda grew up, was married, and moved to a plantation near Richmond.

The big house on Mayfield Plantation, where Marcus was now enslaved, was a tall red brick building in the Georgian style, set well back from the James River. It had two main doors, one faced a drive and the other had a courtyard, facing the river. The hipped roof was fitted with dormers, and the whole pile was surrounded on both sides by a smoke house, a summer kitchen, laundry rooms, and a stable. Slave quarters were set far from the big house, closer to the river. It was one of the oldest of the James River plantations, having been established in the late 17th century by the Johnston family.

In the time of Marcus Aurelius, it also had one of the largest populations of enslaved people, nearly three hundred all told, counting the children, of whom there were many. Records do not indicate this, but at the time, it is likely that the Johnstons of various generations were raising slaves to sell, the former tobacco lands having worn out.

Word of the sharp-witted young man called Marcus Aurelius was known to Johnston, and Marcus and Lucilla and his sisters were housed in slave quarters near to the kitchen, which had an upper story. Lucilla by this time had established herself as a good cook, and her two daughters were being trained as scullery maids, even the eight-year-old girl, Mingo.

One day, when he was seventeen, Marcus was asked to deliver a cake to the kitchen at the Mary Plantation, which was the nearest plantation down the river from Mayfield. When he arrived, he saw a slim teenaged girl outside the back door there dressed in an osnaburg cotton frock and a floppy slouch hat with the brim turned up in front.

"This the back door to the big house kitchen?" Marcus asked, knowing full well that it was.

"Well, it ain't the front door," the girl said.

"Big house kitchen has no front door, Missy, and you know that. What's your name?"

"Tilly."

"Tilly?" he asked. "Tilly?"

"Yeah, that's right, Tilly."

"Tilly Tarry Till the Sun Go Down…"

"What you talking, boy? And what's in that box?"

"I brought you a cake."

Tilly put her hands on her hips and looked at him sidewise, smirking and nodding her head. It was a cynical, knowing look that she had learned from older women, half rejection, half flirtation.

He loved it.

"If that cake be for me, open that box and I share it with you," Tilly said. "You take the first bite, I take the second."

She had outfoxed him. He admitted that it was for the Massa's wife, from Mistress Johnston, and after another short exchange, Marcus said he had to get back and they said goodbye.

Tilly delivered the cake to her mother, and when she came back, Marcus was still there.

"What you lingering around here for, I thought you had to get back," Tilly said.

"I can't remember how to get there," he said.

Hands on her hips again, and the knowing nod, only this time she was smiling.

Two nights later, he came back. Then he showed up a week after that, and then there were more visits.

Tilly and Marcus began meeting after dark, after the field hands came back to their sorry meals of corn bread and bacon. Then they began meeting more regularly, and in time, as the relationship developed, the night visits increased and no doubt sustained Marcus all the day long as he went about his chores.

And all the while, they talked. They talked about their pasts, they talked about love, they gossiped about incidents on their plantations, and often, freedom—always freedom. In time, the night visits became more intimate, they talked about how they would run away together someday and get to Canada—or, as Marcus said, to a country on the other side of the Atlantic called France, where Black people were free.

Traditionally, when enslaved people made a successful final break, it tended to be well planned and permanent, and their masters and mistresses could never comprehend why they would run. They were such good servants and so well treated, why would they run away. Some slaves waited all their lives to make a break.

Tilly was such a woman, good but bad. She would destroy things, break china plates and cups in such a way as to make it appear pure accident. She would spit in stews, throw cakes and puddings on the floor and call in the house dog and blame it. This Marcus Aurelius, whoever he was, was just the sort of man she had been waiting for, a loyal slave boy on the surface—a rebel at heart.

And determined to be free.

There was a landing dock at the end of a path from Tilly's cabin, and one moonlit still summer night, the two walked down to the dock and sat with their ankles in the water.

"You know how to swim, Tilly?" Marcus asked.

"No, but why you ask?"

"I've been teaching myself to swim, in case I run away some time."

"Why?"

"Dogs," Marcus said. "If you can run to the water and swim away, the dogs can't smell you. Keep going, as long as you can, and they'll lose your trail."

"I knew that. Big Bill, man we knew here, he swim away one day, all the way down the James, and when he got out, there was the paddyrollers catched him up."

They were silent for a while. Then Marcus said he was going to have to run away someday.

"Yeah, me too. I'm a' go to Canada."

"What are you going to do there? I don't know. Sing?"

One of the things commonly known about Tilly was that she was always singing while she worked, so much so that her mother would sometimes tell her to stop. Old Mistress asked her once why she would sing all the time.

"I can't sing, might as well throw me in the slave pen," she said.

"Everybody sings," Marcus said. "You've got to do something more than that."

"I know—everybody sing," Tilly said. "I don't know what else to do."

Tilly told him a long story about overhearing Missa Washburn and some white ladies talking about how her 'workers', as she called them, were actually happy, since they sing all the time.

"They ain't sing 'cause they happy," Tilly said. "They sing to escape."

"Why do you sing?" Marcus asked.

Tilly thought for a bit. "I don't know. It feels good. You can't tell ole missus what you feel or think, but you can sing it."

"Actually, you know that Amanda told me once that in Paris and New York, there are people who get paid to sing," Marcus said.

A breeze picked up and ruffled the waters of the river.

"You want to run away with me someday, Tilly?"

"Sure I run away with you, Marky. But give me time. I got to help Mama a little longer. She's going to run off too someday. There's a free man, lives in Charles City and sometimes he come down here and camp in the woods. She goes out and spends the night with him. He told her he's gon' carry her home with him someday."

"That'd be good."

"Yeah. Then we run off, you and me."

"Yes, but first I have to run. Then I'll come back for you."

"Promise?"

"Yes. Promise. I don't think I'll be able to stop myself."

******

Due perhaps to the lack of sleep, Marcus began fumbling at his house work, and also at the time, in the manner of young men his age, he developed a certain resentment to his condition, which he tried his best to conceal. There were perhaps a few clipped responses to the mistress's orders, or a deliberate, passive response to commands. Either way, the family kept a closer eye on this former good boy and eventually, Marcus was caught at his night visits. Horace Johnston took him aside one day and delivered a lecture on behavior. Marcus reformed. But then resumed the visits, and then was caught again, and finally, in order to teach him a lesson, he was whipped.

This was the first taste of the cat for Marcus. No one had ever even struck him.

The overseer at the time was a local white man named Mr. Green. He was responsible for the production of crops and control of the enslaved workers and the general management of the plantation. He was the son of a James River ferryman and grew up in deplorable conditions in the river bottomlands. The job of overseer was a step up for him, and in his early years he did well, crop production improved, and although a strict disciplinarian when it came to control of his workers, he was not irrationally overbearing.

But as the soils began wearing out and the tobacco crops diminished, he came under more pressure from old man Johnston, and with his position threatened, he grew bitter. He had two drivers under him, two trusted slaves whose job was to keep the pickers from slacking. True to form, Mr. Green was out in the fields on horseback every morning shortly after the first horn was sounded, indicating that the slaves should make for the fields. Accompanied by his drivers, Green would circle the fields, whip in hand watching for shirkers, of which on Mayfield there were quite a few.

The one aspect of Mr. Green that kept the slaves ever watchful when he was in view was the fact that Green himself chose to do the whipping, and unlike the drivers or the other whipping boys, he seemed to enjoy laying on the lash.

Marcus was taken out to the whipping post, stripped to the waist, his hands bound around the post, and with the house staff and a few field hands watching, he waited, eyes closed, for the first bite.

Mr. Green came up behind him and uncoiled a short handled whip with three-foot long rawhide strands, and asked Marcus if he was ready.

No answer.

"I said, you ready?"

"No sir, I am not ready," Marcus Aurelius said firmly.

A brand of searing fire burned across his back.

"Ready o' not, here it comes, Mr. Marcus Aurelius," Green said.

Another slash, and then another.

Marcus clenched his teeth and pressed his cheek hard against the whipping post, but he did not cry out. At the fourth lash, he felt faint. And at the fifth, the world spun around into darkness. And then it was over.

Mr. Green, per orders of Horace Johnston, had delivered only ten lashes, far fewer than the traditional nine and thirty strikes for most slaves. This was perhaps out of pity on the part of Daisy Johnston, who had heard about the whipping and pleaded with her husband to go lightly.

More likely—with future sales in mind—Mr. Johnston may not have wanted to scar the back of so fine and saleable a slave as Marcus Aurelius.

The indignity of it all was the worst of it: Marcus Aurelius, handsome, young, and popular with slaves and plantation whites alike, stripped to the waist and publicly lashed. Marcus was eighteen at the time, still young and impetuous, and a few days after that first beating, without much forethought, he ran away.

Before his flight, Marcus walked downstream to Tilly's garden, supplied himself with enough onions and carrots to hide out for a while and then proceeded farther downstream to a swampy bottomland forest with an understory of reeds and an island of higher ground. Here he made a camp for himself and spent the first night.

He woke the next morning hungry, and consumed the carrots and an onion and then sat in the sun and started to wonder what to do with himself now that he was free. He thought to build a snare to catch a possum or a rabbit, and then realized he wasn't sure how to construct such a thing, nor how to skin whatever he caught, nor, for that matter how to cook it, since he had run away without a steel and flint, and unlike some of the field hands on the plantation, did not know how to make a fire drill.

He had spent ten or so years as a house boy, carrying trays, cleaning off tables after dinners, polishing silver, and entertaining Amanda when he was younger. None of this served him now. Nor did his facility with language, nor his ability to read and write, nor his playful dueling skills. He did know how to cook, inasmuch as he had spent time watching Bandie, a favorite house slave of his, but without fire, nor any skills at fishing nor trapping and skinning animals, he was lost.

That night he went back to Tilly's garden and helped himself to more carrots. As he was about to dig up a mess of onions, Tilly's mother appeared at the door. She hissed, and waved him in, and told him to stay away—'they looking for you'—she said, and what's more, she didn't want Tilly to get in any trouble. The master knew he had run and had a good notion of how to catch him, and he was going to get a good thrashing when they did, and then she gave him a hunk of bacon, and a few squares of corn biscuits and told him—go, and keep moving, the posters and bulletins were going to go up if he did clear out in a few days, and the paddyrollers were coming to get him sooner or later. But then she trapped him. She told him Tilly'd been wailing off and on since he run off. This was the hardest news of all.

He went back to his swamp, slept until late in the morning, ate some onions and cornbread and a chunk of bacon and went back to sleep. He woke in mid-afternoon and sat there doing nothing, slept some more, wandered around the swamp at dusk and spotted a snake at the edge of a woodland pool. It slipped into the water and wriggled off, and he could see that it had a wide triangular shaped head, the form of a cottonmouth, and even though it was probably only a black water snake (for which cottonmouths are often mistaken), its presence near his camp frightened him.

The following morning, he went back to Mayfield.

******

He showed up at work that day, as if he had never left, perhaps hoping that no one had actually noticed—this in spite of Tilly's mother's warnings. Marcus had, after all, once been a good boy and his neat clothing and his wit and his ability to dance and play the fool endeared him to the whites of the big house, especially the women. Daisy Johnston, the matron of Mayfield in particular, had a soft heart for her charges, especially young Marcus. Slavery was indeed, as the popular Southerners termed it, a peculiar institution.

Shortly after his flight and return, Horace Johnston summoned young Marcus Aurelius into an empty room behind the cook house and instructed him to sit down in a rickety chair. Johnston stood glaring at him, and then began pacing the floor menacingly. Marcus was certain that the serious thrashing that he had been warned about was in the offing. His heart was hammering and he had to pee. But he sat still, eyes down.

Johnston stopped his pacing, cocked his left leg onto a trunk near the chair, and tapping the floor with a narrow bamboo cane, began to question Marcus. He had been such a good boy. What happened to him? Why would he run away when he had such an easy life and was so appreciated by the family?

"Why?" he asked.

Marcus glanced up. "I don't know, sir. You see I—I was hurting. I'm sorry I ran now, I'm truly sorry. I was hurting and I was not thinking clearly because of the pain I was suffering and so, unthinkingly, I just ran off and then I kept running without forethought and I won't do that again, sir, I can assure you I have learned my lesson now."

Johnston snorted and shook his head tiredly. "You sure can talk, boy," he said.

Marcus stared and the floor and shook his head sadly, as if he was about to cry. In fact, he was brewing anger.

"You're sorry you ran, and you just run off without thinking, you say?" Johnston asked. "And yet you go down to the Mary Plantation and raid Serena Washburn's garden and steal food before you go."

"I was hungry, sir. The pain made me hungry and caused me to suffer pangs and do those things which I should not have done and I am truly sorry for that sir and I won't do that again, sir."

"Get up," Johnston said.

Marcus rose. Eyes down, wringing his hands below his chest.

"Get over to that wall, turn around and pull your pants down and put your hands up on the wall."

Before he had even placed his hands above his head, he felt a painful strike against his buttocks. And then another.

"What happened to you, boy?" Johnston asked. "You were well recommended to us by Mr. Maxwell."

Another smack. "You were a good boy. What happened?"

Another hit.

Marcus remained silent.

"What happened, I say?"

Another swat.

Marcus turned and looked at Mr. Johnston. Green eyes filling with tears. He tried another strategy and resorted to the language of the fields.

"I'se so sorry, Massa, I don't mean nothing evil 'bout dat. I jus' run, see. I don't think no forethought."

He began to sob bitterly. (Crocodile tears! He was raging.) Johnston began to laugh. "You sure can act when you have to," he said.

He shook his head, turned toward the open door and looked out across the yard and laughed again.

"You are one sneaky little monkey son of a bitch, aren't you, Mr. Marcus Aurelius. They told me about you and Miss Amanda, and your playacting and all that, and you dancing and fiddling and making like you speak Latin. I've a good mind to sell you and get you off my hands. But then the ladies wouldn't like it, would they? You and the ladies! I would get no end of complaints from Mrs. Johnston and Aunt Maria and Sally. I can hear it now: 'Why did you sell that good boy, Horace? Why did you get rid of that nice young man. He's just going through a period, and all that…'"

"You and your sweet talk, smart little darkie dancing around like a fool, you know the fact is I can't get over you, Marcus Aurelius. I never did own a slave like you. But it's all over for you now. You're going to the fields and that's that and I don't care you know how to clear a table and decant wine, you're going to the fields and I don't care what the ladies say. Get on, then," he said.

He turned and walked out the door, still chuckling, as if in amazement.

*****

This marked a major change in the life of Marcus Aurelius. He once wore white gloves, dressed in silks and brocade, knew how to carry trays filled with sundry delicacies balanced on the palm of his upraised right hand. He knew how to stand and wait, how to walk and how to use proper English, with (whenever he deemed it fitting) a few choice words of parlor French thrown in. His hands were smooth and uncalloused, and his back was unmarked, lithe and supple. But, in spite of his stature—he had grown to about five foot nine by that time—he was not strong. The field work, especially in the beginning, was hard for him. So was the schedule.

In the big house, his work schedule began an hour after sunrise. In the cabin of the field hands, where he now slept, a bell was sounded an hour before dawn to wake the work force, the idea being that their main meal would be breakfast, before dawn, so that they could work all day in the fields as long as there was light. An hour later after the waking bell, after the slaves had eaten, a horn was blown to send them to the fields. This would be around first light, and the work day lasted until sundown, with a short noonday break, a fourteen hour work day in summer. The hours were long; the work of the tobacco planting and harvest—then the major crop on Mayfield—was not as arduous as the work on the sugar plantations and cotton fields, but it was tedious.

On the Mayfield Plantation, there was a short break at midday, and then it was back to the fields until dark when the slaves returned to their cabins, started the cooking fires, ground their corn meal, cooked their dinners, ate, and promptly slept. On moonlit nights during the harvest, they could be forced to pick until late in the night, sometimes returning with barely enough strength to feed themselves. They went to bed late and were up again before dawn on summer mornings and back to the fields, and all this with no hope of respite or retreat or shelter from the storm of enslavement.

At Mayfield, the slaves had Sunday off and were more or less free to do what they wanted. Some would tend private gardens, some would sneak off to the woods to hunt or collect wild greens, or dance, and some would go to meeting.

There was a white preacher, and also a Black preacher at Mayfield, and Marcus would always attend services. But at this point, having seen what he had seen, he had no faith. If, he reasoned, there was in fact a god, then he was a devil, otherwise why would he let people suffer so. He went to meeting for the language, not the religion. He listened carefully to the readings from the Scripture—not the sermons. And he enjoyed immensely, as did the Black preacher and the slaves, the story of the Hebrew bondage. Freedom by that time was always on his mind, day and night.

Tilly was also always in mind. In spite of the dangers of another beating, he restarted his night visitations. He would nap after his return from the fields and then get up late in the night tramp down through the night woods and whistle for her.

One moonless night they headed over for a clearing near Serena's food depot. Runaways had spent time there in the past and the ground was smoothed and clear and they lay down and began to nuzzle one another, when they heard close at hand, a soft hooting and garbling of a barred owl. They sat up and looked around at the wooded wall of sweetgum and beech. It was a cloudy night, but at that point, briefly, the moon cleared the cloud rack and bathed the clearing in a bright silvery light. It was just a quick flash, so clear it seemed almost unnatural, as if this young couple were selected from the one million enslaved Africans by some powerful controlling force, free from the world of the drudgery of their day to day life. It was almost frightening and they both felt it and drew together in a tight embrace. Then the cloud curtain drew in and the light faded.

They sat, almost breathless.

"You ever feel that suddenly, at a certain age, you get memory, and then you realize that you are a person?" Marcus asked.

"Yeah, I get that. I hide up in that closet with the window in it overlooking the summer kitchen and the yard, and I see people walking back and forth doing things, colored people. Then I see ole Billings, the foreman, standing there talking to some other white man and he's got that coiled whip at his waist, and I'm wonderin': what is all this about anyway, and what am I doing here. How did that happen."

They fell silent again. Clouds ripped by over the treetops. "Maybe it just happens," Marcus said.

The owl called again.

"Maybe there's no meaning at all. No reason," Marcus said. "And no god either. Just an accident. Most human beings on earth are free."

On the heels of this statement, the cloud curtain parted again and the moonlight flashed over Tilly's face. Marcus looked over at her and she was staring at him with a seriousness he had never witnessed, as if she had never seen him before.

"They can't do that," she said.

She was silent then, her dark slanted eyes fixed on him steadily.

"Tilly?" Marcus said.

She said nothing, unmoving.

"You alright, Tilly?"

She held her gaze for another few seconds and then suddenly threw her arms around him and buried her head into shoulder and held him in a grip so tight and so prolonged he almost lost his breath.

****

Having endured regular light beatings and then two serious whippings by the strong arm of Mr. Green, Marcus began planning to make a final escape rather than the spontaneous flights he had taken on previous occasions.

On a late summer night, he slipped out of his cabin and made his way downriver through the fields and a woodlot to the slave cabins of the Mary

Plantation. The cabins at the plantation were lined up along a rough cart track, shadowed, rude plank structures with wattled chimneys, no windows and dirt floors, with benches and pails and field tools scattered here and there or leaning against cabin walls. He crept down the line, stopped at the third one at the eastern end of the cartway and went around to the back, through a tangle of bull briars, squatted down in the shrubbery and started whistling the warbling, repetitive song of the mockingbird.

She appeared shortly thereafter, a slim girl of fifteen or sixteen, her hair still twisted in a cluster of Bantu pigtails.

"You leaving?" she asked. "You really leaving this time?"

"Yes. But I'm coming back, Tilly, like I said. I'll be back. You just wait."

"When?" she asked. "When you comin' back, Marky? And how I don't know that the paddyrollers gonna catch you on your way and then kill you for good measure? And here I am, still waiting?"

He grabbed her around the waist and laughed.

"Don't you worry. I'm coming back someday. You'll hear that mockingbird singing, and I'll be there. Tilly tarry till I come," he added.

She pushed him away. "Get on then."

"Walk me down to the river," he said.

There was no moon that night, which was the reason Marcus had chosen this day for his flight, and they made their way down through the dark woods and the half lit fields to the docks. They embraced again. Kissed, embraced, and kissed some more, and then he separated himself, climbed in the punt, pushed off and just sat there, looking back at her.

Tilly, uncharacteristically, began to cry.

"You come back now, you hea'," she whimpered.

"I've half a mind not to go, Tilly." He was serious for once.

"No!" she said emphatically. "You go! Get on. Get yourself free and then you come back and carry me off. Go. Please."

He pushed off and rowed out toward the middle of the river and stopped. He called back, "No goodbyes, Tilly. I'm coming back. I'm coming back and I won't be in chains when I do."

"Go," she said. "Leave."

He pulled off into mid-river and let the current carry him downstream.

The Great Dismal Swamp
The Winter Interlude

There were nearly three hundred slaves then working the tobacco fields of Mayfield, and it took one of the drivers the better part of the day to determine that Marcus was no longer in the fields, and an evening to summon a group of patrollers, and more than a week to post the broadsides and newspaper escaped slave ads.

By that time, he was deep in the Great Dismal Swamp. On his first full day of freedom, as Marcus slowly came to consciousness in late morning, he realized there was a figure standing a few yards away staring at him with her arms folded. It was a young cocoa-colored girl, about his age, dressed in a loose white smock, much soiled by ash.

"*C'est temps the lever*," she said. Then she burst into gales of laughter.

He blinked at her, shading his eyes.

She flung out a long incomprehensible sentence:

"*Moun sa yo di m 'ou pa renmen manje chen. Jis sonje ti gason. Chen sa yo apatni pou moun blan an, ou pa manje yo, yo manje ou. ou antreprann. De tout fason, sa yo chen yo se bondye pou ou.*"

"Sorry, what did you say?" he asked.

"*Jis di say o chen yo se bondye pou ou.*" She snapped her jaws and barked like a dog. Then she laughed again.

"Dogs?"

"*Oui, chen.*"

"French?" he asked. "*Mange.* Eat? You speak French? *Tu parles français?*"

She laughed again, and snapped her fingers and pantomimed biting her forearm.

"*Un peu français*," she said. "*Aussi ingles*."

"English?"

"Ya ingles." She 'bit' her arm again. "Dug," she said.

He was lost. It was too early to comprehend where he even was, let alone understand what was being said to him, and why. But as they struggled for a common tongue, a young man came over. He too was laughing.

"She say you no like de dog meat?" he said in broken English.

"It was all right. I was too hungry to care. But I never ate a dog before," Marcus said.

He translated for the girl, then said, "Dog belong white mon. You na et hem, hem et you."

Marcus laughed. "In that case, that was a delicious *repas,*" he said.

"You come," the young man said.

He led Marcus over to a group of villagers standing around another stewing pot. Marcus prayed he would not have to eat dog again. But this turned out to be, as far as he could determine, a normal stew consisting mostly of roots and garden vegetables. Once more, he wolfed down his meal. Then feeling fatigued again and slightly ill, he went back to Queen Nanda's wickiup and fell asleep.

He woke shortly after noon and came out into an empty village. But the stew pot was sitting over the coals, so he helped himself to more.

In time, a group of women reappeared, accompanied by dogs and children. They carried more roots, stems of green leafy plants, three rabbits, and a possum. They joined him at the fire.

There was a tall African woman with them.

"You 'wake now finally?" she said in comprehensible English.

"Finally, yes," he said. "I haven't slept so well in a week."

"Where you run from?" she asked.

He explained, telling his whole story for the fourth or fifth time and when he finished, she said, "Don't seem so bad to me. Mos' these people got worse."

She turned her back on him and lifted her camisole. Her back was rucked with scars.

As the women set to cleaning the vegetables and gutting the possum and the rabbits, a group of men came in with more fare, including a few dripping combs of honey, which they passed around. People chomped down, comb and all, passed it along and sat licking their hands and wiping their cheeks.

The pretty cocoa-colored girl came over and sat down next to him. "*Yo been reveille now*?" she asked. He answered her in broken French and English, and they chatted for a while, searching for a common language. Then her apparent partner came over and joined them.

They talked for a while, asking Marcus about plantation life and if he knew of the escaped slave, Nat Turner, who was in fact the only outsider they had heard of, even though he had been long since captured and executed. The three of them were about the only people in the group who were the same age as Marcus. There were older people, young people and even more little ones—many of whom had been born in the swamp and had never even seen a white person.

The young man, who called himself Barco, had better control of English than the girl, Nyala, but the more they talked, the more Marcus was able to understand, with occasional help from Barco, what Nyala was saying. They did not apparently have any parents in the village.

Over the course of that evening and part of the next day, when they met again, he learned that, Nyala, like Queen Nanda was also brought over from Haiti with her parents when she was very young and had been put to work on one of the Sea Island indigo plantations. At one point, when she was still young she were sold away from her parents in the Charleston slave market to work as a maid on a cotton plantation somewhere south of the Dismal Swamp.

Barco was originally Jamaican but he too was purchased and brought over and sold to the same North Carolina cotton plantation, where he met Nyala. While they were teenagers, they decided to run away together. It was a spontaneous and wild adventure, but somehow, partly by the kindness of other plantation slaves who clandestinely supplied them with food, they had carried on for weeks in a random flight. They eventually learned of the maroon community in the Dismal Swamp and, aided once more by sympathetic informants, made their way north. They barely survived.

But one of the shingle cutters working at the southern end of the swamp found them asleep one morning, hid them, and then arranged for a guide to take them to the maroon village. They had been living there for four years.

Their story made Marcus wonder if he should have insisted that Tilly run with him. But, she had refused to leave her mother.

Barco was about twenty but already had a little network of scars across his back. He had been a field hand but was rebellious, feigning incompetence at harvest times, and failing to keep up with the other pickers.

The two of them lived next to Nanda in a small wicker hut. Nanda by then was beyond childbearing years, and she had more or less adopted them and taught them the local survival skills.

After many years of African, Haitian and North American experiences, Nanda had become the combination midwife and *houngan* or priest doctor for the group. She had early success after settling in the village calling down the *loa,* the spirits of the upper airs and talking to the ancestors for guidance. In time, she became what the resident Chickahominy people called a 'saunk' or woman leader for the people. The village people eventually gave her the English name, Queen.

Within a week, Marcus began to adapt to his new way of life. This was far from anything he had ever known. Life on the fields was hard and tedious, but generally safe, unless of course you slacked off or exhibited even so much as a hint of insolence toward the driver. There was a regular, albeit scant and tedious diet, barely enough corn meal, beans, ham to keep one fed well enough to work ten hours a day in the hot sun. While he was enslaved, Marcus would supplement his diet by stealing from the big house gardens and trading stolen food supplied to him by Tilly for the occasional possum or raccoon that the old men, who were free from the fields, were able to hunt in their off hours.

But, free though he was, the hunter-gatherer life of the maroons was challenging for him. There were garden plots, and there were feral hogs in the swamp turned out from the village by the maroons to forage and breed. These reverted to the scrawny razorbacks that they hunted, along with what were known as cattle beasts, wild cows and bulls that had escaped from local farms and were also living in the swamp. The people also hunted white-tailed deer, the occasional bear, turkeys, ducks and geese, and smaller game such as possums, raccoons, and muskrats. Also snakes, turtles and frogs, and all this supplemented by a host of edible wild plants, ramps and skunk cabbage in the spring, groundnuts, hog peanuts, cattail stems, wild nuts and berries throughout the summer and autumn. The diet of the maroons was much more nutritious than the plantation fare, and with it, Marcus began to regain some of the weight and strength he had lost in his year of fieldwork.

True to form, he grew interested in the people who were hiding him and made friends with a few of his original rescuers. They were, to say the least, a diverse group, some as young as fourteen, some old former slaves carrying a network of raised whip scars on their backs, some with cropped ears or noses, and all of them bushy-haired and bearded, and dressed in motley. Their language ranged from an incomprehensible, Gullah-like dialect, to perfectly good English, and also a language of their own employing local Wenackta words, such as *permico*, which Marcus soon learned was both a greeting and a compliment, along the lines of 'well met good fellow'.

His keeper and guardian, Queen Nanda, was not exactly a leader of the village, but she knew more of the world than most of the locally escaped slaves. She was born in Haiti, but during the revolution, was carried off by her master, a French planter who kept her as his concubine and had business in Charleston. As were many enslaved people in such situations, she was kept in the slave pens by day, while her master went about his business in the city. While she was there, rumors spread in the pens of an impending slave revolt and the imprisoned slaves were taken to more secured pens outside the city. On the way, Nanda managed to slip away along with another young woman, and the two of them fled southward toward Florida.

Nanda had not a word of English and was soon recaptured, by which time, in spite of his efforts to catch her, her master had returned to Haiti without her. She was put on the block and sold to a family that had a rice plantation on one of the Georgia Sea Islands where she remained for the next two years, kept as a cook for the big house.

In the summer, part of the family would return to Charleston to get away from the summer flux and the mosquitoes, and during one of these trips she escaped again to the mainland, this time heading north, following the Drinking Gourd. She had a rudimentary, hand-drawn map of a couple of safe houses, and here she met an experienced runaway named Wilson. He was much disfigured by the lash and had had his left nostril clipped and was reported to be a known killer who had twice escaped from the patrollers, having on the second occasion, dispatched two of them with a stolen axe. Wilson was headed for. The Great Dismal Swamp, and agreed to guide her. Wilson knew all the survival tricks, and although they experienced some close calls in the Carolinas, they finally reached the swamp.

Wilson and Nanda lived with the maroons as a couple for five years. But one day he was bitten by a cottonmouth and in spite of the application of a variety of cures by the local 'snake doctor', a native African herbalist, he succumbed.

Nanda took Marcus on as a protégé and began the work of un-civilizing him. All the Christian lore and the knowledge of table settings and silk and silver were supplanted with training in herbs and boar hunting, snake lore, African dialects, poisons, dog killing methods, and man traps to foil the few patrollers and hunters who entered the swamp. He was a quick learner and soon became a sort of go-between for the village, informing them of the larger world beyond the swamp. They had not had a stranger in their midst for years, and there were young people, born in the village who had never known bondage, nor anything about the aborning movement of abolitionists.

The older people did know, however, of Nat Turner, although they had no real knowledge of the fear and the reactionary violence against the innocent enslaved people that followed his killing spree, but they refused to let Turner know of their secret village. They understood he was dangerous to know.

In his first weeks there, Marcuse, as they took to calling him, was invited to join a deer hunt.

Accompanied by a scrawny pack of dogs, a group of men and women set out shortly after dawn to an area where one of the men had seen the tracks of a deer herd a few days earlier. The group hiked briskly toward the site, and after twenty minutes or so halted and began searching the dry ground. From the center where they had stopped, they fanned out in a thin circle, and soon one of the men called out and they all gathered. He had found the first tracks.

Marcus himself could see nothing at all that suggested that a deer had been there. But Barco showed him a faint indentation in the mossy ground and then another a few feet away. Following some unseen signs, and led on by this time by the dogs, who were tied to vine leashes, they started slowly following the trail, which was at one point join by the tracks of more deer. This tracking went on for what seemed to Marcus nearly half a day until finally everyone halted and one of the men went off singly, with one dog. He returned to say that there was a herd resting on a hammock a few hundred yards away.

The group then made a wide circle around the site, and then at a whistled signal they freed the dogs who charged in wildly barking and scattering the deer. The herd rose as a body and bounded away, only to be met with a rain of arrows and spears. Barco himself got in a good spear cast. It was a little low, but the deer stumbled briefly on the spear shaft and was instantly pierced by arrows and two more spear casts.

There were about twelve deer in the herd, and the hunters managed to kill five, which they immediately began to butcher. Marcus noticed that, as they had with the dogs they had killed when Marcus first came to the camp, the group cut out and consumed the entrails first, the raw heart, liver and kidneys, which squeamish as he still was, Marcus politely refused when offered.

There was a lot of private laughter at this point. Barco explained that, according to their tradition, hunters were bound to bring home the day's catch and share it with whole village. But in fact it was a tradition that was more often overlooked and the innards of wild animals were considered more nutritious that the actual meat.

As they were preparing to leave, one of the women noticed a tiny newborn fawn hiding in the underbrush. There was a lot of hallooing over this and they caught the fawn and bound its legs with vines, preparing to carry it home. A large women named Calpurnia picked up the young fawn and made a sort of cradle for it from her satchel and slung it over her back. The fawn bleated and kicked but it eventually wore itself out as they made their way back to the village.

Barco explained that they would give the fawn to a woman named Toque who was nursing a baby. She would adopt the fawn and nurse it along with her human child. The fawn would grow up tamed and stay in the village, Barco said, more or less a mascot. "But hard time come," Barco said, "we eat him up."

Over the course of the autumn and winter, Marcus acclimated himself to the primitive living conditions, the healthy diet, and the customs of maroons, some of whom had interesting and successful escape tales. And in spite of the primitive living conditions he came to enjoy life in the woods. Ironically, even though the maroons were living as hunter-gatherers in subsistence conditions, Marcus had never had so much free time. He calculated after a few weeks that the people as a whole only actually worked about four or five hours a day. The rest of the time they would sit around doing nothing, or sleeping, or playing with children and telling stories.

By November, thanks partly to Nyala and Barco, Marcus had become more familiar with the local territory. Under his friends' tutelage, he sharpened his knowledge of local edible plants and also learned a few tracking techniques. He took to rambling off on his own from time to time and whenever he was stumped by a track or what he perceived to be some animal sign, he would question Barco or Nyala. At one point, during one of these lonely excursions, he spotted what appeared to be the tracks of a bare-footed human being. Whoever it was had emerged from a shallow pool in the swamp, wandered aimlessly through the muddy ground, and at one point seemed to have stopped and turned over a log before moving on. Marcus was mystified, and in fact slightly unnerved by the strangeness of the signs. He came back later in the day with Barco and showed him the signs.

"This a bear," Barco said. "When he put his foot down flat on the ground, he look just like a man."

They proceeded to follow the tracks but lost them at a spot where the bear had entered a thorny tangle of bullbriers.

On another excursion, Marcus ranged farther north in his territory and noticed ahead of him, a bright clearing. He approached and halted abruptly. He had come to what was the edge of the cypress woods. Beyond lay the borderlands of the more settled land where, as he well knew, there could be farms and roads, and possibly, patrollers. He retreated. But on his way back he ran across more tracks, these consisting of a shoed human being in heavy brogans. These too he followed. Whoever it was had ranged along the edges of the swamp as if looking for something, either a lost cow or, as Marcus realized to his horror, a runaway slave. He returned to the village and reported the tracks, but Barco explained that occasionally white hunters would enter the swamp, but they rarely penetrated more than a few hundred yards into the interior.

In the many free hours of what he thought of as his time of *rien faire*, he would wander off to some sunny, dry glade and sit down in the winter sun and spend hours, day dreaming and reviewing the course of his life so far and thinking often about Tilly and what his next move would be.

Easy though it was in the swamp, he realized that he was caught between two conflicting desires. One—the main one—was freedom. The other was his love for Tilly. These two emotions had been in constant conflict ever since his last escape. The loss of freedom was unthinkable, but so was a full life without Tilly.

He had also come to realize that he was in some ways almost a prisoner of his past. His early childhood years were easy and even fulfilling, mainly because of Amanda, but his adult years as an enslaved person were insufferable. He had witnessed the abject cruelty of lives governed by the whip and sometimes brutal torture. But he had heard, via Amanda's descriptions, of the seemingly easy life in European cultures. He had also witnessed a facsimile of French culture from his time working as a house boy.

In spite of the ever present, illiberal, even perverse and cruel underpinnings of the day to day life on a plantation, Southern gentry blithely aspired to an aristocratic European-based civilized style of life. They wore the latest Paris fashions, enjoyed good wines and fine dishes, held costumed balls, and outfitted their plantation houses with imported furniture and other accoutrements of wealth. They led a life of comfort, a model of nobility and civil behavior. And all supported by a system of bondage, sustained by the whip. Considering all this, it came to Marcus that his past was his prison. If he had been raised as a field hand and was illiterate, and knew only the land and farming and the threat of the lash, he might have been contented to live forever in freedom among these peaceable maroons for the rest of his life. But as it was he longed to see the world. He longed for a life of true freedom with no necessity to remain secretive in a dismal swamp.

By late winter, he had sorted things out: He made up his mind to leave the swamp at some point and make his way north, settle, and then return to Mary Plantation and rescue Tilly. And then he would take her to France, a country about which he knew very little save that they spoke a soft language, were fond of dueling, and mainly—according to Amanda—the fact that Blacks were free there.

By the time spring arrived, he became even more restless, and finally decided it was time to resume his flight north to freedom and an equal and literate life.

He announced his decision to Queen Nanda and his friends and allies in the village, and they all encouraged him not to chance a life in the world beyond. They had all heard, or knew first hand, what life was like 'out beyond' although it seemed to Marcus that their fears were greatly exaggerated. They told him that hundreds of men on horses, accompanied by packs of huge dogs continuously circulated through the countryside in a constant search for dark-skinned people.

"Dem catch, dem kill," they told him repeatedly.

Nonetheless, in late March, with Barco and Nyala serving as guides, Marcus left for the northern edges of the swamp.

There were many goodbyes among his new friends and many well wishes and invitations to come running back with his tail between his legs, so to speak, but they all understood. His was a brave move.

By that time, he and Nanda had found a common language, a mix of French and her Haitian patois, and their parting was, as it seemed to be with all the women he had associated with, a bittersweet farewell. She too understood his dilemma, having seen more of the world than many of her fellow villagers, but she was sad to see him go.

"*Ale fò, pitit gason m nan,*" she said, holding him by the shoulders and fixing his eye. "Be strong, my son."

"*Mwen pral, Mamman, mwen p'ap janm bliye ou,*" he said. "I will, Mother, I will never forget you."

They embraced, he kissed her cheeks, and she drew back and held him by his shoulders again. Then she flung her heavy arms around him and rocked him from side to side.

"*Ale fo mon gason*," she said. "*Ale fo*."

Marcus was dressed for his flight in the trousers and a striped cotton overshirt and doublet he had worn when he joined the village and which he reserved for the time when he would have to sortie out into the dangerous world outside the swamp. And he was armed with the Navy sword he had when he arrived and a dagger he had fashioned from the leg bone of a deer—well-armed in other words against dogs and, if necessary, the patrollers.

He left shortly after dawn with Nyala and Barco, and the three of them made their way slowly northward, sticking to the hammocks and high ground until, after a day's travel, they stopped and made camp. Here they spoke mostly in low voices and whispers, none of the signing and chanting and laughter he had known back in the village. They were not far from a shingle cutters camp according his two guides, and even though these people were generally sympathetic, semi-free workers, they could not be entirely trusted. So they stayed quiet and the next morning made their way toward the northern border. By late afternoon, they could see the brighter light of the open fields beyond the dense forest, and here they slowed, then stopped and then said their farewells.

Nyala fell into his arms and wept, and there were tears in Barco's eyes as well. And although they understood his flight, they were sad and there were many invitations to change his mind and run back. But Marcus, appreciative though he was to these two, was not so moved. He had other lives to live and other loves driving him.

Mary Plantation
Steal Away

The day after Marcus left, Tilly asked her mother to tell ole Mistress she was too sick to work. She had whimpered on her pallet all night, and once her mother left for work, she cried off and on for most of the day. She went to work the next day but after racing through her chores, she went up to her closet hiding place and cried some more. When she reappeared, Mistress could not help but noticed her puffed up eyes.

"What's wrong with you, girl?" she asked. "You got the fever?"

"No, ma'am, I just sick and weak. Something gnawin' at my ankles," Tilly said.

It took Tilly another week to fill the big hollow she felt in her stomach, and she cried herself to sleep every night for the next month. By mid-autumn, she still missed him and uncharacteristically, she slowed down at work and no longer sang to herself, and, also uncharacteristically, she stopped misbehaving. She was tired all the time and hid in her closet whenever she could and whimpered. She found that she was soothed by whimpering, save that she began to suffer headaches.

Her mama tried to calm her. She made her teas of St. Johnswort, and managed to steal plasters for her headaches, but try as she might, nothing worked. Even the staff at the big house noticed and tried to be kind to her. Mistress herself allowed her rest periods during the day, but word got out that it was nothing more than the escape of Marcus Aurelius that was causing all her physical problems. And that changed things in the big house.

One hot autumn afternoon, Master Washburn himself came into the kitchen and told Tilly follow him. The two of them went around to the woodshed behind the kitchen.

Washburn grabbed her by the shoulders, shook her, and then violently pushed her back against the woodshed door.

He was a big man, nearly six feet tall, forty-six years old. She was a slim girl of sixteen.

"You listen up, girl," he said. "We've had enough with you, you hear? You got the whole house turned topsy-turvy, you got Mistress Washburn weeping about you to me every night telling me to take care of that girl, let her rest for a week or two. She won't let it go, it's Tilly this and Tilly that, I can't quiet her down and furthermore we're up to your tricks, smashing plates spilling puddings and then telling us the dog did it, we know all about you and if weren't the Mistress I'd sell you down the river tomorrow. So you quit your moping around here like a tired old dog and snap out of it. You unnerstan'?"

He pushed her back against the wall again.

"Get yourself together, girl, or I'm going give you something to cry about. That old whipping post looks lonely out there in the yard."

Tilly began to cry again.

Washburn slapped her hard across the cheek. "I said stop that crying!" He slapped her again, lightly this time.

"I cain't help it, Massa," Tilly whimpered. "Just cain't help it."

"Well, you better help it," he said.

He slapped her again, harder this this time, so hard he knocked her head back against the woodshed wall and she saw stars. Then he kicked her legs to the side so that she fell to the ground and then he gave her a kick and stomped off, cursing under his breath.

Henry Washburn should have known better than to beat a girl like Tilly. People of her ilk are not broken easily. Love, the loss of true love might undo her, but violence begat rage and rage begat a desire for revenge.

She lay on the floor for another ten minutes, weeping. Then she sat up, leaned against the wall and whimpered for a while longer, sniffling, and then she scraped up some of the deep sawdust from the floor and ate it, still whimpering. Then, suddenly, she spit out the dirt, hammered her open hand against the floor, got up, and began to run.

She didn't consciously know where she was running to, she just ran. And ran. And then, breathless, she slowed and walked and realized she was on the long curving drive that led out to the Charles City road and realizing this, she ran again and when she came to the road, she turned right and continued to run until at one point she saw ahead of her an approaching carriage and so she turned into the woods and scrambled through the bullbriers and young hollies and continued to run and scramble and run more, tearing her dress and scratching her shins and knees until she tripped over a root and fell face-forward on the ground.

And then, as if to punish the very earth she began to hammer her fists on the ground and cry again, this time in anger—she was beating ole Massa to death, and she snatched up a rock and finished him off, he with his clean linen suits, his finely trimmed white mustache, his silky blue eyes and serious countenance; she hated him; she hated her mistress; she hated Billings the overseer, she hated the white people who sat on the porch in rocking chairs, enjoying cooling drinks, the very same drinks she sometimes used to spit into, and most of all, although she never consciously considered the reality of her condition since she had never known any other way of life for sixteen years—she hated enslavement.

At dusk that day, she was missed. Mistress couldn't find her, nor could any of the house people, nor even her mother. Word went out that she had run away. Washburn got the news and began cursing her again and raging that she was going to get the beating of her life, sold down the river, and then he told Billings to go catch her, which Billings did, or tried to do.

He let loose the hounds from the kennel, mounted up and rode off, whip in hand.

The dogs set off down the drive, noses to the ground, baying, and then they turned right on the Charles City road, then turned right again into the woods, while Billings sat on the road listening to their route.

Judging by the barking, he realized she had run to the river. Then the dog pack turned right again and ran along the river trail back toward the plantation, baying all the while. Billings headed the horse back along the road, and made his way on a foot tract through the woods to cut her off. But by the time he reached the river, Tilly was back in her cabin. And she was no longer crying.

She was plotting.

James River Bottomlands
Follow the Drinking Gourd

According to Nyala and Barco, within a day or night of following the first road he came to, Marcus would arrive at a crossroads. If he turned left, in the first farmhouse, there lived a white couple who were sympathetic to runaways. They would put him up in their barn and give him directions to the next station, they said.

And so, well supplied with roots, the strips of dried venison and berries they called pemmican, at dusk he set out, walking to the northwest, guided now by the Drinking Gourd.

A week later, he found himself wondering whether he should have stayed.

Toward dawn, he found a spot in a stand of woods and made his first camp. He ate and then cleared a dry spot and slept on the bare ground, warmed later in the morning by the sun. He woke, ate some more, thought about his mission and then at dusk, carried on.

Early the next morning, he came to a narrow hard-running river he had been told about. He hiked downstream, as he had been directed, and in time came to a rickety wooden bridge, which he crossed. Here, beyond an open field, he saw a small white house surrounded by a picket fence. Tentatively, he approached and knocked on the door. An elderly man with wired-rimmed glasses, dressed in a dark suit opened the door a crack and asked him what he wanted. Marcus borrowed the story of the old enslaved man attempting to deliver the silver goblet and asked if the householder had seen him passing by with his wagon. He had been sent out by his owner, Marcus said, to search for the old man.

"Now, I too am lost," Marcus said, "and I wonder if you could spare me some victuals and a place to sleep for the day. I've been wandering lost all night."

The householder stepped out the door, smiling privately. It was clear that he didn't buy the story, but it was clear too that he didn't care.

"Come along, then," he said and led Marcus around to the back of the house where there was a small horse barn. Inside there were two clean stalls, a swept wooden floor, and beams and rails hung with tack. A ladder led to a loft half filled with sweet-smelling hay. Marcus had not seen so neat and clean a place in months.

"Thou may'st stay here, friend," the man in the dark suit said. "In the evening, we will deliver thee a plate and cider." He then led Marcus to an empty stall and showed him a trapdoor.

"But a word of warning," the man said. "Shouldst thee hear a commotion of horses enter the yard, get ye down this bolt hole and do not come up until we call thee. Patrollers have been in this area. And e'en though one may have letters of passage, many of the patrollers are illiterates and will carry you off in chains, no matter, be'ist thou free or bonded."

"I understand, sir," Marcus said, dropping the field hand accent he had used earlier. "And I am truly grateful. I'll be on my way tomorrow night."

The owner left, and Marcus climbed into the loft and lay in the hay, his thoughts whirling with images—Nyala and Barco, the dark shadowed swamp, Nanda, cooking fires, the hunt. The whole winter interlude had all seemed an unreal dream and now, here he was back in dangerous territory, an alien world.

Toward dusk, he woke with the thought that he should maybe go back.

He had not seen a white face since autumn, and this kindly old white man confused him. So did his manner of address. He sounded like a character out of the novel, *Ivanhoe*, that Amanda used to read to him.

Later, at dusk, he heard the barn door open, and a soft whistle.

"Come down, son," a woman said. "I've brought thee dinner."

Marcus looked down from his perch and saw an elderly woman in a poke bonnet and a high-waisted, long-sleeved dress carrying a tray with a glass and a plate of food. He descended and stood with his right hand on the ladder.

"Thank you, mistress," he said. "I won't bother you for more and I'll be off later tonight."

"And where art thou headed, if I may ask?" she said.

"I'm taking a message back to Greenwood Plantation on the James River. I've an errand there."

She considered this for a second or two. “And then what? Art thou a captive or a free man?”

Marcus threw off all caution. “I’m a free man no mistress, and I intend to stay that way.”

“We thought as much. And we know of the old man with the old horse and wagon who had lost his way. He passed by here last fall. We directed him as best we could, but as far as we could determine, he was headed in the wrong direction. But I must warn thee, there be patrollers all over this region. They have a militia of sorts and they ride at night in armed groups searching for the likes of you. They are uncouth men and violent. Be wary.”

“I understand,” Marcus said.

“Leave the plate beside the door, but cover it with hay,” the woman said, “and pull up the ladder when you leave. Patrollers have entered this barn in the past, searching for runaways. And they are not fond of my husband.”

“Why not?” Marcus dared to ask.

“We are Quakers. We do not believe in human bondage, and the small holders and plantation owners around here don’t trust us.” She paused for a second. “Rightly so,” she said with an ironic smile. “And please—God forbid—if you are caught, don’t tell anyone you slept here. There is a dark hill covered with pines just to the north. It’s well off the road and dry. Tell them you slept there. And good day to you and best of luck in thy travels.”

“Goodnight, my lady,” Marcus said, imitating the language of Ivanhoe.

She laughed. “You speak well, sirrah.” She closed the door quietly, and then opened it again. “Dost thou know the next safe house?” she asked.

“More or less,” Marcus said. “I had rough directions from friends of mine who are hiding in the swamp.”

“Well, you’ll be headed northwest from here,” she said, and then gave him a detailed description of the landscape he should follow and the next station on the Underground Railroad.

Marcuse thanked her profusely.

“No need for thanks, young man; it’s God’s work we do.”

He found the family she had directed him to, and found the next station, as well, which was, he calculated, somewhere southeast of Richmond and not that far from the James River where he had started. Directions to the next station were vague, though, and he spent that day in the woods and set out again at night. By dawn, he found the station. He approached the house and knocked on the door, and a large white woman came out and eyed him suspiciously. What did he want, she asked, and Marcus put his case. She continued to eye him and said, finally, she couldn't take him in and told him to be on his way. A man, presumably her husband, came in from the barn at that point and stopped short. He looked Marcus up and down and questioned him again, and then countermanded his wife and said he could stay one day in the barn if he liked, and head out that night.

Marcus took them up on the offer and went to sleep in the hayloft. Toward late afternoon, the farmer came back and called him to come on down now, which Marcus did.

In front of the barn, there were three armed men on horseback. A tall gaunt-faced man, armed with a dragoon revolver dismounted, came over to Marcus, put his hand on his chin and turned his face up to his.

Green eyes!

They had their man.

As it turned out, these three men were not official slave catchers called out by a local plantation owner to track down a runaway. They were renegade kidnappers who would pick up any lone African man or woman, and resell them to an auctioneer or a slave trader, even if they were carrying legitimate passes. Not that that would make much difference anyway. Marcus did his best to talk his way out of his arrest. He produced his well-crafted pass and handed it over to one of the men, who inspected it, and then tore it up.

Marcus carried on in his glib way, insisting his owner had sent him on an important financial mission, and that he was to explain to anyone who interfered, that any help provided as escort to Green Willow Plantation near Norfolk (a venue of Marcus's own spontaneous invention) would be rewarded handsomely.

"My master is a generous man, I can assure you. But I'm afraid I'm lost, so if you could assist me he would be most grateful. This is a very important transaction and the reward is substantial…"

"That right, boy? You sure enough are one fine talker," the tall man said. "But alright then, you just come along with us—we'll take you there." Whereupon one of the other men dismounted, bound Marcus's hands behind his back, and walked him over to the horse and tied a long rope around his neck and tied the other end to the saddle horn.

They walked all that day, stopping once at midday in a shady grove beside a slow stream. They tied their horses and unwrapped a parcel of corn bread, a piece of which they threw on the ground in front of Marcus.

"Eat up, boy," the lank man said. "You got a lot of walking ahead of you."

"My hands are tied, Massa, loose me, would you."

"Dog'll eat from the ground," he said, laughing. "You ought to be able to do that too."

The urge to kill swept over Marcus.

One of the men took out a bottle from his saddle bag and passed it around, and they lay back beside a black willow tree and packed their pipes. Marcus was in the sun, about twenty yards away. He had not yet eaten his chunk of corn bread, nor did he intend to. Eventually, his captors, one by one, fell into an afternoon nap.

The whole morning, Marcus had been surreptitiously working the bounds of the rope, trying to loosen them, but not making much progress. Now, with his captors half-drunk and sound asleep, he began working more furiously, twisting and raking down the ropes from one wrist then the other. This he calculated was his best opportunity for escape. The stream was not more than a few yards away and the horses were just behind him, but try as he might, although he managed to loosen the bonds slightly, he couldn't get them off before one of the men woke up and then rousted the others.

They were on the road again, and all the while, Marcus continued desperately working the knots, calculating that at some point they would stop again before dark. But it was not to be. Before sundown, they came to a rundown farmhouse, the yard strewn with broken tools and barrels and a barn with a half-caved in roof. Here they chained Marcus to a stall post, untied him and brought him some gruel.

"Git youself a good sleep, boy," his keeper said. "You got a long walk tomorrow."

He left without explaining. Marcus got very little sleep. He spent most of the night plotting an escape and trying to figure out how to get himself free from the ankle shackles they had fitted him with, again to no avail.

The next day, they marched about fifteen miles to a village with a few shops, a post office and a slave pen, a brick building with an iron gate across the door. Inside, in the half-light, he saw three or four figures, all young men, leaning against the walls.

He had thought the maroons were a sorry, ill-clad lot when he first met them. But these young men were even worse. They were clothed in rags; they all had whip scars, one had a slit nose, another was missing an ear. They were so broken and downcast, they barely spoke when he was thrown in with them—just a few desultory grunts. More gruel was served, and the keeper brought in a tub of water and a dipper and disappeared.

Marcus was so hungry and tired by this time that he deigned to eat and drink, and then fell into a long uncomfortable sleep. The next morning, the boys were brought out into the sun and marched to and fro along an empty back street for an airing. In the daylight, he could see his fellow captives more clearly. They were all younger than Marcus, some as young as thirteen he calculated, and they were all failed runaways. One of the young men, a boy about eighteen, had been caught twice. This was his third escape and he had learned from another captive, that this was no ordinary holding pen. The children were not destined to be returned to their plantations—the usual destination for runaways caught by the patrollers. The men who had caught Marcus were going to sell him themselves—a much more remunerative action.

He spent nearly a week in the pen with the captive boys, and then one day they were taken out, chained in a coffle and marched overland for a week to what Marcus realized was the Richmond slave market. Although he barely remembered, he had been here before when he was sold to Greenwood with his mother.

En route, it became clear to the head slave catcher that Marcus was a cut above the other captives. As a result, they began to favor him. They fed him a little more gruel than the others. And they kept him at the head of the line, and even chatted with him as they marched. They would rest two or three times a day, eat, drink, march on, rest, eat, drink and march along, some of the boys humming or chanting dirge-like moans to the rhythm of clanking of chains and shuffling feet.

When they got to Richmond, they were taken to the Shockoe Bottom district slave pens where the enslaved people were held, sometimes for weeks before an auction. They were placed in another slave pen, a large one, with older men. Here the food improved; they were given a stew of vegetables, an occasional chunk of boiled beef, grits, corn meal and black-eyed peas. Gossips among the enslaved there was rich with horror—tales of cruel masters, lash-happy foremen, rapists and sadists, and lives so terrible there were no alternative choices but to run. Others had run because they were lonely for their past plantations, where many of them had family. Others, Marcus among them, had run simply because they had heard of a land to the north where there was no slavery—Mother Canada, somewhere beyond the Drinking Gourd.

Once a day, the slaves were taken out and marched around in the sunlight. On one of these occasions, Marcus saw a discarded book, or part of one, lying on a wall. Surreptitiously, he snatched it up and stuffed it under his shirt. Those in the pens had more or less staked out little spaces for themselves, which they repaired to for the night, or the idle moments in the day. When he got back to the pens, Marcus went to his spot and took out the book. The cover was missing, and so was the title page and the first twenty pages or so, but reading on, Marcus guessed it was a translated French romance novel that someone had lost or abandoned. Word got out in the pens that he could read, and some of those imprisoned near him asked him to read aloud to them, which he did.

People in the pens came to enjoy the readings and twice a day, Marcus would read to the assembled. It appeared to be a story of lost love. A beautiful young maiden, very much in love with some local man above her class, had been somehow been betrayed by the man. At the point in the novel, when the hero was about to join Napoleon's Grand Armée and had come to say farewell and apologize for his wayward behavior, the gate to the slave pen opened quietly and a white man stood in the doorway and witnessed the scene. He began laughing.

"What are you doing there, boy?" he said.

"Nothing, Massa. I just fooling around," Marcus said.

"Y'all come up here, boy, and bring that book."

Marcus rose, wove though the crowd, and the two of them stepped outside.

"You know how to read?"

"No suh, I don't read," Marcus said in a field accent.

"Yeah, you don't read but I seen you reading there to the others."

"I'se just pretending, Massa," Marcus said.

"Let's see you pretend then," the guard said.

Marcus took the book and, holding it upside down, pretended to read. The guard snatched the book away, and turned it right side up and read some lines himself, where the pages were opened.

“Now, sir, lemme ask you this,” he said, chuckling. “If you can’t read, how is it that I heard you saying the words I’m seeing on this very page? How does happen?”

“I don’t know, suh—I just guess.”

“You sure enough are a good guesser. It’s all right. You keep the book and keep on guessing. Keeps the darkies quiet.”

He handed the book back to Marcus, and went off laughing quietly and shaking his head in disbelief. Watching from the gate, Marcus could see him telling the other guards about him.

Finally, after two more weeks, a group of the men, including Marcus, were taken to the site of the slave auction house, a large wooden building with a wide stage-like front porch and fitting rooms in the back. Here there were piles of clothing. The men were washed and shaven, and clothed in clean garments. As they were dressing and cleaning, the lanky tall man, his original captor, came in and took Marcus by the arm.

“Y’all come with me now, they’s someone I want you to meet.”

He took Marcus out the back door and walked him down to a little park-like square near one of the canals. Sitting on a wall by the river there was a middle-aged man in a top hat and a dark suit with a green waistcoat. He wore rimmed spectacles and a black silk ascot, and he was staring at the warehouses across the canal.

“Mr. Coffin,” the lanky man said, “I got your man here.”

“Bring him over,” Mr. Coffin said, standing up to greet Marcus. “Now young man, my name is Mr. Caleb Coffin, and I have a question for you,” he said. “I’m told that you have the ability to read. Is that true?”

Marcus was worldly enough by this time, and a sharp enough judge of character to calculate the situation. This was no auction; it was a prearranged potential sale.

“Yessir, I can read,” he said, dropping his field hand accent.

“And where did you learn?” he asked, and immediately corrected himself, realizing that a true answer would indict someone. “But never mind that,” Coffin said. “Can you read, for example, the words of Charles Dickens?”

“I have not read anything by Mr. Dickens, although I believe he stopped by the plantation where I once served when I was young, or so I’m told.”

“What is it that you were reading to the enslaved servants in that pestilential prison where you were held?”

"I don't know the name of the book, sir, it was missing its cover and the first few pages, but I would say that it was written by a woman. It seemed to be the story of a young unmarried woman of a lower caste who is somehow involved in a romantic relationship with an upper-class gentleman."

"Rather complex, I should say," Mr. Coffin said. "A novel of society matters, perhaps English, perhaps French. Can you add and subtract?" he asked.

Marcus hesitated, not sure how to answer. He was not as good with numbers as he was with the written word. "A certain bit, but in my time of imprisonment, I have been working on my multiplication tables."

"Very good, then. And I take it you have the ability to write—since you seem to be literate."

"Yessir, I can write."

Marcus, student of social interaction that he was, could see where this was going, and if, as he perceived, this was an interview prior to a sale, he played his part in order to be bought. He liked this Mr. Coffin better than any white man he had ever had dealings with; he seemed to be a considered man.

"And history?" Mr. Coffin asked. "You seem, by whatever means, I will not bother to investigate—you seem to be well read. Do you know your history?"

"Yes, a little. But mainly from novels. English and Scottish. Plus a little Roman history."

"From Sir Walter Scott, I take it?"

"Yessir. *Ivanhoe*. Also a little French history. My mistress used to read French novels to me."

"In English?"

"Yessir. But sometimes in French. She was a student of French."

"French, is it?" he said with surprise. "Now allow me to ask you another question. *Est'ce que tu parles français*?"

Marcus hesitated for a moment at this, not sure whether he should reveal too much at this point. But he gambled. "*Oui, monsieur, je parle un peu*."

"*Et tu peux lire*?"

"*Oui monsieur, mais aussi, un peu seulement*."

"*Attends ici s'il te plait*. Wait here please. Actually, I never was given your name. *Comment tu t'appelles*?"

"Marcus Aurelius," he said.

"Marcus Aurelius? The Roman Emperor, the Stoic philosopher? What a name. Who gave you that name?"

"I suppose the wife of the master."

"And why did they call you Marcus Aurelius?"

"I'm not sure, sir."

In fact, he knew perfectly well—from Amanda. It was because all the family thought he was so wise for a little pickaninny.

"Please wait here then, Marcus Aurelius," Mr. Coffin said.

All this while, the lank man, who Marcus now learned was named Jedidiah, was standing by, listening and suppressing a smile. In fact, he was very pleased by Marcus's presentation.

Mr. Coffin and Jedidiah stepped off slightly out of earshot and huddled together in an agreeable discussion, after which they shook hands.

Jedidiah came back and ordered Marcus to come along with them. They walked up Market Street and then wove their way through the city, Marcus walking between the two men. In time, they came to a small neat cottage and went around to the back where there was a walled garden. There was a pantry-like room inside the back door and they instructed Marcus to wait there.

This was the chance he had been waiting for. The door and the garden gate were unlocked, and he could easily let himself out. But he sat in the cool room, lined with jarred preserves and considered his situation. He didn't know the streets of Richmond. He had no papers, and it was still morning, no cover of darkness. But then he thought that if he could hide somewhere and then get to the river after dark and steal a punt, he could row downriver until he came to Greenwood.

But then what? Back to Tilly's garden? And then? And then he thought about Mr. Coffin. Life with him would be far easier, he reasoned, than if he had been sold on the block as a field hand. Whatever Mr. Coffin was, it was clear than he was not a plantation owner, nor a slave trader. The work would be easy, he reasoned, and if necessary, he could escape from this thoughtful, somewhat doddering, elderly gentleman.

As he was pondering all this, the two men returned "Please come into the garden," Mr. Coffin said. "We have some news for you."

Marcus followed them out to the gate.

"Well, so long, Mr. Marcus Aurelius," Jedidiah said cynically. "You are now the property of Mr. Caleb Coffin."

Saint Mary's County
Mr. Caleb Coffin

Mr. Caleb Coffin was from a Quaker family who owned a few coastal trading vessels that sailed out of Shelter Island, in New York. His father's business expanded and he began investing in more vessels and eventually settled on an estate on the Potomac River, in Saint Mary's County and began trading vegetables, fruits and dried cod to Cuba, and Haiti, or so Caleb was told.

This was in the years of the Haitian Revolution, and inasmuch as he was a Quaker (or was supposed to be, in fact he was inclined to suspend his faith in the interest of profit), William Coffin began illegally running supplies to the rebel stronghold in Jeremy, and by the time of the successful liberation of the island, to Port au Prince.

After he completed his early schooling, Caleb was sent to Brown University, where, rather than business courses, as was expected, he became interested in comparative literature, and went on to graduate studies at Yale. After graduation, he somewhat reluctantly joined the family business and was trained in the business by his father.

He had always known that his family was in the shipping trade. But he had presumed the business was trading goods to Haiti and Cuba and would return with molasses. But then he discovered the real source of his family's wealth. Along with fruits and vegetables they were always involved in the Atlantic slave trade.

He was shocked by the news and learned also that his father had been expelled from the Friends. But he joined the business anyway.

Caleb was a sharp, even a somewhat hard-nosed trader, and after his father died he took over the trade, even though the Atlantic slave trade had been declared illegal in 1808, he carried on. But on a trip to Haiti, he was exposed to the realities of the business he was profiting from. Human life was cheap in

Haiti. Unlike the United States, where slaves were held for life, slaves in Haiti were worked to death, and when they succumbed, the plantation owners would simply replenish their work force.

Successful though he was in the business, he began to have doubts—he was, after all, more interested in ancient history, French and English literature, and transcendental philosophy, than he was in account books. On his second trip to Haiti, something happened. Instead returning home, he sailed to France and from there disbanded his father's company, sold three of his four ships to a New England packet line. He later returned to America and started a trading company of his own as an independent merchant in the tobacco business in Saint Mary's County.

His business expanded again, and he began trading in European ports, mainly France.

Mr. Coffin was considered a generous and good man who, inasmuch as he was a Quaker was, in theory, opposed to human bondage, but not so opposed that he deigned to keep a slave for himself, but with a twist. He quietly, on a personal level, became an active abolitionist, albeit in a small, undercover way. He would buy a slave, educate him in bookkeeping and secretarial work and then free him. He did this with women as well, although the one experiment in this area, the purchase of a cook named Janey B stayed with him after she was freed. Marcus Aurelius would be his fourth clerk.

******

The day of the purchase, Mr. Coffin led Marcus into the Mr. Coffin's Richmond house to show him around and introduce him to his future chores. There was a small chamber on the west side of the pantry with a narrow cot and a window giving onto the garden gate and a view of the street beyond.

"You will sleep here," Mr. Coffin said. They moved on to a kitchen with a long yellow pine table set along the north wall. "Miss Janey B will give you your meals here," he said. They proceeded down a hallway to a sunny room wide a wide standing desk and shelves of log books on one side. The desk was stacked with a pile of papers on the left side and a long gray accounting book on the right, an ink stand and a quill pen lying on an ink stained blotter on which someone had sketched a primitive drawing of a schooner.

“This is where you will do most of your daily work,” Coffin said. “Come here after breakfast and I will give you the assignments for the day. For the time being, you will work as a copyist, and as you learn the trade, you will be expected to take over some of the bookkeeping, plus errands, plus some orders and receipts. You are free to take periodic breaks from—what I will admit—is tedious work, and I would encourage you at these times to step out into the garden. It is my belief, you see, that fresh air and a short constitutional, sharpens the mind. But for today, please rest. You perhaps need some relief from that hell hole in which you were imprisoned. Miss Janey B will come later in the day and give you a supper.”

Mr. Coffin then led Marcus back to the bedchamber.

There was a pile of blankets on the cot and a clean feather pillow. Marcus looked around the room. There was a wooden table beside the cot with a single candlestick with a new candle. He noticed a clean chamber pot under the bed, and a wooden panel of hooks on the south wall. Next to it was a washbowl with a pitcher of water.

Marcus took off his shoes and stretched out on the bed. The window was opened slightly and a light breeze, scented by the rose garden was filtering in. It was clear to him that he had made the right decision not to bolt. He had seen accommodations of this sort when he worked as a house boy, but he had never experienced such comfort, and within minutes, he fell into a dreamless sleep.

He woke later in the afternoon, not sure where to go nor what to do. Mr. Coffin was not in the office, and he dared to snoop around the desk, and the bookshelves.

There was a smell of cooking in the air, so he pushed open the door and poked his head in the kitchen. There was a middle-aged Black woman sitting at the table with the chair turned to face the stove. She wore a red bandanna over her hair and was dressed in a rough osnaburg cotton dress and a thick apron.

She turned her head when he entered.

“You the new boy?” she asked.

“I guess,” Marcus said. “Are you Janey B?”

“Ain’t no one else. You sit down, boy,” she commanded. “I got coffee brew here and Marse Coffin, he say you gonna need coffee. You been asleep all day.”

Marcus obeyed and took a seat at the table.

He was familiar with women such as Janey B from his houseboy days—worldly, bossy women with a controlling attitude but kind hearts. She poured some coffee from a blue pot on the back of the stove and put the cup on the table.

"Drink that," she ordered.

There was a tabby cat curled on one side of the stove and when Marcus sat down it came over and rubbed its cheek on his leg. He reached down and scratched its head and it jumped into his lap and curled up.

"Get off'n there, cat," Janey B shouted. "Get that cat off a' you; I'll throw him out the door."

"No, it's alright," Marcus said. "He's purring. Nice to have purring cat with clean fur like this one. Cats I knew were horrid scrawny mousers with matted fur who would run as soon as they saw you looking at them."

Janey B asked him where he was from before and Marcus proceeded to tell the outline of his story, including an account of his winter in the Great Dismal Swamp.

Janey B gave a grunt of disgust. "You eat dem possums and dogs like dat?"

"Yes ma'am. You're always hungry when you're on the run, you'll eat anything you can get."

She snorted. "I know 'boutdat," she said, without elaborating.

They chatted for a while about plantation life, as opposed to the hard life of runaways, which required constant quest for sustenance and secrecy. Marcus asked her if she had ever run off.

"Once," she said, again without providing any further information.

"But you're here owned by Mr. Coffin?"

"Yes and no," she said, and nothing more.

Then she asked him where he was before he ran to the Great Dismal Swamp. Marcus related that story too. The real one this time.

"But how about you? Are you from Richmond?"

"No," she said.

"Neither am I," Marcus said.

"Yeah, I know dat."

"You from Charleston?"

"No."

"Uidah?"

"What you going on about?"

Finally, she relented.

She said she had been raised by generally indifferent people on a James River plantation. Her mother was a cook, and when she grew old enough she too picked up the work. She had a husband who was a field hand and two children with him, a girl and a younger boy. But when the children were ten and twelve years old their owner sold her whole family away, leaving Janey B alone in her kitchen.

"You don't got no children?" she asked.

Marcus told her no.

"Well then, boy, you don't know whatdat's like—lose your children like dat, and you husband too. You cry all night, dat happens. You cry in the morning. Cry at the stove, cry in bed, you cry like you never cry before in you' life. Why live when you don't got no family and you got to work for the devil what done that to you. First you cry. Then you plot to kill."

Pure hate sustained her in her daily life after that, hate and a strong desire for revenge kept her going. She said she had always thought her mistress and master were good people. Then they sold her family without even telling her. She began spitting in their stews. Then she thought to poison them. One day a cat brought in a dead rat. She skinned it, cut its head off and put it in the stew.

On another occasion, she found a dead cat in the barn. This too she skinned, chopped up and put in the stews. Another time, she took all the sweepings from the kitchen and pantry floor and seasoned a roast with it. Things got worse. She told Marcus that she took to packing a pot with sweepings from the chicken house floor and dumping that in the stew. One day she mucked the horse barn and added the mix of straw and horse manure to a sauce and cooked it for half a day. But none of this managed to kill her owners. Then one evening, after a long day preparing for a big upcoming dinner, she fell asleep on a chair near the stove. When she woke up, Jesus was standing there.

"I thought I died," she said. "Jesus come down to me take home."

"You saw Jesus?"

"Yessuh I seen him, clear as I see you now. I even smell him. He take me in his arms, and he's wearing this long shirt made of clean rough cloth and I can smell that heavy fresh smell 'a soap or something clean and fresh, like good air."

"What does Jesus look like?" Marcus asked. He was, of course incredulous, but the details were rich.

She thought about this then said, "You know, he looked a little like you, 'cept that he got this long black curly hair. He got colored skin, color of cocoa, but he also look like a white man."

She said Jesus admonished her for putting all those nasty dead animals in the stew. He told her she should cleanse the bitterness from her soul and forgive her master. Brighter days would come, he said.

"So I axed him when dem brighter days a'coming? And he say, 'not yet. But soon. You be free someday.'"

A few days later, through the inter-plantation slave gossip, news came that her children were enslaved at the Rose Plantation on the James River, not far above Norfolk, so instead of trying to kill her owners, she decided to run away. She spent a few days putting up hunks of cold cooked beef, some carrots, cooked potatoes, and corn bread, and then one moonless night she walked to the river landing, turned downstream, and hiked along the banks, staying on dry land.

"I'm free at last but yearning to see my little ones no matter what."

Three days later, the patrollers got her. They took her back to the plantation, and the next day the foreman took her out to the barnyard, tied her wrists to the whipping post, stripped her to the waist and gave her the traditional nine and thirty lashes.

"You know I'm gonna run again after dat."

"I do know," Marcus said. "I did the same thing."

She was caught a second time. Whipped a second time, and then they judged her incorrigible, took her up to Richmond to be sold.

"Best thing ever happened to me," she said. "That family bought me was nice people. He a doctor don't have no plantation, just four or five house slaves. They took me up to Maryland. And instead of keeping me all the time, they rent me out to other families to cook for them. That's how I meet Marse Coffin. And then, next thing I know, Marse Coffin buy me. Fine with me. He's a good man, Marse Coffin. Real good man. Better than you'll ever know."

"One morning he come to me and tells me to sit down. I sit down at that table and he puts a piece a paper in front of me. 'Janey B,' he says. 'I'm setting you free. These papers here, you keep dem with you at all times. You don't got to work here no more. You can move north if you like. You is free,' he say."

"That day throw me in a spin. I don't know what to do. Can't go back and see my little ones, 'cause they catch me again. Can't go north, I don't know the way. Don't know nobody anyhow. So a few weeks later, I go to Marse Coffin, and I say, 'Marse Coffin, I just want stay with you for now.' And you know what Marse Coffin say? He say all right. 'You free now. And free people don't work for nothing. So I'm going to pay you every week. I'll keep that money for you in a drawer, and anytime you want it, you come and get it, and I show you how to use it.'"

"See what I mean. Ain't no better white man than Marse Coffin. Not in this world anyway."

The following morning after breakfast, Marcus went to the office and Mr. Coffin told him to take a seat at the big desk. He selected a letter from the top of a pile of sheets on the left side of the desk, laid out a pen and the ink well and told Marcus to begin copying word for word the contents of the letter in his own hand.

"Call me back when you're finished," he said. "I'll be out in the garden."

This was more of a challenge than Mr. Coffin realized. Marcus knew that his handwriting was hardly very well developed, but nevertheless he took up the pen, and rather than attempt his own hand, he carefully drew each letter, as an artist might do. It was a slow tedious process, and in fact there were many words in the letter that Marcus did not know. He was not even sure what the letter was about. But he carefully copied it and then went looking for Mr. Coffin, who was sitting in the garden, reading.

They returned to the office; Mr. Coffin adjusted his glasses and carefully read over the letter.

"Is this your normal handwriting, Marcus Aurelius?" he asked.

"No, sir," he said. "I thought you said to copy that letter, so that's what I did."

"I did say that, but I meant for you to copy the letter in your own hand. But this is fine. All the better, in fact. Those who know my handwriting will think it's from me."

He handed him another letter and told him to keep going.

"But I want you to stand up and make a circuit of the garden from time to time. My belief, as I may have said, is that a short constitutional refreshes the mind and relieves strain on the eyes."

Marcus returned to his work ever more carefully.

This routine carried on for the next week, work interspersed with periodic turns around the garden, a midday meal prepared by Janey B, more work more circuits of the gardens, a rest, a coffee with Janey B, and then a supper and bed.

On the bookshelf beside the desk, Marcus noticed an edition of Webster's Dictionary and he got into the habit of copying, on a separate piece of paper, words he didn't know from the letters and carrying the dictionary back to his room after dinner to look up more words. The word 'sackcloth' occurred in one letter, for example, and he looked that up and then reading not far along in the 'S' section, he ran across the word 'slave' so he looked that up even though he thought he knew what that meant better than anyone, save for the other slaves in the United States.

"…a person held in servitude as the chattel of another. In the early state of the world, and to this day among some barbarous nations, prisoners of war are considered and treated as slaves. The slaves of modern times are more generally purchased, like horses and oxen."

He slammed the book shut. "Horse no more, Mr. Webster," he muttered.

The daily routine in Richmond carried on for another month and then by the end of April, Mr. Coffin announced that they would be returning to Saint Mary's County. The house in Richmond had been rented for the winter while he completed some important local trade deals. What these were was not clear to Marcus save that he presumed there were some sort of financial exchanges, he noticed phrases such as 'letters of transit, banknotes, remuneration, receipts', and the like all of which he had to look up.

Marcus's workday changed at this point and he spent a week packing papers valises, clothes and other items belonging to Mr. Coffin. Then in mid-April, he helped load the trunks on a wagon and the household rode down to Norfolk. Here they boarded a steamship on the Old Bay Line and sailed up the Chesapeake Bay to Baltimore, where they disembarked, hired another wagon and rode south to Saint Mary's County.

Here, set beside a creek with a boat landing, they turned up an oyster-shell drive through a border of peach trees. They came to a sizable gambrel roofed house with three dormers and two brick chimneys on the gable ends. A brick lined walkway led up to a two paneled Dutch door with two double-hung windows on either side. The drive ended at a sizable carriage house and stable and here they unloaded the wagon at the back of the house and an elderly Black man with cottony hair dressed in a dark suit and waistcoat came out and greeted them.

"Good evening, sir," he said. And Mr. Coffin introduced them.

"George, this is Mr. Marcus Aurelius, our new clerk, I hired him in Richmond."

Marcus greeted him, but he was slightly confused, inasmuch as this was late morning, not evening, and George said 'good evening' again. But he let it go.

There was a big vegetable garden just beyond the back door of the main house, a small slab-sided cottage behind the garden, and two backhouses set off to the side. On the opposite side of the carriage house, there was a large ornamental garden and behind the property was a cleared meadow where a few sheep and two horses were grazing.

"That cottage back there is your house," Mr. Coffin said. "You'll find there such necessities as you may need inside. But first do come in; we'll unload and I'll show you around the house and your new work space."

Marcus and the wagoner carried the trunk into the house, Janey B carried in her carpetbag and a bundled bandanna, and George went to the wagon and carried in a rake.

"Not that, George," Mr. Coffin said. "That belongs to the wagon."

George turned and slowly carried it back.

Marcus had very little baggage at that point. Mr. Coffin had given him a couple of his old shirts, a frayed waistcoat, and a somewhat moth-eaten cutaway and a pair of trousers, but other than the clothes on his back that was all he had. His Navy cutlass had been left behind in one of his flights. And he had lost a brace of pistols he had stolen on an earlier escape. But he was content. If this were to be his state of bondage, he could tolerate it.

Inside the house, Mr. Coffin gave him a tour. Inside the front door, there was a wide stairway with mahogany banisters that led up to a balconied second floor. On either side the entrance there were two rooms, a parlor on one side and a book-lined library on the other, with a two chairs and table set in the middle of the room. The parlor was set with an Empire daybed and Louis XV set of chairs. There was a fireplace with a brass-railed fender and Dutch tiles depicting maritime scenes and above the mantle, there was a portrait of a beautiful young mixed-race woman. She was depicted in three quarters view and she had dark eyes and red ribbons tied in her hair and she was smiling broadly. Marcus was struck by her beauty and wanted to stay and admire her but the tour moved on.

Between the kitchen and the dining room, there was a short hallway leading to another book-lined, spacious room with an elaborate Jory writing desk with a central drawer and two sets of stacked drawers on the sides. As in the Richmond study, this too was strewn with stacks of correspondence, and an ink well and blotter.

"This," Mr. Coffin said, "is where you will work. It will be the same travail as you experienced in Richmond. You will continue your multiple copy work. I will instruct you on record keeping and as we move along I will teach you on some simple bookkeeping. You will also be running local errands for me, but not to worry, I will supply you with letters of passage, and people in this town know me, so unless some piratical slave catchers appear in the town, no one will bother you. When you are ready, we will begin daily French lessons. Much of the correspondence here is between the United States and France, and you will have to learn the proper accents while copying, and later, I am hoping, you will able to return short notes in French."

A door on the left side gave onto a spacious dining room with a fire place and a black marble French clock on the mantle. There was a swing door leading to a pantry with the kitchen beyond, and there were two sizable sideboards against the walls and an imported Chinese screen showing scenes of herons in the south-west corner.

They moved on to the kitchen, a large room with a long French farm house table and chairs in the middle of the room, surrounded by cupboards, drawers, and a large cast iron cook stove. Janey B was already in the room, putting things away in the cupboards and George was sitting with one arm on the table, his long legs crossed, staring into space.

"Now, if you will step this way," Mr. Coffin said, "I will give you are short tour of the grounds. Please feel free to undertake walks here on your own once you begin work. As I believe I have said, the efficacy of fresh air and exercise cannot be overestimated."

(Marcus looked up the definition of 'efficacy' that night.) They went out through the kitchen door, which gave onto a colonial style herb garden planted with rue and lavender, edged by boxwood. Nearby was an extensive kitchen garden, which was now sprouting shoots of green peas, beds of sprouting lettuce and spinach.

“I like to work this garden myself,” Mr. Coffin said. “And you are welcome to help me if you are so inclined, I take it you know something of kitchen gardens.”

“I do, in fact,” Marcus said, thinking back on Tilly’s mother’s garden back on the Mary Plantation. That time seemed years past to him, save for the face of Tilly.

“You know it is said that the Renaissance nobleman Lorenzo di Medici worked often in his garden along with his peasants.” He stopped himself. “Not that you are a peasant, Marcus Aurelius, although your namesake may also have undertaken tasks of manual labor.” He stopped himself again. “Actually, I’m mistaken, it was Virgil who was not opposed to working the land. But be that as it may,” he added, dropping the subject.

Marcus was lost, but intrigued.

They moved on to the cottage, and Mr. Coffin let himself in.

“These will be your quarters here,” he said.

The cottage consisted of one large whitewashed room with a bed against the back wall and two glazed windows on the side. There was a table with a lantern, and a candle set near the bed and a row of coat hooks on the left side of the door. A large French armoire was located on the south wall.

The ornamental garden lay on the south side of the main house. It was also laid out in the colonial English style, with a central allée, laid out with oyster shells, and two transecting narrower paths. At the end of the main allée, there was a statue of a goat like thing, it had the body of a man, but shaggy goat legs and hooves, and a narrow smiling face and curling goat horns. Marcus had never seen such a beast and was a little taken aback. “Pan,” Mr. Coffin said, noticing Marcus’s reaction. “He was the Roman god of wild things. I brought him back from one of the old Italian villas they were tearing apart.”

They turned around and walked along a hedge that ran behind the cottage. There was a pasture beyond the shrubbery where the sheep and two horses were grazing. At the north end on the property they came to a gate to the pasture, turned east to an elaborate carriage house and horse barn. Mr. Coffin swung open the doors and stepped in, followed by Marcus. There were two carriages, including a two person Stanhope buggy and on either side of the building there were neat horse stalls, presumably for the two horses in the pasture.

“Are you familiar with carriages and equipage?” Mr. Coffin asked.

"No sir, I'm afraid I'm not. I know how to ride a little and I can drive a wagon team, but I've never had to do the harnessing."

"Well, maybe George could show you some day."

"Is George one of your—one of your—servants, Mr. Coffin?" Marcus asked.

"No, not really, he just lives here. He helps out from time to time. Or tries to."

Marcus wanted to ask more. He also wanted to ask about the portrait of the beautiful mixed-race woman of the parlor wall. But the timing did not seem appropriate.

They walked across the road, to a small open space above the creek, set with chairs overlooking the waters.

"This is a pleasant and reflective area here where I sometimes come to contemplate the vista across the creek and the ebb and flow of tides. You may wish to come here at times on your own to gain perspective on life," Mr. Coffin said.

"How do you mean exactly, sir?"

"I mean, every man must stop and step away from all this getting and spending and laying waste, and consider the larger picture in the course of human events. I mean to say, for your part for example, here you are, 'enslaved' as they say, my property, according to the American Constitution. And yet, are you not a man? If thy master pricketh thee, do you not bleed, as William Shakespeare, writing in another context, points out."

"I would encourage you to consider your position here, and even discuss it with me if you like. In my eyes, you are not legally my property and if you wish to negotiate your position here at any time, you are welcome to. I will listen to your proposal."

Marcus was nonplussed. The only other white person who had spoken to him in this manner was Amanda and then she was only imitating characters from her readings.

Marcus hesitated and then said, "Thank you, Mr. Coffin. Thank you very much. I-I'm not sure what to say."

In fact, he was not even sure what Mr. Coffin was talking about. But it sounded good.

“Not necessary to thank me,” Mr. Coffin said. “Why don’t you get your things and take them to your dwelling? Janey B will have some dinner in the kitchen later, if you like.”

They walked back to the house; Marcus picked up his bundle of clothes, went back to his cottage, sat on the bed and, unaccountably, suddenly burst into tears of happiness.

*****

The days with Mr. Coffin went by as they had in Richmond, work in the mornings, a midday meal, work, an afternoon break. A light dinner and sleep. The big difference was that every day, after lunch, Mr. Coffin set aside part of the early afternoon for an instruction period, language, rhetoric, literature, and philosophy. Mr. Coffin himself was an autodidact. He had had traditional schooling, and was trained, as were so many in that era in Latin, Greek, the classics, and English literature. But when he began traveling to France for his trade business, he realized he was lacking in certain aspects of European culture and made a point of educating himself. He soon became comfortable in the business world in Paris, and by extensions in the courts and the salons.

He was not the only American in Paris society at the time, there were many American artists studying in the French ateliers, also notable figures such as Samuel Morse, James Fennimore Cooper, as well as American doctors and traders and shipping merchants. But Mr. Coffin, who was more of a Francophile in his way, was a popular, if somewhat eccentric, figure in Paris society. What he traded exactly was not clear. He had started in the tobacco business, but as the Virginia tobacco fields began to wear out, and the cotton fields of the Deep South opened up, he had moved on the other trade goods. Whatever his exact business was, he was required to travel to France for extended visits. He traveled while he was in Europe to the major banking centers in London, Amsterdam, Geneva, and Milan.

There was perhaps another aspect of his shift in trade goods. He was brought up in the Quaker tradition, a cultural group that was active in the abolition movement and the Underground Railroad. Mr. Coffin appears to have been something of a lapsed Quaker, as not a few were when it came to financial matters. Quakers were skilled merchants, wealth was a sign, they believed, of

God's approval, and if owning a slave or two was necessary in the pursuit of lucre, so be it.

For that matter, Mr. Coffin had also seen the irony in the fact that many businesses and merchants in the northern states, including some of the abolitionist families, were involved in the cotton and woolen mills, as well molasses trades, and were also, in earlier years, active in the trans-Atlantic slave trade.

As he had apparently done before with other clerks, Mr. Coffin set out to give Marcus Aurelius a cultural education. Part of this may have been genuine altruism, but it was also useful to have a more worldly figure as his assistant. And Marcus was a willing student, something of budding autodidact himself.

Once Marcus grew comfortable with his business tasks, Mr. Coffin set out to improve his reading skills and lent him books to read at night from his library. He started with a translation of Stendhal's *The Red and the Black*, and when Marcus finished that—it took him more than a month to get through it—gave him a newly translated edition of Balzac's *Père Goriot*. That took another month. But by the time he was finished, he had a little better sense of French history. Mr. Coffin thought he might enjoy *Oliver Twist* and then he gave him a copy of *The Last of the Mohicans*, a book that Marcus enjoyed thoroughly; it kept him up half his nights reading it.

Along with his reading, Mr. Coffin started an after lunch period of French lessons. He had discovered that Marcus's French was far from fluent, mainly conversational, and having learned what French he knew from a southern belle, his accent was *afreux*—terrible. Mr. Coffin himself still had a slight American accent, but he was thoroughly fluent. They began with simple congregations in the present tense, moved on to the past tense, and then the future, the conditional, imperfect and finally, the proper use of the subjunctive.

Marcus found the process tedious, but he did enjoy the method that Mr. Coffin used to improve his conversational French. He would ask Marcus to relate to him in French the action of whichever novel he was reading in English.

With the hot summer moving in, Mr. Coffin changed the schedule slightly and began spending the French conversations in the evenings, sitting out on the little terrace over the creek hoping to catch a breeze coming in over the bay. And here, the French recitation often lapsed in the relaxed sultry air, and the boundary between master and servant began to slip.

Conversations on these evenings often involved descriptions of life in France. And Mr. Coffin's asked Marcus about plantation life from his point of view, and encouraged him to share his life story from his earliest memories of the first plantation and his mother, to the last plantation, from which he had fled. Mr. Coffin was intrigued by Marcus's description of the maroons and life in the Great Dismal Swamp.

It was clear from Marcus's narrative that from his earliest years, France had loomed in his imagination as an almost idyllic place where life was better—the weather was never too hot nor too cold, the food was rich and plentiful, people wandered on the streets and in country parks doing nothing save walking their dogs, chatting amicably with one another, and all the people were handsome, the men in summer whites, and the women attired in the latest fashions. All of this came from a single source—the vivid imagination of the twelve-year-old girl—Amanda.

Mr. Coffin knew the realities of France in those days. The violence, the riots, the peasant revolts, the brutality of the government and the royalist forces, but he was happy to share his stories of France. Paris was indeed filled with white people, he said, but not all of them were handsome and well attired, nor were all of them well fed. There had been in fact bread shortages.

"Bread, you should know, is a staple in France," Mr. Coffin explained, "a little like corn bread here, or grits, but even more popular."

A high percentage of the poor lived on bread alone, he explained, and bakeries were in some ways the most important industry.

"I have traveled through towns that for one reason or another, have lost populations, very few people living there, but there will always be a bakery open. That, and a post office. But life for the rich is very different," he said. "The French love art and music passionately. There are sometimes small riots in the theaters or art galleries, opposing a certain composer's work. And there are one or two painters there who caused a great uproar because they are not detailing their work; they merely give the impression of a scene, not the actual subject. And, as you have learned from reading Balzac and Stendhal, life is not always as easy as was described to you by your friend Amanda."

On one of these evenings, inspired perhaps by an after dinner glass of cognac, Mr. Coffin began sharing a bit more of his personal life: how he had worked for his father in the family trade, and taken over the local coastwise trade, and then, for reasons he did not go into, how he had moved on from the family business, and had ended up exporting tobacco to England and France.

"Before I came to Paris, my family was shipping fruits and vegetables and cod to Haiti. Then after the Haitian Revolution, my father set up an office in Port au Prince and took me with him to further familiarize myself with our business. I loved Haiti. The sultry air, the lively people, the colors, the trade winds in the palms. I was twenty and ready to grasp all there was of life. And then in the midst of all this, I met a young Creole woman of exquisite beauty."

"She had what struck me as the oddest of names, she was called Papagena. I learned much later that Papagena was the name of a bird-catcher girl in Mozart's opera 'The Magic Flute'. Her opera-loving father, a French colonial, had given her the name."

He went on to describe Papagena. She was born in Haiti, he said, the child of a sugar plantation owner and a local woman. She had come over to France with her father who had enrolled her on one the official schools for colonials.

"I was an innocent abroad," he explained. "I had never encountered such a person as Papagena. She used to laugh all the time. She thought everything was funny. She thought I was funny. She called me her stone man because I dressed all in gray in those days. I did not know how to dance; she tried to teach me, and when I stumbled, she laughed. She laughed at my halting French. She laughed when she described the antics of the little dogs she owned. She laughed at everything."

"Where is she now?" Marcus asked. He had an idea where this was going.

"She died," he said. "You would not believe that such a being, so full of life, could die at so young an age."

"I am sorry to hear that," Marcus said.

Mr. Coffin fell silent at that point, and Marcus did not press for details. He suspected the portrait on the wall was Papagena.

A light cooling breeze, redolent of marsh grass and salt, wafted in. Neither of them spoke. Night herons called from the marshes along the creek. The moon rose. A warm breeze ruffled the waters.

"It's late, isn't it?" Mr. Coffin said.

"Don't know," Marcus said.

A silence.

After a while, Marcus broke the silence. "Mr. Coffin, that portrait on the wall in the parlor, is that by any chance Papagena?" he asked.

"Yes, it is. I had it commissioned shortly before we were to sail for America."

"I'm sorry. She was beautiful."

"I know. Twenty years old."

Another silence descended and Marcus did not presume to ask more. But his trust and respect for Mr. Coffin deepened. He had previously thought of him as a cold, but honest and trustworthy man. Then he thought of him as a mentor. And then as a sort of father that he had never known. But now, he thought of him as an equal, a man of sorrows.

****

As the French lessons moved on, Marcus and Mr. Coffin began attempting to converse in French. And as his reading skills improved, Coffin added more complex French texts, starting with parts of Diderot's *Encyclopédie*, and he even introduced him to the theories of Beylisme, a contemporary French empiricist philosophy that held that knowledge comes from sensations, perceptions and experience, not from some inner, personal source, as other philosophers of the period held. One day he gave him a copy of Diderot's *Jacque le Fataliste*. The plot involves the story of a master and his servant on a journey to an unnamed place. In the end, the servant makes it clear that the master cannot survive without the servant; the servant becomes the master.

Marcus waded through it and was lost from time to time, but he did finish it.

"Did you get to the end?" Mr. Coffin asked him one evening, down by the creek after dark.

"I did," Marcus said.

"And what did you think?" Mr. Coffin asked.

"Well, it was interesting, a bit of a surprise. But I don't think that sort of thing could happen here, if that's what you're thinking. A slave is a slave and can never turn the tables and be more powerful than his owner. It's a matter of color, unfortunately."

"Well, that may be true here. But stories of intelligent slaves becoming masters of their masters go all the way back to Roman times."

Marcus laughed. "Well, that's good to know; but we're not in Rome."

"Nor France," Mr. Coffin said, somewhat mysteriously.

That summer was perhaps the most instructive and happiest of his life so far. In one of those few hours of solitude, when he was free to simply sit and think, he calculated that although he was working for free, he was in fact bartering for his education by his labors. He couldn't escape the reality that he had been purchased, like a piece of furniture or a horse, but he liked to fantasize that he was, in a sense, free. He was certainly better off than ninety-eight percent of people of his race in the American South. And it was not only training in arts and culture and language that he was learning, he also learned to sail and swim and acquire some of the finer aspects of horsemanship.

George the stableman was a good rider; he seemed somehow to fit with whichever horse he was riding, as if he were part horse himself—a sort of Black centaur. He taught by example, demonstrating in mumbled French how to hold the reins properly, how to post and work a horse with his heels. The horse, Billy, and his companion, Camino, were good saddle horses that could also take a harness and pull a light buggy.

Mr. Coffin had a twenty-foot sloop tied up at the dock and periodically he and Marcus would go out for a sail down the river to the Chesapeake Bay. He first learned how to handle the sails on a tack, and then was encouraged to take the helm, and then, finally, allowed to make decision as to which tack to take. He also learned how saddle a horse and harness up a team, and on these occasions he got to know George a little better.

Janey B, thought George was once a groom on a big estate somewhere, although, she said he often claimed that he owned saddle horses himself and fine carriages and even owned slaves. He was an old man, early seventies and she presumed he was confused in his senility. Whoever he was, he was not the best of teachers. He took Marcus out to the stables and brought out Bobbie, a sturdy bay gelding with a white blaze. He tied him to a rail then slipped the collar over his head and made it fast. He then hitched on a breast collar, fixed the traces and the bellyband and the crupper, and all this while he mumbled to himself, presumably giving directions.

"Like that, you see," George said when the horse was fully harnessed. "Now this horse, he is named Bobby, and he an amiable horse. Won't run off with the carriage."

They took the carriage out for a ride along the road beside the creek, turned up a street leading down to a shipping dock and then turned left through the town, then left again back down to the creek. The white locals may have wondered what they were seeing here: two seemingly free Black men, one old and frail, the other upright and young, riding through the town in a classy Stanhope phaeton.

Once they were back to the road beside the creek, George turned the reins over to Marcus.

"Don't fret, now. Bobby, he knows the way home," George said. Marcus was not fretting, he did know a little about how to drive a wagon, but he couldn't help wondering about George. He noticed from the little that he said, that he had a slight French accent and sometimes spoke to himself in a language that sounded like French, but wasn't.

When they got back to the stable, George unharnessed Bobby hung up the tack and gave Marcus a brush.

"You know how to curry a horse?" he asked.

Marcus did know a little about carriages and the care of horses. Amanda had a little pony and a ralli car with a rear facing seat; she would handle the reins and Marcus would sit in the rear seat, facing backward. He loved the rides through the country lanes, and they would sometimes ride up to the Porter Plantation, about a mile upstream from Greenwood to pay a visit. On these occasions, Marcus would stay with the pony near the barns and listen to the gossip of the stable boys and watch them work.

Marcus curried Bobby and put him in his stall, then went out and found George sitting on a bench outside the barn, staring into space. Marcus joined him.

"From where you come, son?" George asked. "You don't seem like the others Mr. Coffin bring home."

This was the first time George had ever directly addressed Marcus.

Marcus told his story—again—a shortened version. George seemed particularly interested in Marcus's sojourn in the Great Dismal Swamp, especially Marcus's description of Big Nanda.

"She is coming from Haiti, you say?"

"Yes, at least she was born there, left when she was about eighteen."

"She speak the English?"

"No. She talked some kind of patois. A version, I guess of Creole, a dialect maybe. But why do you ask?"

"I am coming from there too, originally," George said.

Marcus prompted him and, somewhat dreamily, speaking in his soft accents, he went to share part of his story.

He had owned part of a sugar plantation, but he did not make clear any details. It did not appear that he was enslaved, but Marcus didn't dare ask. Thinking it over later, Marcus figured that after the 1791 Haitian slave revolt, he must have managed to have gotten some land of his own.

George was not sharp with present-day matters, and he didn't seem to do any work around the Coffin property except for tending the horses. But he was fluent on his past—to a point. He was apparently freeborn and was seemingly integrated into Haitian French society.

"I was involved with shipping, and *j'avais beaucoup d'amis blancs là, gens de France, Angleterre, et les Etats Unis.*" He had a lot of white friends, he said, slipping into French without apparently noticing, as if he had drifted back into that period in his life. He continued—still speaking in French and singing the praises of French society, which at that point had liberalized the *code noir*, the laws controlling Blacks. George explained that he had a daughter in Haiti, a smart girl, very beautiful, and when she turned seventeen his family sent her to Paris.

"Then, my wife die. So I sail to France to live with my daughter. We have a good time there, like the rich of Haiti, only better. I am meet Mr. Coffin about that time."

George carried on with a seemingly unrelated but detailed story about some failed delivery that must have taken place in some distant port and had nothing to do with his daughter and her school. He was apparently losing track of his narrative.

Marcus dared to interrupt, "So you were living in France with your daughter?"

"Yes, she was thinking to study the ballet there. She was a beautiful dancer, she wore red ribbons."

"What was her name?" Marcus asked, knowing full well by this point.

"Papagena," he said. "She wore red ribbons and she was popular in the courts. She studied dance and music, and she changed her named to Papagena there. We met all sorts there in Paris, foreigners from England and America. But he lost money, Mr. Coffin, because the ships got held up in the port in Switzerland."

"Switzerland?" Marcus asked.

"Yes, or maybe it was Genoa? He is selling tobacco and trading money. You know, in Italy. Mr. Coffin, he could speak Italian. He was a handsome man in that time then, dress himself always in gray. He can speak German, Italian, and English. Also French. Also American. He was like a man with no country."

Marcus was able to understand most of George's French; the jumps in time and place were confusing him, but he caught the gist of his ramblings and he knew what he wanted to learn from all this, so he came to the point.

"Did Papagena know Mr. Coffin?" he asked in English.

"No, I do not think so," George said, also in English. "She may have met him at some dance somewhere in Paris maybe. She died. I mean my wife, she died."

"Who died?" Marcus asked. "Your wife or Papagena?"

"Yes," George said. "That was a long time ago, wasn't it? Do you remember? Weren't you in Paris then?"

The story became even more tangled and Marcus pressed no further.

But Marcus was familiar with the situation. Back on the two plantations where he had grown up, there were wizened old men too old to work in the fields who sat in front of their cabins all day, doing simple chores when they could. When he had time, Marcus liked to talk to them. Some had gone senile and would lose track of time and place and which plantation they were held in the stories they told him. A couple of these older men thought they were back in Africa, and from their descriptions, life in Africa was not much better than it was in America—constant inter-tribal wars, ritual murders, a struggle for food in certain seasons, and constant fear of slave raids.

Marcus was by then bent on self-improvement, and he looked to his tedious work copying out Coffin's letters, making entries in the account books, and adding up long lists of figures as practice. He told Janey B that whenever he got his mathematical calculations right, he felt contentment, a sense of having accomplished something. This was perhaps because accounting was his weak point. He was at ease with languages, reading and writing, not figures.

His afternoons there were taken up with French lessons, work in the garden, and tending the horses with George, all of which he rather enjoyed. Furthermore, Caleb Coffin had the strange habit of giving Marcus two days off each week, Saturdays and Sundays, an unheard luxury on the plantations where he had been enslaved. At first, it was difficult to know what to do with himself.

Even in the winter in the Great Dismal Swamp there were always little chores to tend to, plant gathering, crafts, fletching arrows, preparing gut bowstrings, leather work, chipping arrow and spear points and all the other work that was required for those living in primitive conditions including, of course, the hunt.

But the easy life with Mr. Coffin was a little unsettling. It took him a month to realize he was free to do whatever he liked on weekends. Not only that, Mr. Coffin would often invite him to go crabbing in the shallow waters, and also rake oysters. They would carry home baskets full of blue claws and Janey B would clean them and prepare crab cakes. On some Sundays, they would spread the catch out on the kitchen table and all eat together, smashing the crabs with hammers, cracking the claws, and drinking pitchers of beer or switchel.

It was a strange family he found himself in. A wise, semi-literate local country woman, the cook, a demented old Haitian man, the hostler, and the upright white owner, Mr. Caleb Coffin, eating at the same table with his slaves (who, by the way, he always referred to as his servants). Marcus once overheard Mr. Coffin refer to George as his 'assistant' while he was chatting in front of the house with a local white man. In fact, Marcus suspected that George was, in fact, his father-in-law.

One September afternoon, shortly after his daily French lesson, Mr. Coffin, speaking in French, told Marcus that, as he may have noticed, he had had a lot of correspondence from a certain monsieur Henri Fabre. These letters, he said, made it clear that for business reasons, Mr. Coffin would have to return to Paris.

"You have spoken often of Paris, Marcus," he said, still speaking in French. "How would you like to go there? Your French is good enough now to tend to the required work and I would not have to train a new French assistant."

Marcus was overwhelmed, a little frightened even, scared but excited. His fantasy was about to become a reality.

The Sea Voyage Across the Western Ocean

They set sail from Baltimore, bound for Le Havre on a bright September morning with fair breezes and flying clouds. Marcus had never been offshore and in the first few days he hung over the rails, watching the seas run past. They hit a little rough weather after a week, but the wind was still with them, and Marcus got in the habit of spending as much time as he could stretched out on the bowsprit so as to better watch the ship plow through the foamy waves, with the jibs billowing overhead like willing white horses. He loved the bite of the salty air, the smell of brine and the thought that they were getting somewhere without fear of slave catchers, furtive night flights, and the persistent, edgy thought that he was living in an alien nation among dangerous enemies.

The 'Vanity' was a sturdy 400-ton ship, carrying a variety of passengers the more fortunate of whom were assigned to the upper decks. They were housed in small cabins surrounding a main saloon with a long table running fore and aft, and larger, more accommodating cabins aft. The galley was located on the starboard side toward the bow and in the stern there were more spacious cabins for the captain and first mate. The crew slept forward in the fo'csle.

Below decks in his sleeping quarters was another matter, a little more like the squalid slave pens where Marcus had spent some time. He was quartered up under the foredeck in a tight little upper bunk that stank of musky oak and the foul air of his fellow cabin mates, some of whom were often seasick. They lived mostly on gruel, tea and coffee, and an allotment of three quarts of water per day. The only air they were able to catch came through the main hatch, which the crew shut during periods of rough weather, making the air all the more fetid. Marcus was reminded of the stories Jemma used to tell him of his memories of the Middle Passage when he lay in a narrow bunk next to a stranger with no common language.

On board the 'Vanity' on that particular crossing, there was a strange contingent of about twelve American Indians all stacked up together in the bunks. They were dressed in their native clothes, feathers and furs and fringed animal skins and they had the bad habit of singing themselves to sleep in monotonous, monotone chants. They reminded Marcus of some of the people he had known in the Great Dismal Swamp, and he tried his best to talk with them to find out why they were sailing to Europe.

One of them, a man named Sampus, was the apparent chief of the group and had some English. He explained that he and his people were members of the Iowa tribe of the American Plains. They were traveling to Paris with an American artist who had lived with them and used to paint pictures of them in their native costumes. He had persuaded them to come to Paris with him where he said they would meet the king and perform their dances. Although some of them were seasick at the beginning of the voyage, they too were quick to come on deck with Marcus and take the air. They were fascinated by the sea and seemed also to appreciate the wide sky. Sampus said it reminded him of home on the Plains.

In fine weather, Marcus was joined on deck by Mr. Coffin, and they would pace together fore and aft and then back again, speaking now solely in French and talking of the realities of the city of Paris, as opposed to the dreamy imagined city that Marcus had fixed in his mind back on Greenwood Plantation via Amanda's long descriptions.

Marcus spent as little time as possible below decks, until the third week out, when they hit a patch of nasty weather with driving rain, hammering northeast winds that lifted the little vessel skyward and then brought it crashing downward, waves sweeping the bows and rushing aft along the gunnels. He was confined below at these times, either tucked in his rancid bunk or sitting uncomfortably for hours at the saloon table, listening to the gossip of his fellow passengers.

There was a large, talkative, and very active woman among them, who was, so she claimed, the daughter of a Scottish laird. She spent a lot of time complaining about the conditions, but she also was not averse to working. She somehow obtained vinegar and sail cloth and set about with three other women cleaning the main salon, scrubbing and polishing and getting everyone to move out of her way so she could or the others could work.

Marcus came to enjoy her energy and her nearly incomprehensible Scottish accent. Unlike some of the other passengers, she seemed indifferent to race, and whenever she stopped moving Marcus would engage her in conversation about her life in Scotland.

She told him her father was a tobacco trader and the owner of a large estate called Thainstone, in Kintore, just west of Aberdeen. Her grandfather and her great uncle had set up the trade in the mid-seventeen hundreds and amassed a fortune, she said, which allowed her all sorts of explorations. She had traveled in Cuba and the Caribbean Islands and was now off to France to take the waters at Lourdes.

There was also a pinched little man who was terribly seasick and generally remained in his bunk night and day moaning. And there was a contingent of three Frenchmen who also spent a lot of time on deck even in foul weather. They were returning to Paris after a grand tour of the United States. They were hunters and outdoorsmen and they too had spent some time with Indian tribes. They even dressed like American pioneers in raccoon caps and fringed Indian deerskin shirts. They had with them a good supply of rum, which they shared with the passengers, and, as did the Indians, they would sometimes sing late into the night entertaining themselves with old French folk songs. Marcus missed much of the lyrics of these but he caught enough to understand that some of the songs were decidedly off color.

Sometimes in late afternoon, he was joined at his post in the bows by a dark-skinned African sailor named Dagger. He too spoke a number of languages, including Fon, Spanish, French and enough English to converse with Marcus. He was not enslaved in any nation. He had escaped Senegal fifteen years earlier as cabin boy on an English cutter that was hunting down slave ships and had worked his way up through the hawse holes as the expression has it, to foretopman. He was liked by the crew on all of the ships he had sailed on. He always had a tambourine with him, and if things got dicey with the captain or the first mate, he would play the fool and dance to the beat of his tambourine, all the while singing improvised parodies of whatever was troubling the relationship between the officers and the crewmen.

He told Marcus of one ship he had served on—an English vessel. The captain was a notoriously cruel and vindictive sort, ordering whippings and even on some occasions keel-hauling, on very little excuse. The crew was considering mutiny and were planning what to do with him once they had taken over the ship. But for some reason the captain started sleeping late and failing to come on to deck to give the day's orders. Then he began sleeping in the afternoons, and retiring early to his quarters. The ship was home bound for Falmouth, and when they landed, the crew deserted en masse. A group of them met in a pub before they dispersed and shared stories, including the mysteries of the sleeping captain.

Dagger was working in the galley on that particular voyage and when the discussion turned as to why the otherwise overly energetic captain took to his cabin, Dagger admitted he knew the answer. He had spiked the captain's dinners with a powerful sleeping potion he had picked up in Zanzibar.

The 'Vanity' plowed eastward day after day, some days clear and bright, riding comfortably downwind with the westerlies, sometime battling through periodic spells of stormy weather. Finally, one fair morning, Marcus came on deck and went to his post in the bow. There, ahead of him on the horizon, he saw a slim strip of green.

That thin line grew taller as the day wore on in light winds, and when he went out the next morning it was only slightly larger. The wind had veered to the east at that point and weakened to a light headwind, forcing the vessel to tack, making very little headway.

For another two frustrating days, they worked their way eastward. More and more passengers joined Marcus on the foredeck, staring hopefully eastward at the jagged coastline—first the green strip, then a view of distant hills, then little red-roofed towns, and then the forest-like crowd of masts on the harbor of Le Havre. And then, finally, they were in France.

******

The chaotic hours of customs passed in a blur for Marcus; he was totally confused. Their passports were taken to be reviewed. There were crowds of passengers, unintelligible porters handling trunks and baggage, draymen and coachmen vying for takers, much noise and the air sauced with the odor of dead fish, horse manure, and garbage, contrasting sharply with the cleansing winds at sea. They took rooms in a nearby hotel for the night and the next day boarded a coach bound for Paris.

Once out of Le Havre, the more pleasing landscape of rural France made itself apparent. Squares of neat hedge rows, apple orchards, interspersed with pasture lands dotted with sheep and cows. Small neat villages with rough farm cottages beyond, and clear fresh air.

The noisy Scottish woman was with them in the coach and she found fault with the French for half the journey. "A dirty people, they are," she said. "And atrocious food, no matter what they say. Eating frogs and snails and such like. I was sick here on their oysters once."

Mr. Coffin, who had remained curiously silent during the first part of the voyage, finally spoke up. "But what about haggis, Mom?" he asked.

"Oh haggis. I know, I know everyone talks about haggis and those who complain have never tasted it. Not a bad dish, not a bad dish at all."

Mr. Coffin merely grunted and stared out the window at the passing landscape.

Toward late afternoon, the landscape began to change, the towns grew larger, the air grew heavier, and darker, and the after seven weeks of forward motion, they finally made a full stop.

They were in the center of Paris.

Paris
The City of Light

If this was the bright free world he had imagined, Marcus was to have his first lesson in reality. From the center of the noisy crowd, Mr. Coffin and Marcus, followed by a porter made their way through a veritable herd of people. Marcus had never in his life seen so many people in one place all at once, and all making all manner of noise. He could only catch a few phrases in what seemed a Tower of Babel of incomprehensible words. Furthermore, all of the people were white. Never before in his life had he seen so many white faces in so brief a time, and yet, not one of them seemed to notice that he was a man of color.

The crowd seemed more interested in Mr. Coffin, with his top hat, black tailcoat, tight trousers and shiny boots. Mr. Coffin appeared to be searching for someone in the mass of people and noise and it was all Marcus could do to keep up with him. He seemed to have forgotten that he had a newcomer to Paris with him. But soon they heard someone calling out for a 'Monsieur Coffan' and saw a smiling little balding man in striped trousers making his way through the crowd. He and Mr. Coffin shook hands warmly, and, with Marcus following on their heels, made their way out of the crowds to a waiting fiacre.

It was only then that Mr. Coffin seemed to remember he had someone with him, and he paused long enough to introduce Marcus to his sometime assistant, Jean Claude. They set out, Jean Claude at the reins, Marcus and Mr. Coffin together in the cab, and made their way along the River Seine, then turned on the Rue de Saintes-Père and carried on going this way and that through some squalid side streets lined with shops and little cafés. In time, they stopped at a sizable structure with a wide gate-like door. They left the carriage and mounted a marble staircase and entered through two larger double doors. Inside, on the next floor up. they entered a spacious foyer with sitting rooms on either side and a narrow hallway leading to a dining room on the right and on the other side of the entrance, a series of bedrooms and an office and library overlooking the street.

"Jean Claude will show you to your room," Mr. Coffin said. "You can rest a while if you like and then come down and ring. If I'm resting, Charmaine will let you in. I'll give you the door keys later."

"*Alors, allons-y mon enfant*," Jean Claude said, and began chatting in a patois that was all but incomprehensible to Marcus. He thought he knew French, but this was a different language altogether, as confusing as the Haitian patois of Big Nanda and Nyala.

But he got the point. Jean Claude was a friendly little man with a lot to say and didn't seem to comprehend that Marcus was missing most of what he was holding forth about.

The two of them entered a doorway in the hall and ascended a narrow winding staircase and climbed another two floors to another narrower hallway. On the left side, Jean Claude showed him into a small room, also overlooking the street, with a narrow bed on one wall, and armoire on the other, and a table stand with a basin and pitcher.

"Your room," he said. "Very nice here, although there is sometimes noise on the street. But you will get used to it. And Mr. Coffan, he is the most generous of men, so do not worry. He will take care of you."

This was all delivered in garbled fast French, but Marcus caught the drift and thanked Jean Claude, who shook his hand warmly and said goodbye.

Marcus slept longer than he had intended. The sleepless night on the carriage had fatigued him. He woke in late afternoon and went down to the Mr. Coffin's apartment and twisted a brass turnkey that sounded a jangling bell inside. No one came to the door. He waited a bit and tried again. Nothing. So he knocked a few times. Still no one.

It was a custom of his at that point in his life whenever he found himself in danger of capture, or a whipping, or any other challenge, to make alternative plans even before the misadventure occurred. This was a slightly different situation, but just as he started considering a solution, the door opened and standing with one hand on the door knob, he saw a young woman dressed in gray. She had high cheek bones, black hair tied up in a lose bun and bright blue eyes, and she looked him up and down quickly before speaking.

"*Alors, c'est vous Monsieur Marc Aurèle*," she said. This was a statement, not a question.

"*Entrez s'il vous plaît*."

She stepped aside and let him pass. He could feel her eyes on him as he entered. She was only slightly older that he, and had a definitive coquettish air.

"Come with me, Monsieur Marc Aurèle," she said with somewhat mock formality. "Mr. Coffan, he told me to show you into the office. He will be along soon."

She walked smartly down the hall, swung open a heavy door and ushered him into the large airy office.

"Here, then. You wait. Mr. Coffan, he will be here soon. You will be having tea."

"Merci, madame," Marcus said.

"Mademoiselle," she snapped, and walked back down the hall.

He sat down at a large writing desk in the center of the room and then got up and stared out the window. He could see a row of neoclassical residential building across the street, and below, carriages and fiacres and a few wagons were passing to and fro. People were walking in the street or loitering in front of the arcades of the buildings. They were dressed mostly in black, the men in top hats and redingotes, and the women in daytime carriage dresses, some carrying parasols.

Where were they going, Marcus, wondered, and what were they doing? This was essentially his first exposure to a city, other than the blur of the narrow streets of the port of Philadelphia, and the noise and barrels and chaos of the ports. Here he was able to think about what he was seeing. But soon enough, Mr. Coffin came in.

He had seemed preoccupied, worried even, when they first arrived. But now he was back in his old, world-wise, pedantic form.

"We'll be having tea soon in the front parlor. I want you to meet a friend of mine and learn more about daily life here. You'll be following the same schedule more or less as we did back in Maryland. But you will have a little more free time here. I want you to learn the city and something of the French culture. It will make it easier for you to conduct the business you'll eventually be attending to."

They proceeded to the parlor and sat together on a narrow Empire divan. The maid, who was introduced to him as Charmaine, set a Chinese brass tray down on the table and, standing behind the divan waited until Mr. Coffin excused her, whereupon she sauntered out wordlessly.

"Charmaine is an independent young woman," Mr. Coffin said, "but she is very efficient and keeps track of me."

No sooner had she left, when she returned. "Madame de Latour has arrived," she announced, and on her heels, a striking, tall woman in a gray silk day dress strode into the room. She was all in light gray, light gray eyes, gray hair swept up in a full chignon, and high rosy cheeks.

Mr. Coffin rose quickly took her hands and kissed her on both cheeks. Marcus Aurelius knew enough of politesse to rise as well, and she held out her hand to him, palm down. He knew the routine at this point as a result of Amanda's training and took her hand and raised it to his lips. She too subtly reviewed the figure of Marcus Aurelius when he stood to greet her, he noticed.

"*Enchanté*," she said and took a seat opposite the divan. She was clearly familiar with the setting.

"This is Madame de Latour, my friend I wanted you to meet," Mr. Coffin said, speaking in French. Then he switched to English. "She is from a noble family from Normandy who supported the revolution, and then had to flee their estate in spite of their loyalty to the Council and their support of the execution of the King, who was said to be some sort of cousin of her family. Her brother and father were guillotined during the Terror, but she escaped."

Madame de Latour snorted cynically. "Do not believe a word," she said in English. "I am a mere peasant."

"Ah oui," Mr. Coffin said. "*Une paisanne de l'isle des belles*!"

She blew out her lips. "*Menteur*—Liar. Monsieur Aurèle, do not listen to this man."

This banter went on in French and English, and the interplay was not lost on Marcus. He had rarely seen Mr. Coffin so animated, and so quick with rejoinders.

Charmaine returned with a tray of aperitifs in tiny fluted crystal glasses. They drank, and the banter continued, and then Madame de Latour changed the subject abruptly.

"But tell me about your life, Monsieur Marc Aurèle; what was it like to be held in bondage, and did you have miserable, sadistic lords and masters who raised a whip against you and sold your mother and siblings like cows?"

Marcus was taken aback. So blunt a question, so much to say.

"I don't know where to begin, Madame," he said in his broken but comprehensible French. "Yes, and no. I had a good master, and a bad master, and an even worse overseer. But I also knew kindness, sometimes from the mistress, and most especially from a young woman of the plantation family who took me under her wing and taught me to read and write and handle a sword."

"A sword?" Madame de Latour exclaimed. "A woman taught you the art of fencing? Impossible. How can this be? Was she an Amazon?"

Marcus missed the reference. "She was different," he said. "She was a, how would you say, a romantic. She lived in a fantasy world. She thought she could do anything. Why not she would say? Look at Jeanne d'Arc. She read a lot, especially French and English novels; she believed she could duel and made me play out scenes from literatures of the past, using sticks she cut for swords. She taught me French. She instilled in me a desire for freedom. I wept when she grew up, married, and moved to another plantation. From her, I learned the freedom."

"*Liberté, egalité,*" Madame de Latour said, and snorted cynically again. "France may be not be all she thought it was," she said.

"We are somewhat involved politically here," Mr. Coffin said. "We sometimes have gatherings, a salon of sorts. You will meet them. We invite you. Freedom is still in mind. And what is freedom in any case. A word? An idea? A reality? Is anyone ever truly free?"

Marcus took a risk at this point. "But you cannot know the true nature of freedom until you have been enslaved," he said.

Madame de Latour and Mr. Coffin, who had been firing out playful exchanges, fell silent.

"You will do well in our little group," Madame de Latour said after a brief pause.

****

In the first weeks in Paris, Marcus and Mr. Coffin fell into a routine: work on Mr. Coffin's papers in the morning, a midday meal, and then a walk through the Jardin des Plantes, or the Tuileries, or sometimes, with Madame de Latour, an excursion out to Saint Germain or the hunting grounds at the Bois de Boulogne. Then tea or an aperitif chez Coffin, or at the Café Procope. Another stroll, and then dinner either at Le Tour d'Argent or some other well-appointed restaurant. And also, on certain evenings, a little circle of friends and a discussion of current affairs, or literature, or bad art, or what constituted bad art in their view. Also philosophical questions, such as the nature of reality or the pursuit of pleasure and Stendhal's concept of Beylisme, a philosophy that defined happiness and the necessity of moral indignation in the face of all the political turmoil of that period in France.

Marcus noted that Mr. Coffin, the American, remained silent during these sometimes heated political conversations, but also paid attention and even made notes. Marcus too paid attention, attempting to follow the quick repartee and the references to figures he had never heard of such as someone they often talked about called Cavaignac.

This was a strange group. There was a little man with a withered arm who was an authority on Sanskrit and other ancient texts. Also young dandy with a goatee and a curled mustache who fancied himself an art critic. There were three different women, one of whom was a novelist who dressed like a man and smoked the little cigars they called cigarettes, and another who was politically opinionated and was the consort of an older member of the nobility named Marquis Marcel de Moreaux who had also escaped the Terror and was still something of a royalist. He seemed to be of the opinion that the July Revolution of 1830, which ousted King Charles was a big mistake and the country should return to a constitutional monarchy. No one in the group agreed with him but they listened anyway. The Marquis had escaped the guillotine by feigning serious illness and lying low in a pseudo-hospital north of Paris that required a handsome annual entrance fee. The salon often teased him about this.

And then there was Charmaine. She was everywhere, clearing glasses, filling glasses, standing beside the pantry door, with a tired indifference to the conversation. Marcus noticed that at one point she leaned again the door frame and propped her foot up, and yawned. She cut a fine figure in Marcus's view. Small, well-formed, big blue eyes, and a way of fluidly moving through the room in a balletic walk. Not only that, he caught her looking at him periodically during these evenings. And once, early on, she saw him looking at her and she tilted her head and winked, as if to say, we two know this is all just monkey chatter.

The days passed. Marcus soon familiarized himself with the work, which was essentially the same work he had carried out back in Maryland, save that, as Amanda had told him, here in France he was technically free even though he had no plans for quitting his work with Mr. Coffin.

The talk at Mr. Coffin' salon was often beyond the sphere of Marcus's understanding. This was 1845 and pressure was building against the king Louis-Philippe; economic depression was looming. One night there was a long discussion at the salon dealing with the old code noir, the 17th-century set of laws governing Blacks, both free and enslaved. Marcus was called upon to give more details of the life of an enslaved person in America. The subject had come up earlier in other meetings, but this time the old rightist, the Marquis de Moreaux, a legitimiste, who favored the *ancien regime*, tried to argue that Africans enslaved members of other tribes and then sold them as chattel to the Arabs and Europeans and later in history to the Americans.

"There is nobody who is innocent here," he argued. "Not one of us, no matter how much you speak of freedom and equality. I am wearing a cotton shirt. Who is it who picked this cotton? I have sugar in my coffee. Who cut this sugar cane? What do we do? Stop drinking coffee? We are all oppressors. But you, Marc, only you can tell us who cut the sugar cane," he said. "Only you, who knows the debasement of the ox."

"It was tobacco I picked. And hard though it was, the work was not the problem," Marcus said. "It was the chains of hopelessness that enslave you. You pick cotton for thirty-five years and then you die and there is no way out."

"But nonetheless, you, Monsieur Marc, you break out, you," the cigarette-smoking woman said.

"Luck," he said. "Luck and determination. I could have died, I could have been whipped to death by an overseer and no one would even think to charge him with murder, although my owner would perhaps be upset that he had lost a strong back for which he had paid good money."

Madame de Latour spoke up, "Tell them, Marc, what you told us a while back. Your life and your understanding of what it means to be truly free. You people here, myself included, of course, we speak of liberty. But what is it, freedom? Only the enslaved can know, as you say."

Marcus was encouraged (again—he was often questioned on matters of liberty) and told again his story and the nature of enslavement.

During this particular exchange, Marcus noticed that Charmaine unabashedly fixed her eyes on him, as if understanding for the first time that he had once been a slave. Later that night, after the salon had disbanded and he was preparing for bed, he heard a little scratching at his bedroom door; the door slowly open and Charmaine poked her head in.

"You are asleep?" she asked.

"No. Not quite," he said.

"I can come in?"

He hesitated, sensing what was about to happen but nodded.

She came in and sat on the bed.

"You are a poor boy, you. You are beaten and whipped by cruel masters with hate."

"Well, yes, but that's over now."

"But I was listening to you tonight. I feel so sorry. You are nice boy. A nice man. And the fat pigs whip you and I hate them too." She put her hand on his cheek. "You are a gentle boy. You do not deserve the whip."

Marcus shrugged. "It's over now," he said.

She drew his head forward and kissed his forehead. "Poor boy," she whispered.

Marcus thought this was coming since their first encounter. He reached around her back and drew her in.

Mary Plantation
The Taming of the Bull

During this same period, back in Virginia, Tilly never did recover her former energetic, devilish misbehavior. Mainly, she grew bored with behaving badly and getting away with it. In short, she was growing up. No one had ever beaten her before, mainly perhaps because she was protected by Mistress. She went about her chores steadily, and she still took to her closet to daydream, but now her thoughts had changed and her deviltry became more directed.

In a weedy patch behind the corn crib, there grew a plant her mother called Jimmy weed. She told Tilly to stay away from that plant when she was picking wild herbs. Jimmy weed was poisonous, she said.

"They was some snake doctors back on Corby Plantation where I was held 'fore you were born," she explained. "Those snake doctor women, they sometimes make paste from that plant an' rub it on they tongue. You don't eat it or you die. But they told me, you taste it and you can fly. Makes you crazy, they tol' me but you do that and you can talk to Snake. You know Snake? Back in Afriky, he was God. He help guide you. He come crawling out from the bush and talk. You can see the Ancestors then and caste spells."

In late spring, Tilly went out behind the corn crib and collected some Jimmy weed. Following the instructions her mother had told her about for other herb cures, she mixed up a paste. Then she watered it down to a tea, put the tea in a jar and hid the jar in the bottom of a cupboard.

The Washburns had a few guests over one spring afternoon, and Tilly's mother baked some tea cakes and prepared two pitchers of grog. Tilly carried the tray to the porch, laid out the tea cakes, poured the grog, and served the guests. Her back to the guests, she slipped a vial of Jimmy weed tea from her camisole and poured it into Massa Washburn's glass.

At dinner that night, Tilly and her mother heard a terrifying bellow from the dinner table. Tilly walked out and placed herself beside the dining room door, as if waiting to be called to serve, but mainly to see what was happening.

It was a wild scene. Mr. Washburn had snatched up the carving knife and was attacking the curtains and stabbing at the walls and shouting about—of all things—snakes. A vast company of huge serpents had invaded the dining room, hissing and writhing and striking at the air. Some were able to fly and Washburn went after them too, racing around the table bellowing and cursing, swiping the air with the knife, and Mistress was screaming, and their two boys Winslow and Jefferson, terrified and shouting at their father—there're no snakes, Papa, sit down, Papa, there are no snakes in the dining room—and the older boy raced out of the room and summoned Billings who arrived but merely stood wide-eyed at the doorway, in shock.

Washburn was on the table now, cutting at the chandelier and a lit candle had fallen onto the table threatening to light the whole room, and all the while Washburn was red-eyed, a terrible uncontrolled elephant in must, wreaking havoc.

"Do something, Billings," Mistress screamed. "Do something. He's gone mad."

Billings was a slow-moving man, and he approached cautiously but before he could reach the table, Washburn collapsed onto the floor, panting and spitting and groaning.

Eventually, he calmed down, rolled on his back and lay there, eyes fix on the patterned ceiling. Then, suddenly, as if he had seen something on the ceiling, he leaped up again and began to rant:

"Yes," he shouted to the wall. "Yes! Oh sweet Jesus yes, the snake, the holy snake yes Lord, all ye snakes and frothy cataracts, waters of the earth roll on sweet Jesus devil-sent snake Oh Holy snake king snake, snake of god, roll on snake and all lions and wolves and leopardswolf of deceit all beasts of air and earth, roll on until the end of nowhere!" He paused breathless, then began again more softly, "Come to me now waters of the skycome python come elephant red-eyed and terrible, come, take me home. Elephant take me home. Snake wurrums everyside!" he said. "Our durlbin is swarming in sneaks! Holy snakes. Saint Python. Those slimes up the cavern door around you, keenin God?"

He paused again.

"Horseman pass by…" he said and collapsed.

Then he sat up slowly, supporting himself with the leg of one of the dining room chairs, shaking violently, his eyes rolling up, drooling and snorting and then, mercifully, he fell back and passed out.

Billings and Jefferson, the older boy, carried him up to his bed and laid him down.

Unbeknownst to Tilly, and even to her mother, was the fact that Tilly had fed Washburn *Datura stramonium*, the Devil's Snare, the consumption of which causes wild hallucinations and occult, bizarre visions and can induce long-lasting flashes of disorientation. In fact, Washburn was lucky to have lived—ingesting too much of the plant can be fatal.

As it was, the incident altered Washburn's behavior. He became subdued and disinterested in managing the plantation. He would rise in the morning, eat his breakfast and settle on the front porch, staring into space and then on some days he would dash down the steps shouting at nothing. He could engage in normal conversation for a while but periodically he would slip back into mania. His family came to recognize the onset of the symptoms. His eyes would widen and then he would push back his chair and flee the room, bellowing and raving. Furthermore, even in his lucid periods, which could go on for a week or two, he developed an irrational fear of snakes and ordered the flowerbeds and trees and shrubs near the house cleared.

His wife wrote for a doctor from Richmond, but when he arrived, Washburn was in one of his lucid states. He himself had no clear memory of his outbursts, but from the description from Mrs. Washburn and the children, and also Billings, the doctor diagnosed what he thought to be and serious case of myasthenia. None of them (save Tilly) knew he had been poisoned with Datura. The doctor prescribed rest, altered with physical activity, and a tumbler of whiskey before bedtime.

The behavior carried on nonetheless but, as far as Tilly was concerned, it worked. He never bothered her again.

But then, a new problem arose in the form of unwanted attentions from the younger son, Winslow.

Paris
The Fateful Duel

As the weeks passed, Marcus began to acquire a few acquaintances outside of the salon through errands and correspondence with the local people, some of whom he met through Mr. Coffin, some he befriended in the shops and cafés. He became a known figure in the district around the Pont Royal as the *intendant* of the American, Monsieur Coffin, himself a well-known figure in the arrondissement. And after some time, in the local café gossip, the tryst with Charmaine was exposed—probably via Charmaine herself. No one was concerned very much, not even Madame de Latour and Mr. Coffin, who found it mildly amusing.

"Not his first, I don't think," Mr. Coffin said. "He spoke often to me of a young enslaved miss back in Virginia, before his final escape."

Madame de Latour snorted. "I daresay. He cuts a dashing figure."

But one afternoon, while walking in the Tuileries, a young foxlike sans-culottes of questionable reputation confronted Marcus and told him in no uncertain terms to stay away from Charmaine. He spoke in quick Parisian *cant*, the street argot of petty thieves, but Marcus caught his drift and, actor that he was, he pretended not to comprehend.

"I am so sorry, my good man," he said in English, drawing himself up, "but I'm afraid I do not speak your language."

This enraged the aggressor even more and he repeated his command in a louder voice, as if shouting would get Marcus to understand.

Marcus raised his forearms, palms open, and tilted his head apologetically. "*No capisco signor,*" he said in Italian.

There followed another blast, and the man grabbed Marcus's lapels and drew him down to his level. He was a short little fox compared to Marcus, who pushed his attacker away. The fox stumbled backward, regained his balance, and counterattacked. He should have known better.

Marcus delivered a swift kick to his crotch and when he doubled over, sent him reeling with an uppercut. He went down on the ground. Marcus stood over him, watching him writhe.

"I'm so sorry," he said in French. "I misunderstood you. I hope, monsieur, you are not in pain. Will you accept my apology?"

The fox merely snarled.

"Sorry, I didn't understand that," Marcus said. "Accept?"

No answer. At this time, Marcus had been well attired by Mr. Coffin and wore high leather boots with pointed toes.

"I say," Marcus inquired politely, in English "I was unable to understand your response monsieur, do you accept my apology?"

He followed with a mild kick to the fallen man's ribs.

"*Oui o non, mon vieux*?" Marcus said.

"*Oui*," the fox said weakly.

Marcus had been kicked by Mr. Green while he was struggling on the ground after a beating, but he had never had the opportunity to kick back.

"*Merci, je vous en pris,*" Marcus said. He delivered another kick to the poor man.

Among Marcus's café friends, there was an Italian man named Scarafaccio, a sallow, well-dressed gentleman with ties to the underworld. Marcus told him about the attack a few days later and Scarafache, as he was known in French, said he thought he knew the man. He was a former lover of Charmaine, long since dismissed by her, but who still maintained an obsessive attachment.

"If you see him again, beat him up on general principle and tell him you will have him killed if he continues to bother her."

Marcus's affair with Charmaine was fading at the time but they were still friends. In fact, she was a good source on the demi-monde of the Rue Saint-Denis and the Left Bank. She remembered this scruffy fox.

"He is a twisted little man, easily offended. He is nothing to me, tell him you will kill him if he continues to bother me, or if he bothers you, for that matter."

For his part, Mr. Coffin considered Marcus's sometime association with questionable types and the streets as part of his education. But when he heard of the fight, he had a talk with him.

Shortly after the event, there was an interesting salon discussion of the future of the Republic. There was larger group than usual that night, with newer guests in attendance, including a pale, lank gentleman with a hooked nose, a pianist and the consort of the novelist. In spite of a persistent cough, he too smoked cigarettes. There was also another French-speaking American man who dressed in deerskin like a Western pioneer and was said to be a famous painter of birds.

Late in the night, after the guests had left, Mr. Coffin poured two glasses of *marc* and asked Marcus to join him in the study. He began talking at length about recent French history—the Revolution, the Terror, the power of the masses when pressed by hunger, or the state reluctance to continue the hard won revolutionary reforms.

"But in among the real people, you understand, there are bands of thieves and scofflaws who will take advantage of any political disruption to rob. We must be careful not to trust everyone. Listen. But be wary. For example, I know this Scarafache, he is the lover of an English woman, a revolutionary, who supports violence and travels between England and France stirring up foment on both the right and the left. You may have seen her, blonde, very beautiful, with high cheekbones, always well attired. But these two are dangerous. Stay on their side and feign indifference, or better yet, incomprehension."

"I know that woman," Marcus said. "Mary somebody. We speak in English together about slavery and the Haitian Revolution. Her mother has donated money to the cause. Mary often praises Toussaint Louverture and his allies. She even likes pirates."

"The very same. There was a price on her head when Charles X was king. We didn't see her for a year or two. But I have been meaning to talk with you about a new plan."

"I want you to continue to work for me, of course. But I also want to enroll you in one of the *ècoles des noirs*, the very good schools for people of color from the colonies. They have excellent teachers in these schools, so good that local people sometimes send their own French children there. You'll be older than the others, but there are all ages there, and you won't have to attend all the time. But you will get a very good background in French cultural history—

politics, art, literature, music, that sort of thing. And furthermore, since you are already fond of swordsmanship, I have a friend, an excellent fencer who can refine what you already seem to know. It never hurts, even nowadays, to be handy with a foil. And then also, I have arranged for you to take a few violin lessons. This isn't entirely selfless generosity, you understand. The more familiar you are with European contemporary culture, the better luck you will have with our business dealings."

"The fact is, Marcus, I am, I hate to say, aging, and there will come a time when I am going to need a more active and astute assistant."

He chuckled privately at this point.

"And one other thing," he said. "Be careful with your choices of lady friends."

******

Marcus had experienced three fortuitous events in his twenty or so years of life. The first was his friendship and tutelage by Amanda. The second was his purchase by Mr. Coffin. The third, and most useful, was his European education.

With Mr. Coffin's encouragement, and driven by his own ambition, he read voraciously in contemporary French literature. The school he attended was below him, although he did pick up a solid, though simple outline of French history, and through his older acquaintances at the salon, including one of his teachers from the school, he was introduced to society. He began to attend balls, where, having been trained as a little boy in ballroom etiquette, he became a sought after dancing partner.

At one of these balls, he encountered a young woman about his age named Bettina who was studying at the Royal Academy of Music. She had big dark eyes and curly blond hair and was the daughter of a female painter who specialized in portraits of the nobility, mainly women and children. Bettina's parents owned a chateau in Saint Cloud, and periodically Marcus was invited to spend a weekend there. He and Bettina would often go horseback riding out into the surrounding countryside during these visits and find a secluded spot to linger and share their love. She was an imaginative young woman, cut in the same style as Amanda, and as did Amanda, Bettina liked to invent and act out theatrical scenes, mostly for operas she said she would write someday.

One day in June, they rode out to the forest of Marly le Roi and settled in a clearing. The wildflowers were all were in bloom that day, the thrushes and the cuckoos were fluting, and the air was still and soft with a few high clouds drifting slowly overhead like an armada of sailing ships. They had brought with them a basket of bread and cheese and a bottle of Sancerre, and they settled in to enjoy the afternoon.

Here they were, as yet unrealized, and suspended in time, one sheltered enough by money and connections to have skipped through the street riots of the July revolution and the subsequent political turmoil, and the other, having spent his formative years as a farm animal, sold and purchased at a cattle market, beaten when necessary, his mother sold like a cow, his father unknown and his future as a work horse determined, except for the fact that he had had the good fortune to escape to France.

They knew nothing of what was to come, these two, but that day they didn't care.

Later in the afternoon, having shared the bottle, Bettina began, as she sometimes did, to imagine the plot for a new opera.

"The libretto is a story of intrigue and Barbary pirates," she said. "You will sing the role of the prince, the son of a ruthless Pasha, and I am your favorite concubine. We fall in love—uncontrolled romantic love. Then, against your father's wishes, we flee the courts and ride off to live free of society and all its laws and cruelties."

"But why?" Marcus asked. "If I am soon to be the Pasha, why would I throw it all aside?"

"Because you love me passionately. Because your father looks down on me, because I am but a lowly white slave, not worthy of you, the prince, nor anyone else."

"White slave? There is no such thing."

"Ah, but no, there is, or was. The Barbary corsairs used to capture beautiful English and French girls and sell them to the pashas. I was one of these, you see, but you rescued me."

"And then what? Do we marry and live boring lives of quiet desperation like so many others?"

"But no. We seek revenge. You and I, we become corsairs. We have a galley with a loyal crew of English oarsmen, and we attack the ships of the other corsairs, take their silver, rescue their captors and sail back to England

and set them free. We are rewarded with a chateau on the south coast and here we raise a family, a happy family."

"Very nice," Marcus said.

He lay back on the grassy glade and stared dreamily upward at the passing clouds for a while, then sat up abruptly.

"I say. I've got another plot for your opera," he said.

"What? What could better?"

"The first part is perfect," he said. "But the end is different. We do run off, taking most of my father's wealth. Then we hire a French brig and we assemble a loyal crew of pirates and buccaneers and we sail west to the United States. En route we encounter an American slave ship. We attack, free the slaves, put our first mate as captain of the slave ship with the former slaves as crew and throw the crew overboard, along with their captain. Then we come across another slave ship. This too we attack, free the slaves and throw the crew overboard."

"Then we catch another and then, having armed the crews, we have an armada of three ships and we sail on and land in Florida. Then, with our renegade army, we sail northward, attacking cotton and indigo plantations and freeing their slaves too, who join our army. We continue northward, gaining recruits all along the way, until we come to Virginia and the big river there, the James River, and we sail up the river and we free all the local slaves from the plantations, land our army of renegades and march on Richmond, a big city on the river. The government of the United States sends the military to stop us. But the soldiers are from the North, and they rebel; they don't like the institution of slavery any more than we do, so they switch camps and join us, and then by that time, their king, the president of the United States, albeit reluctantly, decides to abolish slavery. In exchange for our leadership, we are given one of the big James River plantations, and we start a university there to educate the former slaves. Only then can we live happily. Only then can we rest."

Bettina was silent for a while. She looked over at him, his green eyes were fixed on the horizon as if he was living in his plot. She knew his situation.

"That's crazy, you know," she said quietly. "*Vraiment fou*, but I love it."

She jumped on him and kissed him on the lips.

"I love it. We shall spread the revolution," she said. "We shall give back to America the idea they gave to us. Liberty. Egalité. Only this time, under our rule—everyone is free, not just a few rich people."

"If only," Marcus said.

******

Marcus was not Bettina's only suitor, as it turned out; there was a certain nobleman, Count Philippe de Montclair, an older gentleman who often escorted her to operas and fine dinners at Le Tour d'Argent. She was in fact more drawn to Marcus and his perceived exoticism—an escaped American slave—but she did enjoy the operas and the dinners—although not so much the company Monsieur Philippe de Montclair kept. They were mostly legitimists, members of the nobility who, through artifice or self-exile, had escaped the guillotine. They were a self-righteous band, privileged and uncomfortable with the rabble and suspicious of the artists and writerly types that were a part of Mr. Coffin's salon. Bettina, wisely, thought it best to keep her affair with Marcus secret.

But this was Paris and their world was small, and in due time, de Montclair found out.

Toward the end of a quiet dinner with Bettina, he confronted her.

Along with an aperitif, he had consumed most of a bottle of Chateaux Neuf du Pape, and his eyes were glassy. Bits of a napoleon they had as dessert lodged on his finely-coifed curled mustache, and he leaned across the table his face near hers. She knew even before he spoke that he had discovered the affair.

"I have heard," he began, speaking formally, "that there is a certain ambitious colonial in the employ of the American trader the Monsieur Coffan. A Negro, a Black man, a lowly slave who worked the cotton fields before killing his master and fleeing to Europe, having disguised himself to Monsieur Coffan as a humble and intellectually curious student, seeking only to better himself in society. In fact, he is a murderer."

"I have heard furthermore," he continued, "that a certain young lady, a music student at the Royal Academy of Music, has been seen in the company of this Negro. She too, I have heard, has been taken in by his ruse, soon to be used by him in his ambitious climb to respectability. You are advised to cease communication with this ruffian," he said.

"I am 'advised'?" Bettina asked.

"No. In fact, you are forbidden."

Bettina drew back in her seat. Monsieur Philippe de Montclair had set his jaw and his eyes were burning.

"I am 'forbidden'?"

"Yes, forbidden. You are not to see him again."

"You, monsieur, are not my father. I do not believe you are in a position to forbid me to do anything. And what's more, you know nothing of this man. You know nothing of his past, nor his ambition."

"You will defy me, then?"

"No, I won't defy you. I will do what I want to do since you have no rights over me other than the charm of your money. I will not disobey you, since there is no one to disobey, if you take my meaning."

"This is a very big mistake for your friend, Bettina. A very big mistake. I will have to deal with him myself."

"Whatever can you mean, monsieur?"

"I mean to challenge him to a duel."

"O, mon Dieu, Philippe, no, do not do that—please."

"Yes!"

"No! He will kill you."

"I will choose swords; there are very few in the city who can better me with a foil."

"He's a lot younger than you, and strong."

"He knows nothing of dueling."

"But he does. He was taught to fence somewhere back in America."

"Impossible!"

"Perhaps, but Monsieur Coffan has sent him to study fencing."

"Yes? With whom if I may ask?"

"With Pietro Montalban."

Monsieur Philippe de Montclair drew back in alarm, then recovered. Pietro Montalban was said to be the most skilled fencer in Paris. The nobility was careful not to offend him for fear of a challenge.

"Montalban? Well, this Negro is only a clumsy student. What is this Black man's name, by the way?"

"He was named Marcus Aurelius by one of his owners when he was a boy."

At this Philippe de Montclair began to laugh, repeating the name over and over again. He laughed so hard, he began to choke.

"This is the finest joke of all," he said, still catching his breath. "I should like to meet his American master someday—he clearly has a refined sense of the absurd."

"Philippe, do not challenge this man. Please. For your own sake."

"Why for my sake. I would think it would be more for his—and as I can see now, for yours as well, my dear."

"It is you, Philippe. Don't do it. He may kill you. You will at the very least lose face—defeated by an American."

He began laughing again, and called for the check.

"I shall confront him this week," he said.

******

A few days later, Marcus was coming out of the Café Procope with a friend when he accidentally bumped into a man dressed in fine high boots and a silk vest. The man stumbled and then righted himself.

"Are you not the servant of Monsieur Coffan?" he asked haughtily, looking Marcus up and down in disgust.

Marcus was at a loss to respond immediately, he no longer thought of himself as a servant.

"And are you not he who has been seen in the company of Bettina Valcour?"

"I'm sorry, monsieur, I don't understand."

"You don't speak French?"

"Yes, I can understand you. But I don't know what you want."

"You will not see her again."

"Who?"

"Bettina Valcour."

"Why?"

"Because I say so."

At this point, Marcus's friend took his arm and tried to draw him away. "This will come to no good, Marc. Let's go," he said.

“He will not leave,” de Montclair said. “He will first apologize to me for pushing me down. And then he will agree to cease all communication with Bettina Valcour.”

The three years under the tutelage of Mr. Coffin had instilled in Marcus a certain personal confidence.

“And who might you be to tell me what to do?” he asked.

“I am Count Carl Philippe de Montclair, as you should know. As everyone knows.”

At this, he stepped closer to Marcus as if to accost him. Marcus put his hand up and gently pushed him away.

“Done then, you’ve given offense,” said the Count. “I challenge you to a duel. Choose you weapon.”

Marcus shook his head. “I don’t understand,” he said. “You come upon me, put yourself in my path, and then tell me I can’t see my fellow student Bettina, and then challenge me to a duel? And what are you to Bettina, or she to you? You’re not her father; I know him. And then you challenge me. I won’t fight with you, monsieur count no account.”

De Montclair drew himself up, his eyes flaring.

“You are not to address me in a facetious manner, you untutored slave. She is mine, and you are nothing, and you will not see her and I will meet you in the Bois de Boulogne. Tuesday at dawn, and we will decide. Bring a sword and a second.”

“I won’t be there,” Marcus said.

Marcus took his friend’s arm and strode away.

******

Later that evening after dinner, he told Mr. Coffin about the encounter.

“I know of this man,” Mr. Coffin said. “He is a well-known flaneur who favors younger women in the arts. He will soon be tired of her, so do nothing. On the other hand, if you do meet him and best him your reputation in society—if you care about such things—would rise considerably.”

He sipped his Armagnac.

“But let me ask you something,” he said. “Were there other people around when he confronted you?”

“Yes, a small group had collected and were watching us.”

"Were there any fashionable ladies in the group?"

"Yes, several."

"And gentlemen?"

"Yes. We were just outside Le Procope. There was a fashionable crowd there. I think they were amused," Marcus said.

"In that case, Marc, I think he will confront you again. He'll be armed this time, and if you refuse to duel, he may just skewer you. You've made a fool of him, and in his world, that is unacceptable. He has to clear his reputation, especially, and I hate to bring this up, but especially because, for one thing, you are an American and, secondly, a *gens de couleur*. De Montclaire will be laughed out of society."

****

Not long after that, Marcus was coming home from his fencing lesson when a carriage cut him off at a street crossing. The door opened, and Count Philippe, jumped out, sword in hand.

"Monsieur Marc Aurèle, en garde," he said calmly. "Here, or in the Bois du Boulogne tomorrow morning. It is your choice, monsieur, I do you the honor."

A rough-looking carriage driver, armed with a pistol, dismounted and stood beside the Count, glaring at Marcus.

Marcus was silent. He looked at the armed driver, then at the Count, then at the sword in his hand. He had his own sword in his belt, but he was worried that even before he had a chance to draw, one man or another would drill him.

"Very well then, monsieur, I accept your challenge. Where in the Bois do we meet?"

The Count described the location of a certain large English oak, well hidden from the public.

It could have been imagination, but Marcus thought he read in the Count's demeanor a certain air of disappointment. Perhaps even fear.

"You are certain, monsieur le Comte, you want to go ahead with this?" Marcus asked with confidence, as if it was quite clear that the Count would be bested.

"*Bien sur*," said the Count.

After the revolution, dueling rules were loosened and anyone could issue a challenge and dueling with pistols became more common. Seconds were still required however, and Marcus consulted his mentor as to a choice.

Mr. Coffin explained the rules and the choice of seconds, and Marcus immediately suggested the most logical person—his teacher Pietro.

Mr. Coffin smiled, "Yes, but as far as I understand these things, one cannot choose your own fencing master," he said, "you must choose another. Especially in this situation."

"But who?" Marcus said. "I don't know any familiar with the world of fencing." •

"I have just your man, if he will agree," Mr. Coffin said. "The Marquis de Moreaux, the legitimist in our salon."

"But what do we do? Do we travel together, and is there some protocol I should follow?" Marcus asked.

"In the old days, yes, very formulaic, but now not so much. And no matter what you do, you will be looked down upon, save that the Marquis would be your second. He will cast some, some legitimacy to your position. He is well-known and respected by the Count."

Mr. Coffin settled an arrangement with the Marquis, who, it should be said, detested Count Philippe whom he considered an empty-headed fop.

Before dawn on the arranged day for the duel, a carriage arrived at the gate of Mr. Coffin's quarters and Marcus, well-dressed in high boots, a tight doublet and trousers for the occasion, mounted.

As the carriage rolled out over the river and out to the Bois, the Marquis, who himself was not unfamiliar with fencing, chatted with Marcus. "You are ready?" the Marquis asked, smiling.

"Yes, ready, but a little nervous. I've been fencing for years, but never in a real duel."

"Don't worry," the Marquis said, "the Count is an impostor, a nouveau riche from Argenteuil who married well. Plus he's probably been out carousing half the night. Just defend yourself and tire him out. Then, when he seems fatigued, try a few feints, and see if you can determine his condition. Try a point on line, and let him attack, parry, feint, riposte, feint again, and keep him working. Once you have calculated his weakness—attack. Give him a sharp nick on his sword arm, and then nick the other arm. Keep going until you see blood. You have to see blood."

Rules of fencing in those years only required drawing first blood to claim victory. Killing was illegal and the victor could be prosecuted, although, depending on the class of the winner, the sentences would be light. In the case of the Count, if he were to kill Marcus, the charges would be modest; he may even be found not guilty. And if so, the sentence would be light. In the eyes of the law. Marcus was a questionable *gens de couleur* and what's more, the servant of an American tradesman. He would be charged with murder if he killed the Count. Dawn in the Bois that September morning was foggy, and strange wraiths of rising mist rose from the open meadows and the sparse open woods where the large English oak was located. Marcus and the Marquis arrived just at sunrise. They could see a hint of sun, a mere silver coin behind a curtain of fog. The Count's people had not yet arrived.

The two of them dismounted, and the driver drove the carriage off a way, out of sight of the dueling grounds. This was not the first Parisian duel to have been fought at the site.

The Marquis and Marcus stood by the oak, waiting. The light increased in the east. They could hear the incessant calling of the cuckoos and the black thrushes, and the grounds gave off that musky scent of wet leaves and early autumn.

"Where is this impostor?" Marcus asked anxiously. "Was this a false challenge?"

"They'll be here," said the Marquis. "He's probably drunk. Maybe overslept."

"Maybe he forgot?" Marcus said. "What's the protocol if he never shows? Is the challenge settled?"

"I don't actually know," said the Marquis, "but he'll be here. He may actually be worried about you. He has heard things."

"What things?"

The Marquis paused, choosing his words carefully.

"You have become something of a well-known figure in certain circles around the Rue du Bac. Count Philippe is taking a chance. If he bests you, he will be considered a weakling, nothing more than a frightened rabbit, who purposely takes on an inexperienced American Black. But if you win, he'll be ruined. The laughing stock of his class. I know this," said the Marquis, "I know these people."

They waited. The cuckoo calls became bothersome. The misty wraiths faded, and the fog began to burn off.

"How long should we wait here?" Marcus asked.

"I don't know, maybe an hour, then we go looking for him. I know where he lives. We go roust him out and challenge him. I don't know. We wait, I guess."

Ten minutes later, they heard the thud of horse hooves and the creak of carriage wheels and the Count appeared.

He was dressed that day in a fine cambric shirt, culottes and silk stockings and light shoes.

Marcus bowed his head slightly in greeting.

"Bonjour, monsieur le Con—sorry—monsieur le Count," he said. "I trust you slept well in your comfortable bed and are ready for our little sport."

The Count was unamused by Marcus's slip of the tongue. He nodded his head slightly, and the two of them took up their stations, standing at first at the required distance.

"*Allez, messiers*!" said the Count's second.

"En garde," said the Count and held his foil in a straight, point-in-line position. Marcus, whose sword tip was lowered to the ground, lifted the sword and performed a beat—a tap, signaling that he was ready, whereupon the Count immediately countered with a full attack—a lunge straight for the heart of Marcus. Such swift aggression was a surprise, but Marcus parried. This was no feint on the part of the Count, not a false charge in other words, his intent was to kill. Another lunge, another parry, Marcus stepped back, drawing the Count forward. The Count executed a series of three more lunges, followed by three successful parries by Marcus. Again and again, charge and retreat, lunge and parry, one after another. The overall sense of the duel at that point was that he, Marcus, was scared and sooner or later would take a hit, perhaps fatal. But there was strategy in his withdrawal.

The Count was indeed a skilled fencer as he had claimed, but he could not manage to come close to this light-footed dancing, retreating fool. And the harder he pressed, the more breathless he became.

The fog burned off and the sun flashed on the whirling glissades of the foil blades, the scrape a clack of the swords blocking the calls of the cuckoos. Obviously tiring, the Count assumed a recovery, and then another point-in-line. Marcus could see that he was only pausing to rest and he tapped the outstretched sword without pause and executed a feint. The Count parried and attacked with a lunge. Marcus parried and withdrew, feinted again, parried and withdrew, then feinted again—a series of false attacks, which the easily parried by the Count who attacked with vigor.

This went on for nearly twenty minutes, one false attack after another on the part of Marcus, who would then withdraw and continue to parry. At one point, Marcus could see a sweat breaking out on the Count's forehead. He issued an attack, which the Count parried, he was clearly breathing heavily, and so Marcus pressed on, no longer feinting with false attacks—but charging and lunging repeatedly, although not with any intent to end the duel.

Something stirred in Marcus at that point, some distant memory of his days in bondage. He now realized he had the upper hand with the Count, and seeing his condition, he drew closer and began to laugh. He gave the Count a break and made a recovery. "En garde," he said and held out his sword in a point-in line, offering the Count a rest.

"En garde, mon vieux," Marcus said, "You are not tired are you, monsieur? Or have you no spirit for a killing?"

The Count took the bait, tapped Marcus's outstretched sword and attempted a *flech*, a running attack. Marcus stepped aside adroitly and swatted the backside of the Count with his foil. He could easily have drawn blood, but he was not finished yet. He encouraged the Count to fight on.

"Come on then, count no account," he said. "Take up the sword against the upstart nation," he said and offered a riposte, arms outspread offering himself up.

Of course, the Count lunged, and once again Marcus dodged lightly.

"Turn, monsieur le Comte, do your best. Your friends at the Café Procope will be waiting to hear of your victory. Will you kill me then, count no account, or do me a favor and simply draw first blood. Come on then. Up you go!"

The game went on. One taunt after another followed by the Count's attacks, until Marcus, once more deflecting touch after touch, parried and stepped quickly forward, sword lowered, so close he hear the Count's furious breathing and smell his tainted breath. He was uncovered at that point and Marcus could easily have skewered him. But he stepped back again.

"You are tired, monsieur? You are tired? I will kill you later then. Rest now."

He stepped back farther.

The Count stood panting, his sword point down. Then, seeming unstoppable, he resumed his ever wilder, inaccurate lunges. The duel continued. The cuckoos and the thrushes quieted their dawn songs. The seconds shifted at their stations, anxious for this to be over, one way or another. But the Count soldiered on, attack after attack, all of them easily parried by Marcus.

"Monsieur," said Marcus finally, "have you had breakfast? I myself haven't breakfasted yet and I am getting hungry. Shall we retire to the Procope for a café crème and a croissant and perhaps lift a glass of absinth together?"

"*Ta guele sale nègre*!" said the Count. "*Va te faire foutre*!"

Marcus raised his palm to his chest in mock horror.

"Ah well. If you won't join me, I'm sorry then. Allow me to apologize in advance."

Whereupon Marcus stood up straight, his right knee forward, his sword grounded and his left arm cocked behind his back. Then he sprang forward like a pouncing cat and executed an upward lunge that ran his foil through the Count's sword arm just below his shoulder.

The Count let out a low yowl; his sword dropped to the ground, and he stood, wide-eyed and pale, staunching the blood with his left hand. His second rushed forward. "You are struck, monsieur! *Quel horreur. Quels temps, quels mores.*"

The hit was indeed palpable; blood was flowing all across the chest of the Count's cambric shirt.

Marcus had drawn first blood.

****

After two or three weeks, word spread—first through the neighborhood around the Rue du Bac, then outward across to the Left Bank, and then back again to the cheap cafes along the Rue Saint-Denis, and then finally, up to the Café Procope, where most of the regulars found the news of the duel amusing. Count Philippe de Montclaire, himself did not make his presence known. He lay low in his villa, nursing his wound and then saw fit to tour some of his family holdings in Boulogne.

Marcus himself, on the advice of Mr. Coffin, also laid low. He contented himself with his secretarial work, his classes, and even avoided Mr. Coffin's salon for a few sessions.

He did go back to his fencing lessons. The school was located on a side street, not far from the Marais, and the lessons were held in a wide third floor room with floor to ceiling windows. Monsieur Pietro Montalban stood by one of these windows, chatting with a student. When Marcus entered, he looked up.

"Oh mon Dieu," he exclaimed. "Comes the conquering hero!" And he sprang across the floor, his arms spread and embraced Marcus, kissing him on both cheeks.

"My most successful student in years," he said. "Marcus, you perhaps did not know but that fop Montclaire, he is no stranger to dueling, and he usually wins. I've always wanted him to challenge me. But Marcus, *mon enfant*, you have done the work for me. Now, tell me all about it, every detail that you can remember, and tell me what aspect of the Count's duel worried you the most."

Marcus complied, starting with the surprise of the impolite violence of the first attack by the Count, and also the dangerous *flech* toward the end of the fight.

Master Montalban then gave him advice on how to handle each position, "Just in case you have to fight another duel—which at some point I think you will. Montclaire has many shallow friends, and he may encourage them to engage you. Be wary."

He was right in this assessment. After the duel, word began to spread in the legitimiste group and the apolitical social circle of Count Philippe.

Marcus dared to return to the Café Procope after a month or so with his friend, Pierre, the young teacher at the school for colonials. Marcus could feel eyes on him as soon as they were seated. He also began to receive more invitations to festivals and balls. At one of these he met a young German-speaking woman, named Petra, who had visited Mr. Coffin's salon one night. He recognized her at the ball and asked her for a dance. She was small, with dark curling hair, black eyes, and full red lips. She did not look particular German, in fact, more gypsy-like or perhaps Kirgiz, her eyes slanted upward. The gypsy blood was also evident in her skill at the dance. In fact, she was from some well-known family (she claimed, at least) from Vienna where her father was an equestrian in the Spanish Riding School.

But Petra had no interest in horse ballet. Instead she fled to Paris and began studies at the Paris Opera Ballet. This after no small amount of resistance from her family, she claimed. Ballet dancing was hardly a respectable career choice in those times; the girls were often from the streets.

Petra had no English and her French was sketchy, but she and Marcus, were taken with each other. Marcus noticed that she seemed to have a Spanish accent in French. She did speak fluent Spanish, which after some weeks, Marcus managed to pick up.

Sad to say, after the duel, Marcus and Bettina had had a falling out. She had tried desperately to discourage the Count from the duel, partly for his sake—she had anticipated the outcome—and partly for hers. She couldn't imagine that the Count would dare to meet with her after so ignominious a defeat, which was in fact the case. The Count disappeared; Bettina no longer could attend the fine dinners, the opera, and the concerts. This was not exactly Marcus's fault. What could he do? But he didn't expect to lose Bettina.

As it was they more or less drifted apart, without any contentious exit battles. She just began avoiding Marcus, who was now often surrounded with companions, both men and women alike, whenever he was at a café. Marcus spent some time looking for Bettina. And then one day he had a letter from her explaining that she was going to be attending music school in Vienna for the season and wished him luck in his schooling. This last line more or less summed up the situation. Nothing about their shared dreams and ambitions.

In any case, it was not long after that that he met Petra.

Marcus by that time was familiar enough with Paris society to have developed a certain amount of cynicism, and he began to wonder about the veracity of Petra's supposed background. Not that he cared. He loved her gypsy-like soul, her spontaneous out bursts of dance or rage, or laughter. He also got along well with her friends, who consisted of dancers and a variety of theater people, actors who favored the Latin Quarter cafés and dance halls.

With Mr. Coffin's apparent approval, he developed a new schedule that involved less time doing books in the cloistered Rue du Bac study, and more time with the teachers at his school, fencing lessons, and later afternoon, a cinq à sept, then dinner somewhere, and then an evening with Petra and her friends, some of which went on late into the night. Marcus would return, sometimes half-drunk to the Rue du Bac to sleep a few hours before his secretarial duties began.

One night coming home along his usual route along the Rue Jacob, a masked man stepped out of a doorway and challenged him. Marcus stopped, hand on the hilt of his sword.

"And why, monsieur? If you intend to rob me, you have picked the wrong man. I've just spent my all coins on food and drink."

"Not to rob," the masked man said, "to kill. En garde!"

Marcus sized up his opponent. He was a large man, slightly overweight, Marcus judged, and inasmuch as he was masked, Marcus determined that his field of vision was limited. He drew his sword and stepped to one side, slightly beyond his assailant's view.

"You don't want to do this, monsieur, it will not end well for you. Let me pass and be on my way."

In response, the masked man attacked, a stupid and clumsy lunge, which Marcus easily deflected, and waited for the next. Another attack, also repulsed, and then another. This was a joke for Marcus.

"Monsieur," he said, "I don't want to fight at present. I am a little tired and in need of a sleep. Why don't you go home now? You too appear tired."

The answer was another attack.

Marcus was indeed tired, it must have been two in the morning. He executed a false charge, a feint. The masked man made a slow response, so, almost bored, and indeed tired, Marcus attacked and stabbed the shoulder of the man's sword arm.

The confused swordsman stumbled and fell on his back.

"Terribly sorry, monsieur," Marcus said, "but I do want to go home."

He stepped forward and held the point of his sword at the fallen man's throat.

"But before I go, would you be so kind as to remove your mask?"

There was no response, so Marcus touched the man's throat with the point of his foil. The man slowly reached up with his left arm and slipped off the mask, revealing a pasty somewhat rounded face, a weak pouting mouth and frightened blue eyes.

Marcus thought he recognized the face; it was one of the acquaintances of Count Philippe from the crowd that gathered at the Procope.

"*Bonne nuit, monsieur*," he said. "*Dormi bien*."

Paris
The Confession

Carousing notwithstanding, Marcus still made of a point of attending Mr. Coffin's salons. They offered a quiet and enlightening refuge from the sometimes raucous evenings with Petra and her crowd. He also began to periodically take long solitary walks through the Luxemburg Gardens, the Jardin des Plantes, and sometimes out to the Bois de Boulogne. On these occasions, he would spend hours reviewing the course of his past life and his future. These became a means of taking stock. How he got where he was. What to do next and where would it all end. As long as Mr. Coffin maintained his business in France, he was safe, if slightly dissolute. But he sometimes ruminated on what would become of him if Mr. Coffin were to return to America. Under French law, he was presently free. Mr. Coffin had no legal rights to him, a fact that Mr. Coffin himself had made clear to Marcus in the first weeks of their life in Paris. But if Mr. Coffin left, what could he do? He would have no employment, and no source of any funding.

And there was one other thing. A few weeks after his last encounter with a vengeful swordsman, there was another incident. Once again he was out on the streets late at night, this time with Petra on his arm. The two of them were halted by a man in a black cloak and a wide-brimmed dark hat. He stepped out in front of them, flung aside his cloak and drew a sword.

"Step aside, madame," he said in thick Parisian patois. "Your dark-skinned friend is about to die."

Petra was not amused. "And who might you be, you lowlife pig? You step aside, or you will be the one to die—slowly and painfully, if we have our way. One or the other of us will make sure of that."

Whereupon she pulled a stiletto from her sash. Only then she did step aside. But she circled him.

He glanced back at her, and when he turned again, Marcus's sword was at his chest, just below his throat. He attempted a parry, but Marcus was too close. He pressed the sword point in—a shallow cut. The assailant stepped back only to suffer a stab wound in his buttocks.

"Off you go, dirty pig," Petra said, poking him a second time. "Off you go, squealing. And tell all your perfumed friends to steer clear. We have friends of our own if it comes to that, and you would not want to meet them."

The assailant squirmed free and fled down the dark street.

That was the second assault. There were two others, the last an outright murder attempt. A drunken man with a pistol took aim as Marcus stepped out of a dance hall on the Left Bank. He fired and missed, and Marcus and his friends jumped him and began to beat him. He too fled, leaving his pistol behind. It was clear, as his fencing master Pietro had predicted, that Count Philippe was employing his friends and hired assassins to avenge his defeat.

This was another factor to be considered in Marcus's current position. It would perhaps be wise to lay low for a while, and even return to America, if it came to that. It would make a convenient exit.

And there was one other matter. Occasionally on his lonely walks, he would think back of nights on the banks of the James River with Tilly Washburn. He suffered bouts of mixed emotions when he thought back on her life, as compared to his. A rush of love, coupled with pity would well up in him, followed by a veritable wave of anger at the system that doomed her. He thought about her high spirit, her know-it-all confidence and natural intelligence and the fact that, eventually, she would get herself into trouble and suffer the lash. She would age and break and wither and die before she ever got a chance to live.

On one walk in the Bois de Boulogne, alone and out of sight, this fantasy seized him with unusual force and in a frenzy, he drew his sword and began attacking the shrubbery, one slash after another stabbing leaves, slashing twigs, shouting madly, the rage pulling him wildly forward until, finally, breathless and spent, he fell to the ground and rolled over and looked at the passing clouds. A calm descended, and an afterthought consoled him.

What if he could rescue her and bring her to France?

Marcus had been in Paris long enough to pick up the nuances of the language and the mannerisms and suavity of a boulevardier and among some, the reputation of a flaneur. Also a man not to be reckoned with on the dueling grounds. And yet he knew that all that he had achieved in Paris, and in fact in life so far, was due to the generosity of Mr. Coffin. Truth be told, he sometimes wondered what drove his mentor. Two years had passed by then, and why would Mr. Coffin continue to support him even in his youthful follies in the night clubs and cafés.

Late one evening, roughly two and a half years after he had arrived in Paris, Mr. Coffin called Marcus into the drawing room and offered him a *digestif.*

"I have been wanting to tell you something, Marcus," he said, somewhat seriously, and then handed over a folder of documents. "These are your papers of manumission, Marcus. I am setting you free, as I have told you; you can go where you like when you like here in France. But you are still technically bound to me legally under American law. These documents make your freedom official, in case you have occasion to need them—which you won't here in France."

"But I have had letters from America recently, as you know, and for various reasons, some personal, some business related, I have to return to Maryland. I would like you to accompany me and these papers will establish your freedom in the United States. You are also, of course, free to stay here in France, although, speaking personally, I would like you to come with me. But before you decide, I want to share a story with you."

"Papagena and I, as I you may have suspected, were an intimate couple," he began. "We were of different faiths, but neither of us was especially religious, and different races. But love does not see colors. We never did marry. But after a year, Papagena gave birth to a little boy. We named him Moses. He was, you understand, born free under the current Haitian government, which had by then established itself. Moses was a talented young boy. I taught him to read, and he quickly learned three languages, the patois of his mother, French from the white man he called Papa Grande, his grandfather, and English from me. It soon became apparent that if Papagena and I stayed on in the village, where we were then living, Moses, for all his intelligence, would end up working in the timber trade or growing sugar cane."

"Furthermore, as far as we could tell, things were not going well with Haitian independence. The French had imposed a stiff indemnity on the new nation in compensation for the loss of property, including the loss of their work force of slaves. Who knows what would happen to Papagena and Moses. So I decided to move to France."

"We acquired the official papers and booked passage to Bordeaux, and then on to Paris, where we intended to place Moses in one of the schools for colonials. It was not to come to pass."

"There was plague on shipboard. Cholera. One of the crewmen died. Then another, and then the passengers started to die. Moses took sick, then Papagena. I nursed them as best I could. I tried all things, even Papagena's magic potions that she was carrying. They didn't work. My entire family died at sea. My whole family."

"For some reason, I survived, I don't know why—and this had nothing, by the way, to do with a deity; I was not saved for some higher purpose—in fact in Christian lore, I would have been bound for hell. Didn't matter. I would rather have died with them at that point."

"You cannot know, Marcus, the depths of grief I suffered at that time. I landed in France. My French was a sordid mix of Haitian patois, I had only one business associate there, an older acquaintance of my father. I shall tell you there were times in those first weeks that I considered taking my life."

"This was winter; it was gray, the eternal Paris grisaille, as opposed to the warm green sun of Haiti. I have to tell you that I suffered a mental breakdown. I walked out one night and got lost, and I somehow ended up in the Jardin des Plants, and here I collapsed on the ground, weeping. At dawn, one of the groundskeepers found me. I didn't know who I was. I didn't even know where I was. But the groundskeeper sent me over to the Hôtel-Dieu, where I was cared for over the winter. Then slowly—ever so slowly—spring moved in. Flowers bloomed in the Tuileries. There were children in the parks. I was released from the hospital and I started walking the streets. I walked to think, and one day, after a full day of walking, I came to a decision. I decided to get out of the family business and work in a different trade."

"Why would you want to do that?" Marcus asked.

"I wanted to excise myself from the dreadful institution of slavery."

Then, uncharacteristically, Mr. Coffin grew silent.

Marcus did not dare break the silence. He waited, but Mr. Coffin did not explain exactly what his connection with slavery was.

After a period of reflection, he began again, "Through accomplices in France, I landed a position in Baltimore and Annapolis shipping tobacco," he said. "Then later, I began working with currency exchanges. And it was there in the United States, that I hatched a plan to keep myself sane."

"I determined to buy slaves to work for me and then set them free. One after another. No one could stop me from this trade. It was perfectly legal. You, in fact, know some of the people I bought. Janey B, for one. She and George are actually free Blacks."

"One other thing. I think you may have guessed. Old George, senile old George, is Papagena's father. I support him. He is free to leave if he were ever to wish to do so—which he won't do. Why would he? I pay both of them salaries. Old George gets a monthly stipend. Not that he needs it. He has a clean bed and good food and doesn't have to work. For me, it's a question of ethics. A statement, I suppose of the way I think the world should be."

"One day, one of my contacts among the slave catchers came to tell me they had caught a boy I might be interested in. They told me he spoke in a funny language and claimed to be French and was only visiting America. So I bought that boy and his name was Marcus Aurelius."

Marcus shook his head incredulously. The turns of fate. The wheels of fortune. It was too much to comprehend. He was wordless.

Mr. Coffin poured another glass of *marc*, and drew his chair closer to Marcus, leaning forward close to his face.

"Marcus, I have to tell you more thing," he said. Tears suddenly filled his eyes. "You are the same age Moses would be had he lived. I still think of him almost every day and there is nothing I can do, except for one thing." He reached out and took Marcus's hands in his. "I want to officially adopt you and grant you all the rights and privileges of a family member. You will be my son."

At this point, he couldn't help himself, he choked up and let out a sob—a unique expression of emotion from stolid old Mr. Coffin, the Quaker.

Marcus was at first too shocked to respond. Then as the realization set in he could not contain himself. He too choked back a sob and reached over and brought Mr. Coffin's hands up to his cheek.

"Father," he whimpered.

"My son," Mr. Coffin said. Then he recovered and sat back. "But even though you will be my official son, that still doesn't mean you have to come back to America with me. As you know, it is a different world there. No matter where you go, you will be in danger. Take your time deciding. I have booked passage on a ship in three weeks. But before you decide, there is more you have to know about your new family."

There followed here a very long preamble describing his Quaker father and mother and their non-violent pacifist traditions, the persecution that his ancestors suffered at the laws of the Puritan founders—banishment, the whip, prisons, even hangings.

"But there is more," Mr. Coffin said gravely. "Much more. And I tell you this because you have to know something of your inheritance."

Once again, there was a long preamble. But it came down to the fact that his family had owned slaves and that he himself as a boy had seen one of them whipped mercilessly by his father's Irish assistant. The event had deeply affected him, he said.

"She was a maid, a girl only slightly older than I was at the time, only eleven or twelve, that is to say. I don't know what she did, but Corky, my father's assistant, was a large man—I never liked him, to tell the truth, he was not a nice man, a gruff man, and I believe he was fond of the bottle—in spite of the young girl's screams, he laid on the lash."

"I was young and I was not supposed to know about this sort of thing, the whippings took place in the outbuilding beyond the estate, but that day I heard the screams, and cracked open the door. There she was, her wrists tied to one of the studs, stripped to the waist. I could see red gashes across her back, and the waist of her white dress was pooled with blood. And yet he laid on the whip. I tell you this because I was sick. Literally. I vomited. I couldn't help it. I was haunted by bad dreams for months."

Marcus was silent in shock.

Mr. Coffin carried on, "But there is more, my son."

He went on to explain his rebellion from his family trading company.

"My father and mother had kept the family involvement in the slave trade from me. But when I started the work as bookkeeper, it came to light. I said nothing to my parents. I carried on with the work, and as a business we were successful and I was a part of that success. I was a slave trader."

"But it was there in Paris, after the death of Moses and Papagena, that I decided I would get out of the family business. But, Marcus, all you see here, this grand apartment and salon, the large riverside estate in St. Mary's County, the grounds and gardens, the fine horses and equipage, the little teak-decked sloop at the dock, is all based on wealth gained in the slave trade. And as my son, all that ignominious wealth is a part of your own inheritance."

****

For the next two weeks, Marcus walked in shock around Paris on his daily errands trying to comprehend his new situation. A free man. A legalized son with, as Mr. Coffin made clear, a healthy inheritance, an inheritance based on the slave trade. Furthermore, he realized that all this wealth was gained by the family after the Atlantic slave trade was outlawed by the federal government. The Coffins were a family of criminals.

Daily, Marcus set out on the city streets to take stock. He wandered the Bois de Boulogne the week after this news, running through all the possibilities. He knew the dangers if he returned. But as Mr. Coffin had explained, it would only be a matter of months, at most half a year, before they could return to the Paris office.

Here in Paris he was, of course, also in danger. Count Philippe had not forgotten the insult he had received. Assaults on Marcus had become fewer, especially given the fates of his attackers. But nonetheless, here, he was legally free. But then there was his father. He would be separated from the one man he had come to love and trust as no other. And now that man was his legal parent.

And there was one other matter, a major one: Fantasies and memories of Tilly periodically swept over him often after some of his more riotous happy evenings with one woman or another, or out in the cafés with his various friends, and even sometimes during Mr. Coffin's salon events when the conversation became incomprehensible to him, involving the latest political scandal. At these times, he would see himself somehow floating above the gathering, the quick soft music of the French language, the gestures and passions of the delivery of those who were holding forth. It was a sequence of moving images, meaningless, save for the color of the oriental rugs, the gowns of the women, the smell of tobacco, mixed with the sharp scent of cognac.

And following this strange distancing, he would think of the world of Tilly. The hopeless round of work. And to what avail? He knew Tilly. She had as sharp a wit as any of these well-read French liberal aristocrats. Had she been born under a different star she could be here, lounging in a red gown, white pearl necklaces streaming over her dark décolletage, her full rouged lips. "But you are all fools, you players. It's not like that, it's not like that at all, can't you see," she would be saying. At which point, she would split apart the theories of whatever arcane subject they claimed to understand.

If only.

It was on one particular walk in the Bois de Boulogne that the realization struck him. She could indeed be here. He could get her here. With his newfound position with Mr. Coffin, he could either afford to buy her or steal her, carry her back to France, enroll her in one of the schools for colonials, and liberate her, both physically and mentally. He just had to find her and manage to get her out of the ruthless system that bound her.

There was only one way to do that. In the end, he decided to return with Mr. Coffin.

Mary Plantation
Tilly's Travail

Back in America, while Marcus was enjoying the high life of a free and moneyed European man, things at the Mary Plantation were going downhill for Tilly.

The older and more rational son, Jefferson, was sent off to West Point, leaving behind his more rambunctious brother, Winslow.

Winslow turned sixteen that year, two years younger than Tilly. Unlike Jefferson, he had little interest in running the plantation, or schooling, nor apparently anything other than hunting and fishing and carousing with an older crowd in the taverns around Charles City. He would ride off sometimes late in the day to Charles City and not return. Other nights he would stumble in drunk, without bothering tend to his horse, nor even summoning a slave to take care of getting the horse to stall. Billings would find the horse out in the tobacco fields, having ranged around, trampling valuable crops.

On one of those nights in autumn, Winslow came home sooner than usual, sufficiently lubricated. The people in the big house had gone to bed, but the kitchen lamp was burning and Tilly was still up finishing with her sweeping and dishes. Winslow saw the lamp burning, kicked open the door and stumbled in.

"Why aren't you in your cabin, Tilly?" he slurred. "You should be back in your cabin by now."

"I'm going back, Massa Winslow, just a little more work."

"Get back in your cabin, I said, an' get back now, you hea'?" He paused. "Said get back." He stumbled toward her.

Tilly was no innocent. She could see exactly where this was headed. "All right, Massa, I'se going now." She went over to the stove, picked up a poker and raked the fire. Then she blew out the lamp. Winslow stood in the doorway, blocking her exit. She could see him silhouetted in the doorframe.

"Said, go home," Winslow slurred.

"I know what you said."

He stepped forward again. "I'm 'a have to teach you a lesson, girl." He shambled forward, and then made a lunge to catch her.

She dodged to his left, the poker still in her hand.

Winslow grunted, turned and caught the edge of her field dress. She smacked his hand away with the poker and he bellowed, let forth a series of rich curses and lunged again.

Another dodge.

"Teach you lesson…"

Another unsuccessful lunge. But Tilly had had enough. As he came at her, she jumped again to his left, but this time she swiped the poker hard across his right cheek. She could hear the dull smack in the darkened room.

Winslow let out a screeching howl and fell face down on the floor and as he fell, she gave him another whack on the back of his head. Then she fled to the comfort of her mother.

For his part, Winslow regained a semblance of consciousness and, weaving and tripping, he returned to the big house and went to bed.

Winslow's parents were no more approving of his current behavior than any of the slaves on the plantation were. Most were familiar with bad whites in one form or another, either a cruel master or a renegade son, and, often, a rough overseer. All the Mary Plantation people were wary of him.

The next morning, he shuffled into the dining room later than usual and called out for his breakfast. Tilly's mother served him, rather than Tilly herself.

His mother was horrified by his appearance—his right eye was swollen shut and his cheek had a deep purple bruise.

"What on earth has happened to you now, Winslow?" she asked.

Winslow raised his right hand and felt his cheek. "I dunno," he mumbled. "Got beat up at the Bull's Head tavern last night. Gang a drunk patrollers, I think."

In fact, he had been so drunk that night he actually had to stop and think what had happened. But once he remembered, he didn't forget.

He began to pester and make advances to Tilly whenever he could catch her alone. For her part, she learned to avoid him, sometimes hiding when she saw him out in the yard. But then, that winter, things got worse.

Henry Washburn had a younger brother, Conrad, who lived in Richmond. He was a somewhat ne'er-do-well lawyer who currently was not practicing law. Mrs. Washburn and Jefferson encouraged him to come to the plantation to help run things, since Mr. Washburn was more or less useless by then.

Conrad arrived in early winter, and set to work reorganizing the books, paying debts off, of which there were many by then, and trying to get Billings to take a harder line on the slaves. Without the oversight of Henry Washburn, the entire workforce on the Mary Plantation had taken to dodging the normal work schedules and planting orders. They sometimes would purposely sabotage the daily orders by planting peas when they were ordered to plant beans, for example.

Conrad was not much better than Billings at this aspect of the management. Unlike his relatively fair brother (fair being a relative term in the management of any Southern plantation), Conrad took a hard line and would beat slaves himself rather than leave it to Billings or the whipping boy. This had the effect of causing more 'mistakes' and misbehavior of the workforce. And this in turn, led Conrad to drink, his usual retreat in the face of difficulties. It also led him to, eventually, Tilly.

She was a noticeable figure among the slave population of the Mary Plantation, eighteen years old and very pretty compared to the field hand girls of her age. The skinny fifteen-year-old that Marcus had known had filled out to become a shapely young woman, and a woman who was cleaner and less beaten down by hard fieldwork. Now, she had to suffer the attention of both Winslow and his uncle.

Thoughts of escape began to form. It was, she calculated, only a matter of time before Winslow, or possibly Conrad, made a successful move on her.

She and her mother often discussed the situation at night after their chores. Serena agreed, it was probably a good time to get out.

Then in the spring, the decision was made easier by Conrad.

Saint Mary's County
In the Land of the Free

The trip from Le Havre to New York was uneventful, save for a patch of bad weather half way across the Atlantic. Marcus and Mr. Coffin arrived in New York on a windy September morning and landed amidst the noise and smoke of the city of New York which did not seem quite so chaotic as his first arrival in France at the port of Le Havre. If nothing else, he knew the language.

Traveling as master and enslaved personal valet, they took the new train line from New York to Baltimore, and then an overland stage to Annapolis. In an attempt to spare his feelings, or at least soften the harsh realization that Marcus was now considered an individual of a lower order even, sub-human, Mr. Coffin instructed him to speak only in French. He was dressed smartly in the latest Parisian fashion, and at the station, the two of them chatted amicably in French. Nonetheless, public eyes were upon them once they debarked in Baltimore. And on the stage ride to Annapolis, Marcus sat with the coachman, an older Black man dressed in a dark overcoat in spite of the warm weather. The two of them chatted, Marcus speaking in English with a thick French accent and asking the driver innocent questions about America.

"You are held in bondage, here?" Marcus asked at one point in a thick French accent.

"I'm what?" the driver asked.

"You are, I mean, enslaved?"

"Nossir," he said definitively. "I am free. Least I am free as long as I keep to my routine. All kinds of white devils hanging around stations looking to catch a niggaman to sell."

"Oh mon Dieu!" Marcus said. "You mean they catch you and sell you even though you are the free man?"

"That's the way it is with us, you don't never know who's lurking 'round the station house."

"You should come to France, my friend. No one owns anyone there. It is contrary to the law."

At Annapolis, Mr. Coffin arranged to have a carriage pick them up for the trip to Saint Mary's County, and within a day or two, they were settled.

Marcus fell into his old routine. He spent his mornings working on Mr. Coffin's ledgers, strolling in the gardens when he felt the need to stretch his legs, and then, after the midday meal he was more or less free. He helped George in the stables just for something to do. If the wind was right, he sometimes took the boat out, but for the most part, he stayed on Mr. Coffin's property or sometimes wandered along the lanes of neighboring farms, where he was known.

He also went to St. Mary's City from time to time on errands. But this was a slightly risky venture. As long as he stayed within his boundaries, he was safe. Nevertheless, Maryland was a slave state, although the Western Shore did not have the big plantations and since it was a border state, runaways often filtered through. Half the population of the state held northern sympathies, and stations on the Underground Railway were common. Also, as a result, there were patrollers out at night on the back roads and along the river banks.

Marcus was in fact safer here in some ways than he was back in Paris, where h the danger of the continued assaults instigated from time to time by Count Philippe, were still occurring. But he didn't feel that way. In Paris, he was a complete man who could defend himself, here he felt like a refugee, a hunted man.

After a month or two, this limited world, compared to daily life in Paris, began to wear on him. He longed for his old Paris friends and his days and nights with Petra. By contrast, he was pulled to stay on by the thought of his mission to rescue Tilly.

With this in mind, he began by writing to Amanda at the Tucker One Hundred Plantation telling her he was back in the United States for a few months. He had written to her from Paris two or three times but he did not hear back. He was disappointed, but he had reasoned that perhaps in the periodic Parisian revolts and citizen uprisings, the letters had gone astray. Now he asked her if she could possibly help him locate a girl named Tilly Washburn, who was a house slave at the Mary Plantation.

He was sure Tilly would remember him; he had, after all, vowed to come back someday and steal her away, and she said she would be waiting. But that was three years ago.

After a month, Amanda did write back, among other things telling him that she never did get his Paris letters. She wrote that she thought of him often and wondered after his fate. She said, furthermore, that she would make inquiries to see if she could learn something of the whereabouts of Tilly Washburn. She wrote again later to say that she learned that Tilly had run away, and Mr. Washburn, at the behest of his wife, had sent out slave catchers to see if they could get her back.

Correspondence dragged on. There were letters to and fro as Amanda continued to help out. The long hot summer set in. The air over the bay was thick with shimmering night heat, smelling of low tides and marsh grasses. Amanda was having no luck. But her older brother, Robert, was now a Richmond lawyer, and even though she was not supposed to tell anyone, he had attended Yale Law School and had come home a closeted Yankee sympathizer. Robert knew families on the James River plantations. Some of the owners had heard of Tilly, mainly because she was such a lively spirit, but no one knew where she was. He did know, through his northern connections, of some of the safe houses in northern Virginia and Maryland and said he would ask around. But the search was slow and the outcome uncertain. And so it went on. Dead end after dead end.

And all this while, conflicting with the tedium of the dull world of Maryland and the failed mission to find Tilly, was the thought of the night life of Paris—the smell of strong coffee, the good wines, the music and theater, the artists' balls and the ballet.

Furthermore, the reality of the life of a person of color, enslaved or free, in the American South began to make itself apparent in the limited world around Marcus. He could not help but noticed the broken, seemingly craven dark-skinned people he would see in the countryside and in the town. Polite, smiling, perfectly strong men and women, bowing and scraping, and the men snatching off their hats or stepping off the curb, heads lowered whenever a white person passed.

The oppression of his earlier years in America came back to haunt him, also the reality of the world in which Tilly was forced to live in.

He often dreamed of Paris at night, of Petra, and his friends among the professors at the school for colonials. He lost his spirit for work, the gardens, the hot winds of the bay offered no relief. And then he began to worry about Tilly. Was she even alive? Fevers, malaria, the summer flux, even cholera, periodically swept across the enslaved populations. Maybe she had died, or had been caught and sold down the river by kidnappers.

What's more, he had a taste of his former life one afternoon while he was on an errand in St. Mary's City. A beautiful white woman on the arm of a middle-aged man approached him. Marcus glanced at the woman as they passed. Whereupon, unexpectedly, he felt a sharp slap on his right cheek so forceful that it jerked his head to one side.

"You insolent darky!" the man shouted. "You keep your eyes lowered and take off your hat when we pass or I'll take off your head."

Marcus reeled back and his hand went instinctively for his non-existent sword hilt. White rage surged through him. He recovered and looked the man in the eye. The next blow knocked him off his feet and before he could get up, the man and his lady had moved on.

Assaults of this sort were what drove Marcus to new horizons. He set his course.

Mary Plantation
Murder Most Foul

As had many members of the Mary Plantation, Tilly herself by then had been smacked around by Conrad, although she had yet to be seriously beaten.

A few weeks after Conrad arrived, Tilly noticed him watching her while she served dinner. One night after the meal was served, having consumed most of a carafe of a good Bordeaux, he came into the kitchen, and began asking Serena about the oyster stew she had served.

"A little too peppery for my taste," he said. Serena nodded politely.

"Don't put so much pepper in the next time."

"I won't do that no more, Massa," She said.

"Not only that, I had a little problem with the remoulade sauce you made the other night. Same problem. Too spicy. I want you to tame all your dishes."

"Yessuh."

"And you," he said, turning to Tilly, looking her up and down, "what's your name again?"

"Tilly be my name, suh."

"Alright Tilly, I want you to be a little snappier with your service, quit that shambling. Walk smartly. I've heard you have a tendency to drop things. Don't do that anymore."

"No suh, I won't do that no more."

Conrad turned and headed for the door.

"Anything else you want from us'n, Massa?" Tilly called out.

Conrad caught the insolent tone of her question and spun around and glared at her, paused briefly, then said: "You keep down your eyes down when you talk to me, and I don't like your tone of voice. Watch yourself girl."

He walked out and slammed the door.

Tilly's discomfort (and dislike) increased sharply after that exchange. Her guard went up. But so did her anger.

In exchange, probably testing her, Conrad began making absurd requests. He would call her over from her post by the door and ask her to pass the sugar bowl to him, when in fact the sugar bowl was within easy reach. Then he would shout at her to hurry up—one order after another at every meal.

"Get over here with that wine decanter."

"Clear this plate now, not tomorrow."

"Pass that glass properly."

"Hurry up. You are one lazy wench if ever there was one."

All of which served only to cause Tilly to move more slowly.

One evening, when he had clearly had a little too much grog, he slapped her buttocks as she passed. "Get on there," he shouted.

Another night, for no apparent reason, after she had placed his plate in front of him, he grabbed her wrist in a vice-like grip.

"You be a good girl now, Tilly," he said. He was clearly drunk. "When I tell you to jump, you jump." He shook her wrists violently and pushed her away.

The culmination of his behavior came to pass one evening when, flailing his arm in a drunken gesture, he accidentally knocked her forearm while she was pouring him a glass of wine. The red wine spilled onto his plate and splattered over his white waistcoat.

"That does it!" he shouted.

He jumped from the table, grabbed her arm and dragged her out to the grounds where the whipping post stood, all the while shouting for Billings and Tommy, a field hand who was a driver and sometime whipping boy.

Neither appeared.

Conrad pushed Tilly against the post, ripped her dress to her waist and told her to get her arms up around the post, still calling for Billings and Tommy all the while. When they failed to appear, he yanked her around and struck her, sending her into the dust, and began to kick her.

Whatever rage it was that surged through Conrad, rose also to a red heat in Tilly. At the third kick, she grabbed his ankle and jumped up, spilling him into the dust. Then she kicked him hard in the head, knocking him senseless. She looked down at him briefly, sprawled there on the ground, unconscious.

She fled to her cabin.

Serena heard the ruckus and ran to her from the kitchen.

"I kilt him, Mama, I kilt Massa Conrad. Time to go, Mama, get me out of here," Tilly cried.

"You run, girl," Serena said, oddly calm, as if she had been expecting this for a long time. "Run out to the food patch. I bring you a bundle. Just wait there."

Tilly ran off into the borderlands, crashing through the brush, crying and stumbling until she came to a hollow. She slid down to a pile of brush. Beneath the brush was a stash of turnips, beets, potatoes, and onions. She collected a few handfuls and waited for her mother. Five minutes later, she arrived with a bundle of clothes.

"You know where to go, Tilly," she said, he voice still calm.

"I do, Mama," she answered. She embraced her mother, crying bitterly, the tears soaking her mother's dress.

"Get youself to Wilkins place soon as you can. They set you on course. And I'm gonna see you in Waterford someday soon."

Then Serena herself began crying.

"I gotta go, Tilly, 'for they come looking fo' me too." She handed her a small bag. "I been stealing pepper for a year now. For you leave spread this 'round the hollow, and then cover you trail when you take off. But don't use it all up. You may need it again 'for you get to Waterford where you half-sister Bitsy's laying low."

They had discussed Waterford often in their escape fantasies. They embraced again.

"You get on now," Serena said, sobbing. Then she climbed out of the hollow and disappeared.

Tilly sat motionless, head in her hands, still crying. Then she too packed her bundle, climbed out of the hollow, walked around the perimeter, and spread a fringe of pepper. Then she headed north, trailing pepper along the way.

St. Mary's County
Go Down, Moses

One day in late August, Marcus received a letter from Amanda. Her brother had news of Tilly. One of his contacts on the Underground Railroad remembered a teenage girl who fit Tilly's description and had fled the Mary Plantation. The source thought he remembered that she was headed for Waterford, a free town in Northern Virginia settled by German immigrants and Quakers. The source thought Tilly's half-sister was supposedly living there.

The tip confused Marcus even more. He took to pacing the route around the gardens late into the night thinking things over and sitting in the night air by the bay, taking stock. Finally, he made a decision. He went to Mr. Coffin one evening and asked to have a talk.

He began by asking how much longer would they be required to stay in Maryland.

"You are bored, aren't you?" Mr. Coffin asked. "I can see that."

Marcus explained his situation.

"It's worse than boredom," he said. "It's depression, a foggy heaviness," he said in French. "I can't get anything done. I don't feel like I am accomplishing anything new."

"Marcus, the fact is, you are a free man. You can leave here whenever you like. You are not bound to me, if by any chance you are thinking that you should set out beyond the confines of our little world here by the bay and seek adventure. You are free. I know people between here and Pennsylvania who will hide you for a few days; they all know the safest routes."

"I know I'm not legally tied, but I am bound by stronger cords. You are my legal father. My only living parent, for all I know. I am indebted to you for all I have. Everything, including my freedom. So long in my life I have yearned for freedom. Now I have it and I still feel tied."

"Freedom carries responsibility, my son," Mr. Coffin said. "But I must tell you. Love is an invisible magnet. It is hard to resist its pull. I feel the same love and the same ties with you. But at some point, children do leave their families to make their way in the world. I will understand and support you in your decision if you want to leave here."

"It is more complicated than that," Marcus said. "I have had a good lead on the whereabouts of Tilly. She has run away and is believed to be in some town in northern Virginia where former slaves are free. I would like to try to find her. But it would mean leaving here for a while, if that is permissible."

Mr. Coffin pushed back his chair and laughed comfortably.

"But this is excellent news! You must go. One must follow love. I will assist you if I can. Where is she in Virginia?"

"In the north, a small town. Unique. Water something. Waterville, maybe."

"Not Waterford?" Mr. Coffin asked brightly.

"Yes, maybe."

"But I know Waterford. It's a Quaker town. Very sympathetic to the abolitionist cause. There are many free people there of African descent. I may even know people there. You go, my son. She may be there. It is a likely place."

"But there is more to it," Marcus said. "I love Tilly. I am bound to try to find her. But I'm afraid I have been spoiled by my experiences in France. You have no idea what it is like for a person raised beneath the whip of slavery to go into a café or restaurant, take a seat and be served. By a white person no less! My dream now would be to rescue Tilly, bring her back here and then take her with us to Paris. But if necessary, I am wondering if I could return to Paris sooner than panned—once I have saved her, just to get her out of this cursed country and get ourselves free from slave catchers. I could tend to the business affairs there, in Paris. Even if I—or we—leave before you do."

Mr. Coffin rose from his chair and went over to the window. It was night in the garden. The crickets and the katydids were shimmering in the night heat.

"I hadn't thought of that," Mr. Coffin said. "Possibly, the work here is going to take longer than I thought. I would much rather have you as a business partner in Paris. But let me think things through. And I shall make some inquiries into the situation in Waterford."

After that, the days dragged on again. Mr. Coffin seemed to have forgotten his offer to think about a permanent Paris office. The heat rose; the air was warm and dank and redolent of decay and old life. But Mr. Coffin had indeed been thinking about the proposal. He had even lost some sleep over his thoughts. But he finally had come to a decision and invited Marcus to one of their periodic tête-à-têtes.

Mr. Coffin began with one of his typically long-winded didactic prologues about his business affairs in Paris and Haiti, and currency exchanges, German marks, Italian lire, pounds, and notes, the current social revolutions that seemed to be sweeping over all of Europe, Germany, Italy, and the future of the immoral institution of slavery in the United States, the looming war with Mexico, radical abolitionists, the rise of the suffragettes, the Mormon question, the Western frontier, the Indian Wars, and on and on and following on this monologue on the affairs of the world, finally, a single personal statement:

"All that and more—and I am getting old. But my thought is this," he said. "You go off, find Tilly if you can. Come back here with her. But then lay low, while I make arrangements with the Paris connection. Then once the communications are completed, which many take a matter of months, you go back by yourself and take Tilly with you, if it works out. I will stay here and run the American office. You, my son, will be the Paris manager. The fact is, as I say, I am getting old, and the trans-Atlantic voyages are taking a toll on me. I too shall miss Paris, and I may come over permanently if things go the way they seem to be going here in this country. I have seen revolutions in my time—in Paris, but more to the point, in Haiti. The great slave revolt. The institution of slavery cannot last here in my opinion. There are demonstrations in Boston; there is building support for abolition in the new mid-western states. And then, as you know, there was Nat Turner."

"What about Nat? They used to talk about him in the Dismal Swamp," Marcus asked.

"Nat Turner has struck fear into the hearts of slaveholders throughout the South. On the big plantations, the populations of slaves greatly outnumbers that of the whites. It was that way in Haiti and I have seen the aftermath. No one should experience a slave revolt, neither Black nor white. You cannot imagine the horror. The bloodshed. And yet the divide grows here, even now. Something is going to happen one way or another."

"So go out from your haven here. Go in mufti. Arm yourself with disguise. And don't worry about finances. My intent, as it long has been, is to pay you now for all your services since we arrived in Paris. Your funding. It is your money that I have put away in an account for your use. I am not gifting you this money, you understand. It is your money. You earned it. And you will have a French passport if needed. I will arrange that for you and also for Tilly. And you have, if needed, the letters of manumission. I will fix all the papers for you. Do not think of yourself as dark-skinned or impoverished. You are more than their equals now," He paused here. "But do go armed," he said.

He then added as an addendum, a lecture on the nature of freedom and Marcus's obsessive quest to find Tilly.

"It has been, what, more than two years since you left her, standing alone on the shore. And I must ask you before you go off, if you think this is just about Tilly. Or have you in some way associated Tilly with the whole ruthless, inhuman institution of human bondage? From what you have told me, it seems that you have resisted slavery ever since the idea of liberty was instilled in you by that young woman—what was her name…?"

"Amanda," Marcus interrupted, "her name was Amanda."

"Right, Amanda. First Amanda. And then having learned about the rights of man in France, you set out for freedom in a larger sense. But you leave Tilly behind, and so now that you have achieved freedom you go back and risk capture, chasing, perhaps, an idea rather than a person."

"Not true," Marcus said abruptly. "I love her. I love her as a woman, not some symbol."

"So be it then," Mr. Coffin said. "Follow on. I just want to introduce an alternative. And a reality. Given what you have told me about her, she may have made it to Canada for all we know. Or she may have been recaptured and sold down the river to the black hole of New Orleans."

"But you must go. And if I can help, I will. Write to me regularly so I can know where you stand. You go now, follow your leads."

Leesburg, Virginia
Paddyrollers

There was a quarter moon the night Tilly began her flight north, and the trail—such as it was—was indistinct, and Tilly wasn't sure she was on the right route until she came to the outskirts of a plantation that offered a clear view of the northern sky. There, in the northeast, she could see the Big Dipper, and just below it, at the end of the Little Dipper, the North Star. But the route north was tangled and progress was slow and with all the crying and fighting she had been through, she found a patch of clear land, lay down, cried herself to sleep, and spent her first night of freedom in the woods.

The night was silent, save for the crickets and katydids, and she could not hear any baying of pursuing hounds. She had outrun the dogs.

The next morning, she ate a couple of turnips and started north again, keeping the morning sun on her right, and, then toward mid-afternoon, she saw what she thought was the Wilkins farm.

She had heard talk of the Wilkins from other adults, and her older half-sister had fled there when Tilly way about ten.

The farm was a plain brick two-story house with a hay barn and a few outbuildings surrounded by open pastures where sheep were grazing. It fit the descriptions she had heard, but she couldn't be sure and she sat for a while at the edge of the woods, considering what to do next.

Her head ached from crying. Her eyes were puffed; she was lonely and homesick already, and she choked up thinking back on her mother. But her fate was sealed by her character. She could not go back.

Tilly decided, finally, to chance it and go to the house to ask for shelter, but just as she was about to cross the outlying pasture, she saw a group of five armed horsemen ride up the lane toward the house. She ducked back into the woods to watch.

Shortly after her escape, Billings had let loose the dogs to catch her. Conrad had not been killed, only knocked out, and when he recovered, he was determined to catch Tilly, whip her, and then sell her to a slave trader. He called in a posse of local patrollers to find her. They began riding the local roads, and one of the first places they checked was the Wilkins farm. It was a known hideaway.

From her post, Tilly could see the action. One of the men dismounted and a man in a dark suit came out of the house to talk. The two of them stood face to face, and Tilly could see that there seemed to be an argument going on. The other men dismounted; and the apparent leader of the group pushed the owner aside, and the troupe entered the house.

Ten or fifteen minutes later, they came out and rode away.

Tilly was worldly enough to realize what was going on. They were patrollers and they were looking for her and once they left, she dared to approach. Mr. Wilkins saw her crossing the field and beckoned her to hurry, which she did.

This was a good, albeit frightening, beginning for Tilly's flight. The Wilkins took her to the kitchen and fed her a bowl of gruel and coffee. Mr. Wilkins then showed her upstairs to the third floor attic where and assortment of trunks and an armoire and various old pieces of furniture was stored. There was a bureau on the eastern wall, and Mr. Wilkins pushed it aside and opened a panel door. Inside, under the eaves, there was a pallet, with blankets, a chamber pot, and a bowl and water pitcher.

"Thou mayst sleep here, daughter, and be on your way when fit. But you are welcome to stay for a few days."

"Thank you, Massa," Tilly said and began to sob again.

"Daughter, I am not your master. I am your friend, and were I you, I would rest here. The patrollers were just here, and they are scouring this region looking for you. I would give them a few days to satisfy themselves that thou hast disappeared."

Tilly spent the next two days there with the couple, sharing meals and resting, and listening to instructive stories of other escapes. The Wilkins had been hiding people for more than five years. They were experienced station keepers, and along with sometimes entertaining stories of escapees they had helped, they provided her with all she would need and then some. They knew many of the stations between Richmond and Leesburg, and they also knew of Waterford.

Tilly was illiterate, but they gave her illustrated maps of the various routes, and on the third day, they bid her Godspeed.

She left, still crying periodically, but this time it was in relief. She spent several more nights in the woods en route, but managed to locate enough safe havens to replenish herself and get directions to the next station. Most of her helpers were Quakers, but there were two modest houses that were occupied by free Black families. They too were helpful, but more cautious than the Quakers. They hid her in outbuildings, and one family guided her to a nearby camp in the woods and supplied her with food and drink.

In the second week of her flight, she stopped at another large farm run by a sympathetic white family. But unlike the other stations she had been to, there were a number of Blacks living in cabins around the main house, and she could see people working out in the fields. The place had all the appearance of a modest plantation. Even before she got to the house, a friendly young white man with straw-colored hair took spotted her and invited her in. She began calculating another escape. She was certain she had been tricked and would now be enslaved again.

Inside, a light-skinned maid guided her to the kitchen, fed her cornmeal gruel and a side of bacon and coffee.

"You be a slave here?" Tilly asked her, after she had eaten.

"No missy, I jus' live here," she said.

"But the ole Massa keep you here, right?"

"No, I can leave when I want. But they no point. I runaway jus' like you, but it be easy here. Nice folk—religious. You gotta pray and sing hymns with them Sunday morning, listen to ole Massa preach a long sermon 'bout Jesus and that's all. They give all the food you want, tell you to work at certain works 'round here, you got a clean dry cabin, enough fire wood, nice dogs. White neighbors, and even paddyrollers come by here—they all think we be slaves. But we free. Any time you want to leave, they help you. They got a boy here, a little slow in his head, but he know this area and you want to run off, he take to the next station, jus' ask."

After her breakfast, an old stooped Black woman, shuffled in, looked Tilly over. "All right," she said after a long pause, "come on then, honey, you'all follow me." She showed Tilly to a clean back room off to the east side of the kitchen with a cot against a side wall.

"You tired, girl, you rest. Ole lady come by when you wake up and tell you 'bout this place. You don't gotta worry here."

Tilly's trials seemed to be over, at least for the time being. She slept more peacefully and longer than she had on here entire ten day flight. She woke up confused and it took her a while to adjust to this strange situation. She was not sure if this was real or some trick, and she started plotting again how to escape.

When she came back into the kitchen, the younger 'maid', whose name was Pamela, brought her around to the front parlor, and told her to take a seat and wait for the mistress.

In time, a frail older white lady with gold-rimmed spectacles came in and introduced herself as Mrs. MacDowell. "Did you sleep well, then?" she asked.

Tilly told her, yes ma'am, she had slept for a very long time, thank you.

"Well, the Lord be with you, honey," she said. "Now you may stay here for as long as you like," Mrs. MacDowell explained. "Or if you wish to leave, my boy, Jackie, will take you on to the next station. But if you choose to stay, we will ask you to take on certain tasks. We cannot pay you, but if you stay on, I will feed you and clothe you and I will give you rest."

She went on about the work and her family and the crops they raised, and the hens and the cows and the sheep, and then she asked Tilly what she had done at the plantation she had so recently fled from, and hearing this, she told Tilly she could begin by serving the dinner table.

"My Pamela will show you the protocol," she said.

Guided by Pamela, Tilly began working the next day.

******

There were five people in the MacDowell family. Mrs. MacDowell was in her early fifties, her husband, who everyone referred to as 'the Preacher' was a tall straight-backed fellow, with sharp blue eagle eyes and bushy brows. There were two apparently spinster daughters in their twenties and a teenage boy, Jackie, with a messy bird's nest of blond hair and vacant blue eyes.

There was a long grace before every meal. But other than that they were not a talkative family. Tilly noticed that unlike the garrulous chatter and sometimes outrageous behavior of the white people at the Mary Plantation, there were long periods of silence at the dinner table when the only thing you would hear was the tinkling and clatter of the glassware and silverware. Only Jackie spoke, and once he started, he went on and on about the animals he tended: The cow, Sally, was in a bad mood, he would explain at length. The old sow, Queeny, was very hungry so he fed her some carrots that he had picked, and while he was in the vegetable patch one of the hens got in and he had to chase her out, and the dog, Skippy, helped, and then he and Skippy went around to the back pasture to see how the sheep were doing, and the new lambs and on and on in a steady stream, and all the while the other MacDowells ate in silence with an occasional condescending nod or remark from Mrs. MacDowell.

The whole body of workers had to join the family on Sunday morning for services, and then they had the rest of the day off. They were also free on Saturdays unless a harvest or planting season was at hand, and even free on minor Christian holidays, such as Saint John's Day.

Tilly stayed on. The work was easy, but after two weeks, she began to get bored. For one thing, there was no one to rebel against. She no longer was able to enjoy the thrill of spitting in soups and getting away with it. Furthermore, she was anxious to join her half-sister, Bitsie, who had run away two years earlier and was said to be living in Waterford.

Finally in late August, she announced that she wanted to move on to join her half-sister.

Mrs. MacDowell was disappointed. For all her devious ways, Tilly was a lively, entertaining addition to the generally dour Scottish Calvinist family. Waterford was only three-day wagon ride from the farm and they arranged to get Jackie to take her. He had made the trip before and was good with directions and also, if necessary, survival techniques in the wild. Ever since he was a young child, he was in the habit of wandering off and staying out in the borderlands for a day two. He was good with plant identification and he knew how to trap and fish. Rumor was that he was slow, and there was some gossip among the workers that he was adopted, but he was skilled in some areas, and slow in others. He could barely read and write, but he could survive in wilderness.

Two days after Tilly's announcement, he brought a wagon around, filled with hay, supplies, a rifle and a fishing rod and enough dry food to keep them going for three or four days.

The whole body of workers came round to bid Tilly goodbye, and joined by Jackie's constant companion, the mongrel, kippy they set off.

******

Jackie was indeed a talker. He started as soon as they set off and talked off and on most of that first morning. And when he wasn't talking he would sing hymns and folk songs. By the second day, Tilly began to sing with him, and they rolled on along back roads singing the old slave songs, all of which Jackie knew by heart. They made an off-beat couple—a blue-eyed white man and a Black girl of roughly the same age, sitting side by side singing 'Wade in the Water', 'Steal Away', and 'Follow the Drinking Gourd' at the top of their lungs. Singing together, Tilly learned, was one way to keep Jackie quiet.

This was an easy ride, Tilly was permitted to nap in the hay, and she sometimes took the reins while Jackie would take a break from his talking and sleep. But on the morning of the third day, they ran into trouble.

They were overtaken by two armed men on horseback, who rode along with them for a while without a word, and then cut them off.

Who was the Black girl, they wanted to know.

Jackie had been instructed to tell anyone who asked that Tilly was his slave who he was delivering to another plantation.

He faltered with his answer. "She's Tilly, our friend, and I'm taking her to Water—"

Tilly elbowed him.

He turned to her. "What?" he asked. Then he caught himself. "I mean, she's our slave and someone bought her and I'm taking her there. That's right," he said. "She's our slave and she's a good worker and all, but she got sold and so me and Skippy are carrying her off."

"Who the hell is Skippy?" one of the men asked. He was thinking there was another runaway hiding in the straw. He dismounted, lifted a pitchfork from the back of the wagon, and began stabbing at the hay.

"What you doing, mister?" Jackie asked.

"I'm looking for this Skippy," he said.

"He's right there," Jackie said, pointing to the dog, who had been sleeping in the wagon behind the wagon seat.

The man threw down the pitchfork and walked around to Tilly's side of the wagon and grabbed her arm.

"Where you going, missyy?" he asked.

"I'se a gwine to ma new plantation, suh," she said, trying to sound as empty-headed as Jackie.

The second man dismounted and came over. "This your owner?" he asked, nodding toward Jackie.

"Yessuh, dat ma Massa."

"That kid's your master?"

"Yessuh."

"He don't look to me like he's a very good master. Maybe you should come with us."

Seasoned fighter that she was, Tilly starting plotting escape instantly.

The patroller grabbed her by the arm and yanked out of the wagon.

Jackie stood up from the seat. "Cut that out," he said. "She belongs to me."

He jumped out of the wagon and came around to the other side and tried to disengage Tilly's arm. The patroller pushed him away and dragged Tilly toward one of the horses. The first patroller went around to his horse to get a rope, and while he was off, Tilly broke free and made a dash for the woods. Both of them gave chase, caught her, and dragged her back, struggling and biting.

At that point, Jackie joined in the melee, tried to pull one man off, and got hit in the jaw for his efforts. His lip bleeding, he retreated to the wagon, and while Tilly squirmed and bit and kicked, he came back with an axe and struck the back of the head of one of the patrollers with the blunt end. The second man let go of Tilly and drew a pistol from his holster:

Dust in the air, much shouting and screaming, and the horses began to whinny and rear up and Skippy jumped out of the wagon and bit the thigh of the man with the pistol. But before he could shoot the dog—or Jackie—the man went limp. He crumpled to the ground, a pitchfork in his back.

Tilly stood over him, crying and shaking.

"Oh no," she screamed. "Oh no, Jackie, I think I kilt him. I didn't mean to kill him, Jackie, I didn't mean to do that. Let's go quick, 'for that other one comes 'round. Quick. Les' go."

"He's dead too, I think," Jackie said slowly as if in amazement.

He walked over and rolled the man on his back. He lay still. Eyes wide open.

They got Skippy in the wagon and started off, but after only a few yards, Jackie stopped the wagon.

"We can't leave them there on the road," he said. "Next traveler comes along, they'll go looking for more patrollers."

They walked back; Jackie stripped the men of their guns and gun belts, and the two of them dragged the men off into the woods.

They started off for the wagon, then Jackie stopped again and shrugged.

"We might as well take the horses," he said.

And so, stringing the horses behind them, the guns and gun belts under the hay, the saddles in the wagon bed, they set off as fast as they could get the horse to move and rode on for an hour. Then they slowed to an easier pace, and then after a few more minutes, Jackie stopped the wagon. "What you doing, Jackie? Let's get on," Tilly said.

"We gotta pray, Tilly. We have to pray for forgiveness."

"We don't go no time to pray, Jackie, we pray later, let's go."

"Don't tell my Pa we did that, Tilly, don't tell anybody. But I'm not going hell for that, and neither are you, 'cause we did that in self-defense, didn't we, and it says in the Bible, if thine enemy assault thee, defense is alright. Or something like that. So we're not going to hell."

He paused. "I don't think." He stared into the surrounding woods, blankly thinking. "We got to pray for forgiveness," nodding with his decision.

He got down from the wagon, and knelt by the side of the road and began to pray out loud:

"Father forgive us, for we know not what we do," he began. "We are but lowly sinners, Lord, but the agents of the devil did set upon us, Lord, and they sought kill us and take thy dark-skinned daughter into bondage. We acted only in our own defense. Forgive our sins, oh Lord, but we fought them in defense, and we were victorious. Thank you Jesus. We were victorious in our defense. But they were evil men, agents of the devil. But bless them too. Oh Lord and forgive them their trespasses." He rambled on in a long stream of a never-ending prayer.

Tilly sat in the wagon, looking back and forward at the road. Then she called back to Jackie, "That's good, the Lord say that's good, Jackie, Let's go."

Jackie looked back at her. "I got more to say."

"No Jackie. I'se praying too here in the wagon. And the Lord done spoke unto me and he say. 'Go forth, my son and daughter, onto the road, go down to Egypt land and freedom. Forgiveness be all,' he say So let's go."

"He spoke to you?"

"Yess'uh, Jackie, indeed he did. He say, 'thou art my daughter. You and that boy are forgiven.' He tell me to tell you to get back the wagon here and get on the road to freedom. That what He say to me, Jackie. And I believe in Him. Praise Jesus!"

Jackie rose up from his knees and stood for a few seconds and then slowly mounted the wagon and then snapped the reins.

For once, he was silent.

They rode on, only the creak of the running gear and the rhythmic clop of the horse hooves breaking the silence. No singing.

"Just don't tell my Pa," Jackie said after a while.

The struggle took place in late morning. They plodded on all that day and well into the night, not saying much. The moon was almost full and they drove through the night, one or the other sleeping in the hay, spelling each other. The next morning, they stopped for a breakfast, fed the horses, and then started up again.

Late that day, they reached Waterford.

Part Two

Five Points District, New York City
Jimmy Hubbard

On December 18th in 1816, in the notorious Five Points section of New York City, an arrest warrant was issued for a young man named Jimmy Hubbard. Nothing ever came of the notice. Even if the police had followed up, which was unlikely, no one ever would have found the Hubbard boy. The fact is, in all likelihood, no one ever even bothered to try to catch him. Individual policemen would not enter Five Points alone; if they did, they would rarely come out. It was the most squalid and dangerous districts of the city with a population of Irish and freed African slaves who lived crowded together in filthy hovels in frightful, degenerated conditions. The area swarmed with thieves, murderers, prostitutes, pickpockets, beggars, drunks, and dangerous rival gangs, struggling for control.

Troupes of police sometimes entered in an attempt to clean things up, but the gangs would scatter to their warrens, only to reappear a few days later to continue robbing and killing one another. Powerful gangs, the Dead Rabbits, the Shirt Tails, the Roach Guards, and early on in the century, the Kerryonians, a band consisting of natives of County Kerry, Ireland, ruled the district. The Hubbard boy—he could not have been more than thirteen or fourteen at the time—was believed to be a member of this latter group. He had robbed and killed another young man, said to be a member of the Gophers, one of the more violent of the bands of murderers who were the bane of the good citizens of the city.

Jimmy Hubbard's name appeared again in a record of a Methodist mission that had attempted to establish itself in the district. With the lure of a warm stew, the mission ladies had drawn the boy in and given him a bed. He was identified as an orphan who had come over with his mother from County Kerry. Their ship was wrecked on the rocks off Horton's Point at the mouth of

Long Island Sound. His mother drowned, but the young boy was rescued by a sailor and given to a member of the sailor's family who lived in Five Points.

There was one more notice issued in 1821 posted by a well-to-do African-American man named Mr. Richardson who was a member of the vestry of a mission church in the Bowery. The complaint stated that Richardson had been captured and taken back into the Five Points warren and imprisoned, with the intent of carrying him below the Mason-Dixon Line to be sold to another slave catcher. Richardson managed to get word out to some of his friends back in the Bowery. A group of Blacks, some of whom were no less violent that the Gophers, raided the den and dragged the kidnappers off to the Tombs to be charged. One of the suspects identified himself as James Weston Hubbard, sq. He was twenty-seven years of age, swarthy-skinned with a mass of curly black hair and bushy sideburns. Hubbard was a black Irishman who looked for all the world like a mixed-race individual—which in effect is what he was—he was a descendant of the sailors of the Spanish Grand Armada, which had wrecked on the rocks of the Irish Sea. But Hubbard was white, Reverend Richardson was dark-skinned, and the case was dismissed. No charges.

But that was only the beginning of Jimmy Hubbard's career. Working for a larger organization with ties to the police and business entities, he successfully kidnapped a young Black boy who was on his way home from school one day and delivered him to the slave-catching organization that later sold the boy at auction. There followed more captures, each with increasing profits, and eventually Jimmy Hubbard decided to move to Charleston, South Carolina and enter into the slave trading business for himself. He refashioned his identity, he was no longer the rough black Irish punk; he was James W. Hubbard, esquire. He dressed in dark well-cut suits and doublets, a dark silk cravat, collared white shirts and a top hat. And to assist in his trade, he acquired a slim iron cane that he employed freely when necessary. He was described in the historical records as a large, rough man with uncouth manners. He worked the plantations around East Virginia and took his charges down to the big New Orleans slave markets, where prices for human chattel were higher.

Leesburg, Virginia
A Slave and Captive, Now Was I

At this point in the life of Marcus Aurelius, the wheels of fortune, often imagined by Marcus in his more reflective moods, were turning slowly. They continued to turn in Paris, in the Jardin des Plantes and the Bois de Boulogne. They turned after he and Mr. Coffin came back to the United States, and they turned and slowed in St. Mary's County, until a day in November in Leesburg, Virginia where they halted.

One may attempt to control events in a life but the best laid plans cannot account for accidents, unless, perchance, there are no such things as accidents. Mr. Coffin used to cite Greek myths in some of his prolix introductions to a subject, among them the story of the Moirae, the Three Fates, who tirelessly weave the destinies of individual lives on their looms. One never knows what threads will cross, and such was the case with Mr. James Hubbard esq. and Marcus Aurelius Coffin.

Armed with his documents of passage, a leathern wallet of notes, and dressed in the latest Paris men's fashions, Marcus set out to find Tilly. He went to Annapolis driven by George in the farm wagon. From there, he traveled by coach, without incident, to Washington, where he found quarters in Georgetown. From there, again without incident, he boarded a canal boat on the Chesapeake and Ohio Canal to Leesburg. His intent was to make his way from Leesburg up to Waterford, establish himself and begin his search for Tilly if she wasn't there.

Passengers on the canal boat were instructed to board the vessel at the ungodly hour of 4 AM. Marcus managed to arrive on time and was ushered to the men's quarters by a fawning African deckhand. Marcus's disguise, his haughty carriage, his accented English, and his manner of dress were so far working very well. He had had no trouble in Washington or Georgetown, and they worked well on the trip to Leesburg. The sleeping quarters on the canal boat were so crowded and stifling he decided to forego sleep and went out to the foredeck to watch the mule drivers work. Here he encountered curious white passengers on the boat who were interested in life in Paris, and when he reached Leesburg he had no trouble checking himself into a small hotel, although the concierge looked him over cautiously before offering the guest register. Marcus signed in with his florid French script. The next day he boarded a coach to Waterford, and was politely received at a guest house by a white woman named Inga Moser. The German immigrants and Quakers of the village, generally speaking, were opposed to the institution of slavery.

Waterford was a small agricultural center and Marcus had no trouble making his mission known about town. No one had heard of Tilly Washburn, but one informant directed Marcus to a Quaker family named Miller, who lived on the outskirts of the town. As it turned out, the Millers did have an 'employee' who fit the description of Tilly.

Mr. Miller was a stern, chiseled-faced man with a German accent, and his description of his servant matched Tilly perfectly, although the young woman's name was Belle du Bois.

"She was not a good servant," Mr. Miller said. "She would sleep late, or complain that she was sick. She was slow to obey orders and that sort of thing. We had to let her go."

"What do you mean 'let her go'?" Marcus asked, feigning incomprehension. "You mean you set her free?"

"Ach no, not her. We have friends with a plantation back in Leesburg. They are needing field hands for light work. We sent her there."

"You sent her?"

"Well, they have picked her up here."

"And did she go willingly, if I may ask?"

Mr. Miller glanced at Marcus, chuckled and kicked at the straw at his feet.

"You don't know this girl, sir. She did nothing; she does nothing she does not wish to do."

"Was there money exchanged?"

"Yah, there was some money. But why do you want to know all this though, are you the former owner of the girl. Why do you seek her?"

Marcus hesitated then said, "I knew her mother. I have business in Haiti, and her mother is Haitian. This Belle, which by the way is not her real name, if I have the right individual, was stolen when she was a young girl and taken to Virginia and sold. Her mother is associated with the government in the new regime; she is an owner of a large sugar plantation run by paid employees, not slaves. Through the trading company I am associated with Madame Surplice, the mother, got word that this Belle, whose real name is Tillisande Surplice, was held on a James River plantation but ran away a year or so back. Sources in Richmond tell us she made her way to Waterford, thinking she would be free here. You would be interested to know, perhaps, that if this is the right person, she is from a very rich family. I speak English, and so I was sent here to America by the family to find her. There is a very handsome reward for assistance with her return."

"How much?"

"A great deal, to be distributed to those who have helped with the search. Now, could you describe to me what happened, exactly? Did this girl go willingly with her new employers?"

Mr. Miller chuckled again and shook his head. "Hardly," he said.

"What happened?"

He laughed again. "When she found out she was about to be sold, she ran off. Broad daylight, though. People saw her racing through the fields down toward the river. We have horses here. We caught her."

"And then? Did you have to tie her up?"

"Yes, I'm afraid so. She was attempting to bite her captors. We kept her in the barn until the buyers arrived. I want to tell you something, though. This girl is a rascal, a true, untamable wildcat. But you know something? Everybody around here in this town knew of her. They liked her anyway. She was, what do you say in France, *mignonne*?"

"So I have heard," Marcus said. "And what is the name of the plantation she was taken to?"

"If she is still there, it was Wheatlands Plantation in Leesburg, on the Middleburg Road. The family name is Watson. They have many slaves, but they are a fair-minded family. She is in good hands. It's just that we could not control her."

Marcus thanked Mr. Miller and prepared to leave.

"I say, monsieur, did you not tell me there was some remuneration for this information?" Mr. Miller asked.

"What means remuneration?" Marcus asked.

"You know, payment?"

"Yes, yes, indeed. Upon capture, we are prepared to pay handsomely. Let me give you my papers of note." Marcus extracted a leather notebook and prepared to write. "Ah," he said, "a pen. I have no pen. Have you a pen?"

The two of them went into the house whereupon a pen and ink were presented. Marcus tore out a page out of the notebook, scrawled a document guaranteeing payment upon the capture of one Tillisande Surplice, the sum of $250. He then signed it, "Count Marc d'Aurèle Coffin & Coffin, rue du Bac, Paris, France," and handed it to Mr. Miller, who stared at it for a moment.

The two parted, leaving Mr. Miller still contemplating the note. Marcus returned to Leesburg and took up residence at the Horsehead Inn where he had stayed earlier. At the tavern that night, he fell into conversation with a gray-haired man with bright dark eyes and bushy sideburns dressed in a plaid suit. The man professed great interest in Marcus's strong French accent and asked where he was from. The man, who introduced himself as Mr. Judson Barnes, said he had occasion to travel to New Orleans periodically, and spoke a little French with Marcus, who answered with his strong Parisian accent. Marcus claimed to know nothing of the city and the man explained that, although it was technically part of the United States, the population there associated themselves more with France than with the United States.

"If you are, as you say, touring the South, you might enjoy the city, monsieur; it is a lively, if somewhat dissolute, version of Paris."

Marcus professed an interest in the city. The man made a point of praising the beauty of the Creole women of the city, the Quadroon Balls, and the 'guest houses', by which he meant, without saying as much, the brothels.

"I notice you carry a sword, monsieur," he said. "A good thing, if I do say so. The city is famous for dueling. It was France, after all. There is often some dispute after a ball. Duels are common. Do you fence, monsieur?"

"I do," Marcus said. "In fact, one of the reasons I decided to tour your country is because of a duel."

"How so?"

"I was challenged by a well-known Count, a man famous for his fencing abilities. I was reluctant to take up the challenge, but in the end, I agreed, and, after a long and drawn out encounter, in which I continuously merely defended myself, I suddenly changed course and lunged. I drew blood and disabled his sword arm. He withdrew to his estate to lick his wounds. But he never forgot.

He suffered more from the loss of honor than from the wound, and from that point on he encouraged his friends to challenge me, and eventually even went so far as to hire ruffians and assassins to actually kill me. I was often challenged on my way home at night and forced to defend myself, which only served to increase the number of assaults. I thought it best to leave Paris for a while. So here I am."

"You must be a skilled duelist," the man said. "You seem to be interested in the city of New Orleans, sir. I have a friend traveling with me who actually lives there. He's a respected lawyer named James Hubbard. I could arrange a meeting if you like. He's staying nearby."

Marcus explained that he had a former engagement and would probably return in a few days. To be polite, he said he would not mind meeting his friend to learn more.

"And where are you headed tomorrow?" Mr. Barnes asked. "I have a fiacre you could borrow, if you are coming back soon."

Marcus's guard rose. This man, who seemed a perfectly friendly sort at first, now was too friendly. Furthermore, he did not like the mention of New Orleans. He had feigned ignorance, but knew all about the city's reputation. There was perhaps no one among the thousands of enslaved people in the American South who did not know of New Orleans. Marcus demurred and went to bed.

The next morning, he went to a local livery, hired a horse and set out for Wheatlands on the Middleburg Road. A few miles outside of the town, the track curved under the east side of a wooded hill, and shortly after he passed, two horsemen emerged from the forest and began to trot along behind him. He rode on listening to the hoofbeats, and as they gained on him, he turned in the saddle and saw Barnes accompanied by a large, swarthy-skinned man with a mass of curly black hair spilling out from under his top hat.

Barnes hailed Marcus. "I have brought my friend to meet you, monsieur," he called out, picking up his pace. The two of them approached one on either side, and Marcus could see where this was headed and spurred his horse. The chase was on.

Marcus slapped the reigns and kicked his heels into his horse's flanks. He leaned forward encouraging the horse onward, racing for Wheatlands and possible refuge. But the old nag Marcus was riding was no match for the two spirited horses his pursuers were riding, so Marcus changed his escape plans.

As his pursuers drew nearer, he abruptly turned his horse and charged back at them, his sword drawn. As he passed, between the two, he slashed the reign hand of Barnes, rode on, and then turned again and charged down on the dark-haired man. But this devil was ready. He raised a narrow iron cane with which he smashed the wrist of Marcus's sword arm. Then he reached out and grabbed the bridle of Marcus's horse and with his other hand drew a pistol.

"Give over, Frenchie," he said, pointing the pistol at Marcus's temple. "My friend here tells me you want to visit New Orleans. We can arrange that," he said.

The Natchez Trace
The Coffle

The next five days were a blur for Marcus. His wrist was badly bruised, his hands were shackled behind his back, and he was taken back to Leesburg, where he was put in a barn on the west side of the town. He was led into the dusty gloom of a hay barn and deposited, his wrists still bound, the doors latched from the outside.

Spread around him in the shaded interior, he could see other dark forms, some crouched, some sleeping, some leaning against the barn walls. He was familiar with the scene. This was a makeshift slave pen.

He was held there for the next two weeks while Barnes and Hubbard and their accomplices captured more and more dark-skinned people, whether free full-blooded Africans, or a variety of mixed-race men and also women. It was clear the two men were collecting slaves for a drive down to New Orleans.

This was late August and the heat in the barn was stifling and Marcus was overheated in his expensive French-made clothing. But a few days later, a young rough-looking half shaven man came in with a bundle of clothing and instructed everyone to strip and dress in the new clothes. The women were issued calico dresses and the men cotton trousers and osnaburg cotton shirts. Three other bundles were brought in, containing formal suits and dresses, but these were stored away. Marcus recognized the strategy. Once at the slave markets, they would all be cleaned and outfitted in fine clothing for the final sale.

Other goods continued to be stored in the barn, including dry beans and cracked corn, kegs of bacon, switchel, and corn bread. Then a few days later, a pair of workers hauled in chains and hand shackles. Wagons continued to gather in front of the barn, supplied with boxes of tools and canvas tents and tent poles. And then one bright late August day, a band of tough looking characters armed with whips and pistols, rousted everyone out of the barn and instructed them to form a line.

There were about fifty people all told. The men were first in the line, standing two by two, the women behind. Then the crew got to work and shackled the men side by side, attached a chain to the first in the line and ran it down the line to the end, shackling each pair to the chain. There were two men toward the end of the line who were not cuffed but were fitted with iron collars. Bad actors, Marcus later learned. The women were lined up behind the men, two by two, but unchained. There were three fully-loaded wagons behind with their drivers, each of them armed, and behind them there were four horsemen, all of them armed with rifles and whips. Mr. James Hubbard, esq. rode ahead, armed with two Starr pistols, a rifle, a curled whip, and his iron cane strapped to his side. Then, with the caravan assembled, the coffle moved out.

They followed the Middleburg Road southward. Marcus could not help but notice after an hour or so on the road, a large plantation on the left, a large light yellow house set up a rise, the fields stretching off to the east and south. The grounds fit the description of Wheatfield Plantation and he was tortured by the fact that he might be passing within a hundred yards of Tilly. Were he not shackled he would have chanced a break, guards notwithstanding. A feeling of anger and defeat and self-pity welled up in him. He fought back tears and for the rest of that first day the thoughts of why and how this had happened plagued him. He looked forward to nightfall and the possibility of escape.

This was coupled with a desire for revenge. He wanted to kill the slave trader. As much as his love for Tilly, an equally powerful murderous desire to run the brute through with his now lost sword rose up within him. Fantasies of killing the man played through his head for the next hour, and were, curiously, soothing, more comforting than thoughts of self-pity. The sweet solace of revenge. And when the coffle turned west on the Little River Turnpike, near the town of Aldie, his burning anger settled into a smoldering obsession. Hate and love were his constant companions on that journey and became the driving force of his life for the next two years.

******

The coffle walked all day, with periodic breaks and toward evening turned into a long empty field. Here the men were unshackled and instructed to assist with raising the tents and building fires. Pots and kettles were unloaded and then the women were lined up.

One of the guards from the back of the coffle came up and stood in front of them.

"Now, which of you womens know how to cook?" he asked.

No one answered. He repeated the question, but no one moved.

"All right then," he said. He uncoiled his whip and arbitrarily selected a woman from the group.

"I'm 'a beat this here woman, till one you all come forward." Before he could even strike, the selected woman spoke.

"I can cook, suh," she said. (She couldn't. But she thereby dodged the whipping.)

"That's good," he said. "Who else here? I know for a fact that some you is house slaves, so step out or I'll whip the lot of you."

Three more women stepped out. They were put to work preparing the meal.

The evening meal cooked and eaten, the men were chained and driven to the open-sided tents to sleep. The women were sent to a different tent and the guards surrounded the group. The horses were pastured and watered, and slowly, the cricket-loud summer night settled over them.

One of the men began singing a long slow song about old Virginia. Others joined in for a while. Then the women. It was long and sad chant and you could hear some of the women crying, and so the night ended with the sad chorus, the rattle and shush of the katydids and the snowy tree crickets, and somewhere off in the hills, the distant barking of farm dogs.

In the privacy of darkness, strategies of revenge kept Marcus awake half the night.

For the next month, the coffle plodded along, traveling about twenty miles or so per day and camping in fields and groves each night. Early on in the first week, Hubbard brought out an old fiddle and asked if anyone could play. Marcus knew how to fiddle. He had learned folk melodies from Amanda, and in Paris, he had been given a violin, which he used to entertain himself. He was reluctant to admit that he knew how to play, but no one else came forward, and he calculated that in order to play, he would have to be unshackled, so he raised his hand and said he knew a few tunes.

"I should 'a knowed it'd be you," Hubbard said. "Tomorrow morning, you come here to the head of the line and play us some walking tunes. And I want you all to do some singing too," he shouted to the line. "It's been too quiet here. You all understand me?" he asked.

The coffle was quiet.

"I said did you all hear me? I want some singing."

There was a unified, uninspired sound from the coffle, halfway between a groan and a grunt of approval.

Amanda's violin teacher was an itinerant Irish fiddle player who made the circuit of the James River plantations, teaching children to play. Marcus used to sit listening and later Amanda, ever in character, shared her lessons.

Marcus knew some simple classical pieces from Paris, but they were too slow, so he began where he had started—with a few American folk tunes brought over by the Irish fiddlers. He struck up the old melodies from 'The Morphett Rant' and 'Soldiers Joy', and then began improvising on his own. This work fiddling while marching along proved tiring, and he requested a break, which Hubbard granted, but commanded the coffle to sing.

The tedious days stretched into weeks, then months, and still they tramped on. They marched south through the Shenandoah Valley and southwest toward Nashville then turned west to Natchez.

And all the while, Marcus fiddled and marched. Sang and fiddled and tramped and plotted his escape. He eyed the dense forest of the Shenandoah Valley, the steep laurel hells stretching up to the heights. The cover was good, but the riders now rode beside the coffle, leaving the wagons and one guard in the rear. There was no exit, and he lay chained at night. But then, slowly, another possible escape route opened.

In the years following his semi-criminal career in New York City, Mr. James W. Hubbard, esq. had evolved since his first attempt at slave trading. He and his accomplices managed to catch more runaways, and also took to kidnapping free Blacks as well. After two years, Hubbard began to have success and set up his trade in Alexandria, dealing with captives brought to him by his northern slave catchers. Then he began working directly with plantation owners in East Virginia and the Tidewater.

James Hubbard, with his signature iron cane and burly manners, had by that time established himself as a financially successful trader. He had also, unlike so many other traders, attempted to raise himself up in society. Slave traders were considered a necessary, but devious and sordid group. Many of them were violent, ill-dressed whites who had come out of urban centers and hard-scrabble Southern farms. But not Mr. Hubbard. He imagined himself as the sort of gentlemen plantation owners that he dealt with. He was on a quest to make money, but he was equally attracted by the good life, and was planning to get out of the business and establish himself as a settled property owner. He was already on his way. He had a residence in Yorktown, Virginia, as well as a small house on Grove Street in New Orleans, and he had an eye for the French fashions of the cotton traders along Market Street.

Marcus, with his European manners, his language ability and cultured background was clearly one of these; he would make a good butler once broken. Hubbard thought he might bring a good price and began to curry him. But there was more to it than that.

He recognized an elegant model of these types in the form of his captive, Marcus Aurelius, and he began to question him on life in Paris. What did people of means do with their days, he asked. What were the dishes that were favored, what books and plays were popular, and were the women as beautiful as rumored. Marcus, for his part, began to play the same game. He still maintained something of his hauteur, but he willingly shared stories of life in Paris, and especially stories of the women he had known, and the balls he attended, the literary salon he was a part of—and not incidentally—the easy money that could be made with currency trading. Hubbard had some French as a result of his trading in New Orleans, but it was atrocious, heavily accented and ungrammatical. He began attempting to converse with Marcus in French, and even stooped so low as to ask him for corrections.

Marcus was still enslaved. He was shackled at night, and forced to play the fiddle and sing and march by day. But he could see an escape route in his new relationship with Hubbard. He wasn't sure what it would be, be he was cunning enough to spot an exit when it appeared.

******

The line marched on. The days passed. September merged into October, then November, and still they walked and by December they had reached Natchez, where they regrouped.

There were three routes to New Orleans for slave coffles from Natchez. The captives could be herded onto rafts and floated down the Mississippi River, but this was not always the most secure route. The river was notorious for tricky currents, whirlpools and logs and snags and the rafts were ill-constructed, subject to accidents. One encounter with a log or a submerged snag could tip the raft, and if one or two people slipped off, chained together as they were, the whole cargo might follow.

The other route, for smaller coffles, was by steamboat. But this was expensive. The third and the cheapest, but the slowest, was to walk the coffle down the Natchez Trace, a former Indian trail. Now in the mid-1800s, it had been somewhat enlarged and improved by the conquering Europeans. It was this route that Hubbard chose.

He sold a few people on the Natchez docks, resupplied his wagons, paid off his guards, and hired new ones, and after a week of rest, set out again.

More marching. More tedious days. It was December. There were rains. The Trace was muddied and the wagons became mired. The men of the coffle were put to work freeing them. And what could they hope for but more chains, the auction block, and then the cane fields, the worst, the hardest and the most dangerous of the three remunerative crops of the ante bellum South—tobacco, sugar, cotton.

And all the while, when they rested at midday, or at the feeding hour in the evening, or even late into the night around the fire, Hubbard drew Marcus aside to practice his French and pick up tips on the life of a cultured gentleman.

By early January, the coffle finally reached New Orleans.

New Orleans
City of the Dreadful Night

When the coffle reached New Orleans, the group of some forty people were taken to a crowded slave pen on Lafayette Street where they waited for two weeks. The pen was a tall brick building with side walls containing bunk beds. The quarters were decidedly better than the two other slave pens where Marcus had been held, and the business of the trade was far more organized.

Shortly after they arrived, Hubbard showed up with a doctor and bundles of clothing. His coffle was bathed and scrubbed, and the doctor, a man in a stained vest, his teeth much yellowed by tobacco, inspected everyone, checking for signs of disease and making notes of various scars, or missing fingers and brands. Then they were dressed in clean new clothes, the women in calico with bright head scarfs, the men in blue suits with brass buttons and top hats.

While they were dressing, Hubbard came over to Marcus and pulled him aside and told him to come along with him. He had a bundle under his left arm, and he tapped his iron cane on the ground as he stepped out onto the street. They walked a few blocks, turning left and right, and then entered through a gate to a small ill-tended garden with green filigreed iron chairs. Hubbard told Marcus to sit down.

"I don't want you to get no ideas," Hubbard began. "But it is my intention to keep you for myself. I'm not even sure why I even picked you up—man like you don't sell very well. For one thing, you're light-skinned. Buyers don't like that much. Types like you get ideas, haughty sons of bitches who do not believe they should be told what do. Far as I can tell, that's you. 'Nother thing, you're literate. High-yella like you might start spreading ideas about freedom to the other folks."

“But here’s the case. It looks to me like you know your way around financial matters, money trading or whatever it is you claim you used to do. So I’m keeping you. Now don’t you be getting no ideas. You’re bound to me. You’re me property, see. I know that don’t fit well with the life you expected to lead. But you should have stayed up north. Come down to the South here, people get the idea you run away. You don’t got no papers, but you’re dark and you got that kinky hair, and sooner ’n later, somebody would have caught you and sold you. Happened to be me. That may be a good thing for you, if you behave proper-like.”

“You got an easy job. Keeping things in line around the house. Running errands when—and if—I come to trust you. Even seeing to my books. I got a man who comes in and does my accounting. But he charges me a lot. I know you smart enough to do that yourself, ’cept I don’t have to pay you. Get that part straight, Monsieur Marcus Aurelius. You are a slave. My slave. My property. And just in case you don’t understand that—well, you may remember the taste of this here iron cane.”

“Now I brought this bundle ’a clothes here. They’re yours. I don’t mind you speak French and pretend to be a fancy man. Does my business well to be seen around town with a high-yella in French fashion who is my slave.”

Hubbard dumped the clothes out on the garden table and told Marcus to get dressed.

For once, Marcus obeyed. Even before Hubbard finished his lecture, Marcus saw a way out.

****

Mr. James Hubbard, esquire, must have felt very much at home in New Orleans when he first settled there four years earlier. The city was a larger, more corrupt and degenerate town than the small district of Five Points back in Manhattan where he grew up. It was the location of the largest slave market in the United States, for one thing. It had the highest crime rate in the nation in the mid-19th century. Gambling was legal, and when it was temporarily outlawed it flourished anyway, and then spread to the ornate Mississippi steamboats where it bloomed profusely. Prostitution was legal; there were brothels in most districts in the city, and professional ladies were advertised in the local journals. The ads were in some ways similar to the boastful descriptions of slaves in the posted auction notices:

Almost every day, the local papers ran long descriptions of heinous murders. Plus there were notices and descriptions of upcoming public executions, especially when the guilty were well-known members of criminal gangs. Also interesting news events. On one occasion, an elephant in a menagerie killed his owner, lifting him on his trunk, casting him down and stamping on him. Then he killed a camel, and escaped into the nearby woods. A posse formed and the elephant was hunted down and dispatched.

Steamboats blew up at the docks, killing people. Sailors off one of the Mississippi flatboats got drunk and, like the elephant, went on a rampage along Bourbon Street and attempted to burn a brothel they had visited, apparently unsatisfied by the resident ladies in waiting and the 'gypsy beauties' as advertised. And then almost every day around planting and harvest season, announcements of slave sales.

Unlike other Southern cities, there was no central auction block in New Orleans. Sales took place outside the pens where the people were jailed, or at the docks, or commonly, at the famous St. Louis Hotel foyer.

Marcus was not witness to any of this. His enslavement was a private matter and he was not listed in the records of slave sales. He was taken by Hubbard to a house on Grove Street, not far from Congo Square, where every Sunday evening the slaves were permitted to gather and dance, a tradition that developed a few years after the Americans took over the city.

Hubbard's house was a substantial Creole-style cottage with a long railed front porch with ornate filigree posts, upper rails running below the porch roof. The interior was cool and dark, with two living rooms on either side of a hallway that led back to two small rooms and then on to the kitchen. Here, standing at the stove, Marcus saw a middle-aged Black woman in a white muslin dress and cotton apron and bright madras headscarf. She turned and looked Marcus up and down when he and Hubbard came in.

"This here is Maisie," Hubbard said. "Maisie, you say hello then to Monsieur Marcus Aurelius, the French Count, he's taking over from Jones. Show him his room. And you, Mr. Mark, I'll show you where you'll be working later. I got another man named Pikey, lives in the back garden. You'll meet later."

He turned and left the kitchen.

Maisie looked Marcus over again.

"All right," she said nodding, and went back to stirring her pot.

Marcus stood waiting, politely. It looked to him that Maisie was perhaps the boss in this establishment even though she was enslaved.

Eventually, Maisie turned, wiped her hands on her apron, and told Marcus to follow. "And don't get no ideas of running off," she said. "Ole Hubbard beat the tar out of you before you even open the door."

"Yessum," Marcus said obediently. He calculated that it was best to stay on Maisie's side in this new venture.

The room was a small squared space with a cot with a cotton mattress set against the right wall and a grilled window overlooking an untended weed patch garden. He could not help noticing that there was a chain with a leg iron attached to one of the back legs of the cot.

"You'all come out here to the back and I'll introduce you to Pikey," Maisie said. "One thing to know. Pikey ain't all there in his head. He rake the grounds here, bring up the carriage, clean the horses, take care of any mess around here. They don't even know how old he is or where he from. Ole man Hubbard found him lying on the street down by the docks early one morning and drug him here. I nurse him back to health and he here to stay now."

Pikey was a frail old man, with the whites of his eyes yellowed and a game leg. He was dressed in ragged field clothes and walked stooped over.

"Pikey, this man is name Marc Oriole and he gonna work for ole Massa."

Pikey took off his slouch hat, held it to his breast and bowed. "Good evening, Massa," he said.

"You don't got to do that, Pikey. He a slave like us. Just don't look like us."

Pikey bowed again nonetheless.

They returned to the kitchen and Hubbard summoned Marcus to the front room.

There was a wide rude desk set under a window facing the garden that was strewn with piles of accounting paper, in no particular order as far as Marcus could see.

His job, as explained to him by Hubbard, was similar to the work he had first done for Mr. Coffin. First, he was to make sense of the confused stacks of paper that the former accountant had left untended to, apparently for weeks. Marcus was ordered to organize these papers, and then begin work. He was to record purchases and sales of dry goods, purchases of dried beans, corn meal and bacon, sets of what was known as 'plantation clothing' for enslaved men, women, and children, shoes, hats and head scarfs. Also an order from iron mongers for chains and shackles, and finally, set off on a separate section of a hardcover account book, money borrowed from local banks. These funds, which numbered in the thousands of dollars, were for purchases of slaves. These latter were identified in separate columns—some from auctions, some from plantations, and some from people who were kidnapped—a more profitable means of collecting slaves for Mr. Hubbard.

Marcus noticed that the heavy claw-footed desk was also fitted with a chain fixed with a leg iron.

"When I'm out, you wear this," Hubbard said. "I can't have you running off as soon as I turn my back—which I am certain you would do."

Marcus tilted his head politely, indicating that he understood. But he had not counted on this. Nor had he realized he would also be chained in his bed at night.

"Now, I have a pretty little Quadroon lady friend who lives over on Rampart Street, and I visit her often in the evenings for dinner and sometimes don't return 'til late in the night. I'm checking you when I get home, just to make sure you're comfortable. I want you to sleep well, you understand."

Among other things, Marcus learned that first week was something of the 'friend' of Hubbard. Her name was Bebe Leclaire, and she was one of the famous Quadroons of New Orleans. These were free women of color who, unlike other free people of African descent, exhibited themselves in all their finery. They were the stars of the famous Quadroon Balls, popular events that younger white men of the city would attend. These balls were held in the best hotels and dance halls and the tables were set with delectable foods and good wines. The Creole women of New Orleans were famed for their beauty, and the one successful way to the easy life of the town was to match up with a well-to-do gentleman.

Quadroons were a class above the mostly white and Creole women who made up the large population of prostitutes who were residents of the multitude of brothels that were located all through the various districts of the city.

Racist though the city was at its roots, whites, Blacks, and Creoles mixed readily on the city streets. There was a small population of free Blacks, and a larger population of free mixed-race women who would marry whites. Even local urban slaves were given a certain amount of free time, as with the Sunday dance parties on Congo Square.

The Americans inherited from the old French *code noir*, an elaborate rating system of racial types. Lowest in the ranking were the newly arrived Africans, known technically as 'Negroes'. These people were looked down upon by second rank of *gens de couleur*, known as *les griffes*. These were considered lower class by the mixed-race mulattoes, one of the oldest of the racial types, descended from the original Spanish owned slaves. These were ranked below the Quadroons, who were a step below the high class Octoroons, who were for all intents and purposes nearly white.

All these free people of color who ranged through New Orleans were for the most part industrious and law-abiding members of society. They owned property and some of them owned plantations with slaves. They educated their children and even sent some of them off to France to be educated in the schools for colonials. They made up the bulk of the work force in the city; they were merchants and brokers. One step down socially, were the mechanics, shoemakers, barbers, tailors, and chefs. Nevertheless, those with a trace of African blood were aware of their tenuous position in white society and stuck to the rules of the game and led, one presumes, quiet lives.

The only ones who flouted their position were the sexy, free-spirited Quadroons. They dressed in silk and satins and plumed bonnets and cascades of jewelry and at public events they outshone the drab, formal Creoles and white ladies.

As the first weeks and months progressed, Marcus became aware of these unique cultural traditions of the city. He saw in it an opportunity, if not for escape—still very much on his mind, needless to say—but a means of getting by in life while he was enslaved.

He also came to realize through his accounting work how thoroughly integrated the institution of slavery was to the economic health of the city. The realization first came to him in the form of the meticulous records of Hubbard's slave sales, including the cost of the enslaved, as if he were selling furniture, or arms, or horses.

Every aspect of the finances of the town was tied to the trade. Sellers and traders and buyers were only the first in line. But local and national banks were also involved, floating loans to slave traders in order to assemble enough people to make up a coffle, and also loans to plantation owners. Insurance companies offered policies to traders to protect them from potential losses during slave shipments by land or the flatboats on the Mississippi, or coastal trade between Charleston, Key West, Cuba, and New Orleans. Lawyers gained as well, collecting fees for slave transfers. The river steamboat companies and the ships' captains made money on the transport of slave coffles, as did the food providers, the iron mongers, and even the medical professionals who nursed captured slaves back to health after the strenuous overland walk from Virginia to Natchez. All this was meticulously recorded in Hubbard's account books.

The more Marcus learned of this economic system, the more depressed and angrier he became. Sometimes, chained to his bed early in the night, he comforted himself with his fantasy of a huge slave uprising, similar to his imagined libretto for Betina's opera, in which he and his enlisted crew of Barbary pirates would land in Spanish Florida and raid plantations, liberating the enslaved people all across the South.

He sometimes imagined himself the leader of a slave revolt of this sort, a man similar to Toussaint Louverture, leader of the Haitian Revolution.

But by morning, back at work on Hubbard's books, he was totally disheartened by the reality of the national and even international involvement in the business. One of the beneficiaries of the trade were the clothing manufacturers of the North who provided the outfits for the massive populations of enslaved people. He then tracked the exchange to the shipping industry and the slave trade and the European coffee and sugar imports cited by the cynical *legitimiste* Count Marquis de Moreaux back in the days of the salon discussions in Paris. And finally, he followed the institution of slavery to the port of New York and to Wall Street, and the interdependence of big business and political figures, the police, and finally, to the United States government and its Constitution.

All this he learned from his accumulation of knowledge working on the accounts of Mr. Coffin and in the records of purchases and sales of his arch enemy, the scruffy Irish kid, Jimmy Hubbard, now risen in power, and himself operating a sort of metaphorical revenge against the system that had discriminated against him.

What hope could there be for an enslaved race of people woven so tightly into the economic web of Western economies? He fell deeper and deeper into the fantasy world that sometimes swept over him and sustained him in quiet moments. That and the thought of revenge.

Where would it all end?

And then, finally, after two months of imprisonment in Hubbard's office and garden, things changed and Marcus was able to step out into the debauched, amoral, degenerate streets of New Orleans where he began to devise a path to freedom.

Grove Street
The Loyal Accountant

Marcus had proved himself a loyal accountant in the eyes of James Hubbard. He had discovered and reported to Hubbard evidence of minor embezzlement by the paid accountant whom Hubbard had employed before he turned the work over to this far more sophisticated and worldly slave.

It should be added that part of the disclosure of former embezzlement was cover. Marcus himself was squirreling away notes of his own at the same time. He was also secretly copying over and over again James Hubbard's signature. He accurately foresaw the day, if things went the way he planned, when he would be able to forge passes for himself.

Finally, by late spring, the day arrived when Marcus was trusted with an errand on his own—the delivery of a letter to an associate with quarters down by the French Market near the river. Hubbard provided Marcus with a pass.

"Not that you'll need it. People know me here and they have seen you around. But don't get any ideas of making a break. You don't know this country and the slave catchers do. You won't last long."

"Do not worry," Marcus said. "I have no reason to run."

"One more thing," Hubbard said. "If you do run, and I catch you—which rest assured, I will—I don't intend to whip you. I'll sell you to the cane fields. I've got friends out at the Whitney Plantation. They know how to deal with types like you."

Marcus felt a strange weakness rush through him as he turned down the street. Weak-kneed, he leaned against one of the iron fences for a few seconds, breathing. This was not exactly freedom. But it was the beginning of freedom.

******

The errands increased over the next few weeks. He began to meet people, many of them free people of color from whom he learned the art of survival in the world of the white Americans and the complex Creole community. He was at a great advantage in the markets and shops and cafés, since he was fluent in French, the language of the upper classes in New Orleans. Not only that, there were many people on the streets who looked like him—light-skinned, mixed-race men and women who walked upright among the white French and Americans. No craven slouched, obsequious bowing and scraping and snatching off hats.

He began to feel more comfortable in the streets of New Orleans than he had in any other place in America. And with each successful mission carried out, Hubbard's trust in his new servant grew. Marcus was able to get letters off to both Mr. Coffin and also Amanda, explaining his location and current enslavement. He wrote that he would keep up correspondence but asked them not to try to contact him, until he found a trustworthy return address.

And then one evening, Hubbard's confidence in Marcus jumped a few more degrees.

Marcus was instructed to pick up a packet of notes from an associate. The office was located on a side street near Saint Anne's Street, not perhaps the best address in the French Quarter. As he entered the gate that led to the front door, he noticed two Creole men sitting on the curb on the other side of the street. He located the patron Hubbard told him to contact in an upstairs office with a window overlooking the street.

The patron was a white man who had a scar across his left cheek and a squinted left eye that seemed to tear a lot. The man had a wide kali kerchief which he used frequently to dry his cheek and his breath reeked of tobacco and absinthe—not an entirely savory character, in other words. The two of them spoke in French.

They chatted for a while about current events in the town, including the recent escape of the rogue elephant and also Mr. Hubbard and his business.

"He has, as you no doubt know, his hands in many pots," the broker said, "some of them containing questionable substances. He is not a man to be crossed."

The small talk completed, the man opened a drawer and took out a leather folder, tied in rawhide.

"Keep this out of sight on your way home," he said handing the package over to Marcus. "The types around here. Not so good. They know me, they know my business. When you leave, get over to Saint Anne's Street as soon as you can and get in with a crowd. You will be safer that way."

Marcus descended the stairs, the packet stuffed into his belt below his coat. At the glassed front door, he looked across the street and noticed that the two men on the curb had moved on. He opened the gate and turned toward Saint Anne's. But no more than fifty yards on, the two men stepped out in front of him. Marcus did not hesitate, he turned quickly and ran off at full speed. The two gave chase, calling out in a friendly manner, saying they just wanted to help him. Marcus turned at the first street, turned again on another, and then another, not knowing where he was but trying mightily to lose his pursuers. At one point, shortly after turning a corner, he saw an alley and ducked down to a dead end.

To his relief, he saw the two men race past. There was a rough uncared-for garden with a trash heap on one side of the alley. Not satisfied that he was entirely free, Marcus sorted through the junk and found a broken pitchfork handle. He picked it up and ventured toward the head of the alley. Just as he reached the street, he saw the two men pass back. One of them glanced down the alley, saw him, drew a knife and advanced.

Marcus didn't wait. He rammed the splintered end of the rake into the man's face, cracked his knife hand, and then charged at the second man. He let out a half screeching maniacal yowl and struck at the man's face, but his assailant dodged the strike and slashed Marcus's left arm. Marcus kicked him in the groin, hit him on the head with the fork handle and then smashed his fist across his left jaw, knocking him off his feet. He snatched up the fallen knife and stabbed the man in the shoulder, then put the point of the knife at the man's throat. And then he stood up. He looked down at the poor man's terrified pain-racked face, the full lips, the dark eyes and skin.

"Better luck next time, *mec*," he said in Creole.

He stumbled back toward Hubbard's, staunching the blood from his left arm with the cuffs of his right sleeve and turning down one street after another until he recognized a location and staggered home. Maisie met him at the door and fainted.

Hearing the noise, Hubbard dashed out of his office, saw Maisie on the floor and Marcus covered in blood.

"By Christ in Heaven, what the hell happened to you?" he said. "Did they get the money? Did you save the notes?"

At this point, Marcus was dizzy with the loss of blood and collapsed against the wall upright. He too felt faint. He reached in his belt, and tossed the packet at Hubbard's feet. Then he blacked out.

Saint Anthony's Square
Crossed Swords

If nothing else, the safe delivery of the money advanced Hubbard's trust of Marcus even further. There were other loyal errands and ventures over the next month and eventually, Hubbard began to allow Marcus more liberty to be out on the streets on his own, after the workday.

Late one night, Hubbard reeled into Marcus's quarters and told him to get up. Marcus could smell the alcohol on his breath, and he followed him, as he stumbled down the hall to the study.

"Sit down boy," Hubbard said.

Marcus knew something was coming but couldn't imagine what it was.

"You sure are a sharp niggaboy if I ever knew one," he began, slurring his words a bit, his head nodding this way and that.

Marcus figured he was up for a beating for something he had done, but in fact, Hubbard went on singing the praises of Marcus's ability to function in the complicated New Orleans world. Then in his drunken way, he went on to praise his ability with languages, his taste in dress, his comfortable style among people who were better educated and more sophisticated than Hubbard himself.

"You got a way, boy. Now here's a little secret. I don't like this business no more, this catching niggas and then selling them. It just come to me by accident. I didn't mean this business and I want to get out I want to go back to Virginia, get some property and a bunch slaves and retire. Join the plantation society."

"You going to set me free?" Marcus asked. He was already plotting to get a paper and pen and then get Hubbard to sign his name at the bottom of the page and then Marcus would write out his own letter manumission in Hubbard's hand.

Hubbard shook himself awake. "Hell no, boy, I'm not freeing you, not ever. Get that much straight." He dropped his head on his chest. "I'm learning from you. Why would I let you go?"

He stopped talking at that point, slovenly drank a little more cognac, and stared down at the table.

"I didn't grow up on no plantation," he said. He was talking to the table now, not to Marcus. "Didn't ever even know no rich people. Just the streets." He shook his head and was silent again.

Marcus waited. Then Hubbard began to spill out the hardships of his childhood.

"Just a little kid," he said. "Big ugly type comes and tells me—your mother's dead, kid. I didn't have no father neither back in Ireland. No father. I don't remember. Maybe there was one. Must have been one."

He laughed and shook his head again. "Had to be one," he said and laughed, a slobbering drunken bray.

He took another gulp. Then he let out a low, slobbering sob.

Hubbard rambled on, recounting the hardships of his childhood in a series of disjointed, scrambled memories. His narrative became more and more incomprehensible. But Marcus caught the drift. It was a hideous life Hubbard had survived.

Hubbard's speech thickened into a slow stream of mumblings, and then suddenly his head flopped down on the table and he passed out.

If ever there was a time to pack up his things, rob Hubbard's money and make a break it was then. But as it was, Marcus sat there looking down at this pathetic, crumpled figure.

To say he felt sorry for this broken heap of a man would be an extreme exaggeration. But the confession stalled his plans briefly. He helped himself to a glass of cognac and sat there for a while, staring at his master and reflecting on the contrast between his own life and the life of this helpless kidnapper. The Marquis de Moreaux's theory that everyone is a slave came to him. Maybe he had a point. If he, Marcus, had played the game, stayed on as loyal house boy, his life would certainly have been more comfortable. Certainly better off than this ruin of a human being that lay before him, his head sprawled out on the table, drool spilling from his half-opened lips.

In the first few weeks of his less restricted life, Marcus returned to Hubbard's house loyally and at reasonable hours. Then he began to dress himself more formally in the suits and top hats that Hubbard kept in storage for slave auctions. Hubbard noticed the change in routine, and determined that Marcus perhaps had a girlfriend. By this time, with his financial success improving, Marcus's discovery of the embezzlement scheme of Hubbard's former accountant, his fight to save Hubbard's money on the streets, and with the apparent contentment of his lot on Marcus's part, and his lack of interest in escape, Hubbard loosened the reins even more.

By late summer, the tall, green-eyed light-skinned figure with a classy European accent in French became known in the faro halls and taverns of the Quarter. People who didn't know him took him for one of the moneyed Creoles who had been sent to the French schools for colonials—which in fact was the case, in some ways. But it wasn't a girlfriend that kept Marcus out late at night. It was success in the gambling establishments.

New Orleans was famous for its legalized gambling and also for the mountebanks, crooks, schemers and shysters who frequented the gambling halls and the steamboats. For months, Marcus had been clandestinely siphoning small amounts of money from Hubbard's accounts which he hid under his mattress. He started conservatively in the gambling parlors, betting at the faro tables and losing often. But loss was his teacher. He soon learned a few tricks and strategies and slowly began to return home to Hubbard's with more money that he went out with. This continued through the summer, until one August night when he ran into trouble.

He was engaged in a game of faro when a dark-eyed man rose suddenly from the table and accused Marcus of cheating. His accuser wore the recognizable outfit of a professional gambler. He was dressed in e a dark suit and top hat and a frilled white shirt, a gaudy doublet crossed with a heavy gold watch chain, his fingers ringed with gold and diamond.

"I don't like that move, sir," he stated firmly. "Stand up!" Marcus looked up at him and remained seated.

The other men at the table quickly backed away.

"Up, you blaggard cheat, I am challenging you, don't you understand?"

Marcus rose slowly. He unfolded himself to his full height, rested one hand on the table and nodded to the man in silent recognition. This was the last thing he wanted to deal with at this point on his determined path to freedom.

"You are make the mistake, monsieur, I do not cheat," he said in strongly accented broken English.

His accuser switched to French. "I said, en garde monsieur. You have dishonored me. I am challenging you to the duel. Don't you understand? Come out."

This was not by any means a rare outcome in the gaming halls and ball rooms and brothels of New Orleans. Dueling, known locally as the *duello*, was technically illegal in the city, but it was the chosen means of settling arguments, minor disagreements, and most especially any, even hinted, infringement of one's honor. The local Code of Honor was sacrosanct, challenging someone's honor automatically generated a duel.

Marcus attempted though apology to avoid a duel. He did not wish at this point to bring attention to himself. Nor did he wish to win. On the other hand, he didn't want to be skewered. Profuse apologies on his part only deepened the offense, so finally Marcus agreed.

Arrangements were quickly established and they left the hall and made their way down to Saint Anthony's Square, behind the cathedral, where there was a garden surrounded by high shrubbery and trees and hidden from the street. It was a favorite dueling site. Here, the two men retired to fight. But there was one last exit for Marcus. He had no sword.

"As you can see, sir," he said. "I cannot fight you without a sword."

His opponent snorted. "Nor can I kill an unarmed man," he said. "But *attendez*, and we will settle the problem."

He had a second with him, and borrowed his *colichemarde*, a sword cane with a wide upper blade that narrowed to a rapier point. It was the dueling sword of choice in New Orleans society in those years. He carried the sword over to Marcus and cast it down at his feet. When Marcus bent to pick it up, his opponent swiped the grass, scythe-like in front of his nose.

"Can you fence, sir?" he asked.

Marcus demurred. "I've never fought an actual duel, no."

They rose, and took up their positions. Then Marcus thought of another angle.

"I'm sorry, monsieur, that was an untruth. I feel I should warn you that back in Paris, I am well-known for my fencing abilities. I've fought several duels, and I have never lost. I should add that this includes a challenge from the Duc de Bois, one of the better known duelists in Paris. A famous loss for the Duke, I'm afraid. He was forced to leave town in shame and nurse his loss at his country estate. You see, I was trained by Pietro Montalban of the Paris

Fencing School. Surely you know of him, monsieur? He is said to be world-famous. No, I do not know of him, nor do I care, and I can't say I believe a word you say," he raised his sword. "En garde!" he shouted.

Marcus tried another tact. Rather than tally and play the man, he immediately lunged, swirled his opponent's sword off to the side, and touched the man's lower throat with his sword tip.

"Don't move please, I don't want to have to hurt you," Marcus said.

In France, a duel could generally be settled by drawing blood, even a nick. This was also the case in French Louisiana. But after the Americans took over, duels often went on till a mortal wound was delivered. His opponent was well aware of this tradition.

The two men stood there under the shadows of the moon.

"Please drop your sword, monsieur," Marcus said, applying a little more pressure to the man's throat. "I won't say anything about this. Feel free to say you were victorious."

"I misjudged you," his opponent said. "I thought you were boasting. Who are you, sir, and why are you here in New Orleans?"

"I'm just a visitor to your city," Marcus said. "I'm in the cotton trade and have been visiting the exchange and watching the proceedings. Very interesting. I am associated with the Degas family, you no doubt know them. Nothing more. And I will keep silent about this little incident. Your honor will stand. But if you wish to play on—en garde!"

Marcus stepped back and waited; the man lunged, Marcus parried. He lunged again, and then again. Marcus retreated. All around the garden they went, crossing swords, the gambler lunging repeatedly, looking for an opening, Marcus easily, almost casually, defending himself and making an occasional feint, just to keep the duel going. At one point, his opponent dropped his guard slightly and this time Marcus lunged, once again holding the point of rapier at the base of the man's throat.

"I understand your position, monsieur. I have no desire to defeat and dishonor you, and if you will allow me I can demonstrate a win for you. But you must allow me to step back and show you something."

His opponent nodded, and Marcus stepped back, drove his sword into the ground and took off his coat. The gambler relaxed. He stood in contra-posto, his sword at his hip and watched as Marcus carefully rolled up the left sleeve of his shirt, to reveal the still-raised red scar from the recent knife attack.

"This wound, monsieur, is the result of a recent unpleasantness I was involved in a few weeks ago near Saint Anne's Street. If you wish, I am willing to appear in town, my arm in a sling from a wound I received in a duel with you."

"I'm not happy with this outcome. How do I not know that come tomorrow you'll be boasting about besting me in the Saint Anthony Street garden?"

"You have my word, monsieur."

"What good is that?"

"Very well then," Marcus said, his anger rising. He snatched up his sword and lunged, this time the point pierced the shirt just above the man's heart.

"Monsieur. My name is Count Marc d'Aurèle. I don't know you; I don't know who you are. But I daresay no one would be surprised in the circles I normally travel in to learn that while visiting America I was forced to kill yet another man in a duel. This would not by the first time, and I think they would no doubt find it rather amusing, in fact." He applied a little more pressure to the man's chest. "It would make an entertaining entry in the story of my travels."

The gambler shrugged. "Very well, then. I yield."

"One other thing," Marcus said. "In order to identify my victor, I'll need your name, and your trade."

"I am Jacques Biel. I am an importer and the owner of three ships running between, here, Cuba, and Key West and Virginia." He paused here. "And Charleston. If in your travels you need transportation to those ports, it can be arranged."

True to his word, for the next two weeks when Marcus went about town out of sight of Mr. Hubbard, he kept his left arm in a sling.

One evening, at the Barker's tavern, the waiter set before him a glass of absinthe. "On the house, monsieur, from the gentleman in the corner."

Marcus looked across the room and saw Jacques Biel at the card table with a group of men. He raised the glass, and Biel nodded.

The incident was successfully covered up. But some of the people in attendance in the gambling hall suspected the truth. His reputation rose, as it had in Paris. He was not a man to be fooled with.

Grove Street
Congo Square

Over the course of his months of enslavement, Marcus befriended the real boss of Hubbard's domain, Madame Chef, as he took to calling Maisie. He began by telling her stories of old Virginia, the cool greenery, his girlfriend Tilly, his good mistresses and his bad masters, and his adventures in Paris, and the kindness of Mr. Coffin, who had freed him. He detailed how Mr. Coffin would buy people and then free them, sometimes supplying them with funds if they wanted to run north. These stories garnered extra food at breakfast and dinner for Marcus. They also instilled in her, by design on Marcus's part, the possibility of escape.

True to New Orleans tradition, Hubbard allowed Maisie to attend the Sunday evening Congo Square dances and Marcus would sometimes accompany her, mainly to watch.

The first time he attended, Marcus saw crowds of African people gathering. Shortly thereafter, a drummer arrived and started pounding out a rhythm with old cow bones on an empty barrelhead. People moved slowly out into the square and began shuffling around. Then they picked up speed and soon enough they were jumping and twisting, knees up, their feet pounding the soil. Suddenly, with no apparent signal the crowd separated and moved out to the edges of the square, and accompanied by the swaying and stamping crowd, a sole dancer jumped into the center and executed a series of leaps and twists, crouches, slides and turns. She retired to the edges and another woman jumped in. And all the while the bone drummer pounded on the barrelhead, and the people set up a counter-rhythmic clapping.

Abruptly, the drummer stopped and started again with a slow pulse and a woman dressed all in white, with voluminous skirts and a white headscarf, moved with a regal slow pace out into the center and began a slow shuffling around the perimeter of the crowd. She moved step by step, her head tilted this way then that, bent over swaying and all the while moving forward. The rhythm slowed and women decked out in ribbons and head bright scarfs and colorful skirts followed after, a huge line of blurred color snaking here and there around the square chanting in a slow call and response.

Marcus realized that the formal woman in white was Maisie.

He asked a fellow observer about the change and the apparent leader.

"That woman there," the man said. "Be careful dat woman. She Queen Philomena. She the voodoo queen 'round here. She gather the people up by the lake to pray and she know roots and chants and can work the bones."

Marcus was intrigued. He had noticed that Maisie always carried herself with a certain confidence, even around her apparent owner, Mr. Hubbard. He began to wonder if perhaps Maisie could help him with a strategy for escape.

Not long after the Congo Square event, he asked Maisie about the other dancers, and her own formal dance, which, as he pointed out, seemed to indicate that she held a position of authority.

"A man there told me you're a voodoo priestess," he said.

She demurred. "I'm a good Catholic," she said.

"But why'd that man tell me all about you? He said you can work the bones."

"Yessuh, that true. I know the voodoo chants, but I'm a Christian woman," she said. "Jesus taught me at that voodoo."

"To work bones?" Marcus asked.

"Yeh, work de bones. Mix herbs. Talk to plants. Travel around."

Marcus asked if the plants talked back.

"Indeed they do. You address them proper. They will help you. Or they will destroy someone. You just have to know how to talk their language. Ole brother snake the same. You talk to him right he don't bite you. But he bite others if you ask him right or feed him certain roots. Rabbit too. He's smart. So is Fox. Ole bear come down sometimes in dreams. You just have to know."

These conversations went on during those evenings when Hubbard was off visiting his Quadroon mistress, Belle Leclaire. Eventually, at his request, Maisie invited Marcus to come up to one of her services her people would hold up on the banks of Lake Pontchartrain.

Marcus arrived late and went into a large barn-like shanty. The air was smoky with the scent of burning herbs; there were no windows, and the interior was shaded and dark, lit only by rows of candles ringing an altar in the middle of the room, crowded with gourds, statues of Jesus, Mardi Gras masks, and candelabras, all surrounding a cauldron of burning herbs, which an old man in a red shirt fed periodically. There was a dais at one end of the barn and, surrounded by acolytes sat the Voodoo Queen Philomena.

In front of the dais, a crowd of mostly Creole men and women in bright flowered shirts and dresses with ribboned hats and sashes circled rank on rank, holding smoky torches and chanting to clapped and stamped rhythms.

Marcus and one or two other people watched the ceremony. There were one or two whites mixed in with the circlers, including a wild eyed woman, her loose blond hair cascading halfway down her back. She swung her head from side to side maniacally sweeping the air with her locks.

The dance went on. The pace did not change, and still they circled, singing a low repetitive chant a little like the chanted vocables the Haitian and Indian people among the maroons of the Great Dismal Swamp used to do sometimes. The air thickened with the smoke of the herbs in the caldron. This ceremony was endless and trance like. It lacked the spark of the call and response services of the religious gatherings Marcus used to attend back in the days of his imprisonment at Greenwood and Mayfield. But then, after what seemed an unchained length of time, Marcus could not be sure how long, the pace increased, the chants were interrupted by animal barks, and growls, backed by a rhythmic, huffing call from the men.

They began to spin, the smoke funneled upward, people twirling round and round and leaping in the air, and then one of the younger women, stripped open her blouse, threw off her ribbons and sashes and began spinning wildly around the caldron with more and more frenzy, until, finally, possessed, she fell to the ground, quivering and yelping like a puppy, her eyes rolled up into her lids. The women swooped in and lifted her gently and carried her to the dais.

Marcus stepped out of the chapel and breathed in the musky swampy air of the lake shores. He himself was dizzy and confused, unable to think clearly, and he sat down on the ground waiting for his head to clear.

This was a magic he was unprepared for. But he saw in reflection, an opportunity.

After that, Marcus cultivated Maisie more actively, asking her, whenever they had some quiet time together, away from the presence of their master, about her ability to work herbs, and also her ability, as she claimed, to foresee the future.

"Could you predict my future?" Marcus asked her. He knew she could throw bones.

"I could try," Maisie said. "Sometimes the bones don't talk. Sometimes they just give me cloud talk."

"Cloud talk?" Marcus asked.

"You know, could be one thing, but then the way they fall next, could be another. Just cloudy. But you want to try; we'll throw the bones next time ole man Hubbard go off to see his sweet pie."

That night came a few days later, and Maisie and Marcus met at the kitchen table. Maisie bought over a lantern and a small brazier, threw some embers from the stove into it and added some powder from a satchel she wore inside her blouse. A pungent, heady smoke rose. Then she pulled out a little silken satchel, opened it and dumped a small pile of bones on the table.

"These here from Fox," she said. "He knows more than the chicken or the dog or cat."

She picked up the pile of bones and began humming and mumbling, mixing a few Creole words with words Marcus couldn't catch. Then she threw down the bones and stared at them.

She shook her head and rolled them out again.

"Yah, I see it," she said.

"What do they say?"

"I see you leaving here sometime."

"That's good, right? Freedom?"

"Don't know 'zactly."

"Freedom?"

"Yah, but I don't see something."

She picked up the bones and rolled them again. "Um, Um," she said, shaking her head.

"What?"

She shook her head again. "I don't know. One more." She threw down the bones and stared at them for a long time, shaking her head. "Yah, I see it. So, you gonna be free from here, I see that. You be traveling. But there's this blank spot after that. I can't see where you are. But there's cloud out and then, I see some trouble. What come up is a fox. I don't know why. And then I see a hunter with a dog and all kinds a animals chasing that fox. You got alligators, big storm in the sea, some kind of wild girl there like a injun. I don't know what's going on, tell you the truth."

"The hunter is after the fox?" Marcus asked.

"I see that, yeh. There's trouble there somewhere. Not here though, not in New Orleans. Maybe I just can't see so far but it looks like somebody's gonna get killed."

"The fox?"

"No, that's not clear. Could be the hunter. All these animals coming and going. That's all I see with ever' roll. I got no clear answer, somebody chasing somebody."

"Well at least I'm out of here," Marcus said.

******

In fact, however, Marcus was beginning to have mixed feelings about leaving New Orleans. He was coming to love the city and its vibrant night life. It was far more degenerate than the Left Bank artist's balls that he had joined, with bare-breasted Cleopatras parading the streets on floats, slave girls, and princesses, and Roman soldiers and emperors, clowns and donkeys, and on one occasion an Indian princess with a diamond tiara, riding on an elephant.

The two Mardi Gras he experienced were far more celebratory than the Parisian events, with the requisite Cleopatras and Caesars, but also with prisoners, and wild Indians, Venetian masked women, also bare-breasted, throwing coins, and the streets filled with drunken celebrants, and the taverns full every night. Duels somewhere in the city nearly every night. Brass bands, drum corps, the brothels open and busy. The steamboats whistling and belching smoke along the quay, gun shots in the night. Screams in the night, dogs in the night, cat fights, howling crowds. All this he could hear from his bed, or sometimes even participate in. Furthermore he was getting rich. He learned new tricks at faro, and he continued to bet conservatively—always gaining but never boasting. The biggest trick, he came to realize, was learning when to quit. He had friends; he met new people; he was, in spite of his enslaved position, enjoying himself.

But all the while there was the darker underbelly of the whole glorious experiment of the city. People were sold on the streets. Babies were torn away from their mothers. Strong men, powerful figures who could knock over anyone with a single blow, led off in chains. Whippings. Torture. One house on the Esplanade was revealed to be a veritable torture chamber for slaves. Even the white press was horrified. People were murdered somewhere in the city almost every night. The air was fouled with open drains. The mud in the winter streets was gummy and intolerable, the dust in the summer streets choked people.

And then one night, he witnessed the true nature of his master.

Old Pikey had apparently been out on the town without a pass. He was shouting insults about his master, Hubbard, cursing him bitterly, boasting that he was going to kill him with a pitchfork. Patrollers caught him and carried him home trussed up and told Hubbard what had happened. Hubbard wasted no time in administering punishment. He drove Pikey across the back yard, slapping his back with his iron cane and cuffing the back of his head. There were two chains fixed to the wall in back of the kitchen, and Hubbard smacked old Pikey one more time and shackled his wrists to the wall. He gave him one last smack on the back of his thighs with the cane, and then brought out the whip.

It was a short handled cat-o-nine tails. Hubbard ripped off Pikey's shirt, and gave him a light stripe, as if to test the whip. And all the while Pikey was howling and pleading and crying piteously. Then the real beating began.

Hubbard stepped to his left and delivered the traditional nine and thirty lashes. He began on the left, with downward-angled lashes, then moved off to the right and laid on the rest of the whip, leaving a patterned mass of red, bleeding diamonds.

Then Hubbard stepped back as if to admire his work. Pikey's pants were sullied and sopped with blood. Hubbard laid on a few more strikes, and Pikey collapsed, hanging by his wrists, his head lolled to his right shoulder.

From a side window, Maisie and Marcus watched in horror. But Marcus lost control.

"Christ's sake," he shouted. "He's killed him. I'm gonna kill Hubbard!" he shouted and jumped for the door. Maisie grabbed the back of his collar and tipped him backward.

"Don't you go out there, Marcus." she shouted. "Don't go out there. He got a pistol, he just kill you, too. Or he catch you up and tie you up there and kill you too with the whip. Don't go. Just wait. We do something."

Marcus was shaking with rage. "I'll kill the son of a bitch," he said.

"I know, but don't do nothing now. Everybody know him. They'll catch you and hang you. Just wait."

Vengeance, now lit, burned.

Marcus could not sleep that night. He dozed and woke in a rage slamming his fist into his pillow. His hate for Hubbard, always just below the surface, would not resolve itself that night. He plotted tortures and ways to kill the man without being caught. The feeling went on for weeks, and then one night, in the Porter Tavern, the sweetest revenge of all presented itself.

The Porter Tavern
The Sweet Revenge

After the murder of Pikey, Marcus found it difficult to play the role of loyal factotum to Mr. Hubbard. He still kept the books. He still ran errands and he still tried to enjoy himself on the streets. But the reality of the city, the horror of the place, would not let go of him. He began brooding privately, and one day, rather than run one of Hubbard's errands immediately, he took a long walk along the river and came to a quiet bank and a clearing below an old willow tree.

He sat plotting both revenge and freedom. But he also started brooding again with a powerful hate for the whole system of slavery. He knew from his work how deeply engrained the system was in the world economy and he realized how impossible it was for any one person to do anything about it. But he thought back on some of the philosophical discussions he had listened to during Mr. Coffin's salon evenings. These intellectual analyses were somehow comforting to him, a means of distancing himself from reality. During one of these sessions a young man named Belson, a new participant, put forth an idea that had attracted Marcus, during the constant discussions on the nature of freedom. He said in so many words the idea was to carry forward Voltaire's idea of cultivating one's garden—which in original form was a cynical statement of the world condition.

Take that one step farther, Belson had argued. You start a revolution to defend liberty. Individuals rise to power, and when they do, what happens? They become as bad as their predecessors. "Look at the world's first democracy," he said. "They liberate themselves from the British Crown in the name of liberty and justice for all but then keep thousands of people in chains." All one can do, Belson argued, is live an individual life as a model for what we would want the world to be. Not what it is.

“What good is that?” Madame deLatour had asked. “The slide toward destruction carries on. The wars begin again. The people rise up, the oppressors move back in, only with a different name.”

“It’s true,” Belson said. “It’s a conundrum. But it will comfort you. You will sleep at night.”

It struck Marcus that this is exactly what Mr. Coffin was doing. He could not do away with the system. But he could free people, one by one. Whether this idea would catch on did not seem to concern him. He did it for himself.

Marcus went home that evening, feeling slightly better and decided to make a start where a start was possible.

One night, when Hubbard was off with his mistress, Marcus sat down at the desk and in Hubbard’s hand, prepared a letter of manumission for Maisie, signed it in Hubbard’s name, and sealed it in an envelope with her name on the front.

He took it to the kitchen and asked her to share a glass with him. Then he handed her the envelope and explained the contents.

“You hide this and guard it. And if you ever wish to be free, just run off, but be sure to carry the letter with you and if any paddyrollers come after you, just show them this.”

Then he took out another envelope. “If you need money to get started, you use this. I’ve managed to gain some funds in the gambling halls and you’ve been working for free a lot longer than I have. Somebody ought to pay you.”

“What you doin’ this fo’, Marcus. You crazy?”

“No, not crazy. I just want to do it.”

“You don’t owe me nothin’.”

“Yes, I know, but this is Mr. Hubbard’s money. I’ve been hiding it away since he brought me here. It’s your pay. He owes you this. He actually owes you more.”

“I’m not running,” Maisie said. “I got family ’cross town.”

“You don’t have to run. But if you ever want to, you’ve got the means.”

“What about you? Whyn’t you run off?”

“I will. I’ll be saying goodbye to you. Don’t know when, though.”

A few weeks after giving Maisie her papers, Marcus came into the kitchen for his morning coffee and found that the stove was cold. He looked for Maisie in one of the rooms in the slave quarters in the back garden she shared with

Pikey. Marcus thought maybe she had overslept, but her bed was empty and most of her clothes were missing.

He sat down on her bed, laughing quietly and slapping his knee. He hadn't felt such happiness since his days in Paris. Then he raced into the house and knocked furiously on Hubbard's door, shouting that Maisie wasn't in the kitchen.

Hubbard tore open the door. He wore a night cap and a filthy gown, and his eyes were raging. He struck Marcus across the cheek in blind anger.

"I'm just telling you. I think Maisie's run off. I'll go look for her if you want. Can't be long gone. But the stove's cold."

Hubbard came to his senses, let out a stream of epithets, against Blacks, abolitionists, Yankees, Quakers, ministers, and do-gooders.

Marcus acted out equal concern. "I never would have expected Maisie to run. She liked you. She told me when I first came here. You were a good man, she said. I can't believe she's run off. Maybe she got kidnapped."

"Kidnapped?" Hubbard shouted. "How's she going to get kidnapped out of her own quarters?"

"Maybe she's got a boyfriend, took off to see him. Maybe she got caught up in those voodoo rituals and was poisoned. Who knows. Not like her, is it. I don't get it. We were friends. I can't believe this. She must have been kidnapped by voodoo witches."

Marcus too began to curse. He cursed the voodoo priestess. He cursed the Congo Square dancers. He cursed the crooked city.

"Yeah, well, I'm gonna catch her and give her something to remember. I might even sell her 'cross the river. Damn her. Let her wear out in the cane fields and get bit by a snake. She don't know how lucky she was here. I shouldn't never—never—have trusted her, God damn her."

Another stream of invectives.

Later that day, somewhat calmed, he came into the room where Marcus was at work and instructed him to take up his pen and letter paper.

"I'm posting notices. You take this down," he ordered.

Marcus inked the pen and waited.

RUN OFF

MY COOK, MAISIE

DARK-SKINNED NEGRESS, AGED ABOUT 42. HIGH CHEEKBONES TALL

MAY BE AROUND CONGO SQUARE ON SUNDAYS

RUN OFF ON SEPTEMBER 18 FROM GROVE ST

AT LARGE IN THE CITY

GENEROUS REWARD FOR HER RETURN.

SUBSCRIBER

JAMES A HUBBARD, ESQ

"You take that down to the printer, tell them to run it as soon as they can."

Marcus folded the posting in an envelope and walked over to the printer on Lafayette St. but sat around for a while in the Square. Then went home with the notice still in his possession under his coat and hid it under his mattress with his other papers.

"When did they say they'd be ready?" Hubbard asked later that day.

"They said they're backed up but they'd get to it soon."

"All right, now get in there and write up another for the runaway notices in the 'Advocate' and take it over to them, God damn her."

He began to rant again. Mr. Hubbard did not like to be beaten at his own game He stormed out of the room.

Marcus carefully wrote out a new notice and brought to Hubbard for approval. Then he went back to the office and wrote out another version.

Runaway from Grove Street:

My cook: Maisie. Aged 55

Light-skinned, heavyset, walks with a limping gait.

Last seen around the French Market, carrying a basket of greens.

September 18. No passes on her person

Please contact subscriber:

James A Hubbard, esq.

This he carried to the paper, paid for the advertisement, and returned home.

A few days later, Hubbard asked Marcus to go back to the printer and pick up the posters. Marcus went back to the office and this time delivered the original. It was another two weeks before the printed bulletins were delivered to Hubbard. Marcus was then instructed to post them around the Quarter—which he did, in various obscure sites, or posted along with a notice board with many other runaway notices.

A week after Maisie's break, Hubbard came home with another cook, a young woman named Lucinda, who cried all night and wept privately at the stove. She had been purchased away from her husband, Marcus learned. She had recently arrived after a summer-long tramp in a coffle originating in Richmond. Marcus told her his story of having been raised on two of the James River plantations and asked her if she knew of anyone at the big Mary Plantation on the James. She said she did. Before she was sold, she was enslaved at the Tidewater Plantation, closer to Norfolk.

"Did you ever hear of a slave girl named Tilly, whose mother was the cook at the Mary Plantation?" he asked.

"Never did hear of a Tilly. But that cook at Mary Plantation was well known. My brother run away from our place a few years back and he was hiding in the woods near the Mary place. 'Nother maroon hiding out there tol' him how to get victuals from the woods 'round Mary. Ole cook there, he said had a big garden and she send food out and hide it under a hollow. Runaways knew 'bout that place. But that was years ago. I got taken off to Richmond and got sold down the river, where I meet Johnny, my husband. And now they take him off and this Massa Hubbard buy me. I don't know what to do."

Marcus snorted cynically. "I don't either," Marcus said. "Maybe we can get out of here someday."

This time Lucinda was the one who snorted, and shook her head sadly and began to cry.

Hearing these stories of his territory, and the rumors of Tilly's mother, and the fate of so many runaways such as her brother hardened Marcus's resolve to get back and find Tilly.

But first to get out of New Orleans.

With Lucinda in the kitchen, and Marcus apparently as hardworking and loyal as ever, Hubbard went back to his trade and Marcus returned to his former life, spending evenings out at the faro tables and returning to the Pirate's Cove Tavern for a late-night drink.

Periodically, he would meet his former dueling rival, Jacques Biel, and over time they got to know each other. Biel was, as he had pointed out a successful shipping magnate. He had two packet vessels that would carry cotton from New Orleans to New York, where it was unloaded, and then shipped to British and European ports. He also had a smaller topsail schooner, that sailed between Cuba and Key West and Southern ports. Marcus had been wondering how, once he got himself free, he would get out of New Orleans. He thought of booking passage on a river steamboat to Natchez, and from there sailing up the Ohio River to a free state. But the alternative was to book passage on one of the packets that would ship cargo east to Norfolk or Charleston.

He met Biel one day and asked about his packets.

"I ask because I'm thinking of leaving New Orleans at some point," Marcus said. "I've a good sense of the cotton trade at this end. But I may want to return through Baltimore. Do you have vessels that make that run that I could book passage on?"

"But of course," Biel said. "Whenever you want to leave, let me know, I'll give you the schedules. I've got one vessel coming into port sometime soon. She'll be leaving for Baltimore as soon as we get a cargo."

Marcus was determined now to get his final revenge on Hubbard, even if he had to simply murder him and make a quick getaway. But simply killing him didn't seem fair—it seemed too quick. He wanted Hubbard to have a taste of the misery he had caused to the hundreds of people he had captured or bought, and sent down to a living hell.

He thought of knocking him out, or getting a potion through Maisie or her friends to put him to sleep and then chaining him in the slave quarters. Then, ever entertaining himself with vengeful fantasies, he thought of putting word out to the African people around Congo Square that there was a slave trader captured and chained in the slave quarters in the garden behind 58 Grove Street, if anyone would like to pay a visit.

Night after night, he brooded and plotted. And then, one evening at the White Bull Tavern, an opportunity presented itself.

In the second week of September, Marcus fell into conversation with a rough-looking white man, who in spite of his appearance seemed to have a lot of money. He had seen the man arrive with two powerful Negro slaves, who waited outside the tavern door while their master enjoyed a drink.

The man introduced himself as Henry Davis. He was originally from New Orleans but now he was living up the river, operating a large timber cutting operation in the cypress swamps. He had come to New Orleans to buy new slaves as timber-cutters.

Marcus expressed an interest. "What kind of slave are you looking for?" he asked.

"I need bucks. Men only and not just any man. I need powerful types. And it doesn't matter to me if they're rascals who try to run off or kill their masters. I can take care of that. In fact, in my experience, once you break them, and give them enough food. They'll work."

"Aren't you afraid they'll kill you when they get a chance?" Marcus asked.

"You see those two big niggas outside the door?" Davis asked. Marcus said he had noticed them. "That's Poquito and Emanuel. They're my overseers. Nobody crosses Poquito and Emanuel. And they're with me all the time, day and night. Good men. Best I've ever owned."

The conversation as to the work and the functioning of the timber camp carried on. The holding was on the west side of the river isolated from any other properties and consisted mostly of swamp. Davis said he and his crew lived on a high hummock, an island in the swamp.

"That's another thing about the place," Davis said. "Nobody gets out. Slave run off I just wait. They'll come back. And if they don't, it doesn't mean they got themselves free. Means the snakes got them. Or the 'gators. Or who knows what. There are even panthers in that forest. Another thing. Soon as they get there, Poquito or someone tells them about the Moth Man."

"The Moth Man?" Marcus asked.

"It's a kind 'a white spirit. Looks like a huge moth with wide wings. It folds you up and then eats you. Slowly though. Takes them a week or so to kill you."

Marcus was intrigued by these stories. "Are you going to be around here a few days?" he asked.

Davis said he was.

"Well, maybe we could meet here again. I myself own a bad slave like that and I'm not sure I want him anymore. Too much trouble."

Two days later, they met again and shared a glass or two of absinthe.

"What about this buck you own?" Davis asked. "I haven't seen too many types that would do for the kind of work I need done. Everybody's too clean."

"He's still around. I actually kind of let him loose. He will work on his own terms, and I let him out. But he always gets drunk and comes crawling back. I always know where he is though."

"He sounds just right," Davis said.

"Yes, but I have to warn you. He is a tough one. When he's out on the streets, he carries a cane made of iron. Nobody fights him when they see that cane. I heard that he nearly killed another Black man two weeks ago."

"Sounds good to me," Davis said.

"There's one other thing though," Marcus said.

"What's that?"

"He thinks he's white."

Davis tapped his glass down and started to laugh. "I like it. What is he, crazy or something?"

"Well, he's violent alright. The thing is, though, he actually looks white. He's light-skinned. But he's got that black hair and jet black eyes, might be part-Indian. He's a big fellow. Rough-looking. I bought him off a plantation back in Virginia and at a very good price. I thought I could use him for protection in my travels. But it hasn't worked out; I'll sell him to you for a good price."

"How much?"

"Seven hundred, maybe. I don't know, I didn't think about selling him until you came along. Tell you the truth I'd just as soon get rid of him, but I thought I'd have trouble selling him at auction. He's such a nasty type."

After some more questioning and arrangements, the two of them agreed to meet the next evening to arrange the sale. And the capture. Davis would bring the money.

"Fine with me then," Marcus said. "But I feel it's only fair to warn you."

"What now?"

"He's going to fight you. He's going to fight like a wildcat. He's going to start shouting about the fact that he's white. He even sometimes claims to be a trader. I mean I do think he is crazy. You have to know that. He does not know reality. You've got to slap him in irons right away. Knock him on the head if you have to. Muzzle him so he can't talk crazy and haul him off to your pen. He can take it."

"Doesn't matter," Davis said. "You should see the types we have up there in the woods. Half of them are crazy."

They met the next night. The plan was to catch Hubbard as he came out of Belle's cottage late at night.

"We'll stay in the shadows till he comes out. Then you and the boys go grab him. Don't let him see me. Let him think you're just kidnapping another free colored. He knows all about that." Marcus waited at Grove Street house until Hubbard left, after a light supper. He usually walked over to Rampart Street and stayed for the evening and then would walk back between eleven or twelve.

After he left, Marcus returned to the tavern and met up with Davis and his men. Poquito brought around Davis's wagon, and the four of them rode over to the Ramparts and waited.

There was a little open space on the east side of the street across from Belle's cottage, and the crew waited there in the shadows, chatting about New Orleans and Virginia and Paris and other cities that Marcus Aurelius had visited. Finally around eleven-thirty, Hubbard came out.

Belle stepped out with him and they stood there for a while. Then she went back in the house and shut the door. Hubbard set off for home, swinging his iron cane jauntily. He was a picture of a man contented with his lot, well satisfied with himself and indifferent to the reality of his trade. An unexamined life.

"OK, boys," Davis said. "Go get him."

The two of them jumped out of the shadows and ran across the street.

"Watch out for that iron cane," Marcus called after them.

Hubbard heard them coming before they reached him, turned and raised his cane as they approached and swiped at Poquito, who jumped back while Emanuel circled around behind him and pinned his arms. Poquito delivered a hard punch to his stomach, twisted the cane away, and threw it across the street into the shrubbery.

This was no easy fight, though. Bellowing with all the confidence of a seasoned street fighter, Hubbard broke Emanuel's hold and kicked Poquito and then lunged, his fists flying. But Emanuel chopped his neck and boxed his ears, deafening him. Hubbard turned and knocked Emanuel off his feet, whereupon Poquito pounced. He punched Hubbard repeatedly; Emanuel joined in; Hubbard fought back bravely and there followed a fine rumpus of flying fists, kicks and punches. Hubbard, fighting his way left and right, finally managed to make a break with one last uppercut, and raced away down Rampart Street.

“Go get him, boys,” Davis shouted. He ran to the wagon and snatched out one of the loose chains, and gave chase with the others. Marcus, staying in the shadows, followed to watch the fight.

When he caught up to the group, he saw that the three of them had Hubbard pinned on the ground while Davis shackled Hubbard’s wrists behind his back. The two Blacks yanked Hubbard to his feet; Davis circled Hubbard’s waist with the chain and Poquito and Emanuel picked up the loose ends. Then they began to frog-march Hubbard back toward the wagon.

It was clear that this was not the first time these two had captured recalcitrant slaves.

For his part, Hubbard, even though now chained, continued to fight, kicking and charging from one side or another like an enraged bull, only to be brought up short by the ends of the chain they had wrapped around his waist.

Then Hubbard began to shout. “What the hell are you doing? I am a white man,” he shouted. “You can’t carry me off. Can’t you see that? White man! White man!”

This was followed by a stream of curses and another pronouncement of his white background.

Finally, Davis spoke, “White or black, you’re my slave now. I bought you outright.”

“Bought me? Nobody buys me, you son of a bitch.” He lunged, his teeth gritted.

Davis had picked up Hubbard’s iron cane from the bushes, and at this point delivered a swift strike across the side of Hubbard’s face.

“Just shut up and give over, or take a few more licks.”

Blood was streaming down over Hubbard’s chin, but he still raged on as the three of them hoisted him into the wagon. Then the three of them rolled him over on his back. Poquito jumped in and kneeled on his chest while Emanuel shackled his ankles and bound the ends of the chain to the wagon rails.

The fight was over; the raging bull was bound.

Davis walked over to the shadows where Marcus was hiding, and thanked him.

“I see what you mean,” he said chuckling. “That’s one hell of a fighting buck if I ever owned one. We’ll break him though; his type make good cutters.”

They shook hands, and Davis delivered the fee. Then he got in the front of the wagon beside Poquito. Emanuel sat in the back with Hubbard's, iron cane across his knees.

From where he stood, Hubbard was not visible to Marcus. But he knew he was there. He could hear the threatening bellows, the rages and curses as the wagon slowly moved down Rampart Street and turned left, out of sight.

******

Marcus had a lot of work to do after that. He contacted Biel and arranged to meet him for a dinner at Antoine's. It was a quiet evening at the establishment, and the two sat in the back at a table by the wall. Biel guessed accurately the purpose of the dinner invitation.

"You're looking for passage, aren't you?" he said.

Marcus declared that he was and would like to book a cabin.

Biel laughed. "I knew that was coming soon. You know that rogue Jim Hubbard told me that you're no cotton trader. He claimed you're his slave. Caught you up in Virginia someplace and brought you down here."

Marcus threw back his head and laughed heartily, "You believed him?" he asked.

"Well, I don't know why he'd tell me that."

"I do," Marcus said. "Hubbard's from New York. He's wanted for murder there, so he ran to the South and got himself in with the dirtiest trade in the world, kidnapping free people of color and bringing them down here for sale. He kidnapped a girl I loved. She was a light-skinned Haitian Creole, part of a rich family I had business with. She got caught while she was in Charleston with her father. I got word that Hubbard was her captor, and I tracked him to Richmond, only to learn that he had left with a coffle of slaves, six months ago. We think Tilly, my girl, was in that coffle. So I'm here."

"So far, I'm just socializing with Hubbard. I wanted to learn from him who Tilly was sold to and now I know. Turns out she wasn't in that coffle. He sold her to the family that owned the Mary Plantation on the James River. I need to get back there. I'll buy her back if necessary."

"Hubbard was actually useful to me in the end. I told him there was a substantial reward from her family for those who helped locate her, and he was very cooperative."

Now it was Biel who laughed. "Either you spin a great tale, or Hubbard's a liar. And since I know Hubbard, I tend to buy your version. No one in this city likes the greedy bastard. Anyway, I've got a vessel leaving here in a week, the Mary Lane. The little I know of you, I think you'll like the captain and the crew. He's a unique sort of trader with a decidedly unique crew and a mind of his own. Come on down to our office on Maspero tomorrow, and we'll write you up. The Mary Lane is headed for Baltimore, but Captain Maybe has a mind of his own. He may stop at a few ports on the way. In any case, I think you'll enjoy the voyage. By the way," Biel said, "I haven't seen Hubbard around town this past week. Any idea where he is?"

"Yes," Marcus said. "He's driving a coffle of twenty-two female slaves up to the Laura Plantation. He told me he might stay up there for a while making a circuit of other plantations, looking to either buy or take orders for more slaves."

"That figures," Biel said. "Usually, he boasts all around town whenever he's off, though."

The outbound passage established, Marcus began to arrange for his departure. He went to the Canal Bank, and with a forged power of attorney document from Hubbard and letters of intention, he transferred Hubbard's Rampart Street property to Belle Leclaire. This would have been a legal action under a unique New Orleans system known as *Placage* that entitled Quadroon mistresses rights to property and any children of the union. He also took the opportunity to withdraw funds from Hubbard's account for himself.

He then began to pack his trunks with Hubbard's finest clothes, a cache of gold specie and all of Hubbard's movable valuables, including his dueling pistols, his Coulax sword, identity papers, and anything else he could lift that might be useful to him in the future. He then penned a letter to Mr. Coffin and Amanda, explaining that he was now free, and would be making his way back to Virginia to find Tilly. That done he wrote out a letter of manumission for Lucinda and, using Hubbard's account, paid her for the days she had worked.

The Gulf of Mexico
Captain Maybe and Queeny Malloy

The Mary Lane was a trim 170-ton topsail schooner of one hundred or so feet with sleek, raked masts and a black hull. A group of very dark slaves were loading her with supplies when Marcus arrived at the wharf. He was waiting around for a while with his trunks, when a strong young Negro man approached and addressed him in broken English.

"You be da Marc Oerey?" he asked.

Marcus said he was, and the man walked off without a word and came back with two other dark Negro men.

"*Wa bo yeye nda mbolani.*" he ordered.

The men lifted Marcus's trunks up the gangway and carried them aft.

The apparent boss tapped his chest. "*Nda dzam Mokuro*," he said. "Me name Mokuro," and held out his hand.

Marcus took his hand and Mokuro grabbed it in both hands and shook them up and down vigorously. And kept shaking them vigorously. Mokuro smiled warmly, revealing a mouth filled with filed-down pointed teeth like a cat. He also had two zigzag lightening-strike tribal scars on each cheek. "Mokuro. Name," he said again.

"Marc Oerey," Marcus said. "*Falla Portuguese*?" Marcus asked, taking a chance that the man might know Brazilian Portuguese.

"Nao," Mokuro said.

"Haitian?"

"*Non. Fang den Igbo*. English da bes."

Fortunately, Jacques Biel arrived at this time.

Mokuro shook his hand as well—and just as vigorously. Then he executed a short dance, stepping forward then back then turned around and repeated the step.

Biel made an attempt to respond with a dance of his own. This was apparently some recognized tradition among Mokuro's people.

"This crew here you will find very interesting," Biel said to Marcus.

"I can see that," Marcus said. "Where are they from?"

"All over," Biel said. "Gabon, Gambia. Bight of Benin, I don't know. They're all saltwater negroes. I'm not sure whether they've ever lived in any country this side of the Western Ocean. Ah—but comes the conquering hero himself," he said.

Striding toward them on the wharf, Marcus saw a late middle-aged white man with a saber at his hip wearing a tricorn hat festooned with the bright feathers of tropical birds and dressed in a velvet suit, a brocade waistcoat, and scarlet plush breeches.

"Good day to you, sir," he said, shaking Marcus's hand warmly. "Captain William Maybe here." He spoke with a hint of an Irish brogue.

"*Comte Marc Aurèle, ici,*" Marcus said, nodding coolly.

"Count, is it then? *Comte de quoi*, if I may ask?"

"My family is from the Perigord."

"Ah le Périgord, le Périgord, les caves de Périgord, les bon vins du Périgord. I know your country well, monsieur le Comte. I have sailed there in my youth, up the Garonne for *bariques* of Bordeaux. Entre-Deux Mers, Haut-Brion, and all that. Then down the coast past Sicily. Then back. We traded wine there sometimes. Run the barrels ashore in a line, bobbing in the seas they were, like porpoises. But please—to come aboard and make yourself comfortable; you will be my sole *copain* on this voyage. And I'm sure we'll share some tales."

"I daresay," Biel interjected quietly.

Marcus was not sure what he meant.

Captain Maybe then turned to Mokuro and delivered a long sentence in his language—whatever that may have been—indicating that Marcus was this and Marcus was that. Whatever he was saying was pleasing to Mokuro. He looked at Marcus nodding and smiling and showing his cat teeth.

Anyone other than the worldly Marcus would suspect that the two of them were planning to have him for dinner once they got clear of the coast.

As it was Marcus, ever the curious when it came to language, repeated the last phrase Mokuro said in a reasonably good imitation of the accent.

Both speakers turned to him and smiled widely.

"*Wa dzinga Fang*?" Captain Maybe asked.

"No, but perhaps I could learn," Marcus said, catching the meaning of the question by context.

"Well sir, you shall have an opportunity to learn, I daresay, you shall have ample opportunity. The lads here don't have much English or French in their repertoire, save for Prince Mokuro here. Nor Portuguese. And no Spanish to speak of. But you'll get by; they're all good fellows. Now do come aboard and take a glass."

The three of them boarded and turned aft to the captain's quarters. There was a small cabin on the starboard side just aft of the galley. The door was open and Marcus saw his trunks inside.

"Your home away from home, monsieur," Captain Maybe said. "Not a bad nook, does na' leak much in heavy weather, and it's away from the noise on deck. They sing a lot, my boys, and beat the tam-tam all night and they dance and they hoot and they have jolly old time once we've come from port with a fresh cargo and with many a ports and many adventures ahead."

"Captain Maybe runs a loose ship, Marcus. You'll enjoy the voyage; his Blacks are a happy bunch." Biel said.

"Where are they from, *capitain*?"

"Well, I'll tell you. But first, a drink."

The captain's cabin was a well-appointed space, with dark mahogany cabinets all around two port lights, and a mullioned window astern, with a wide bunk beneath. On the forward side of the starboard wall, he noticed a rack of long Dane muskets. And stretched out upright on a patterned day bed, he saw a fulsome mixed-race woman with red lips, a white piqué dress and a veritable horse collar of roped glass beads cascading down her ample bosom, a rose-red turban encircling her hair.

"Now monsieur le Comte, I wish to introduce you to the real captain of the Mary Lane, whose name is Queeny Malloy. Queeny old girl," he said, "do say hello to Count Marc d'Aurèle; he'll be joining us on this little escapade across the wide waters of the Gulf."

"And then a *bonjour a vous, Monsieur le Comte,*" Queeny said in heavily accented Creole tones.

"Good day to you, Madame Queeny," Marcus said in English. "I am Count Marc Aurèle of the Périgord."

She grinned widely. "It is true?" Queeny asked. "Well, I am Mistress Queeny Malloy, late of the English nation and now a woman of no country, attached to this piratical devil who commands this sea swallow of a ship we sail upon. And will you drink, Mr. Count?" she asked.

"I will, Madame, thank you."

Whereupon Queeny rose from her day bed, throwing aside a bright purple chiffon, walked unsteadily across the deck to a cabinet on the port side and brought out a bottle of rum and four glasses.

She had a nondescript, furry little lapdog with her who leaped down to the deck and followed her on her heels.

"Who's that?" Marcus asked.

"That is Yankee," Queeny Malloy said, "and he is the most excellent of dogs. Our most loyal member of the crew."

They raised their glasses.

"Calm seas and prosperous voyage!" Biel said and lifting his glass. "Well, never mind calm seas—to a prosperous voyage," he added.

They drank.

"Now my crew here," Captain Maybe began. "I want you to understand. They na' slaves. They are free men all, and under my command, as free as any English tar that sailed the Seven Seas. They're free to leave in any port we put into. But they'd rather stick with me."

"But how did you find them?" Marcus asked.

"Well, now there's a story, me boy, there's a story if ever there was one. You know the American revenue cutters, well this vessel is one, or was one, or could be one again. I sail with Letters of Marque from the British Crown, as you'll see. And as you well know, monsieur, it's illegal nowadays under American law to transport people of the African race across the Western Ocean, so I sail also under the flag of a revenue cutter of the United States of America when convenient, and if I spy an English or American ship a vessel carrying Africans, well it's back to Africa they go, and if the wheels of justice run smooth-like—which they never do—it's off to prison with the captain and his crew and freedom for said Africans."

He drained his glass and continued, "So one bright day with a fair breeze, just off the Bight of Benin as we then were positioned at that time, what do I espy, but a little brigantine making her way down the coast and flying an English flag. Now I don't like the looks of that flag, do I. I'm not sure why, but something seemed amiss to me. So, flying the American colors of a revenue cutter, I put the helm down and I place a shot across her bow. Now any honest Englishman would round up at that point. But what does she do but lay on sail and make a run to the north, along the coast. So, of course, we give chase."

"Like a greyhound, we were, we give chase, don't we, and the Mary Lane here, as you may have heard, is one the fastest little sea hawks that works the Western Ocean, and so we catch up. Another shot. Then the brigantine, she changes course and comes downwind on us, a little six pounder on the foredeck flashing and billowing like dragon, and so we ourselves heave to port and run for the open seas, as if to escape. The brigantine resumes her course, and then—and then, monsieur, we come down her, blasting away this time with a four pounder and with a lucky shot she splits the main topmast. We're armed, all of us, even Queeny here, who could split a block and tackle with her long Dane as any of us could, all of us, as I say, and we come alongside and give her a whiff of the grape just for good measure. We board, all of us armed to the teeth, and sure enough, there below, what do we see but a cargo of Black fellows, all shackled down in chains—one hundred hearty Africans, eyes rolling and silent in fear."

"Now, I know a few dialects of the African lingo from my days in these parts, I know also the shushing lilt of the Portuguese, the French language and the Spanish language too, but also enough Fon and Fang and Ibo and the like to get by, and so I sing out them, in so many words, I says 'Don't fret lads, you're free people now.'"

"Long story, my son. Long story. But, having made legal deposition back in the barracoons of the Gambia, and turning over the captain and the crew to the British authorities, we take our Black fellows up the green and forested coast. Day after day with nothing ashore save a few clearings and rotting thatch-roofed shacks."

"But you perhaps know of the Bight of Benin, you know what it's like, but then maybe you don't, it being the case that you're a count as you say, but that is not a healthy part of the world for a white man. You know, perhaps, the little slaver's pasquinade:

The Bight of Benin
The Bight Benin
There's four come out
For forty go in"

"So there you have it, Monsieur le Comte. We've lost half our white crew, and more getting sick by the day. Whereas our Black fellows, stressed though they were by weeks in the barracoons, were in good form."

At this point, Biel interrupted, "Perhaps you should come to the point, Billy," he suggested.

"Well, I'm getting there, damn your eyes, Jacques, I'm getting there, can't you see?"

The epic carried on for another five minutes. Basically, they sailed up to the free town of Banjul and put the captives ashore, where under English law, they would be free—at least for the time being. But by that time so many of the white crewmen having succumbed to the fevers, the Mary Lane was desperately short of hands. So Captain William Maybe offered some of the stronger Africans a position on the vessel along with their freedom, plus a share of the revenue from whatever profit the Mary Lane acquired. He signed on a group of men, but they had girlfriends or wives with them and rather than separate them, Maybe took them along as well.

It turned out the women were just as able at hauling sail as the men, and they were also skilled at repairing rigging, ropework, and food preparation. True to his word, Maybe split a share of his profits with his African crew and taught them how to use the money in various ports of call where it was generally safe to have them go ashore without fear of captivity—Mexico, Curacao, and Denmark's Saint Croix, among them. In this manner, he gained a loyal crew of free Africans.

Marcus came to realize that, along with his post as a supposed revenue cutter, Captain William Maybe was not averse to collecting lucre from under-armed vessels of nations he did not favor, mainly the Spanish, whom he would halt and board and then request a little gold and silver, and also lady's rings and necklaces and other ornaments which he would distribute to his female crew He was, in other words, a privateer for no country in particular. He carried the colors of the American flag, British when necessary, France, when expedient, and also the striped flag of an American revenue cutter. Also, it should be said, the Black Flag.

Captain Maybey's story completed, more rum consumed (and this in spite of the fact that the sun was not as yet over the yardarm), Biel bid everyone a bon voyage and went ashore.

Biel drew Marcus aside as they left. "Good luck to you, Monsieur le Comte. It was a pleasure knowing you in spite of our somewhat unpleasant first meeting. And be forewarned, your Captain Maybe can outtalk anyone in any language, even those he doesn't really know. And beware too of his consort, Queeny Molloy, she is said to be one of the offspring of Jean Lafitte and is not averse to a little piracy herself. Rumor has it she knows how to handle a Dane musket and how to swing a saber if needed."

He shook his hand and wished him farewell.

******

That very afternoon, the Mary Lane cast off, caught the outgoing tide and sailed slowly out into the Gulf, under light airs. Marcus stood on the afterdeck and watched the coastline fade into a slim ribbon of green under a yellowing sky. He felt a twinge of regret leaving the city of New Orleans. It had the French flavor of Paris, but was far more colorful and degenerate, replete with voodoo queens, wild chanting and dancing every Sunday afternoon on Congo Square, pirates, criminals, gamblers, prostitutes of all colors, con men and crooked slave traders, and the streets accented by the bright wild colors of the clothing of the free population of the Quadroons—a sharp contrast to the dull, gray attire of the grisettes, not to mention the eternal grisaille of the Paris weather. Furthermore he had never been in a place where so many people looked like him; it was virtually a city of mixed races.

The Mary Lane drifted on in calm tropic breezes, westward toward the setting sun, which that evening built a bright, mountainous landscape of dragon-like clouds, billowing and shifting and throwing out rays of crimson and gold. The vessel was bound for a stopover at Key West, and it slowly came to Marcus that they should be sailing on a southeastern course. He puzzled over this, and at dinner that evening with the captain and Queeny, he asked why, if they were bound for Key West, would they be sailing west toward Mexico.

Queeny had opened a good bottle of Chateau Margaux, and the captain poured himself a second glass, drank, and began:

"It's my crew, lad," Maybe said. "They don't like to go ashore so much in New Orleans for fear of slave catchers and their lack of English or French. I thought we'd go down to Campeche for a spell and let them go ashore. They deserve a little holiday, don't you know. Not only that, we might find a little prize along the way." He paused. "By which I mean a vessel carrying illegal cargo."

That was a cover for what was to come to pass.

The answer was followed by an account of his latest voyage along the coast of Honduras before he put in to New Orleans.

"We saw a little chalupa, flying Spanish colors and headed east for Cuba, so we ran up the American colors and headed toward her. She turned west, into the wind, sailing for a little bay there, trying to outrun us. Now the Mary Lane here is fast in any quarter, and by the grace of God, we caught her didn't we, put a shot across her bow, came up with her and I put the lads aboard. Turned out she was not a slaver as we thought, but I didn't like the fact that she tried to outrun us. So my crew searched the ship. Proud to tell that they came back with a good haul, not a bad haul at all. The crew is burning to spend it."

That was not the end of this particular story. It went on for another five minutes, but the reality of the venture made it clear, as he should have known, that the Mary Lane was neither revenue cutter, nor coastwise trading vessel. She was a corsair sailing under the flag of no less than four nations.

Marcus dared to ask when they would be getting to Key West.

"In due time, sir, in due time. We cannot rush these things, monsieur le Comte, one must proceed with caution and with a view to opportunity. We cannot rush, nor can we can we tarry, nor count on the weathers in these parts. Now just two years ago, here in the Gulf I caught up with a little brig, flying the colors of Ceuta…"

Another twenty-minute tale followed that lasted through the first bottle of Chateau Margaux, and on to cognac and coffee and a few off color tales from Queeny of old New Orleans, and verification of details of her tales by the captain, and a little tiff between Queeny and the captain over which dog it was that they had on board on that particular venture, and how, once off the coast of Venezuela, they came across a strange ghost vessel, her sails still set and not a soul on board, and on into the night until Marcus, pleading fatigue, retreated to his little cabin.

Marcus understood his situation. They would get to Key West in due time and then, presumably on to Norfolk.

****

Around noon the next day, one of the crew members began shouting something and came running back from the foredeck. There followed a quick exchange in one of the African dialects, and the crew member went scrambling up the mainmast and stood on the spars of the topgallant. Then he began shouting again.

"Blast!" said the captain. "A fine sail spoiled." Then he shouted a command to Mokuro, who retreated to the helm. Slowly, the Mary Lane came about and made a run eastward, back toward New Orleans.

"What is it?" Marcus asked.

"We think it's a Spanish frigate we see on these waters sometimes," the captain said. "They know us, the bastards, they know the Mary Lane because of her rig, they've chased us before. So it's off toward Galveston. I feel sorry for the crew."

"Why are they after us?" Marcus asked. The captain glanced at him as if to say you should know that already.

"They're Spanish, for one thing, and years ago the Mary Lane helped Mexico during one of their attempts at independence. But it's probably the little incident with the chalupa," he said. "The captain probably made his way back to Campeche and reported us, damn him."

"What would you expect?" Queeny said. She had obviously been in situations of this sort before. She turned to Marcus. "Our brave captain here, he is no normal corsair. A perfect gentleman is he. He apologizes to the captain, shares a glass, cuts the rigging, and then sails off. One voyage I remember there was a pretty senorita on board. He had the crew strike up a drum beat and asked her to dance the fandango with him before he left. Another time there was a frightened little boy, crying. He ordered Mimba to go below and bring up some sweeties. He gave them to the little boy, kissed his forehead and gave him a ruby. No one walks the plank under Captain Maybe."

All that afternoon, the frigate drew closer and then toward dusk, by now still west of New Orleans, the Mary Lane, changed course suddenly and headed straight for the coast. As they drew near the shores, they came to a network of swampy channels meandering through the bayou ahead of them, and the captain ordered Mokuro to shorten sail. Then he himself went astern and took the helm, steering this way, then that. Slowly the vessel entered the bayou and then Maybe ordered the crew to strike the sails and lower the long boat. The sails furled, eight of the strongest men went astern, lowered the yawl boat, and climbed aboard. Obviously, they had done this before.

Using the oars as paddles as was customary in their native waters, they paddled around to the bow, fixed a line, and struck up a song. The boson sat in the stern, pounding out a rhythm on a tam-tam; Marcus went up to the bow and watched as they slowly towed the Mary Jane deeper and deeper into the bayou. They sang as they paddled, a long repetitive phrase—*Wom 'm bola, Wom 'm bola*, striking the water together on the first syllable.

Mokuro stood in the bows, watching the channels and directing Maybe at the wheel. In time, having twisted through a number of curving channels, they came to a wide bay and paddled out to the middle. And here Captain Maybe ordered the crew on deck to drop anchor.

Marcus joined Queeny and the captain at the stern after the vessel was anchored.

"We'll be taking a little holiday here for a while," Maybe said. "Are you fond of alligator, me boy?" he asked Marcus.

They stayed there for six days. The women worked at repairing sails and running gear, splicing lines and braiding fancy work with twine. The men, those who were good swimmers, did their best to clear the hull of barnacles and ship worms.

There were three children on board the Mary Lane, a boy of about eleven named Papi, who along with a younger girl they called Squeaky, scrambled all over the rigging, swinging and hanging by their knees. There was another child, a boy of about three or four who also attempted to climb, and there was also a toddler and a nursing baby. Squeaky worked in the galley and helped serve food and clean dishes, and Papi ran various chores as cabin boy. But most of the day they simply ran around the deck and the rigging, playing.

The captain and Queeny and Marcus did very little during this interlude. They sat under an awning rigged across the afterdeck, drank rum every evening and told stories. At night, the lanterns lit, the men and women, sang and drummed and danced on the foredeck while a hot smoky half-moon crossed the sky.

It was a pleasant period for Marcus, in spite of the fact that they had headed in the wrong direction. His obsession with Tilly was in suspension here. On the third day, Captain Maybe ordered an alligator hunt.

The same paddlers, joined by a harpooner in the bow, set out upstream, deeper into the bayou. Yankee, the dog, knew what was coming and ran to the afterdeck, barking and wagging his stump of a tail. They took him aboard.

Mokuro sat in the stern, holding three sharpened lances and the crew paddled slowly into the winding channels of the bayou and entered into a swamp of bald cypress, overhung with Spanish moss. Yankee was in the bow, sniffing the air, and then began barking at one point. The crew paddled around a bend and they came upon a muddy south-facing bank where six or seven large alligators lay basking in the sun. The men stopped paddling and Mokuro took a position in the stern, slowly sculling toward the sleeping gators.

Yankee ran to the starboard side and began barking again.

There on the bank, was a big eight footer among the lesser few. The paddlers slowed and steered the yawl boat toward the shore, slowly, not chanting. Clearing his lines from the coiled lines in a tub, the harpooner moved to the bow, his right arm cocked. One or two of the closest alligators splashed down into the waters as they approached. Another one, alerted, raised its head, looked at the crew and slid in. Then the great king of them all lifted his huge jawed head. He was a vast primordial monster out the Jurassic Era, and he started lumbering down the bank, his alternating massive legs propelling him forward. Just before he entered the water, the harpooner let fly.

The harpoon arched across the brown waters and struck the alligator's neck; it dove, and the lines ran out of the tub as the gator twisted, submerged, rose up, and dove again, thrashing the brown waters to a milky froth. The harpooner made fast the line and the yawl boat suddenly dipped her bow and then tipped hard to starboard. Two other crewmen came forward and joined the harpooner and, slowly, having allowed the lines to pay out, they drew the gator back while the paddlers kept the boat steady. When they got him close to the surface, Mokuro stood up, balancing himself amidships and made a cast with a javelin and then quickly sat down; the spear pierced the gator's back on the left side.

The yawl boat was loaded with eight men but nonetheless the powerful dives and twists of the thrashing alligator nearly capsized the boat; the paddlers attempting to compensate all the while, leaning this way and that on the port side. As the men drew the alligator closer, Mokuro made a second cast that struck the gator's neck, and when he was within range, he came forward with the third lance and delivered the coup de grace.

Slowly, singing again as they paddled, they towed the huge body back to the Mary Jane.

Once alongside, they managed to work two blocks and a tackle around his neck and behind his back legs, and chanting again, they slowly hauled him up on the deck to be butchered. It took six strong men working the lines to get him up.

That night Mimba, the cook, prepared a stew pot of alligator gumbo, which the crew fed on for the next two days.

The morning of the fourth day was a Sunday and Captain Maybe announced that there would be church services that day. Marcus expressed surprise. No one he knew, even back in New Orleans, seemed very religious, save for the voodoo queens. He asked Queeny, who at this point had become his interpreter, for the odd course of events on board the Mary Lane.

"Ah oui, monsieur." Queeny said. "You'll see the captain is a very religious man."

She went below and came up with a box of cigars.

The entire crew gathered on the foredeck and brought out their drums and a fifer who played a traditional flute called an *oja* that the crew said could talk. A large man pounded the handle of a marlin spike on a barrel in a slow pulse, and the captain went forward and climbed up onto a fruit locker on the deck.

"Dearly beloved, let us pray," he said, in English. Then he delivered a long discourse in an unrecognizable African language, the equivalent of what Marcus assumed to be a sermon.

"What's he saying?" Marcus asked Queeny.

"Nothing," she said. "It's his version of some language none of them knows anyway. But they get the point. Mimba told me some of them think he's a wizard, what they call a *nunimba* priest."

The sermon ended with an enthusiastic shout, and instantly the drums sounded off. Everyone jumped to their feet and began shuffling, forward, then backward, crouching and lifting their knees high in time with the drums. The *oja* sailed off with a whistling, erratic, bird-like call that rose and fell and trilled off in waves. The people twisted and turned and then formed a circled, still stamping the deck and clapping, and a young bare-breasted woman in a red skirt jumped into the center spinning and leaping and twisting and then withdrew. A man jumped in, turned and spun and did his turn, then another and another, and then at some unrecognizable (to Marcus at least) point in the dance, the drums stopped abruptly, and Mokuro stepped up onto the fruit locker and tore off his shirt. His gleaming chest revealed a scarification of entwined pythons and he stood quietly, only the now lower keyed whistle of the oja breaking the silence of the morning bayou. Two men came out, bowed to Mokuro, lit a cigar and gave it to him. The drums began again with a slower tempo and Mokuro stepped down and passed through the crew with a slow shuffling dance, bowing and circling slowly among the crew puffing smoke, his head down and twisted to one side, his eyes closed.

"What's going on?" Marcus asked Queeny.

"He's the chief," she said. "Back in his country—before he was captured—he was a prince, soon to be crowned. Then the slave raiders got him. He was a no one for a while. Then in the barracoons, someone from his tribe recognized him for who he was. He kept a low profile, we think, until Captain Maybe freed him. Word spread in the crew that he was an *Ogboef*, or something like that—very important. He must have learned his English during the trek to the coast, we think."

The singing and dancing went on for most of morning and then carried down until dusk, when the drums and the signing started up again. The sun slowly sank over the distant cypress and palms while Marcus, the captain, and Queeny sat under the awning in the stern, drinking rum and smoking cigars. It was still, the smoke drifted up in gentle curls, and the scent of curried gumbo rose from the galley. No one spoke for a long time. The wet swampy heat enveloped them, the fresh winds of the Gulf were far off and the damp, still air was redolent of mud and marsh grasses and amphibious creatures lurking in the eel grasses. The drumming in the bows slowed and a long, lugubrious chant began, mostly women's voices.

"By God, it's hot, ain't it, Queeny?" Captain Maybe said.

Queeny merely grunted and sniffed the marshy air.

"Reminds of that time off Constantinople, when you and I were young," Maybe said.

Queeny huffed through her nose.

"What a heat, by God, those were the days," the captain said.

"I wasn't with you in those days," Queeny said.

"Yes you were. You're forgetting."

"No, I was a little girl skipping on the wharfs of New Orleans back then."

One of their tiffs began and eventually Maybe relented.

"Well, anyway, those were fine times, they were, and I was young and salty and I thought I could sail on forever."

His talk, his mellifluous verbosity, began again and flowed on, rich with the sound of the dripping waters of raised anchors, the hum of wind in the shrouds, the cry of gulls, the sea mews, headland and harbor lights, and storm tossed sailors home from the sea, blue skies with fresh fair-weather winds, and square-riggers hull down on distant horizons.

"God bless us all, Oh Lord," the captain sang out, "God bless those of us who go down to the sea in ships and on to distant ports, down the green tropic coasts of West Africa, the white line of surf and the boundless dark forest, and we sailed by for weeks, didn't we, on that first African cruise. It was as if the civilized world had declined into wild forest. Not a village, not so much as thatched roof hut in view..."

"Give over, Captain Maybe," Queeny said tiredly.

"No I mean it, Queeny, you don't remember maybe. [Which of course she did remember, having heard his tales for a thousand and one nights.] I sailed the Mediterranean as a lad before the mast, Monsieur le Comte, I know those parts, those classic seas, the isles of Greece, the storied wine dark sea where every wave throbs with ancient memories, golden days and the shores swimming with amber and rose and aquamarine, and great skipping lines of porpoises—by God if it weren't for family problems, I'd still be there now wouldn't I, back off the Corsican coast and out bound for Constantinople."

"What family problems would those be?" Marcus asked.

"Never mind that, my son, never you mind, that was long ago, and we sailed past Sardinia and down the Sicilian coast, I think it was there on that voyage we stopped to off load wine casks. Sailing out from Bordeaux we were—but never mind. It was a fine old time that was, before I sailed down to the Bight of Benin, and then over the open seas to Brazil."

"What was your cargo on the voyage?" Marcus asked, guessing that it was probably slaves.

Maybe dodged the question. "Coir and jute it was, and a rough crossing as I remember. Freakish head-winds all the way. September I think."

His stories carried on into the hot sub-tropic dusk. The becalmed schooner, its sails tightly furled aloft, lay still under a huge fire sky of setting sun and the night cry of herons and egrets sounding out from the obscured mangrove shores.

"Someday, I'd like to get to Norfolk," Marcus said idly, breaking the silence that had dropped.

"You will, my son, you will, but you're better off here with me and Queeny. It's a poisonous city for a tawny fella such as yourself, young-un. Don't go there," he said.

"He's bound to, Billy; he's got a girl around there."

"Well, that's different," Maybe said. "Who is she, a little Quadroon sprite with red ribbons and a flair for dancing?"

"No, Captain. She's African, she's the daughter of a prince in Gabon, a man said to be of great wealth, sits on a throne of ivory, surrounded by his python priests and his concubines, a terrible man, the dread of all, along that coast, a slave raider himself. But she was his favorite child, and then the slavers got her. He had insiders—he was a trader himself, after all—so he tracked her to the barracoons in the Gambia, where she took ship for Charleston. I met her there. I saw her on the auction block and fell in love at the sight of her, small, lively, and a sharp know-it-all demeanor, she picked me, as much as I picked her. She saw me eyeing her and winked."

"So I bought her. I was going to take her back to France with me, and we were booked on a coaster for New York when she got snatched. Damn them. So then I learned that she got sold down the river, so I came down to New Orleans, only to learn that she had run off, back toward Richmond, looking for me, headed up the coast I guess. I don't know what I'm doing now. But I'm going to find her, damn it…" He broke off here.

There was a pause. A whisper of a breeze crossed the bayou and vanished.

"You don't believe all that, do you, Billy?" Queeny said.

"Sure, why not? I had a girl like that back in Havana. Creole, lively as a young filly…" He was off again.

Darkness fell. The vessel creaked and groaned. The waters lapped rhythmically at the topsides. No one talked.

Marcus began to sing—in Spanish—"*En las noches Sevillianas…*" then broke off after a few lines.

"Go on," Queeny said. "Where'd you learn that?"

"A woman," Marcus said. "A woman in Paris. Andalusian Gypsy I think, although she tried to claim she was from an aristocratic Austrian family. Petra. She was a great beauty, wore a red rose in her black hair, and had a fire in her black eyes."

"Is that really true?" Queeny asked.

"Yes, actually. That is true."

Over the past weeks, a friendship had established itself with this odd group—a young mixed-race man from Virginia, a renegade piratical trader from Dublin, and a middle-aged Quadroon woman, half pirate herself. Queeny had as many stories as the lot of them, but she mostly kept them to herself.

As had other older women, she had developed a certain motherly attachment to Marcus. Sometimes late at night, when Maybe was drunk and half dozing, or otherwise dead to the world on his bunk, she and Marcus talked more seriously. She shared with him a bit of her story.

She was indeed, it seemed, the child of Jean Lafitte, although she said it could have been his brother, Pierre. Whoever he was, he never recognized her. Her mother was Creole, and raised her well, dressed her in the best finery, and then took her to the Quadroon Balls. There she met another sea-faring white man, a trader from Cornwall and she sailed with him to Cuba and back. Also Mexico and the West Indies. She was vague about what trade they were in, but Marcus didn't ask. The couple never married, got into a few sea fights, and it was here that Queeny learned to shoot and fight with a cutlass.

"Only a few times," she said. "I think I killed a sailor in one exchange. I couldn't see—too much smoke and noise. But I didn't like it, *moi, non, je n'aimais pas*. I didn't like that."

"You were free?" he asked.

"No. Who's free? A woman isn't ever free. I weren't owned by no one, but I wasn't free."

Marcus told her about women in Paris, the rich women in Mr. Coffin's salon.

"They argued that question a lot. There was one woman there who dressed like a man and smoked the little cigars. She smoked in public and went wherever she wanted. She had a Polish lover and I heard later they ran off to some island somewhere. He died there."

"She a white woman or a colored woman?" Queeny asked.

"White," Marcus said.

"There you go," Queeny said.

"There was a very rich white man in that group," Marcus said. "He claimed that everyone was a slave of some sort. He said he himself was jailed."

"Who jailed him?"

"He jailed himself. He lived in his own prison, he said."

He was talking about the Marquis de Moreaux.

"I think a lot about freedom since those talks," Marcus said. "A different kind of freedom that all enslaved people think about. I do think we maybe do enslave ourselves in a way."

"Yeah, how's that? I don't believe it. What else put you in chains save a bad Massa," Queeny said.

"Love," Marcus said.

"Love?" Queeny exclaimed. "What's love got to do with it? Sometimes, Marc, you sure do talk crazy."

"No, I mean it. You love somebody, and she binds you. You're never free."

Queeny snickered. "I don't know 'bout that," she said.

******

Marcus had come to enjoy the company of these two, the captain's long histories and remembrances. Queeny's lazy, easy-going style. Theirs was a life he knew nothing about. He determined, thinking things over, that Captain Maybe was old enough to be his father. This begat one of his flights of fantasy—the idea that perhaps the captain really was his father. He had put into Norfolk, or Yorktown, and there he met his mother, who in that time, so he imagined, was a free woman of color, making her living weaving Sea Island baskets. Maybe she went to sea with him. Maybe their vessel was raided, and a slave catcher tried to kill Captain Maybe and then stole his mother and sold her in Charleston. Or perhaps the captain he saw her at a slave auction in Charleston and bought her, then set her free, but once he had to put back to sea there was a raid and she got caught and sold again, carrying Maybe's child by that time.

Where was she now, his real mother, he wondered. The pig, Horace Johnston, sold her and two others slave one morning without telling him—no chance to say goodbye.

This was not a healthy fantasy memory but he threw himself into the memory of that afternoon in the fields when he didn't see her in the line. He asked others, but no one said anything except for one slightly slow-witted man. "Lucilla?" he said. "Ole Massa sold her down the river this morning."

With this memory, Marcus surged into another interior rage and jumped to his feet and smacked the rail and shouted a stream of curses at the empty sky. He cursed everyone. He cursed Amanda's father. He cursed Horace Johnston. He spit in the sea at the memory of Mr. Green. And then he imagined that he would encounter Hubbard again someday, and the pleasures of sweet revenge began again. He challenges him to a duel. Then delivers a stab here, Hubbard fumbles, a slash there, another jab, a broadside slap to his cheek, slowly, cut by cut, he kills him.

And in the backwash of this raging fantasy, Marcus wished he could catch Hubbard again somehow. Go back to New Orleans, steal him from the timber camp and kill him. He wished he could meet him one more time.

As it turned out, he would meet him one more time.

****

Captain Maybe ordered another alligator hunt the next day, and the day after that, the Mary Lane ventured out into the Gulf. The coast was clear, and the winds were fair, and they laid a course for Key West, sailing eastward over the blue green waters, a fine curl off the bows of the schooner. Half way across the Gulf they ran into a rain squall, followed by a little rough weather out of the northwest. They sailed on but the visibility was poor. At one point the dog, Yankee, ran to the stern and began barking furiously apparently at nothing.

"Oh no," Maybe said. "Get ye a lookout aloft," he shouted. One of the younger crew members scrambled aloft and climbed to the topmast.

"What is it?" Marcus asked.

"Yankee here is our sharpest lookout. He can smell a Spanish frigate from miles away. Knows we don't like them and there will be a little unpleasantness. He'll scurry below and hide under a bunk once the guns begin to fire. He hates the noise."

The lookout called down in his native tongue. He could see a tall ship astern.

The rain thickened, and try as he might through the telescope, Maybe could only make out swirling clouds. But Yankee was still sounding the alarm. A minute later the clouds lifted, and they saw a ghostly full-rigged ship. Then the clouds rolled back and the curtain dropped.

Maybe ordered a watch, and they sailed on, not making very much headway in the light winds. They sailed through the night. Then at one point, a crew member knocked on the cabin door and said something in his language.

Maybe got up to get dressed.

"What he say?" Queeny asked.

"He said he thought he saw running lights astern of us."

Maybe went up on deck in the rain, took the glass and went astern. All he could see was darkness. Then the mists lifted slightly and he saw the lights of another ship. He watched the area for a while, searching with the spy glass, and then saw, or thought he saw, the vague form of a square rigger, apparently closing in on them. When the vessel faded again Maybe told the helmsman to change course and head south Cuba.

The following morning the rain slowed to a drizzle. The wind had shifted toward the northeast, and then veered farther to the east by midday. The Mary Lane had to sail into the wind for the rest of the day. That afternoon on a port tack, they saw the ship again, a dark etching on a gray canvas. Maybe himself took the helm at this point and came about on a starboard tack. The frigate followed.

Marcus went astern and asked the captain what was happening. There was a lot of scurrying on the decks.

"She's either the Spanish frigate or a pirate," Maybe said. "I've ordered the guns brought up."

The crew carried on deck the four pounders the Mary Lane carried, and set up the swivel gun on the foredeck.

Slowly, out of the mists, the square rigger emerged.

"All right then," Captain Maybe said. "We'll just ask a few questions."

He ordered the crew to hoist the vertically striped flag of an American revenue cutter. Then he bore off on a south, southeast course. Then once out of sight of the frigate, he veered north, then sailed back downwind toward the vessel until the frigate appeared in the fogs and the Mary Jane's flag of an

American revenue cutter was in view. Maybe then shouted something in Fang to the gunner on the foredeck and a billow of smoke and flame burst out and flung a shot across the bows of the frigate.

Instead of heaving to, as an allied vessel would do, the frigate let out a blast of her own with two shots, both of which fell short.

Maybe put the helm down. More shouts in Fang from Maybe, and the crew scrambled aloft and cracked on more sail, and the little Mary Lane showed her heels.

"At least we know what we're up against." Maybe said. "It's the bloody Spaniard."

He ordered the swivel gun brought around and let fly a few parting shots, one of which ripped a hole in the ship's outer jib.

Then they laid a direct course for Key West again.

The rest of that day and into the night they beat on. The following morning was clear and calm, with light breezes out of the south and there, not far abaft, to the northwest they saw the Spanish frigate again. The day would turn out to be a race for Key West.

Spain and the United States were not getting along well in those years, and Key West was a naval port to the U.S. with a fleet of swift revenue cutters and a number of naval vessels, not a port a Spanish frigate would necessarily venture into, even to catch a renegade pirate.

The lighter and smaller Mary Lane was theoretically a much faster vessel, but this frigate was a trim barkentine, and no dawdler herself. She was unable to catch up with the Mary Jane, but she was dogged, and clearly attempting to get within firing range. At one point, just to let the Mary Jane know the Spaniard's intent, the frigate fired on the Mary Jane, even though it was obvious that she was out of range.

Marcus had been in any number of life-threatening situations in his life, but nothing like this. Wars and international conflicts, not to mention piracy, were far removed from beatings and shackles, duels, and even street fights, as well as the constant weight of his race threatening him everywhere he went on U.S. soil.

Somehow—at least so far—the maneuvering skills of Captain Maybe, the rain and the fog, and the roll of the seas, the thunder of a distant enemy gun was thrilling to him.

Hour after hour, the vessels drew closer. And then, just off Key West, Maybe spotted another sail and ordered the crew to run up the American flag. An hour later, he saw that this new boat was no less than the cutter 'Swift', one of the most feared revenue cutters out of Key West and she was headed for the Spanish ship. Now Maybe changed course again, and the two American vessels closed in on the Spanish ship, which turned on a southerly tack and laid a course for Cuba.

Once clear, Maybe left the work to the 'Swift' and sailed into Key West harbor.

The crew unloaded the jute sugar bags the next day, and then stayed in port. Key West in those years was a free town. Maybe left the yawl boat at the wharf and anchored out in the harbor off Caroline Street. Here Maybe, Mimba, Queeny and Marcus remained for the evening. After dinner, they lounged on the decks, listening to the drumming and singing drifting over the waters. The crew did not return that night. Marcus wondered if they had run off.

Maybe laughed. "Run off?" he said. "Why would they run off? There's good money in this line of work. The best they could ever hope for here in the South…" Here he paused. "Well, you know what it's like," he said tiredly.

They rested out in the harbor most of that day and in the late afternoon, they could see the Africans returning, paddling with their oars, in their inimitable way, not rowing.

They left Key West two days later and laid a course for Nassau and picked up the Gulf Stream. Why they were headed for Nassau was a mystery to Marcus but by that time he had stopped wondering about Captain Maybe's erratic course. He took to lying out on the bowsprit, watching the flowing sea, mesmerized by the changing patterns of the waves and the whispering voices of the waters coursing the bows—white-maned horses. Sometimes there he fell into a sort of half sleep in which he seemed to forget exactly where he was and what he was doing and he would drift into a singular state of an eternal present—no past, no future, only the wide sea, the smell of salt air, and the whispering voices of the waves, signifying nothing.

He would return from these sessions feeling calm and even happy with where he was. He enjoyed being at sea. The Mary Lane was an island in the stream, a separate reality for him.

They were hit with another squall a few days out, and after it passed a bright, hot calm descended.

Now the Mary Lane herself was cast into suspended animation; she drifted aimlessly, her sails hanging lifeless in the rigging, carried along by the Gulf Stream.

Marcus was daydreaming at the bow one afternoon when he heard a shout from one of the crewmen who was working aloft.

Captain Maybe came on deck and climbed into the rigging to have a look with his spyglass. There, off to the east, he could see a lone Bahamian fishing smack. It appeared that the recent squall had dismasted the little boat, and Captain Maybe could see a lone dark figure supine on the deck, leaning on his elbow, seemingly resigned to his fate—un-masted, rudderless, and alone in the empty sea.

The captain ordered the helmsman to make for the boat.

The man they picked up was a fisherman from Nassau, blown off course the recent series of squalls, and then dismasted by the most recent blast. They took his boat in tow, Mimba fed him a good stew and gave him water—he had not eaten in three days, and he had finished off his jugs of water earlier.

"I thought I was a lost man," he said. "All around me there were hungry sharks, just waiting."

"But that's life, ain't it," Queeny said. "We at sea, all of us, surrounded by the sharks."

The rescued man, whose name was Billingsworth, looked at her, uncomprehending.

Billingsworth slept in the foc'sle with the African crew, but he shared no common language with them and spent his days on the afterdeck, talking with Marcus and Queeny about the life of the free people of Nassau, many of them refugees who over the years had escaped from the United States. His ancestors had once been enslaved on the Georgia Sea Islands and had stolen a sloop and made their way to Andros Island.

******

The Mary Lane made New Providence Island and Nassau two days later. Once again, the African crew went ashore for a day or so. Then they returned, picked up a shipment of salt and rum, and set sail for their final destination, Norfolk. Or so the captain claimed.

Marcus was almost reluctant to reach port by that time. He dreaded the return to what he viewed as enemy territory and the work that he knew lay ahead of him.

Part Three

At Large Norfolk, Autumn 1855

A tall cocoa-colored man with green eyes, wanted for assault on the subscriber. Goes by the name Marcus Aurelius. Last seen aboard the schooner, Mary Lane, leaving New Orleans. Believed to be en route to Richmond.

Contact:

James Hubbard

Port City Hotel

1855

Richmond Va.

Seeking my runaway, Marcus Aurelius. Last seen Shockoe Bottom.

Often dresses in culottes and a silk waistcoat in the style of a French gentleman. May feign to have limited English. Also goes by the name Mark Coffin, a free man of color.

Caution: This man is armed and dangerous. Is wanted for murder in New Orleans. Report sightings to the local militias or the subscriber:

James Hubbard

Colonial Hotel

Richmond
Eliza and Mary Lou

Wanted: Charles City

Ran away from the Mary Plantation, October 10

Our girl, Tilly, aged 18. A pretty, dark-skinned girl, often wears an oversized slouch hat and has darting black eyes. A female rascal. Tilly is a quick-witted chambermaid, and can be devious, a fast talker. She was a favorite in our household.

Generous reward for her return: $75

Henry Washburn, subscriber

Mary Plantation

Havre de Grace, Maryland

1856

I am seeking a tall, green-eyed mulatto who calls himself Marcus Aurelius, my former slave. Often assumes the disguise of a French nobleman with limited English. May have papers identifying himself as Mark Coffin, a cotton trader.

May be accompanied by a young Negress named Tilly, escaped from Mary Plantation, Charles City autumn, 1855.

Warning: Marcus Aurelius is guilty of murder and abduction. Is armed and ruthless. Do not attempt to apprehend unless well-armed.

Report any sightings to:

James Allen Hubbard sq.

Care of Harbor Inn

March 1856 Philadelphia Enquirer

WANTED For MURDER

A tall light-skinned Negro man, with distinctive green eyes who goes by the name Count Marcus Aurelius. But also may call himself Mark Coffin. He is wanted for murder and abduction in New Orleans. He was a constant and ambitious runaway who lived in France in his youth. Is fluent in French. Escaped New Orleans aboard the packet ship Mary Lane, arrived Norfolk VA in 1856 Last seen in Richmond around the Church Hill district.

This man bears watching. He is well-armed and strong, likely to identify himself as an official French currency trader, associated with the firm Coffin & Coffin, Annapolis, Maryland.

This man is a murderous impostor, carries a dueling sword at all times and is a skilled fencer.

Likely to be attired in the latest French fashions.

If sighted. Report to local authorities. Do not attempt capture.

Late in the afternoon in mid-October, the Mary Lane arrived in Norfolk and docked at the Port of Virginia. The African crew unloaded the freight, but rather than go ashore, they stayed on board in order to avoid capture. The next day, Marcus boarded the steam packet up the river to Richmond.

Marcus, Queeny and Captain Maybe said their farewells on the wharf. It was a sad parting—at least for Marcus.

Captain Maybe took Marcus's hand and put his left hand on Marcus's shoulder and looked him in the eye. "Be brave, me son," he said. "Find your lady love and carry her off, and if you can find us again, we'll take you aboard and carry her home to Haiti."

"I'll do that," Marcus said, knowing full well it was not a possibility, although with Captain Maybe, it seemed that almost anything was possible.

Then Queeny said goodbye and kissed Marcus on both cheeks.

"*Allez, mon enfant. Soit fort,*" she said.

Marcus was wordless for once; he spontaneously took Queeny in his arms and embraced her. These two had become almost like parents to him—albeit wild and unruly parents, but kindly and solicitous. Also entertaining.

"Goodbye, then," he said. "Goodbye to both of you. And thank you for everything. I wish I could sail with you."

"You do that," Queeny said. "We'll be here for a couple of weeks. Go catch your lady and bring her back and we'll be off."

Using his best French tourist disguise, he successfully made it to Richmond, and here he landed and began his search for Tilly. Still in his French attire, carrying a French passport, as well as papers of identity, letters of introduction to important political figures in other ports all along the East Coast, he managed to secure a room in the new Colonial Inn for a week, making sure of his position by tipping handsomely and issuing bribes to the various concierges and maître d'hôtel as insurance whenever expedient. He had learned this trick from an Italian visitor in Paris as a means of getting top service or keeping certain things under cover or more commonly, both. He also took to lightening his skin with makeup and keeping his head covered at all times.

He eventually managed to find suitable rental quarters on Broad Street and finally, after nearly two years, he had a mailing address. He wrote again to Mr. Coffin and Amanda, telling them of his whereabouts and his continuing attempt to find Tilly and bring her north, and if she was willing, return to Paris with her. If not, he would at least set her free.

Given his precarious position in Richmond—Virginia had passed regulations banning free people of color—he tended to stay close to home in the first weeks, walking the neighborhood, and confining himself to a pleasant garden in the back of his house.

Finally, he heard from Mr. Coffin. In fact, he had four letters from him written at different periods since his capture and disappearance. Mr. Coffin had calculated accurately what had happened to Marcus and was wondering where he might end up. He said he felt sure that if Marcus was still alive, he would hear from him at some point. In his absence, Mr. Coffin too had taken up the search for Tilly, partly to see if he could find Marcus. He had written to his acquaintance in Waterford, and learned that Marcus had been there, but that Tilly had been sold to Wheatlands. Marcus had come close to finding her. She was there when he was caught by Hubbard. He learned further that he and Marcus were not the only ones looking for her. The family at the Mary Plantation had sent out slave catchers to bring her back.

Not long after Marcus was captured, they had found her and brought her back to the plantation. Mr. Coffin presumed that she was still there—unless, of course, she had run away again.

Then Marcus heard from Amanda. She wrote in French—the language he had been corresponding to her with to keep her husband in the dark—

congratulating Marcus on his escape and telling him to contact her once he was settled in. She wrote a second letter, reminding him about her brother Robert, now a lawyer in Richmond, who although not active, was sympathetic to the abolitionist cause. She gave Marcus his address and encouraged him to get in touch. She added that she was writing also to Robert to explain the situation. He may have remembered the smart little 'pickaninny' with green eyes they had renamed Marcus Aurelius. With this in mind, Marcus paid Robert a call on a Thursday afternoon.

Robert was Amanda's older brother and had had very little interest in his younger sister and her pet houseboy she used to cater to. But he did remember Marcus.

Robert was a handsome middle-aged smooth-shaven man in a frock coat, a white shirt, and a black silk ascot. He rose and shook hands with Marcus and greeted him in poorly accented French.

"I was told that there was a certain French count coming to see me," he joked. He knew Marcus's story from Amanda. "Last time I saw you, I believe you were about ten years old. I can't say I envy your life, but it sounds like you've had far more adventures than I. All those years in Paris! All I do is sit around here and sign papers."

"I would trade at this point. But if I were in your position, I daresay I would go back to Paris," Marcus said.

"Well, maybe I should do that if things go the way they seem to be headed here in America. Maybe."

After a little more banter and catching up, Robert grew more serious.

"I can't say I like what's going on in this country at present. Amanda has probably told you my position. No civilized nation can carry on as we are here in the South."

"I agree," Marcus said. "But I was the bookkeeper for this devil trader Hubbard, and I have seen firsthand the international economic entanglements. Everyone hates slavery, and everyone depends on it."

"Save for the enslaved," Robert added.

Marcus chuckled. "Point taken, sir."

Then they got down to business. Marcus knew that Amanda was married with children and living at the Tucker's Hundred Plantation and wanted him to visit her there. Robert said that John Tucker was aware of the fact that

Amanda had a 'French friend' who lived in Paris who often wrote to her. Robert told Marcus, he should go in his best French disguise.

"Old John Tucker is—how shall I say—a traditional man. He grew up on the family plantation and never left."

Marcus caught his drift—a staunch believer in the peculiar institution.

"As you've heard, I'm here looking for Tilly who was enslaved on the Mary Plantation," Marcus said. "She ran away, but we think she's now back. Amanda told me you know people there. Do you think they would sell her to me?"

"I do know the family," Robert said. "But I don't think they'd sell the girl to you. I heard they were looking for her. They went to a lot of trouble to get her back. I don't know how Tilly feels about it, but they love her, or at least her mistress loves her, and my understanding is that now she is more or less the person managing things. Old Henry Washburn suffered a stroke or some other mental lapse that disjointed him. He goes out shouting at things no one else can see. Tilly was purchased along with her mother and they raised her from babyhood. Old Mrs. Washburn loves her as her own child and forgives her no matter how much she misbehaves. This Tilly girl is a bit of a wildcat, I gather."

"I know that," Marcus said, smiling in remembrance. "It's why I'm here."

"Ask Amanda about her," Robert said. "She may know more than I do at this point."

Robert rose from the table and went over to a set of bay windows. The building was set on a rise overlooking the Capitol. He stood there briefly, staring out the window. "I know people in that building," he said reflectively. "Friends even. I don't know what's going to happen here. I've got a son. You know of the talk of secession—I take it."

"I do," Marcus said. "It's why I want to get out."

"That son. He's keen on one the Harrison girls here in town. You know the family?"

"I've heard of them, yes."

"Well, that daughter—Lelia—she's another wild thing like your Tilly there. A great beauty. And I just worry my son's going to get himself in trouble because of her. Get into a duel over her. Or worse. He'll go off and work to defend the sacred Cause, just to impress her."

He paused here, still staring out the window. "Damn them. Damn them all," he said. He returned to his desk and sat down heavily, then turned his attention back to Marcus. "I've got papers here," he said quietly. "Keep this to yourself by the way. I've got papers here manumitting Tucker's slaves. All of them. I'm just waiting."

"For what?" Marcus asked.

"Word from Amanda. She's got to convince Old Tucker," He paused again. "You see—how to say it—there's trouble in that marriage."

And with that, he cut himself off. "I don't know why I'm telling you all this," he said.

"It's all right, I'll keep quiet."

"I know you will," he said. "You know, I wonder if it's because, see, I do remember you. Little scrappy houseboy. I knew what Amanda was doing with you. You know, you were some kind of social experiment she had going. She and I used to talk sometimes about slavery and the different slaves on the plantation. She had this thing about you. She'd argue with me and tell me she could teach you to read and write and learn to hold yourself up like a white man. She used to think there was a slim difference between whites and the coloreds. 'Just look how we used to play out in the barn with colored children; we didn't even know they were colored, till we were taught,' she'd say. I didn't disagree with her. But I said that might not be a good thing for her to teach you all this stuff."

"Why would that be?" Marcus asked.

"You know better than I. You know what it's like to be a free colored. You could be another Voltaire or Rousseau, and you come down here to Virginia, and they'll slap you in irons and sell you down the river. But if you play the game, like so many on these plantations can do, you can lead a quiet life."

He paused again.

"The quiet life of a sheep or a cow?" Marcus posed.

"Right you are! You know I am acquainted with a young woman in this town, in fact two young women, not much older than you. One is a fashionable white lady, the other is her slave—except that she's not really her slave. She's actually free, but for political reasons, she pretends to be her slave. She got jailed once here because the court thought she had broken the local laws for being at large without a pass, always a danger for Black people who aren't enslaved, as you know. These two are adventurous sorts. They may be able to help you out in some way. Come back in a few days and I may be able to arrange an introduction. The white woman is a friend of my son, among other connections."

At the end of the week, arrangements were made, for a meetng and, as instructed, Marcus walked up to Grace Street in the fashionable Church Hill district to meet the two women. He passed many stately houses, searching for the right address, and at one point, passing a front garden, he saw a blond-haired woman dressed in the latest Paris fashions, talking with a Black woman in a red bandanna and a calico dress. They both looked up as Marcus passed. He was well dressed in his French silks that day, and wore a top hat tipped jauntily to the right.

Marcus nodded and touched the brim of his hat in greeting as he passed. The women both seemed interested.

"Well, how do you do, sir, I haven't see you around town," the white woman said with a flirtatious Southern lilt.

"No madame, I am new to this city, a visitor," he said in a thick French accent. It struck him that these were the two he was looking for but just in case, he carried on with his French ruse.

"And where might you be visiting from, monsieur, would it be Paris?"

"*Mais oui*, madame, but how did you know? Have we met?"

The two of them laughed.

"Are you by any chance the famous Count Marcus Aurelius so recently arrived from the fair city of New Orleans?"

"I am indeed he, well, not famous, perhaps infamous in the eyes of a few I know," Marcus said, dropping his fake French accent.

The white lady introduced herself as Eliza and then introduced the Black lady as her foster-sister, Mary Lou.

"Welcome to Richmond, Monsieur Marc, do come and have tea with us," Mary Lou said in an unaccented educated voice.

The two women invited Marcus up to the porch for tea and they sat in the late morning light, catching up on their stories. They knew from Robert the history of Marcus and were very interested to hear of his recent adventures in what they termed the 'pirate trade'. They explained that Mary Lou was born as a slave to Eliza's family, but had been freed after Eliza's father died and sent north for an education. She too had traveled, in fact she had spent time in

Liberia but hated it and had returned to stay with the family as a free person. They kept her out of trouble by registering her with passes as their slave.

"You think this Tilly girl is here in Richmond?" Mary Lou asked with genuine interest.

"We think she was sold here, yes, but people are telling me she is probably on one of the downstream James River plantations, the Mary Plantation."

Eliza said, "I know the place. It's owned by the Washburn family. You think Tilly is there?"

"I do. Amanda Tucker wrote to me and said she thinks Tilly ran off but got caught and taken back."

"Well, *Monsieur le Comte*, perhaps we could help you," Eliza said after all the gossip was covered. "We know our way around this town, and there are certain places you perhaps should not go, at least not without a chaperone and letters of intent and introduction."

"That would be very kind of you, *mesdames*, but I do have identification papers," Marcus said.

"That may be, but this is not France. This is not even New England."

Mary Lou spoke up, "You obviously don't know us, sir, but we have done this sort of thing before—many times in fact. You should let us supply you with the letters. We have managed to free a number of people."

They went on to explain that Virginia had just passed laws expelling free people of color, and without proper papers he could be arrested even though he was a French citizen.

"We'll buy you," Eliza said, laughing. "You will be my livery boy, we will write passes for you. That way you can go where you like. If you're stopped, just show the authorities my letter. They will probably know me, or at least my family. We'll write a group of them, stating that you are out on one errand or another."

"*Oh mon dieux*, you mean I will be a slave again?" Marcus asked with feigned horror.

"Just a trick," Eliza said. "You like tricks, don't you, Count Marcus Aurelius?"

Eliza laughed—these two seemed to laugh a lot. "Mary Lou's a slave. She's a slave to the idea of freedom," she said.

"So am I," Marcus said. "I guess."

They invited him into the drawing room and brought out pens, ink, and papers and began writing different passes. Marcus told them where he would like to go in the city, and they furnished him with the necessary documents and warned him about slave catchers who would perhaps act as friendly helpers, and then, when the opportunity presented itself, nab him. Marcus, of course, knew all about this sort of thing.

******

Later in the week, still in his French nobleman disguise, Marcus first went to the office of the register of slave sales and scanned the records for Tilly. After an hour or so, scanning the roles he found Tilly's mother, Serena, who had been purchased ('with a daughter, Tilly, age 5') in 1834. That was the original sale, but there were no records afterward.

He then went down to the slave market at Shockoe Bottom thinking to perhaps pick up some gossip. Although he had only vague memories of the event, it was here that he and his mother were spontaneously purchased on a whim and taken to Greenwood Plantation, where he fell in with his mentor and inspiration, Amanda. At the auction house, he got into a conversation with a half drunken auctioneer named Porter Jackson, a garrulous sort with a scruffy blond beard and bleary eyes. He knew nothing, of course, of a slave named Tilly, how could he? Thousands of young girls had been sold off in this market in the ten years that he had worked there. But he did know of the Mary Plantation.

"They're good people out that way. Take good care of their slaves, 'long as they abide by the rules. I believe they had a crazy son there who inherited the place when the old man died. He got ideas in his head and then set all his slaves free. Then he died. Next generation come along, showed up here to buy a whole new batch. But that was years ago."

"Did you ever hear of a slave trader in these parts named James Hubbard?" Marcus asked.

"Hubbard!" Porter shouted. "Sure we see him around here from time to time. Mean son of a bitch. He used to carry a cane made of iron. Ugly sort of brute, not from these parts. I think he came down from New York. Ole Teddy Benson saw him down here a few weeks ago."

"A few weeks ago?" Marcus asked with as much composure as he could manage.

"Yessir. He goes by another name sometimes. People call him Black Jack Gamble. But that's Hubbard. He's from New Orleans."

"Who is Teddy Benson?" Marcus asked.

"He's just another ne'er-do-well, hangs around here watching the girls at auction. Never buys nobody. He likes to look. He knows evr'body, though. Evr'body an ev'thing. Why you want to know about Hubbard, though?"

Marcus spun one of his cover stories—how he was sent by authorities to find a Haitian girl named Tilly, who was kidnapped from a rich family and sold here in Richmond.

"Would this Teddy know anything about her, maybe? Or Hubbard? We think he was one of the ones who kidnapped her."

"Well, you go ask him. We got a big sale here tomorrow, he'll likely be here."

This was the first shock that day. The second took place when Marcus was walking back to his quarters on Broad Street. On a wall just up the hill from Shockoe Bottom, he saw a poster:

RUNAWAY SLAVE
Believed to be in Richmond
A tall, green-eyed mulatto who calls himself
MARCUS AURELIUS
WARNING
This man is guilty of attempted murder and abduction.
Report any sightings to:
James A Hubbard sq.
Care of Krueger Hotel

There was a man coming up the street behind Marcus and after he passed and turned a corner, Marcus tore the sign down, crumpled it up, and stuffed it in his pocket.

Then he went home to think. Finding Tilly was the least of his problems at that point. His main problem now was the presence of Hubbard.

Church Hill, Richmond
The Hounds Set Free

According to records set down sometime after the New Orleans events, Hubbard had managed to contact friends back in Yorktown where he had been based before he left for New Orleans. Somehow, through the network of slave traders and buyers, an individual familiar with Davis and his apparently notorious timber camp managed to convince Davis that the wild man he had kidnapped was indeed white as he had always claimed, and also rich. Friends in Virginia were prepared to buy him back.

In the end, money was not exchanged. A New Orleans trader had brought in what was then known as a salt water slave, a man fresh out of West Africa. This particular captive was incorrigible, he was thought to be Watusi, or some tribe from the distant interior; no one could understand a word he said, not even the local Africans. In any case it didn't matter, all he did was rage. He was shackled and collared, but if any white man came near enough, he would lunge and attempt to bite, so he was fitted with a wider collar with spikes. But chained, collared and masked, he still raged, growling and shouting in his incomprehensible language and heaving at his shackles whenever a white person came into sight. No one wanted him. But he was huge and muscular in spite of the hardships of the Middle Passage and was known on the wharfs and in the auction houses as The Gorilla. Sometimes as a joke, they would haul him out to the auction block for entertainment and allow him to rage and growl and spit in his chains. Needless to say no one would ever bid on him. But he was just the sort Davis favored. He told Hubbard's friends if they would buy him as a replacement, he would let Hubbard go.

Now, though free, it was James Hubbard who raged and spit for revenge. He was determined to catch and kill Marcus, and using funds from his Virginia accounts, he set out to find him.

He learned from Jacques Biel that Marcus had shipped out with the Mary Lane, but true to form, Captain Maybe never did follow a given itinerary once he put to sea so Biel didn't know where he ended up. For all Biel knew, Marcus could be in Mexico where slavery was illegal, or Key West. But Hubbard had an idea that he was back in his old stomping grounds in Virginia, looking for the girl he always used to talk about.

******

For the next three days, rather than range through Richmond or the James River plantations, Marcus retired to the garden behind his house to plot his next moves.

The first action he decided to undertake was to get rid of Hubbard's posters. With this in mind, dressed in a cloak and a wide-brimmed slouch hat pulled down over his eyes, he ranged the city by day, marking the locations of all the posters he could find. Then he went out at night, and one by one, tore them all down.

Then he decided to lay a trap for Hubbard. Using a pseudonym, he posted an anonymous letter to Hubbard at the Krueger Hotel address, stating that he believed he had recently seen this Marcus Aurelius at Mayfield Plantation. The letter stated that there was a foreman there named Jack Green who had assisted Marcus Aurelius in his last escape and knew where he was now hiding. The letter stated further that Green was a rough customer and would surely deny any knowledge of Marcus, but ironically, given the fact that he himself was free with the lash, the one thing he dreaded most was a severe beating. The writer instructed Hubbard not to hold back. Green would give in after a good thrashing.

Hubbard took the bait, hired a horse and rode out to Mayfield and found Mr. Green. The two of them chatted in a friendly manner, and Hubbard explained politely that he was hunting a runaway slave named Marcus Aurelius, and was told that he was here at Mayfield.

Green seethed at the very name. He said he remembered and hated the smooth spoken uppity field hand with his houseboy manners.

"And where is he now?" Hubbard asked.

"Don't know," Green said. "Wish I did."

“Mr. Green,” Hubbard said, “my old man used to say to me, ‘Don’t Know was made to know.’”

“The hell you mean by that?” Green asked.

Hubbard swished his iron cane in the grass casually. “Don’t Know was made to know, Don’t Know was hung. Don’t Know was put in a pot and boiled till he was done,” he said.

“Is that by any chance some kind of a threat, sir?”

“No, not at all. I’m just curious. Where is he?”

“I told you, I don’t know. Now, I think you better mosey on off the property, with your Mr. Don’t Know and all that.”

“I think you do know.” Hubbard said.

Mr. Green carried a revolver in his holster and reached for it. “I told you—get out…” he said.

Before he could raise his pistol arm, the iron cane slashed down and broke his wrist. Green yowled and struggled to get the pistol into his left hand, but that too, was incapacitated with a swift cane strike.

The pistol fell to the ground. Hubbard picked it up and went over to Green’s horse, and uncoiled the whip.

“So where is he?” he asked. He laid a whip stripe across Green’s shoulders.

Green was undaunted; he charged Hubbard with a head butt, a choice fighting method of men of his class in that era. He was stopped by Hubbard’s knee and sent sprawling. The whip fell again, and then again, followed by a hefty slap across his back with the iron cane. Then after a second or two, another strike.

Dazed and struggling, Green staggered over to his horse, leaned on its flanks and turned to face Hubbard, the blood soaking the horse’s hindquarters.

“Listen to me,” he said weakly. “I hate that son of bitch just as much as you do. If I knowed where he was, I’d be the first one to tell you. You lay off beating me and I’ll do my best to help you catch him. God’s truth, I do not know where that man is. He ran off three years ago, and I haven’t seen him since. No one has.”

“I have,” Hubbard said.

“Where?”

“New Orleans. He was my slave until he run off. He’s wanted for murder and abduction. If the law catches up with him, he’ll get himself hung. But I’d rather kill him myself.”

"Well, good luck," Mr. Green said.

Green's extreme hatred of Marcus was part theater. He didn't hate Marcus any more than he hated any other slave.

Hubbard returned to Richmond to continue his search. And Marcus returned to his garden sanctuary, to plot another means of throwing Hubbard off his trail.

****

During this period, Marcus would periodically take tea with his neighbors Eliza and Mary Lou. He shared the stories of his quest with them, and they listened carefully and even told stories of other people they had set on their way to freedom. Escape was easy part, they told him (as if he didn't know), staying free, that was the problem, especially since the passage of the Fugitive Slave Law.

"She won't be safe until she gets to Canada," Mary Lou said.

"Or France," Marcus added.

They advised Marcus to go out to the Tucker Hundred and pay a visit to Amanda and collect as much information as he could about Tilly's situation. Then they said they would get to work freeing Tilly. For all Marcus knew, they said almost apologetically, she may have another partner, she might not want to leave.

A week later, armed with a variety of documents of passage in case he was stopped, Marcus hired a trap and rode out to the Tucker Plantation.

The big house was set at the end of a long drive lined with live oaks hung with Spanish moss, and as he turned up the drive his heart began to pound. He had written to Amanda to say he would like to visit and she encouraged him to come the following week, when her husband was planning to go up to Charles City on errands.

The plantation big house sat among tall cedars with a balconied second story and a wide verandah. Even before he dismounted, a dark woman in a voluminous skirt came out onto the porch, then turned and went back in. Amanda appeared as he approached.

He caught his breath when she stepped out. The sight her, the face he had known in his childhood years, the memory of the gardens and lanes of Greenwood overwhelmed him. But he recovered and approached.

Amanda was dressed all in white, her dark hair swept up in a loose chignon, and her wide blue eyes moistened with tears. She held her right hand at her breast, just below her throat—the white benevolent queen of a corrupted kingdom. Marcus had never seen so beautiful a woman. His impulse was to run to her, throw his head on her breast and weep bitterly for all she had for done him, all her lessons of the past, everything he knew, all his success in life, were bound in this singular girl and her wild youthful spirit, now seemingly tamed.

But as it was, smiling, with all the demeanor of a French count, he bowed deeply and formally, his right hand across his waist, his left cocked at his hip. It was theater again, he was playing the part.

"*Bonjour madame, après toutes ces années, bonjour.*"

"*Bonjour*," she said, laughing, and executed a brief theatrical curtsey.

She barely recognized Marcus. He was fourteen when she last saw him, and the dashing twenty-two-year-old French 'count' in a Riverdale linen suit and a Paisley cravat was hardly the little boy she last knew, save for his distinctive green eyes. The old flame of love that she once felt surged in her, her admiration and sympathy for him was nearly overwhelming and difficult to hide. She could barely hold back tears. She invited him in and they sat in an airy front parlor on the right side of the main foyer.

"Now *monsieur le Comte*, tell me all about Paris and your life there," she said. She clearly enjoyed his successful disguise.

He recounted stories of his life in Paris, leaving out his affairs and his duels and focusing on Mr. Coffin and his salon, and the freedom he experienced in the restaurants, balls, and cafés.

She listened dreamily and said she would love to go there again.

"Why don't you?" Marcus asked. "I want to get back there when I'm finished with my business here. Come and visit."

"I don't think I could do that, actually," she said.

"Why not?" Marcus asked and tilted his head and spread his hands indicating the luxury of her well-appointed home. She was rich enough, in other words.

She told Marcus of her family situation, her two children, her responsibilities with the social life of the plantation set. Not to mention the responsibility and, in her case at least, the burden of living in luxury while keeping by seventy-five people of African descent working in the blistering tobacco fields six days a week, with no pay and no rights while she enjoyed mint juleps on her wide verandah with her society friends.

She discreetly left out the fact that, according to her brother, she was trapped in a marriage to an older man with limited imagination nor any desire to travel, and not much humanitarian sensibility to boot.

After tea and crumpets, and an hour or so of conversation, Marcus raised the subject of Tilly. Did Amanda know the people at the Mary Plantation, Marcus asked, and Amanda said they are a very nice and polite family, good to their field hands. But she did not know of the enslaved girl named Tilly.

"They have over a hundred people working there I think. I can't say I know any of them by name. They have an excellent cook, well known in social circles," she said.

Marcus laughed.

"That's Tilly's mother," he said. "I know her."

Now it was Amanda who laughed. "I know a thing or two about her also," she said.

"What's that?"

"Well, I've got a talkative maid here in the house; she tells me things I shouldn't know, because she knows I like the stories. Tilly's mother feeds the family, but she's also feeding half the runaways that live out in the woods around here. She's got a drop-off place out in the borderlands where the extra food gets left. Runaways come by and help themselves."

"I know about that. I've had dinner there myself in the old days," he said. "But let me ask you this. If you knew about that. Why didn't you stop her?"

Amanda snickered. "You know me Marcus. I've changed, but not entirely. We've got our own runaways living out in the woods. I know where they are, but I don't say anything to Mr. Tucker."

A silence fell between them at that point.

She looked up at Marcus, and a tear was in her right eye, and she dotted her eyes with a silk pochette.

"What?" Marcus asked.

"Nothing. I'm sorry," she said, recovering. "I'm just so happy to see you as you are."

In fact, the tears were for her situation. She could no longer bear the scream and wails of slaves at the whipping post, the beaten down fatigued demeanor of people returning from the fields at dusk, and the dull indifference of her husband. Marcus had evoked in her a memory of her younger years.

"Seeing you reminds me of our past," she said. "My present situation has become uncomfortable, I'm afraid. I guess I never did like living the way my family and my friends did. Now it's even worse, knowing what I know."

"I'm sorry," Marcus said. "Nothing you can do to change, I suppose."

"No," Amanda said. "Not now. Not yet."

Marcus remembered the letter of manumission that he was not supposed to know about but said nothing. He sighed. "Maybe someday, somehow, all this will end," he said.

"Not soon enough," Amanda said.

"Could you help Tilly escape?" he asked.

"I would, if possible. But I don't know what I can do. Why don't you go there and talk to the family? They're very gracious. They may even sell her, although I know Mrs. Washburn is very fond of her. I don't know about her husband. But that doesn't matter. He's no longer in control. He went crazy a few years ago. Just sits on the porch all day, talking to himself."

The conversation carried on until Marcus announced that he probably should leave.

The two of them went out onto the verandah and stood by the front steps. Marcus started to leave and then turned and faced her, his voice quivering with emotion.

"I'm sorry, Amanda, I can't help it, all these years and all these turns of good luck and all this is because of that little eleven-year-old girl who had the wisdom and sensibility and sympathy and all that is kind and honest in you to see in me a human being and not an ignorant African slave. You can't imagine…" he said. He was fighting back tears at that point. "You just can't imagine."

"I didn't know what I was doing back then," she said. "It began as a game, I just didn't know," she whispered.

The desire to step forward and take him in her arms surged, but she stopped herself and looked him in the eye.

"Now I do know. I don't regret a whit. I wish I had done more. I wish I could do more," she said softly, speaking more to herself than to Marcus.

Just as they were about to part, they were interrupted by the sound of hoofbeats on the drive.

"Dry your eyes, Marcus; that would be John, coming back from his errands."

A well-formed gray-haired man in a riding habit with black leather boots rode up and dismounted. A Black boy came running out as he arrived and took the horse by the reins and led him away.

Mr. Tucker crossed the yard and stood at the bottom of the stairs.

"John, this is Count Marc," Amanda said, "the Frenchman I've talked about so often. He's come out from Richmond."

"How do you do," Tucker said; he nodded coolly and mounted the stairs. Amanda had never mentioned the fact that her French friend was a man of color. Nevertheless, John Tucker was cordial. It's possible that he perhaps thought that all Frenchmen were a different shade.

"I am pleased to meet with you, monsieur," Marcus said in a thick French accent. "It is the very pleasant establishment you have."

"We like it," Tucker said.

The small talk carried on half in French half in English with Amanda translating for Marcus who would stumble along in broken English and then turn to Amanda for assistance. At one point, he managed to slip in—in French—the fact that he would be in touch with her soon about a visit to the Mary Plantation.

Marcus noticed that at one point in the idle conversation, Mr. Tucker fixed his eye sharply and his formerly polite tone changed.

"What is your business in Richmond, Mr. Aurelius?" he asked.

"I am a cotton trader," Marcus said. "I had business in the cotton exchange in New Orleans, where I still have cousins. You perhaps know of them, the Degas family."

"Can't say that I do," Mr. Tucker said. "We got out of the cotton trade here years ago."

"Well, when my business was completed, I came up to Richmond where I also had family from way back."

"How did you meet my wife?" he asked. This was a test, Amanda had already told him many times. Now she broke in and saved the day.

"You remember that, John, I've told you before. He was just a little boy, and his family was visiting Greenwood from Paris. I was eleven or twelve, and we used to play in the fields with my little dog Miss Pixie. I was studying French then, and he had no English. I helped him. You all remember that, don't you, Marky?"

"But of course, madame, how could one forget?" he said in English. "Monsieur Tucker, you should know that your wife was so very kind to a lost little French boy. She is my fondest memory of my first visit to the America."

Mr. Tucker nodded.

The change in attitude did not go unnoticed by Marcus. They parted formally, Marcus shook hands with Tucker, who looked him in the eye without smiling. He then Marcus raised Amanda's hand to his lips. "*Au revoir, Madame, j'espère qu'on pourra communiquer encore un fois.*" he said, indicating that he would be in touch.

On the way back to Richmond, Marcus stopped in Charles City, which was in fact no city at all, just a few supply stores, a bank, and a tavern. Marcus went into the tavern for a glass, but on his way out, he saw the cause of Tucker's change in attitude. Tacked to a telegraph pole, he saw another wanted notice:

Charles City, VA December 7, 2023 I am seeking one Marcus Aurelius, my slave. Escaped New Orleans September, 1854.

Believed to now be in the James River area.

Light-skinned, with distinctive green eyes. An impostor who may feign ignorance of the English language.

Speaks in French

Report sightings to

James Allen Hubbard, Krueger Hotel, Richmond

Attention: This man is armed and a known criminal and dangerous. Do not attempt capture without support.

******

At tea, not long after his return to Richmond, Marcus and his closeted abolitionist allies reviewed the situation: Tilly was almost certainly back on the Mary Plantation. Hubbard was in Richmond, actively searching for him and, so far, the only satisfaction Marcus had experienced was the fact that the ruthless Mr. Green had been thoroughly beaten. The worry was that, now hardened he, Green, might actively assist in the hunt for Marcus.

His allies found this story of retribution hilarious, and expressed their admiration for Marcus's imaginative revenges. First and foremost, the sale of Hubbard to the cruel timber operator and now his revenge on Mr. Green.

"You should work with us when this is over," Eliza said.

"I've thought of that. It's what Mr. Coffin does in his own way."

He described Coffin's strategy of buying slaves and then setting them free.

Eliza and Mary Lou laughed.

"That's exactly what Edward does," Eliza said. "I've got a rich brother in Charleston. When he's in town, he sometimes goes down to the auctions and whenever he sees that a family is about to be broken up, he buys the whole family. Then we set them free and help them with passage."

Marcus told them about his encounter with an auctioneer and the man named Teddy, who knew a lot about Hubbard's modus operandi. He told them he wanted to get in touch with the man to see what he could learn. You should do that, they said.

So the next morning, cloaked and hidden by a wide-brimmed black hat, at ten in the morning Marcus went down to look for this Teddy.

Unlike the other well-appointed plantation buyers who attended auctions, he was told that Teddy had a disheveled unshaven look, and usually dressed in a rumpled dark suit, his shirt open at the neck.

Marcus searched the crowd of buyers, spotted such a man and introduced himself and explained his mission.

Teddy, who was clearly a friend of the bottle, said Hubbard was there that very day.

"He's right up there in front of the stage. Come on over, I'll introduce you."

Marcus weaseled his way out of the meeting and retreated to the back of the crowd to watch.

At one point, the auctioneer brought out a muscular man of twenty-five or so, much scarred, with cropped ears and a face brand, clearly a rough character, prone to run at his first opportunity.

"We got a strong boy here, name is Jeremy," the auctioneer began. "Big buck like this can be useful as a driver once he's broke in, even as an overseer or foreman. You break him and he'll be loyal. I can guarantee you that gentlemen. He's got a lot of years in him, make a good bodyguard if you needed one. Don't see many like this. Do I hear five hundred?"

No one wanted to buy such an obvious risk.

But Hubbard bid.

"Five hundred," he called.

The bidding began. "Do I hear six?" the auctioneer shouted.

"Seven hundred," someone from the back of the crowd called out.

Hubbard bid eight hundred.

The man in the back bid a nine hundred.

There was a silence.

"A thousand then," Hubbard called out.

Another silence. The auctioneer began the countdown.

"Twelve hundred," the man at the back called out.

Silence.

Hubbard kicked the dust. He wanted this type of slave, but the price was growing. He bid again.

"Fifteen hundred, then," Hubbard shouted.

Instantly, the man in the back bid: "Eighteen hundred."

Hubbard looked over his shoulder to try to see who was bidding. He did not like to come out as a loser, no matter what the situation. Clearly, whoever it was in the back of the crowd was competing with him for some reason. The slave perhaps had something going for him that the auctioneer didn't know about.

"Two thousand," he signaled.

"Two thousand five hundred," from the back.

God damn it, Hubbard said to himself. "Three thousand," he called out angrily.

Another silence.

"Three thousand, then," the auctioneer called. "Do I hear more?"

A silence.

The auctioneer tried for more. He knew perfectly well from the records that this Jeremy would bolt as soon as he got a chance. Rumor was that he had actually killed a slave catcher. None of that, of course, came out in the sale.

"Sold then to the gentleman with the cane," the auctioneer called.

Hubbard paid the house, chained his purchase and led him off to the Goodwin slave jail in Shockoe Bottom, where he intended to keep him and use him when needed.

Before Hubbard left, he encountered Teddy and asked him if he had seen the man in at the back of the crowd.

"Yessir, I seen him, a tall man in a black slouch hat. He was looking for you he tol' me," Teddy said.

*****

Back with his Church Hill allies, Marcus recounted his adventures at the auction.

"It was satisfying to see him lose his money," Marcus said. "But I do feel sorry for the man he bought. He didn't look like the type who knows how to play the game and gets himself beaten up all the time. He had a brand on his left cheek."

"Where is he now?" Mary Lou asked.

"Hubbard put him one of the Shockoe Bottom pens."

Mary Lou looked over at Eliza.

"What do you think?" she asked her.

"What's up?" Marcus asked.

"What was his name?" Mary Lou asked.

Marcus told her.

"You all come around for tea tomorrow. We'll talk about this," Eliza said.

Marcus spent the rest of the afternoon in his garden, plotting and wondering what the Church Hill gang had in mind. He went back the next afternoon, and the three of them retired to the front parlor. Mary Lou brought in a tray with tea and short bread. Marcus had noticed that for all her apparent liberty, Mary Lou did do a lot of the menial jobs around the house.

"So this Jeremy," Eliza began. "You say he is a big man with a lot of scars?"

"Yes, cropped ears and a brand."

She asked which of the several slave pens in that quarter this Jeremy was held. Marcus described it. "Goodsell's, or something like that," he said.

Eliza said she knew that jail. She knew the man who managed the pen. Bill Henslow.

"A horrible character, if ever there was one," she said. "As bad as your friend Mr. Hubbard. And you think Hubbard is just storing him there while he's staying at the hotel?" she asked.

Marcus said that was his understanding.

“Well, let us do a little more exploring. We know you like revenge, maybe we can get this Jeremy free and set him on the road north.”

Marcus laughed heartily and slapped his knee. “Perfect,” he said. “Perfect, what do you want me to do?”

“Nothing,” Eliza said. “You just stay out of it. We’ll manage.”

The next day, Eliza and Mary Lou went to the Krueger Hotel and inquired if there was a man named James Hubbard in residence. Eliza’s ‘slave’ stood near a table near the door where there were letterheads and a stack of bills advertising the hotel.

And did Mr. Hubbard have a slave accompanying him, Eliza asked. She was informed that he did not, but he would commonly visit the slave auction whenever one was announced.

That established, the two of them walked up to Marcus’s cottage on Broad Street. They found him in the back garden, reading.

The garden was laid out in a square, and off to one side there was a small shack, presumably the slave quarters.

Marcus invited them to sit and they described their plan. They intended to free Jeremy.

“Are those slave quarters serviceable?” Mary Lou asked.

“They are,” Marcus said. “Whoever lived here before me had a slave.”

“Well, let’s go back the house,” Eliza said. “We have some paperwork to do.”

Marcus followed, and the three of them went into the study left of the main foyer.

“We’ll need you to write a letter,” Eliza said. “Just in case someone asks, can you by any chance imitate Hubbard’s hand?” she asked.

He said he could. Whereupon they sat him down at the desk and told him to write a letter from Hubbard:

While they were chatting with the hotel concierge, Mary Lou had snitched a few hotel letterheads. Eliza spread them out and dictated a letter stating that Hubbard had instructed his wife, Letitia Hubbard, to conduct his newly purchased slave, Jeremy, to his residence at 108 Broad Street.

“See that he is well shackled and bring him out to my carriage,” the letter ended. “Signed James A Hubbard.”

“You stay at home tomorrow,” Eliza said. “We’ll bring him around to you and hide him in the slave shack.”

"Then what?" Marcus asked.

"We'll take care of that. I will write him a notice of manumission and we'll take him up to the nearest safe house and set him free."

"Do you think he can make it? He's a rough-looking character."

"You never know. But we have a loyal band of conductors to get him as far as Philadelphia," Eliza said.

The following day, Eliza, dressed in her finest Paris fashions and her 'slave' Mary Lou, clad in calico and a bandanna, took Eliza's carriage, driven by an apparent associate of the family, a Black man named Henry, down to the slave pen, and told Mary Lou to deliver the letter. She rapped on the door, and a brutish, low-browed white man stepped out. Mary Lou delivered the letter. The man squinted at it, looked over at the rich woman in the carriage.

"You sure you want to take this buck with you?" the guard asked. "He's a rough customer."

"So is my Massa," Mary Lou said. "Jus' make sure he shackled hand and foot 'fo' you bring him out."

The guard looked back at the carriage, shrugged, went back into the pen and closed the gate.

Eliza and Mary Lou waited.

And waited.

Just as they were beginning to wonder, the door open and two guards brought Jeremy out, squinting in the sun. They shackled him on the roof of the carriage, behind Henry, and the carriage moved through the streets and carried Jeremy back to the Broad Street house.

Still shackled, they led him around to the back garden and sat him down at a table in the garden. Eliza explained carefully that they intended to free him, but that he would have to lie low for a few days while they set up the network. She told him they might want to keep him shackled for a day in case he takes it in mind to run off before they got a chance to help him.

Marcus and Henry helped Jeremy off the carriage and led him around to the back garden and they all sat down and Mary Lou explained the situation.

Jeremy was thoroughly confused and sat squinting in the sun, looking from Mary Lou to Marcus, and then to Eliza.

"You two be her slaves?" he asked Mary Lou and Marcus.

Mary Lou explained again. He couldn't seem to understand, but anything was better than the slave jail, so he just wondered on.

“You hungry, Jeremy?” Mary Lou asked.

Jeremy nodded, saying nothing. Marcus was instructed to stay and talk with Jeremy while they were inside getting food for him.

“That man who bought you,” Marcus said. “He’s a slave trader. One of the cruelest in these parts. He held me as a slave in New Orleans for nearly a year before I got myself free.”

“You was his slave?” Jeremy asked. He was still cool and stand-offish, not sure who to trust.

Marcus explained, “Don’t worry about these two women here. You can trust them. They’re the ones who figured out how to get you free. Remember the auction? I was the one bidding to drive up the price for you. I did that just to get back at Hubbard. Then these two women here said they could do more to get back at Hubbard. They would free you, his purchase, then set you on your way north.”

“I done that before,” Jeremy said tiredly. “Got snatched every time.”

“This is different. These two have connections.”

They kept Jeremy for a week, feeding him and strengthening him and then, when they thought he was strong enough, they brought around papers for him. Eliza had written up four letters of manumission, one for each region, and all of them signed by different names. They told him to show the letters to the conductors and they would instruct him which letters to use.

Early one Sunday morning, Henry, who seemed to be a freelance employee of Eliza, possibly a former family slave, brought the carriage around. They gave Jeremy a package of food and carried to the river to a landing. Here, they loaded him on an empty iron ore barge that was headed up to Lexington.

The last Eliza saw of him, he was sitting in the stern, looking forward, not back at his liberators.

“I can’t imagine what he’s thinking,” Mary Lou said.

The escape of his newly purchased slave, and most especially the method by which Jeremy was liberated, enraged Hubbard. And the fact that he now suspected all his recent spells of bad luck—the fruitless beating of Green, the outbidding of his purchase, and now the theft of his property—caused him to believe that his arch enemy, Marcus, was in Richmond and all this was his work. Then he noticed that all the bills that he had posted around the city had disappeared. He published more and posted them. He wrote up a long notice in the runaway slave column in the Richmond Enquirer, and he searched the registries of all the local hotels and boarding houses.

It never occurred to him that Marcus would have rented a house of his own, nor that he would spend his time up on Church Hill, the most fashionable section of the city. He also grilled the auctioneer and Teddy Benson, both of whom had met with Marcus. Finally, he began to walk the streets, swinging his iron cane and burning for revenge.

Then he thought of a trap. He would find this slave, Tilly, who Marcus talked about so often, either buy her or kidnap her, and post a public for sale notice. If Marcus saw it, he would surely attempt, no doubt by subterfuge, to buy her.

But first, he had to find Tilly.

So now, there were two people looking for Tilly.

******

In the meantime, Marcus and his Church Hill allies put in play another strategy. They had seen the new runaway slave bills all over the city seeking Marcus, and they all determined that now would be the best time, by one means or another, to free Tilly and get out of town. Freeing her was the easy part. Getting her out of the city with Marcus, who was now more or less a marked person, was another.

It was Marcus himself who figured out how do manage the flight. He would come up with a new disguise. Changing his clothes and his French persona was the easy part; his green eyes were the giveaway. But he had an idea.

He announced his plan at tea one afternoon.

"I'll go as a blind man," he said.

Of course, the two women laughed; they laughed at everything.

That settled—for the time being—they plotted a means of getting Tilly out. First they had to determine if she was in fact still at the Mary Plantation. Then somehow determine whether the Washburns would sell her, which seemed unlikely. So the Southern belle, Eliza, decided to pay a social call on Eleanor Washburn, ostensibly seeking funds for the Army of Virginia Militia.

The social butterfly, Eliza, was a successfully closeted abolitionist. Although she was considered somewhat eccentric, no one in her social circles suspected her of northern sympathies.

A date was arranged by courier, and on the appointed day, Eliza and her man Henry rode out to the Mary Plantation.

Mrs. Washburn, a pleasant, stout woman of a certain age, with a mass of graying curls, received Eliza and the two of them enjoyed a tea service, brought to them on a silver Queen Anne tray by a pretty housemaid with a devilish sparkle in her eyes. The conversation flowed easily between these two: The latest Richmond social gossip. The unpleasantness brought on by the Yankee abolitionist movement. The constant trouble managing what Mrs. Washburn termed her 'workers'.

The pretty serving girl, having left the parlor, stood just outside the door, listening.

"You must have some good people?" Eliza asked.

"Well, yes, we do, many of the older ones, who know their place. And then we have some lively-minded ones who are good workers, but can get a bit saucy from time to time. One of them ran off six months ago, one of my favorites. My brother-in-law, Conrad, agreed to hire slave catchers to go get her. We had a good idea that she had run up to a free town in Northern Virginia where she had a half-sister."

Mrs. Washburn lowered her voice and leaned forward conspiratorially. "It's that pretty thing who just served our tea."

"Why, she sure enough is a cute little thing, isn't she," Eliza said. "What's her name?"

"Tilly. She is a sly little vixen if ever there was one. But I love her. She's the daughter of our cook. And you'd think she'd be better behaved, that cook is such a strong, bossy woman. Nobody crosses her. And she's as loyal as they come. She's been with us most of her life."

"Why don't you just sell Tilly, if she's so much trouble?"

"Sell Tilly!" Mrs. Washburn exclaimed. "Never in all my born days would I sell Tilly. She's my little girl. Always was a good little girl till she came of age. You know how it is. She'll get better when she grows up a little."

"Do you ever try beating her? A taste of the cat might straighten her out," Eliza asked. This, of course, was cover. One of the things that had set Eliza on her abolitionist career was the fact that she had witnessed a brutal whipping of a young man when she was ten years old.

"Oh my gracious, no! Never. I wouldn't let anybody lay a hand on my Tilly," Mrs. Washburn said. "Against my wishes. Conrad beat her once, or tried to, but she turned on him and nearly killed him with a hoe. Then she ran off."

Out in the hallway, Tilly rolled her eyes.

The conversation moved on to other subjects—horses, Paris fashions, and the Washburn children, of whom there were two, one of whom was at West Point, and a younger son who left the plantation was now living in Richmond, a twenty-year-old boy name Winslow.

"I worry about him," Mrs. Washburn said. "He's fallen in with the wrong crowd since he left the plantation."

The tea slowed, the afternoon advanced, and finally Eliza and Mrs. Washburn parted company, without mentioning the fund-raising donation.

Charles City
Go Down, Moses, Way Down to Freedom Land

The whereabouts of Tilly established, and the unwillingness of Mrs. Washburn to ever sell her, the Church Hill gang plotted their next move. First they had to arrange for the 'blinding' of Marcus. Eliza had a friend who dealt in eye glasses, and she arranged to obtain a pair of smoked dark glasses for a friend from Charleston, for a 'recently arrived blind man'.

That done, they fitted Marcus out in a dark suit, a silk cravat, and a white ruffled shirt and a plain doublet—an average, if slightly dark-skinned, middle-class gentleman, in other words. Then they lent him Eliza's father's light bamboo walking stick. He turned himself into a not uncommon figure in the city in those years—a white society man with what the gossipy local ladies cynically termed 'a touch of the tar brush'.

Marcus explained that the Mary Plantation had a landing on the James where there were often several punts and pulling boats tied up.

"I got away in one of those boats on my final escape from Mayfield," he said. "I could maybe get her out some night and row downstream, to another landing."

The group discussed the idea but an overland escape through the cypress swamps might not be easy, and they would surely let free the dogs. They decided to take her back to Richmond in a carriage.

"You know the plantation grounds, do you not?" Eliza asked.

Marcus said he did, but he was not sure how to get her out to the road. He would have to get word to her to get ready for flight, say goodbye to her mother and all that. They had no way to get this information to Tilly, save through Marcus.

So, traveling in less obvious clothing, dressed in his wide-brimmed slouch hat, and armed with passes and a pistol, Marcus set out. He boarded the ferry to Charles City, carrying a carpet bag and a supply of food and sufficient passes to explain his presence. In this guise, he leased a trap in Charles City, rode down the Landing Road later that afternoon to a convenient drop-off place in the scrub lands just upstream from the Mary Plantation, and set out. He knew the way from his past night visits and went straight down to the river, then circled around along the bank and cut back up to the row of slave cabins. Tilly's mother's place, if she was still there, was the third cabin up from the riverbank.

He emerged from the woods, and scratched on her door. To his surprise, Tilly herself opened the door.

Marcus's heart jumped. He could hardly breathe.

"What you want here, boy?" Tilly asked sharply.

"Tilly, it's me, Markie, come for you like I said I would."

"Marcus?" Tilly said. "You ain't no Marcus, he run off years ago."

"No Tilly, it's me. I come back. I told you I would. Remember down by the river, and I rowed off to freedom and I said I'd come for you. It's me, remember?"

She looked at him. "I do remember. But you ain't he. Now git on out."

"Tilly, please."

"What, please?—git!"

Then he sounded out the warbling mockingbird call he used to use to summon her. "Remember that?" he said.

"Marky?" she said. "That you?" She started to pant. "That truly be you, Marcus Aurelius. You? It can't be you, you run off somewhere. You run off, I never did hear from you and I run myself. And it can't be you."

"It's all right, it's me. I come for you and I love you and I'm off doing all this running around, everything and everywhere and it's just you I love. You've got to believe that it's me."

She reached out, pulled up his chin and stared at him.

"You wait here." she said firmly, and she went back in her cabin and came out with a lighted ember and held it up to his face.

"Oh golly Moses, it be you. I can't believe it. Marky. How you do this after all these years, Marcus Aurelius. Come in, boy, don't let no one see you. Marcus Aurelius, you just come in here and tell me everything 'bout you and why you come back, and, and…" She broke off. "Oh sweet Jessa, I can't believe this," she said to herself. "I jus' can't believe this." She started to sob.

She was breathless now. "You come back for me?" she mumbled.

"Yes."

A huge dizzying wave broke over her, and she fell into his arms and began to cry harder. "You going to take me off?" she whimpered.

"Yes, if you'll come."

"I will. I will. When?"

"Whenever you want—now if you want."

"You wait here," she said. "You wait 'round back of the cabin. I'm going off to say goodbye to my mama and get my things. You wait. Don't go nowhere. Promise?"

Marcus laughed. "Promise?" he said. "Promise? I promised I'd come back years ago. I'll surely wait another few minutes."

He settled in the brush at the edge of the woods. This was an unexpected venture. His intention was to tell her mother that he was back, and if Tilly wanted to run away with him, he could arrange it. Now she was here—unplanned. He tried to figure out what to do. How to get back to Richmond with her.

He had boarded the ferry with his walking stick and his shaded glasses in his vest pocket, and with this disguise he thought of a plan. Tilly would be his slave, acting as his eyes. She would hide in the brush while he returned the trap. And then they would spend the night in the woods and board the ferry for Richmond the next morning, he traveling as a blind gentleman of a certain class, Tilly as his slave girl guide.

By this time, the night had progressed, a cloudy half-moon rose, and Tilly did not return. Marcus began to wonder. Could it be possible that she had been caught. Did her mother forbid her to leave? Then his imagination took over. She didn't believe a word and had gone to get the overseer. He would be captured again and sent to the fields. Maybe she had a new man, a powerful field hand, and she'd bring him around to drive Marcus off. All manner of dark thoughts passed and so he got up and went around to the front of the cabin.

There she was, still stuffing clothes into a wrap.

"Let's go, boy. Let's get out before the dogs start barking."

Which they did.

No sooner had they made their way down to the river, than the kenneled dogs started barking. Tilly and Marcus started running, and then Tilly stopped and listened.

"They're still penned. You hear? They ain't moved yet. They do that some nights. They hear old 'coon scrambling around the corn cribs and they set to yowling. They're still penned up. I think," she added.

They walked on, and then the barking changed. Instead of yapping and barking, they began with a lowered howling bark, a sound all too familiar to runaways, the yelp of dogs on a trail.

Tilly and Marcus started running again. They ran down the riverbank for a few hundred yards, and then Marcus turned left through the thickets to the spot where he had left the trap and horse. They jumped in and started up the road toward Charles City, and soon left the yelping dogs behind.

They had lost the scent.

At Charles City, they hid in the woods away from the river. Tilly unloaded her bundle and Marcus left his carpet bag. They spread out Tilly's clothes and lay down on the forest to rest. They didn't sleep that night. They talked till dawn. They talked after the sun came up. They talked and they talked and finally Marcus thought it time to take the trap back.

Marcus explained his strategy for getting themselves back to Richmond—he, disguised as a blind man, she, his slave and guide.

"I your slave?"

"Yes."

"Don't make no difference to me. I be your slave anyway."

"Yeah, well, I'm enslaved to you."

He returned the trap and walked back, put on his shaded glasses and took up his walking stick, and the two of them proceeded in this manner, she guiding him by his left elbow, he sweeping and tapping the ground in front of him as they walked down to the ferry landing and waited.

The ferry ride was uneventful and the walk up to Church Hill did not attract any more attention than just another blind citizen of Richmond would, guided by his slave girl. With Marcus leading the way, they walked up to Church Hill to the house of Eliza without incident. Had they passed Mr. Hubbard himself en route, he would not have noticed.

On the way, Marcus stopped and showed Tilly one of the posted bills advertising himself.

"See why I have to be blind," Marcus said. "Not many green-eyed people in this town. White or black."

Eliza and Mary Lou welcomed Tilly, and the four of went around to the back garden. Tilly herself had dressed in her house servant's dark dress, buttoned at the neck, and looked more formal than the Church Hill gang expected. That she was clearly uneducated was not lost on them, and the contrast with the philosophical Marcus with his Paris manners and his worldly travels was problematic, although not, apparently, to Marcus.

That same afternoon, they began studying the coastal shipping departures from Richmond to Annapolis or Baltimore. It was Marcus's intention to return to his work with Mr. Coffin and begin the process of liberating Tilly in a larger sense, starting with reading lessons. He had not thoroughly explained this to Tilly, but when he did, she accepted the idea.

"Anything better than where I was all my life," she said.

In fact, as it turned out, she was not entirely illiterate. Her Quaker owner in Waterford had started to teach her to read, but he was such a taskmaster and stickler for detail, she grew bored and quit.

Later that afternoon, Henry came around with the carriage and took the couple down to Marcus's house. Marcus had neighbors close at hand, and so for propriety's sake they made a show of setting Tilly up in the slave quarters, but that was merely cover, in fact she moved into the main house. And there they lived for the next two weeks. Not traveling far afield save for teas at Church Hill, and only venturing out to the market and for strolls along the waterfront and around the Capitol. They might have stayed there forever, save that Marcus and Hubbard were in the same town, and it was not entirely convenient to go traipsing around the city pretending to be blind.

And as it was, Hubbard had not given up on his search.

*****

Marcus received an obviously quickly composed letter in French from Amanda telling Marcus to pay a call to her brother—there was news, she wrote. Guided by Tilly, Marcus went down to Robert's law offices to learn what was going on.

"More trouble, I'm afraid, in the Tucker family," Robert began.

John Tucker had confronted Amanda on her familiarity with Marcus, pointing out to her that the man she so admired was a runaway slave and a murderer. She was therefore aiding and abetting a fugitive slave, which, after the recent passage of the Fugitive Slave Law was illegal, according to federal law.

Amanda denied any knowledge of his background and claimed she had mistakenly fallen for his subterfuge—which, of course, was a lie. She knew all about his escapades and had enjoyed his revenges, especially the act of selling his own master, an accomplishment unequaled in all the imaginative escape strategies of runaways. Nonetheless, Tucker had reported the presence of Marcus to the authorities, which had in turn alerted the private militia who worked the city and its environs. The big danger, Robert pointed out, was that Tucker would discover his Richmond address via the exchange of letters. Fortunately, Amanda had been hiding his letters, and Marcus purposefully had not included a return address on the envelope—only in the body of the letters. But the end result of all this was that they would have to leave the city sooner than expected.

A few days before he got Amanda's letter, old blind Marcus and his guide Tilly were walking back from the Capitol grounds when a man swinging an iron cane turned a corner ahead of them and walked in their direction.

"Keep walking, Tilly," Marcus said in a lowered voice, "and don't look at this man coming toward us, it's Hubbard."

Marcus proceeded, hunched over and gingerly tapping his walking stick, his blind eyes searching the ground. Tilly kept her eyes down and Hubbard walked by and glanced at the couple as he passed.

A few paces along, he stopped and turned and looked back at them. Some obscure intuition or some familiar detail must have alerted him, but he couldn't place it.

Marcus did not turn, but he could feel Hubbard's eyes boring down on his back.

This situation was made all the more dangerous a few days later. Mary Lou reported seeing a man with an iron cane walking slowly up and down Church Hill, looking at houses. From what she had heard about Hubbard, she figured it was he, looking for Marcus. Like an obedient slave, she stepped aside and lowered her eyes as he passed. He carried on, then called her back.

"Missy, you ever see a well-dressed foreign looking gentleman around this neighborhood?" he asked.

"Yessuh," she said, "they was a high-toned man be visiting down de road someplace but my missa say he done lef' this town an' went off to see his people."

"Did your mistress say where he went?"

"No suh, he jus' go—'bout two weeks back, I don't see him no more. He gone back to sea."

****

There were daily steamship departures from Norfolk to Baltimore on the Old Bay Line and so collectively, the gang decided that Marcus and Tilly should leave as soon as possible.

Two days later, Marcus paid off what was left for his rent. On the day of departure, he abandoned his blind man disguise and traveling in style, a French count with a serving girl. Unfortunately, before they boarded the coach, Teddy Benson spotted Marcus and came over to talk. In point of fact, he was more interested in Tilly than Marcus. He was chatty old lecher and asked Marcus where he had found her.

"I never did see a pretty young wench like that on the block," he said.

Marcus said that she belonged to his family; he was delivering her to the family plantation.

The conversation carried on for a while and then Benson mentioned that James Hubbard was looking for Marcus.

"He knows you're the one who outbid him. Plus that buck he bought somehow escaped before he could even use him. He thinks you done it, somehow. He thinks you stole him from the pen."

"Well, if you see Mr. Hubbard," Marcus said, "you just tell him to come around to my place to talk. I'll be back in a couple of days."

He gave Benson a false address on Broad Street, and a few minutes later, Marcus and Tilly boarded the stage, Tilly, the slave, riding on top with the driver.

The next day, they arrived in Norfolk, in time for the departure of the steamboat Polly Ann, bound for Baltimore.

What Marcus did not know is that Benson saw Hubbard a day later in Shockoe Bottom and told him he had seen Marcus leaving on the Norfolk stage.

St. Mary's County
The Calm Before the Storm

From Baltimore, Marcus and Tilly boarded a ferry to Annapolis and from there traveled down to St. Mary's County. Marcus had written earlier to Mr. Coffin, telling him that he had finally rescued Tilly and that they would be traveling soon to return to him.

Their arrival was a welcome homecoming. Old George was the first to greet them as Marcus brought the hired trap around to the stables. George was confused and stood by the door, shaking his head in disbelieve.

"That is not you, is it, Marcus? That can't be you gone all these years. You married now?"

Marcus explained, but George stood there, slowly shaking his head.

Next to spot them was Janey B. She came out of the summer kitchen rubbing her hands on her apron, and then halted, hands on her hips, also shaking her head in disbelief.

"You look like you ain' eat nothin," she said. "And who that skinny girl there?"

"That's my girl, Tilly, come all the way from the James River," Marcus said.

He introduced them and then entered the house through the kitchen where Tilly lingered briefly, as if unsure whether to enter the front parlor.

"Come on, girl," Marcus said. "You've got meet my second father."

Mr. Coffin was already out in the hall, having heard the commotion and he greeted Marcus warmly, shaking his hand. "And this must be Tilly," he said grandly, "the famous Tilly Washburn."

Mr. Coffin thought it best the give these two separate sleeping quarters. Tilly was set up in Marcus's former cottage and Marcus was given an upstairs bedroom.

"Just for propriety," Mr. Coffin said to Marcus privately. "I don't want Janey B and George to get upset. You can sneak off at night if you want, just don't let Janey B catch you."

Over the next two weeks, Mr. Coffin arranged a new schedule for his 'family'. He himself began schooling Tilly, and Marcus returned to his old work, keeping books. Schooling and work took place in the mornings, and after the midday meals, their afternoons were free.

Tilly was a reluctant and suspicious student in the beginning. Mr. Coffin started with the alphabet, then using objects around the room and the house cat, his spaniel, and the horse, he showed her how to use the letters to form words. The old dislike for learning influenced by her hardline Quaker master, Mr. Miller, slowly dissolved, and Tilly soon gained the ability to read simple sentences. Then Mr. Coffin began teaching her to write. She followed along as best she could but half the time she spent thinking about the coming afternoon of total freedom.

Tilly had never known freedom. She had been put to work in the big house back on the Mary Plantation when she was seven years old, and she had been working six and a half days a week all her life, with Saturday night and Sunday afternoons free. Now she was free, but it took her awhile to understand free time. In the beginning, she was uncomfortable with her liberty—what, after all, does one do with free time, stare into space? To busy herself, she would work in the garden, or catch crabs and the local diamondback terrapins.

Marcus took her sailing in Mr. Coffin's sloop and taught her to steer and handle lines. They walked by the river, hand in hand. They rode horseback around the countryside—carrying passes—riding double on the docile old mare Dacey, Tilly dressed in an rude straw wide-brimmed hat and a loose blouse, holding onto Marcus's waist.

Marcus knew of an isolated pasture belonging to the inland farm behind Mr. Coffin's property and they would dismount there and chase each other through the grasses, wrestle and kiss, and break away and laugh. Cynical Tilly did not laugh often back on the plantation, but now, she laughed when Marcus grabbed her, threw her down in the grass and tickled her and did childish things—pretend to be a cat pouncing on Tilly, the mouse. They would also talk at length. Tilly had never been a child after five or six years of age. Joy did not come easily to her. In effect, Marcus had liberated her twice, once through physical escape, and then mentally on free days at the Coffin property.

The one area where Tilly excelled was her singing voice. Now, free in the fields, she sang the old spirituals. She had a low contralto voice, but a very wide range, and could jump to soprano notes with ease, sliding smoothly up and down the scales, as she felt. She would make up her own songs for Marcus, singing in Gullah or maybe making up her own words, Marcus couldn't tell, but Tilly loved to sing. She sang all the time.

Sometimes, in the quieter times when they would retreat to the riverside garden to talk, Marcus would tell her again of the white girl, Amanda, who was the one who taught him the art of free play and imagination.

"You can't imagine what I learned from her," he said. "She was a free spirit, not only free because she was a white girl, but set free by her imagination. There were set rules of behavior for young white girls in her world. Rules she was supposed to live by. But she somehow set herself apart from all that."

Tilly and Marcus had so much to say to one another. Or at least Marcus had so much to say. He told Tilly all his old adventures from his Parisian life and about duels, and Mr. Coffin's meetings and visits to estates (leaving out for the time being his female companions) and life in the streets of New Orleans, and his adventures at sea with Captain Maybe, Queeny, and the African prince, Mokuro, and the wild African crew. She told him about her escape, and flights with Underground Railroad conductors, days hiding in attics and cellars. Then during one of her escape tales, she grew serious and stopped.

"You wanna know something, Marcus?"

"Of course," he said.

"You don't tell nobody 'bout this."

"No," he said. "I won't."

"Me an' this white boy name Jackie," she began. "We done kilt two paddyrollers."

Marcus was curiously silent. "You sure you killed them?" he asked finally. He was clearly shocked.

"They dead fo' sure. Jackie kilt one with ax, and the other went for his pistol to kill Jackie, but Jackie's dog jump up an' bit him, and in all the fighting, I get a pitchfork an' stab him in the back. We drug 'em over into the woods. Jackie steal their guns and they horses too. Then he get down on his knees and set a praying to the Lord for forgiveness, it being that he a religious man. I'm scared they gonna catch us and hang me, but we made it to Waterford."

"What about Jackie?"

"He went home. I don't know what happened to him. He afraid of his Pa. He was a little slow in the head, but that white boy—he save my life."

She went on the explain how she eventually reached Waterford where her half-sister was living and found a place with the upright Quaker religionist, Mr. Miller, who, although he never beat her, was a strict taskmaster. She said she felt more enslaved by him and his lectures and reprimands than she had back on the old plantation, where she at least had friends and her mama, and where she knew how to get away with things. Plus, old Mrs. Washburn was a kindly mistress, favoring Tilly above all others, including, in some cases, her own children.

"Sometimes at night, after I done something bad like spit in the stew and get away with it, I lay down on my pallet and I feel bad about what I done because of ole Mistress. Even when she catch me, she don't say nothing. She just tell me not to do that no more. She some kind of grandmother to me. One day when I was about eleven-year-old, I go up to her bedroom just snoopin' around, and she's in there and she's a'crying. She see me and she say, 'come over here, chile, and sit here.' Then she take me in her lap and kiss my forehead, and hold me in her arms and she say 'the day I die, I'm gonna set you free, Tilly girl. I'm 'a write a will that say Tilly Washburn is a free woman.' I don't know what's going on with her, why she crying, but I feels bad then that day."

"Could have been the fact that she's living among slaves," Marcus said. "Sometimes you get a sensible, loving woman comes along and realizes how bad it is to make people work all day and beat them till they bleed. I know this because that's what happened to Amanda. We had a long talk about the old days, and then she started to cry. I wasn't sure why she was crying, but she told me she couldn't stand to hear people getting whipped anymore."

"Yeah, I know 'bout that," Tilly said. "That ole lady love me. I feel like I love that old lady myself. I feel sorry I leave her like that. She just don't understand why I run off. Mama told me after I run away, ole missus was in tears for days. She up in her bedroom crying all the day long."

They were quiet for a while after that. The wind out on the river dropped and the late summer air was thick and redolent of marsh grass.

Their relationship, the attractive charge of opposites drew them closer. They spent days and nights together, talking and loving and laughing in a world that was new to them both.

Seeing this, Mr. Coffin grew concerned that Tilly would get pregnant. One day, like a concerned father, in a carefully worded statement, he warned Marcus to be careful.

Marcus assured Mr. Coffin that Tilly knew what she was doing.

"Her mother was a food provider, but she was also an herbalist. She knew, I was told, how to keep the plantation girls from getting pregnant. Tilly learned from her," Marcus said. "She brings in seed heads from certain plants she collects on our walks. She crushes them, soaks them in water, and drinks that after we've—after we've been together," he said carefully. "It's a lacey-leafed plant with a big white flower head. And it smells like licorice. She calls it 'binda plant' but I think that's the Gullah word."

******

The autumn set in, the migratory ducks, geese, and swans began to settle on the river. The green marshes faded to yellow, then to brown, and Mr. Coffin and his little family of dark-skinned people grew closer. With winter arrival, they took to eating in the kitchen together, talking of the seasons, the harvest and also, of the coming deluge in Washington, which was a consuming interest for Mr. Coffin.

Things were heating up in the United States. France and England were watching, Spain was watching. Slavery in the European colonies waned and then waxed. The interstate slave trade carried on even though the international trade was technically illegal (a fact well-known, of course, to Captain Maybe).

One certain evenings, at Mr. Coffin's request, Marcus related again and again, his adventures at sea, his adventures in the streets of New Orleans, and, at Janey B's request, the story of his sale of his master, a favorite of everyone.

"You wouldn't do that to me, would you, Janey?" Mr. Coffin asked jokingly (Janey was in fact already free; Mr. Coffin was paying her for her work).

"Yessuh, I would, I'm 'a take you down to Richmond, put you on the block, say—'who here would like to buy a nice old white man…'"

Everyone laughed, although George was a little confused by this family banter, but he did very much enjoy the stories of piracy.

There were periods during that time on winter afternoons when Mr. Coffin and Marcus spent hours together in the office talking over the business. Currency exchange rates were fluctuating wildly in Europe in those years. Italy was in turmoil over unification; Germany was attempting to liberalize and was at odds with the monarchy, and Britain and France were at war with Russia over the Crimea.

Here at home, the political pot had been simmering thanks to William Lloyd Garrison's journal 'The Liberator' and the establishment of The Anti-Slavery Society. The abolition movement grew, fueled further by the voice of traitors to the Southern cause such as the Grimké sisters, daughters of well-known Charleston plantation owners, and also the thunderous voice of the former slave, Frederick Douglass. The Mexican War broke out and the United States obtained Texas and other territories, opening up the possibility of the addition of more slave states. There was bitter fighting in Kansas between the pro-slavers and the abolitionists. Then Congress passed the controversial Fugitive Slave Law and the pot began boiling. And then, finally, Harriet Beecher Stowe published *Uncle Tom's Cabin* and the pot boiled over.

It was not an easy period of history—if it ever was in the United States—for free people of color, yet alone the enslaved.

It was difficult to deal with all this from the little estate on Smith's Point in Saint Mary's County. Maryland was a slave state, and in the town and the countryside people of color, even those who were free, were always suspect and in danger from bands of patrollers or kidnappers. Furthermore, Mr. Coffin's cover trade with American tobacco was slowing. And what's more, Mr. Coffin was aging. He was now sixty years old, and the trans-Atlantic voyages were difficult for him, as he often made clear. Now he officially proposed the plans they had been considering.

Marcus himself had been privately considering all this as well. He was hungry to get back to France, where he could breathe. And then Mr. Coffin proposed an idea that Marcus himself had been thinking about for months.

Marcus was familiar enough with the business end of things to keep the firm running himself, and one afternoon in February, after one of his long preambles, Mr. Coffin suggested that Marcus take control of the Paris office while he, Mr. Coffin, managed the firm from home.

"I'm of a mind to slow the trading business down and live off the Amsterdam Exchange for a while," he said. "You could keep an eye on the rates but lay low and live off our investments until the European financial markets stabilize, then get back into trading."

"What about Tilly?" Marcus asked.

"Take her with you, of course. You were more literate than she is now when you first came here, but you still had a lot to learn, as you very well know. I'll continue her lessons here, and then in Paris you can enroll her in one of the schools for colonials."

This was, as far as Tilly's personality was concerned, slightly far-fetched, but Tilly was smart, there was no question about that. She could pick up French even if she didn't go to school.

Marcus pointed this out.

"That may be, Marcus, but you've heard Tilly sing. It may be that she would take to singing lessons. She might take to opera or French art songs even if she has no interest in reading and writing."

"Doesn't sound like the Tilly I know," Marcus said.

"Well, there's always the popular theater, or the cabaret—perhaps a little more to her style."

A music career was an angle Marcus had not considered, but of course, all this planning by these two men was up to Tilly, and Tilly, being Tilly, would do whatever she wanted when she got to Paris.

On one of their trysts, Marcus brought up the subject of a possible move to a country that she knew nothing about. She had heard all this before, but now it was about to become a reality. She was uncomfortable leaving all she had known, dangerous though it was, but Marcus's repeated stories of what it's like to live in a place where she could breathe freely with no slave catchers haunting her was tempting. So was the idea of making a living by singing. This was hard for her to understand. No one in the world that she knew ever made money by singing.

******

Mr. Coffin was not so devoted to his work and family that he was devoid of a social life. He had a circle of friends in and around Saint Mary's County and also at a stage stop tavern just outside the town, and here he would meet with a group of his old friends and acquaintances. Most were local land holders. But he would also travel occasionally up to Annapolis where he had another group of friends associated with finances, trade, as well as ship owners and sea captains. He and George would also sail across the bay to the Eastern Shore where he would stay for a few days at a big estate on the Chester River, owned by another trader who had a fleet of coastal schooners that traded vegetables to the river towns.

Discussions at these meetings at some point would always involve the widening gulf between the North and the South. Even though Maryland was a slave state, there were those on the Western Shore who were sympathetic to the abolitionist cause, and this was often the main subject of discussions in those years. Mr. Coffin was careful during these meetings with his friends to keep his political opinions to himself. He was known among his friends as the questioner. He was always offering challenging opinions, albeit in his friendly somewhat bumbling, pedantic manner. He did, in fact, like to hear other people's views even though he might not agree with them.

One wintry day in mid-February he returned from Annapolis, and asked Marcus to come into the office.

After his usual preamble, he announced that he had seen a bill posted near the Capitol describing Marcus and identifying him as a runaway slave wanted for murder. He also found a notice in the runaway slave column of the Baltimore Patriot.

"It's this Hubbard's work, of course," Mr. Coffin said, "but I commented on the poster with my friends who work around the Capitol and one of them told me he had overheard a group of ruffians, clearly hired slave catchers, also discussing the posters. It was clear that they were the ones who had put the bills up."

"They're working for Hubbard, obviously, and he's offering a very generous award, $750 alive, $500 dead. The question is, how does he know you're around here?"

Marcus was not sure; he had never told Hubbard about Mr. Coffin, let alone his Maryland connections. The Church Hill women and possibly Amanda's brother, Robert, were the only ones who knew he was headed for Baltimore, and they had no connections with Hubbard, and even if they had, they would never have given him any information.

And then it struck him.

“When we were at the stage stop in Richmond,” Marcus said, “I was approached by a local drunk I knew who had helped me locate Hubbard. He must have realized we were taking the stage to Norfolk for the Baltimore packet. Maybe he told Hubbard. That would be like him. He was a tipsy gad-about, damn him.”

“Well, the fact remains, it doesn’t matter how or why Hubbard suspects you are around here,” Mr. Coffin said. “He may have gotten his crew of slave catchers to post notices all up and down the port cities for all we know, and even around the stage coach stops. But I think we’re going to have to change our plans. You may have to sail from New York instead of Baltimore.”

The Chesapeake Bay
Row the Boat Ashore

The news of Hubbard's slave catchers upset the peaceful interlude that Marcus and Tilly had enjoyed over the autumn and winter. The hound of New Orleans was once more on the trail, and his dog packs everywhere. So far, Mr. Coffin had only heard from friends of the bills and newspaper runaway ads describing Marcus. All the former bills had portrayed Marcus as a pseudo-Frenchman, traveling in style and well-armed.

But worse news came in from one of Mr. Coffin's allies about a runaway slave notice he read in the Baltimore Patriot. Marcus was portrayed in all his various disguises, and worst of all, one notice suggested that he was traveling with a young Negress. The newspaper column even described his faux blind man disguise.

"What to do?" Marcus asked.

Mr. Coffin said they will have to figure out some way to get Marcus and Tilly up to Philadelphia or New York and hope that Hubbard's network doesn't spread that far.

"He apparently understands, or believes at least, that you'll be shipping out on the scheduled packet run from Baltimore to Le Havre. But how to get to New York when all the stage stops and coastal packet ports are being watched?" Mr. Coffin asked rhetorically.

"How about a captain?" Marcus suggested. "We'll disguise Tilly as a boy. And I'll go as captain and his cabin boy, headed to New York."

"I don't want to be no boy," Tilly joked.

"Of course not," Mr. Coffin said. "But there's another problem. Your green eyes. All the notices mention them."

"Damn my eyes, as old Captain Maybe used to say," Marcus joked.

The discussion carried on throughout the rest of that day and on into the night. The easiest solution seemed to be to escape into the free state of Pennsylvania, although even there, because of the Fugitive Slave Act, catchers were abroad. Kidnapping free Blacks was a lucrative venture and New York City was proving prime hunting ground for kidnappers. It was the worst of times for free people of color. But the first problem was getting over the border because of all the local posted notices.

The normal route on the Underground Railroad was not possible because of all the luggage Marcus and Tilly had; they were, after all, attempting to get out of the country altogether and set up housekeeping in Paris.

Late in the evening, it was Marcus who came up with the most feasible solution. "What if we sail from here?" he asked.

There was a long pause while Mr. Coffin pondered.

"My boat is too small for three or four of us, plus your trunks," he said. "But let me think."

With this, they retired and agreed to figure it out the next day.

The next morning, Mr. Coffin had come up with a possibility. Marcus and Tilly could sail up the bay to Havre de Grace where there was an active station on the eastern route of the Underground Railroad and an easy access to Pennsylvania or New Jersey on the eastern bank of the Susquehanna River. From there, they would have to make their way to Philadelphia and find a packet to France, or barring that, they would have to travel to New York City. But it all depended on getting a boat. Finding a sympathetic and reliable captain and crew in Annapolis was unlikely. But Mr. Coffin thought his friend on the Eastern Shore might be able to help out. He owned a fleet of coastwise trading schooners and a couple of two-sail bateau oyster boats with plenty of room for passengers, crew, and baggage. If he would lend or charter a vessel, and they could find a sympathetic crew for the return trip, they could manage.

With this in mind, the next day George and Mr. Coffin sailed across the bay and paid a visit to his friend, John Crowley. They returned two days later with a suitable plan.

Crowley was a somewhat reluctant slave owner, familiar with Mr. Coffin's philosophies, and he had a loyal crew of Black sailors who manned his various schooners under different captains. Crowley offered to lend Mr. Coffin a vessel and a couple of sailors, and Mr. Coffin could sail up to Havre de Grace, leave off Tilly and Marcus, and return.

The arrangements were settled for the following week.

Marcus spent his last days at Beechwood organizing the books he would need, packing his trunks and engaging in long, bittersweet talks with his mentor.

Given Mr. Coffin's age, the rising political tensions between the North and the South and the rumors of war, it was not clear how long it would be before they would see each other again—if ever—and their last dinner together as a family was strangely subdued. Tilly was the only lively one and kept questioning Marcus and Mr. Coffin about France and what it was like, and could she really walk freely in the squares and eat in restaurants. She was warming to the idea, having by then heard so much about Paris. As Marcus had when he first heard Paris described by Amanda, she had begun to think of France as some kind of Black paradise. Marcus tried to add a soupçon of reality, but the lure of freedom was overwhelming.

Marcus and Mr. Coffin had a smooth sail across the bay, where they met the crew, three young men in canvas trousers and striped sailor jerseys. Marcus was introduced to John Crowley, a portly, jolly man, with a substantial belly set on spindly legs who dressed in a plaid vest and narrow trousers. He had spent some time at sea and yachting out on the bay and he and Marcus had a fine chat about Marcus's adventures on the voyage up from New Orleans. He especially liked the story of the loyal crew of Africans.

"My boys are a little like that," he said. "They're loyal. They've got girlfriends and wives holding them here, and they're free with passes when they're not out on the bay. Plus they get around to visiting on other plantations and realize how lucky they are here."

Mr. Crowley, the crew and Mr. Coffin spent some time together charting the course to Havre de Grace. There were apparently some shallows around the mouth of the Susquehanna they had to watch out for, but other than that it was a pretty straight run. Plus the crew had been there a few times themselves on deliveries and knew the waters.

The arrangements made, they boarded the schooner, a clean little forty foot vessel named the Break of Day and set sail for Saint Mary's County to pick up Tilly and their baggage.

They left the next day.

It was a sad departure for Janey B and Marcus who had become close over the time that Marcus was with them. There were tears, but it was partly tears of happiness and hope for Marcus and Tilly. Janey B knew they would be happier. In the short time, she had been with them, Tilly herself had formed a bond with Janey B and they embraced—with more tears.

The waters off Beechwood were a little shallow for the deep-drafted schooner, so they had to truck Tilly and the baggage down to the public wharf. The crew loaded the schooner and everyone got on board, including George, and they chatted for a while on deck waiting for the tide to change.

Marcus was anxious to be off. He had noticed a couple of rough-looking urban fellows watching the proceedings from a bench set back from the docks. He was perhaps by this time a little overly suspicious of this sort, but they did not approach the crew and make casual conversation as slave catchers were wont to do. Nonetheless, he didn't like their looks.

Eventually, the tide turned. George disembarked; the crew raised the sail, and Mr. Coffin took the helm and the little schooner moved slowly down the river.

Marcus and Tilly stood with Mr. Coffin in the stern sheets. It all seemed to be going smoothly; they were off at last. But Marcus did not like the fact that as the Break of Day drifted toward the open waters of the Potomac River, he could see the two ruffians talking with George.

By the time they got out into the bay, the breeze was fair and they sailed downwind toward Havre de Grace.

*****

The banks on this stretch of the bay were lined with farms and forested areas with many tree-lined tributaries and a few sandy beaches and small towns on some of the larger rivers that fed into the bay. This was March, and the bays and inlets were blanketed with migrating waterfowl, scaup, shovelers, black ducks, Canada geese, snow geese, and swans. At one point, the Break of Day flushed a huge raft of Canada geese and they rose up, setting in motion a separate gathering of geese and swans off on the starboard side. That set off another flock on the port side and soon the whole sky ahead of them and over them was clouded by birds.

This happened again later in the day and one of the crew, a young man named Peter, went below and brought up a shotgun. As a low flight of geese flew over, hardly aiming, he fired into the flock and brought one down. Mr.

Coffin steered the boat into the wind and Peter snatched it up with a crab net. They gutted it and plucked it and cooked it for dinner that night while they lay at anchored in one of the smaller unhoused tributaries.

It was a four-day sail up to Havre de Grace, and there was a little rain on the second day. One of the crew members took the helm and Tilly, Marcus and Mr. Coffin sat below in the cabin, chatting somewhat sadly and drinking coffee. These were the final hours for Marcus and Mr. Coffin and they were both feeling low. Only Tilly kept their spirits alive with her lively chatter.

"I don't like that Peter fellow," she said at one point.

"Why not?" Mr. Coffin said.

"He got eyes on me," she said.

Marcus laughed. "Who wouldn't?" he asked.

After learning the purpose of Marcus and Tilly's flight, the crew began sharing their stories.

Peter seemed to hold rank above the two other crew members, Phineas and Chester, who were a few years younger. Peter and Phineas were both born on the Eastern Shore and were sold to Mr. Crowley's family when they were teenagers, but Chester was a runaway who had come up as crew on a vessel from Norfolk and had jumped ship when they landed in Oxford and worked his way north intending to get to New Jersey. He got caught near Centreville, but learned that if he could get over to Crowley's plantation, Upper Heathworth, on the Chester River he could shelter, no questions asked.

They all spoke favorably of their owner, Mr. Crowley. He was an easy-going, lazy man, indifferent to politics and married to a woman who enjoyed making the rounds of local plantations, driving herself wherever she went in a well-appointed trap and sometimes riding horseback on the back roads and trails. In recent years, Mr. Crowley kept telling his 'boys' as he called his crew, about the changes that were afoot in the north.

"Someday soon, you all going to be free. But if I was you, I'd stay here. It's a nasty world out there beyond these shores."

Mr. Coffin explained that when he was younger, Crowley had left the plantation. He went north to college at Yale, then studied the law and came back to Maryland to work as a lawyer in Baltimore, dealing with property cases. He never was a very good lawyer, he kept misplacing papers and the like, and when his parents died he came back, slowed down the plantation farming operation and began breeding horses, and then began letting his slaves run off if they wanted to. He bought a schooner and became a produce trader.

"He never did make much money," Mr. Coffin said, "but he didn't seem to care. He had enough."

The next day was sunny and fresh, a classic late spring morning; the wind had shifted to the southwest and they skipped along brightly, a little wake curling off the bows. They passed empty river mouths, sailed through flocks, scattering birds to flight, and then on the second evening, turned east up a larger tributary. They carried on upstream for a while and then came to a cove and anchored for the night.

Peter and Phineas took the shotgun and rowed up the river for a while out of sight around a bend to hunt for ducks. Back on the Break of Day they heard gunshots. Then later, a couple more.

But the skiff did not return. The evening closed in and still they had not come back. "Should we worry?" Marcus asked Chester.

"Don't know," he said. And then they saw the crew rowing furiously toward them in the half-light.

"We gotta get outta this cove," Peter said as soon as they were in hearing distance. "We gotta get out fast."

On the way up the river, he said they had rowed up a little side stream and had come across a small half-ruined riverbank farm, apparently abandoned. Peter went ashore to explore the place and when he was within a few yards, the door swung open and a scruffy white man with a long black beard stepped out, took one look, ducked back in, and came out with a shotgun.

Peter raced for the skiff and jumped in as the first shot let fly. It missed, but Phineas picked up his shotgun and fired back. The white man was charging down the bank at that point but stumbled, then jumped up, reloaded, and fired again as Peter heaved away at the oars. Phineas fired back again, and this time apparently hit the man. He grabbed his shoulder and dropped his gun, just as Peter rounded the first bend.

The crew hoisted the sails of the schooner and the fugitives made for open waters.

Out on the bay, the wind was light and there was a half-moon, and they coasted along the eastern bank until dawn, at which point they sailed up another tributary and anchored.

Mr. Coffin questioned Peter further about the incident. Were there other houses around, he asked. Were there cleared fields around the house. Was the man alone? No woman there?

"If there was a woman, she would surely have come out screaming, after he got hit," Mr. Coffin said.

"Nobody around, Massa, save that ugly white man," Peter said. "And that old wreck of a house was set under the river willows, covered in vines, and scratchy miserable lands all around. No fields. No cows."

"And were there cultivated fields on the stream bank anywhere?" Mr. Coffin asked. He was trying to determine if anyone on a neighboring farm had heard the gunfire. On the other hand, gunfire from off the waters in the bay region was not uncommon when the duck and geese were in residence. The white man must have been some lonely old hermit.

Mr. Coffin figured they were safe.

Later that afternoon, after a rest, they made sail again, until, at dusk, they coasted into another isolated cove for the night.

The next day, the wind was in the southwest quarter again, and the little schooner plowed on steadily, mile after mile. There was traffic out on the river, although not as much as there had been on the lower reaches. They passed or sailed downwind from coastal schooners and sloops. They saw two-sail bateaus near the banks, dredging for oysters, and open crab boats working along the banks of the tributaries, also from time to time, the little punchy workboats and at one point, close-hauled to the eastern bank they saw a single man in a narrow punt gun boat, hunting waterfowl for the markets.

The favorable weather held for the next two days and they sailed northward, Peter at the helm, the crew handling the sails. The wind was steady and there was not much to do but lounge on deck. Tilly and Marcus got into the habit of spending time in the bow, leaning over the rails and watching the curl of the bow wave. Or they would lie back across the deck, their heads propped against the gunnels, facing the warming spring sun and listening to the cry of the gulls and the shushing sound of the waters. Tilly was content in the moment. This was her first taste of real freedom. She did not think of what was to come, nor what was past, but drifted along in a seemingly eternal suspended state of water and wind and open air.

Marcus too tried to enjoy the moment, and when not daydreaming, as usual, the two of them spent their time together talking. They talked about how they could live out their time there hunting and gathering and growing their scant crops in season.

"I'd like to do that, Marky," Tilly said. "Let's get us some land in the north and just be farmers. We raise some hogs and chickens, plant corn and live out there and let the world we used to know just move on. Don't matter to us 'long as the sun rise."

Marcus did not tell her the realities of such a hard-scrabble life. He knew the hardships of winter, even with the well-stocked larder of the wild foods and local crops of the Great Dismal Swamp. During the winter rains, they sometimes had to spend days in smoke-filled huts with damp fires that threw no heat. And from late spring to fall, the biting insects plagued them and the windless, damp heat made the air barely breathable. He didn't tell her about that. But he did engage her with more stories of life in Paris. The biggest city she had ever been to was Richmond. It would have been hard to describe the shock of what she was soon to see in Paris, let alone New York, if they sailed from there.

As it was, in spite of the pleasant voyage on the bay, Marcus was worrying about what they would do once they reached Philadelphia, free city though it was. Mr. Coffin had given as much direction as he could about getting around in the port and where to find the shipping offices. And he also told Marcus of a hotel near Rittenhouse Square where he would stay whenever he was in town. But he was more familiar with the port of New York. Marcus also had sharp memories of his brief time there, and he thought if necessary, he could find the hotel they had stayed in while waiting for a ship. But he was hoping they could get out from the port of Philadelphia.

One evening as they drew closer to the head of the bay, they anchored just inside the mouth of a brackish tributary. The tide was rising and Tilly went forward and leaned on the rail watching the sun sink over the lowlands across the bay.

At one point, as a fiery red sun dropped slowly toward the horizon, she started humming to herself, then as the sun dipped lower, she began to sing—just low vocables in her sultry contralto, improvising on the melodies of old the spirituals like 'Go Down Moses'. And all the while the sun dipped lower and lower, and as it touched the horizon, it spread out a sheet of red orange light across the greening, distant shores and the gray-blue bay. Then it set and briefly, a strange, bright green flash swept over them, as if this little crew of people, caught in the midst of a chaotic period of human history, had been somehow consecrated.

They were all quiet that night as they sat around eating their oyster stew. No one said much. They knew they were near the end of the voyage: The crew would return to the Chester River for more cargo. Mr. Coffin would sail back to Saint Mary's County, and Marcus and his spirited partner, Tilly would set off toward some unknown future.

In late morning the next day, the wind hauled around to the south, and they had a comfortable sail downwind. By midday, they could see the spires of a church above the horizon. By late afternoon, they reached Havre de Grace and anchored in the harbor for the night.

Havre De Grace
The Inheritance

The next morning, before they made any decisions, Mr. Coffin rowed ashore to make inquiries. What he found out was not good. James Hubbard's hounds, probably calculating that Marcus would use one of the known Underground Railroad escape routes, had posted notices around the port.

Mr. Coffin wandered around the docks for a while, talking to local watermen about the river currents and the river depths, and later toward midday went into a local tavern for lunch. Here, as he had hoped he would, he managed to fall into conversation with a likely looking older man, the kind of weathered sailor and local gad-about who had retired from the bay to spend his days reminiscing. Mr. Coffin bought him a glass of ale, and he was all too happy to talk.

Mr. Coffin verified what he had heard about tides and the water depths, and then he brought the conversation around to people like himself who were only passing through, and then, subtly, and with a certain amount of indifference to the subject, he asked about the Underground Railroad. He phrased this in such a way so that his position on the matter could not be identified. He said he was trying to find a slave trader from these parts who might be able to help him find a slave.

"His name is James Hubbard. He's a big black-haired man who carries an iron cane wherever he goes."

"Big man with a walking stick? Mean-looking?" the old man asked.

"Yes, that's the man."

"Well, a fellow like that passed through here last week with a gang of slave catchers. They said they're after a light-skinned man claims to be French. He put up wanted posters all over this town."

"Is he still around?"

"Nossir, he and his gang went upstream to Jackson Landing. Some runaways get over to New Jersey that way. They're coming back, though. That's no way to cross. That's why they went up there. Man they're looking for takes the most unlikely routes."

Mr. Coffin was now poised to get the information he was after.

"How do most runaways go?" he asked.

"They all go up the Elk River to the Chesapeake and Delaware canal across to the Delaware River. Then on up to Philadelphia."

With this unfortunate information, Mr. Coffin returned to the Break of Day and explained the situation. He told the crew it would be best to sail back to the Elk River and on to Chesapeake City and board a packet for Philadelphia there.

"Other than that, we could hire a mule team and get a tow on the Chesapeake and Delaware canal over to the Delaware River. Then book passage up the river," he said. The crew was not particularly happy about the detour, but they set out then next day, beating upwind now, down to the mouth of the Elk River. They anchored again that night and then the next day sailed up to the port at the western end of the canal. Once again, Mr. Coffin went ashore to scout for passage. He returned shortly to say there was a packet leaving the next day, so they anchored offshore and spent the night on board. They were still in slave-holding territory and didn't want to make themselves apparent.

There was another sad dinner in the cockpit that night—sad, at least for Marcus and Mr. Coffin.

After dark, Mr. Coffin called Marcus to come up to the bow for a talk. He began with one of his preambles, speaking more quietly at this point and saying that they may not see each other again.

There were rumors of war in the air in those years both in the United States and Europe, and Mr. Coffin was not sure of his business situation since there was talk of blockade of Southern ports.

"I may join you in Paris if war comes," he said. "If not, however, I want to give you this." He withdrew a large envelope from his coat and handed it over to Marcus. "I want you to guard this at all times, and I have mailed a copy to you at our Paris address. But do not open it until you get news of my death. Keep both copies in different locations."

"What if you come over during the war, if there is a war?"

"The same rules apply. I will die in Paris—with you at my side, I hope. Then you may open it."

Marcus knew better than to ask what was in the package, but he suspected it was a copy of Mr. Coffin's will, and he suspected he was a beneficiary; he was, in effect, Mr. Coffin's only relative.

There was another sad departure the next morning. They went ashore to the canal boat landing with their baggage and prepared to board. Marcus and his adoptive father were disconsolate. But Tilly was happy to be off on her last leg to freedom, and the crew was happy to get back to their girlfriends.

They knew Hubbard was somewhere in the region, but the escaped slave notices Mr. Coffin had seen did not mention the disguise of a blind man, so Marcus and Tilly resumed the ruse for as long as they were south of the Mason-Dixon Line.

Mr. Coffin and Marcus stood apart from the others in a sad farewell. They were too formal to fall in one another's arms, weeping disconsolately.

Mr. Coffin took Marcus's hands in his.

"God speed, my son," he said. He started to say something more, and then looked away and fell silent. When he looked back, silent tears were cascading down his cheeks.

Seeing this Marcus too broke into tears, He lifted Mr. Coffin's hands to his cheek and held them, sobbing bitterly.

"I can't talk," he said. "Just can't talk." He looked up into the sky and slowly turned his head from side to side.

"Goodbye—Father," he said. "Just goodbye."

From a distance, Tilly and the crew watched.

"Something mighty big going on there," Tilly said.

Mr. Coffin and the crew returned to the Break a Day, boarded, while Phineas sculled back down the river. Then the crew raised the sail and they drifted off down stream.

Marcus stood on the shore watching them leave.

Mr. Coffin could not face him.

Philadelphia
The Hellhound

The packet boat was a steam-powered three-masted schooner and made good time and got to port in Philadelphia late that afternoon.

Some of the whites on the vessel were from Philadelphia and they took pity on the odd couple—a traveling blind French Count and his Black guide. One pleasant couple recommended a good and safe hotel down by the port, which was populated with a mix of racial types, also visiting Europeans.

Once the steamer was docked and the trunks unloaded, Marcus removed his shaded glasses, hired a carriage, and traveling now as man and wife, the two of them, without incident, booked a room in the Hotel Britannia, not far south of the port. There were no questions asked; other people of color as well as whites were staying there. They ate dinner in the hotel restaurant that night.

This was the first time in her life that Tilly had been seated in a restaurant, let alone served by a Black waiter, a skeletal, somewhat haughty man with long spidery fingers. She watched Marcus and the diners around her and did her best to imitate their manners. All of this bright new world was exciting for her. She had never been on water; she had never known the friendship of a white man who did not own her, and she had never met so many free people of color. And the next day out on the streets by the port she was, as was Marcus when he arrived in Paris, overwhelmed by the sea of white faces that swirled around her.

It was a fresh late March day with sun and high flying clouds, and the river was crowded with steam and sail and sleek small oyster boats. They strolled the wharves—a tall foreign gentleman, with an attractive lady on his arm (aka, Madame Tillisande Lavendre from Port au Prince). Eventually, they got down to the business of the day and stopped in a booking office to see about passage to Le Havre.

There were regularly scheduled crossings to Liverpool aboard somewhat second ranked ships that carried Irish immigrants to America. But the shipping companies in Philadelphia had no scheduled trips to France.

Marcus and Tilly walked back toward the hotel, but on the other side of the street, they witnessed a scene that made them uncomfortable. Three ill-clad young whites were proceeding down the street, when a lone, younger Black man turned the corner, spotted the group, and ducked into an alley. The move made Marcus wonder what was going on and after the whites had passed, he crossed the street and went down the alley to find the man and engage him in conversation.

The young Black man seemed as nervous in the presence of Marcus as of the white gang, who he had judged, probably accurately, to be kidnappers, but Marcus calmed him and explained his situation. He was new to the city, Marcus told him, and he too was on the run. The two of them, joined now by Tilly, stood back on the sidewalk chatting. Marcus explained that he was passing through, looking for a ship and wanted to know if the city streets were safe for colored people free or on the run.

"Nossir, not whatsoever. They's slave catchers and kidnappers all over this town. You got to keep your head up and your eyes down, hats off and step aside. But stay around here long enough, you get to know who is who and who to watch out for. Like that gang I just seen coming down the streets, something told me—Johnny, you better get youself out a sight."

Marcus thanked the young man and he and Tilly went back to the hotel to talk things over. Philadelphia was not as safe as they thought it would be. Just as Marcus had been told repeatedly by the Church Hill gang, "You won't be truly safe until you get out of the country."

On his way back from the port, they had seen a few escaped slave notices posted on telegraph poles, and, feigning complete innocence as a foreign traveler, Marcus asked the concierge about them in his thick French accent.

"It is not a free city here for the Negro? I have seen the signs telling of fugitives," he asked.

The concierge, a polite, but formal man with iron gray hair brushed back from his narrow forehead, explained that it was a free city, but since the passage of a new law a few years earlier, criminals were ranging through border states looking to kidnap people of color to sell.

"Any people, free or enslaved," he said. "There was a famous Black man here a year or so back, a well-known writer and public speaker and former slave himself. Slave catchers, as they are called, came up here from the Eastern Shore to try to catch him—sent here by the man's former master."

"Did he escape?"

"Yes. But he had protection from whites. Abolitionists."

"Abolitionists? What is?" Marcus asked.

"People who want to abolish slavery. They too are all over this city."

"We are living in interesting times here, monsieur."

At dinner that night in the hotel dining room, he and Tilly discussed the situation and decided to go up to New York where there were many scheduled crossings to French ports.

And then, as if the situation were not bad enough, there was more to come. The next day, Marcus bought the local newspaper and on the back pages, he came to a few pages advertising runaway slaves. And there he was on page thirty-two.

WANTED For MURDER

A tall light-skinned Negro with distinctive green eyes who goes by the name Count Marcus Aurelius. May also call himself Mark Coffin. He is wanted for murder and abduction in New Orleans. He was a constant and ambitious runaway slave from Virginia who lived in France in his youth and now assumes the role of a visiting tourist. Is fluent in French. Fled New Orleans aboard the packet ship Mary Lane, September 1852, arrived Norfolk in April 1853. Last seen in Richmond, around the Church Hill district.

This man bears watching. He is well-armed and strong, likely to identify himself as an official with a French currency firm associated with the American office Coffin & Coffin, in Annapolis. He may claim to be in Philadelphia on a business trip.

This man is a murderous impostor, carries a dueling sword at all times,is a skilled fencer and is armed with a revolver. Wanted for criminal abduction and murder in New Orleans in 1849.

Likely to be attired in the latest French fashions.

If sighted, report his whereabouts to local authorities. Do not attempt capture. Danger.

Signed,
James A Hubbard, subscriber
Independence Hotel, Philadelphia

Marcus slammed the paper down on the table with uncommon violence. "*Merde alors!*" he muttered.

"What is it, what does it say?" Tilly asked, alarmed at his violent response. She had never witnessed such a reaction.

"It's Hubbard again. It's an escape notice, claiming I'm wanted for murder and describing me in detail. That's settles it. We go to New York."

****

They booked passage on a coastal packet the next day, fled the city, and arrived in New York City a day later.

New York City
The Dance of Death

If Philadelphia was confusing to Tilly, New York City was even more so. Noise, smoke, people rushing, almost running everywhere. No one moved that fast where she came from. Also dirty—trash, broken pottery on the streets, ragged white urchins, bared-footed and dressed in deplorable rags, some smoking little cigars, some sitting on the curbsides, staring into space, empty-eyed. It was not the freedom she had expected.

They found the Hotel Utah where Marcus and Mr. Coffin had stayed years ago before they sailed for Paris, and the concierge even remembered Mr. Coffin. He often stayed there while waiting for a ship. It was not an entirely up-scale hotel, but Marcus noticed that there were other mixed-race people staying there as well as many middle-class white couples. The next day, Marcus bought a copy of the New York Herald and scoured the shipping news. He found a packet leaving for Le Havre the following week. That very afternoon, they went down to the port and booked passage.

"One more week, Tilly, then you're truly free," he told her.

There were not many passengers signed on and Marcus was able to purchase a sizable cabin just aft of the main saloon. But like it or not, they would have to spend the week in the city, which in the 1850s was in turmoil, especially if you were a person of color.

In those years, slave catchers were swarming over the city, kidnapping runaway slaves and free people of color alike and carrying them over the Mason-Dixon Line for sale. The hotel concierge was polite enough and civilized enough to take in an apparently moneyed Black couple to rent a suite of rooms. Count Marcus Aurelius was sophisticated enough to know that money was blind to race and he tipped the maître d'hôtel and the waiters handsomely.

They spent three days shopping for clothes for Tilly and buying staples to sustain them on the voyage across. But they stayed as best they could in the better neighborhoods around Washington Square, where they spent most of their idle hours, eating in local luncheon spots and taking tea in the afternoons.

They also went down to Wall Street and spent the day wandering the streets, taking in the locale. As long as they stayed away from the more isolated impoverished streets, they enjoyed a certain freedom. People did not stare at them around Wall Street, or even the Bowery and Washington Square. Elsewhere south of the Mason-Dixon Line, there were eyes on them all the time, or at least they felt so. New York, squalid, noisy, busy, rude and crowded as it was, was far preferable. But they heard that there were slave catchers everywhere in the city. There was even a well-connected group of whites who formed an organization of slave catchers they jokingly termed 'the kidnapper's club' that consisted of a network of well-funded supporters of the trade and who enjoyed a certain indifference from the local authorities.

Occasionally, Tilly would tire of their afternoon jaunts and the constant motion and business of the city and rest in their room, practicing her reading and her new accent and vocabulary. She had come to appreciate the benefits of learning and carriage, whereas, earlier, she had scoffed at what she thought of as useless frivolities. She understood that it was easier to be free if you were able to at act free.

During these quiet times, Marcus would tour the wharves. He found the bark they were to sail on, 'Victory', lying at dock, loading cargo, and he chatted with the crew for a while. If winds held fair, as they had been over the past few days, the vessel was scheduled to sail on time.

He returned to his room late one afternoon after one of his jaunts and found that Tilly was not there. She sometimes would take tea in the parlor, but she was not there either. He asked the concierge if she had gone out.

"No," said. "But there was a man here, looking for her."

"What did he look like?"

"A big man, rough about the edges. He left a letter for you."

The concierge rummaged around in a drawer and handed Marcus an envelope with his name on it.

Marcus suspected the worst, but managed to feign indifference, and took the letter into the parlor. Then he read it and instantly crumpled it into a tight ball, his teeth gritted. His hands began to shake and he stood up and went out into the streets and began walking as fast as could, cursing, his fists opening and closing. He walked so long and so fast and with such blinding rage consuming him that he got lost and had to pick his way back to the hotel, still raging.

The letter was from Hubbard. In effect, it stated that Hubbard was holding Tilly at a certain address in the city, and if he wished to pay a visit, he should feel free to come over.

"Alternatively," it read, "if you wish to take ship without her, I will understand. This type of fertile wench will bring a very good price in the New Orleans slave market."

Back at his hotel, Marcus went straight to the hotel bar and ordered a cognac. Then another. Then he went to his room, armed himself with Hubbard's Starr revolver and Coulax sword and went down to the check-in desk and with all the composure he could summon, asked how to get to the address.

The concierge read it and looked up at Marcus. "Why do you want to go there, Monsieur?"

"I have an old friend who is in trouble there and needs some help," he said.

"Sir, I think it only fair to warn you about something. Would you step in here?"

Marcus considered and then followed the man to a small office behind the front desk and sat down. "What is it?" he asked.

"Mr. Aurelius, sir, this address is in the Five Points District. It is not the best section of the city. Outsiders generally do not enter there. Is it an emergency?"

"Yes, my friend is in trouble there, a known criminal has him in hand and is asking for ransom."

The concierge considered this for a moment.

"Normally, you should go to the police with this and ask for an escort. But I'm afraid that would not be feasible. Even the police do not go in there, except in battalions, and even then, some do not come out."

"I'm afraid I have no choice."

"Is this 'friend', perchance, your wife?"

"Yes."

"And is the burly man who left the letter her kidnapper?"

"Yes."

"In that case, sir, I understand, and I wish you luck. His type is a plague in our town. But the police cannot help you, nor can the city government. This is a sad part of our history now, I have to tell you, since you are not from this country. New York City is now a cauldron of corruption. Slave catchers abound here. Theoretically, before someone can be sent back into slavery, there has to be a trial. No such thing exists here, or exists only rarely when there is substantial bribery."

"Officials in this city will do anything to keep the markets running smoothly. High-level financiers and politicians, the police force, judges, plus lawyers, plus, of course, the kidnappers themselves are all bound in a network of crime."

"My point is, sir, you are on your own in this venture; no one will help you. I tell you all this just so you know what you're up against," he said.

Marcus was grateful for the lesson, which, although he did not say as much, did not surprise him at all.

"I understand," Marcus said. "In some ways, it is no different in Paris, the same conflicts. But I have been in difficult situations of this sort in the past. I am prepared. In this case, I know the criminal. He is a notorious slave trader and a murderer. It's me he's really after, not my wife. He's using her as bait, and I intend to bite. And bite hard."

"Here's to you, then," the concierge said.

"Thanks for the warnings," Marcus said.

******

The Five Points District was too far from the hotel to walk so Marcus hired a hackney and asked to be dropped outside the neighborhood.

The driver was an elderly Black man. He turned to Marcus after he was paid. "You not going in there, are you, sir?"

"I'm afraid I am. I have to."

The old man shook his head and mumbled in amazement. "You got a gun?" he asked.

"I do," Marcus said.

"Well, charge it. And good luck."

The passage through the street proved an expedition through an urban version of some ruined, war-torn underworld hell populated with dangerous beasts in the form of cruel-eyed white men in bowlers, carrying sticks and knives and clubs. One man had a dead rabbit dangling from his belt. There were barrels spilling over with garbage; rats scurried across his path as he walked slowly, checking the buildings. The walls of the buildings dripped with dank, odiferous mold that spread onto the very streets. The buildings leaned toward him ominously as he threaded his way through sunless canyons. Crowds of shoeless urchins dressed in rags called to him as he passed.

In time, he came to an open square and a tenement known as the Old Brewery. He entered, climbed to the second floor as directed, and walked down a rubbish-strewn corridor to a door at the end of the hall. More rats scattered as he walked.

He knocked on the door, but there was no response.

Marcus could hear shuffling inside and what sounded like a chair falling to the floor.

"Do come in," Hubbard called out. "The door is open."

Marcus slowly pushed open the door and came face to face with his nemesis.

Time held them in a frozen frame, a burly white man holding a derringer to the temple of young Black girl in front of him, his left hand encircling her waist, right hand holding the pistol. A and facing them, a light-skinned man of African descent, his left foot forward, left hand on his thigh, his right hand holding the half-opened door behind him. The light was dim, the smell of garbage and must filled the air; the room was strewn with cracked furniture and two overturned chairs, as if there had been a struggle.

And so here they stood—two powerful forces, both playthings of the fates, one a descendant of the squalor of Five Points, and the other the child of a legal system of human bondage, faced off like opposing armies before a battle.

"Drop the weapons," Hubbard said in a cool voice.

Marcus paused.

"Drop, I said."

Marcus slowly loosened the sash holding his sword hilt.

"Don't do it, Marky," Tilly said.

"Go on, drop the weapons. You and I are going to have a little talk about the old days in New Orleans," Hubbard said. Marcus was silent; his sword clattered to the floor.

"Marky," Tilly cautioned.

“Shut up,” Hubbard said. “Now get rid of the revolver I see under your coat. And don’t get any ideas about trying to shoot your way out of this or you won’t see your little lady friend here live through it.”

Marcus withdrew the pistol and dropped it, whereupon Tilly suddenly collapsed heavily on the floor in a dead faint.

****

It takes less than a second for a person to fall to the ground, even less time for a man to glance down at her, and one second more for a flying human figure, head down, to butt a burly man off-balance and less than another second to deliver a swift kick to the jaw, and a fourth second to chop the wrist of Hubbard’s right hand and kick a derringer across the room.

Two seconds later, Tilly jumped up from her supposed faint, which was no faint at all, just a calculated diversion. What followed was a scrambled confusion of fighters. Hubbard attacked;, Marcus dodged the charging bull;; Tilly snatched up Marcus’s fallen sword and jabbed Hubbard, who turned on her, only to be kicked in the head by Marcus, who then grabbed the sword and shouted at Tilly to snatch up the derringer and retreat.

And so there they were, the two arch enemies, one armed, the other bleeding from a sword wound in his side and a bruised face from a kick.

Marcus stood apart, his sword in the en garde position.

“Mr. Hubbard, sir,” Marcus said with mock politesse. “I believe you have a sword of your own over by the wall. Why don’t you go over there and pick it up.”

This only served to enrage the fallen bull more. He jumped up and charged, swinging his fists madly. Marcus dodged again and delivered a whip-like swat as the bull stumbled past.

Marcus stepped back and held his sword in the point in line position, standing sidewise, his arm extended toward his opponent.

“My good man,” Marcus said. “You would do better to be armed in this little misunderstanding. Why don’t you walk over there and pick up your sword.”

Hubbard stood facing Marcus his jaw jutted forward teeth gritted.

“Go get your sword!” Marcus said, and nicked Hubbard’s left shoulder with a slight hit, just to urge him along.

At this point, Hubbard was facing an inevitable loss. In the confusion, Tilly had managed to pick up Marcus's dropped revolver and aimed it at Hubbard.

"Dat's right ole Pig," Tilly said. "You git over there, pick up dat sword. Git on now!" She cocked the revolver.

Still glaring with hatred at his former slave, Hubbard crossed the room and picked up his sword and rushed Marcus, his sword raised.

Marcus dodged again.

"*En garde, monsieur, en garde s'il vous plait,*" Marcus said.

Mr. Hubbard responded with another unprofessional lunge, easily parried.

"*Non, non mon vieux*, not like that," Marcus said. "Rather impertinent, if I do say. You always wanted to be a gentleman, did you not? Well then good sir, you must behave as a gentleman."

At this point, Marcus tapped the tip of his sword on the floor, indicating that he was ready for a formal duel.

"Like that, Mr. Hubbard, sir, like a proper gentleman in a fair duel," Marcus said. "*Alors, en garde. En garde s'il vous plait*," Hubbard's response was another lunge.

Another swat from Marcus.

Tilly spoke up again. "Git up ole wallowin' Pig. Git youself up and fight like a genelman."

Her taunts seemed to enrage Hubbard more than the formal, mocking requests from Marcus.

"Come on Jimmy, stop that," Marcus said. "If you best me, I'll surrender. Take your position, please."

This time the response was a stream of invectives mixed in with self-pity. "I taught you all you know, you little rascal. Saved you from the auction block, didn't I? Saved you from the fields God damn you, who do you think you are? You're an animal like the rest of your low life race, an animal just out of the jungle."

"Come, come, now, that's no way for a gentleman to speak," Marcus said. "There are ladies present. "

"Dat's right. Shut you face dirty pig," Tilly said.

Marcus delivered another hit to Hubbard's left shoulder, which was already bloodied. Then he began to taunt the bull with a series of shallow cuts.

"There's for Maisie," he said. "This for Lucilla." Then a more serious stab. "That's for Pikey," he said. "And this is for the glory of Africa." A serious jab to Hubbard's right shoulder.

"I await your response, Jimmy Hubbard." The wild bull's answer was another lunge.

This time Marcus delivered a serious stab, closer to Hubbard neck. His tone changed.

"Fight, will you." he said. "Come on. This is too easy."

Hubbard stood, his sword down at his side, as if in defeat.

"Come, on," Marcus said. "Pick up your sword. Fight."

"OK then," Hubbard said; he raised his sword, and executed two formal lunges, both parried. Then Marcus retreated again, employing his chosen technique of wearing out his opponent before executing a final hit. They swirled around the room, Hubbard charging, Marcus retreating.

"Dat right ole Pig," Tilly called out. "Stop you dancin' an' fight back. I bet you cain't kill dat bad-behave slave of you'n. Come on. Fight him."

Hubbard's response was to turn and charge Tilly in an uncontrolled, irrational rage, his sword raised.

At no more than two yards from Tilly, there was an explosion of sound and a flash of light and Hubbard fell backward, unmoving.

Tilly stood, the smoking revolver at her side.

"NO," she screamed. "NO. I didn't mean dat. I done kilt another white man. I didn't mean to kill him, Marcus."

Marcus dropped his sword and came over and put his arms around Tilly, comforting her.

"It's alright. That hit is for all of us."

He stared over her shoulder at the fallen body stretched out on the squalid floor of a Five Points tenement house, a gaping bullet hole in the middle of his chest.

The life of Jimmy Hubbard had ended where he began.

"The poor, broken son of a bitch," Marcus said to himself quietly, turning his head in pity.

On March 3, 1857, by order of a United States Supreme Court decision, all people of African descent were denied American citizenship and therefore any legal standing. If you were Black, you were powerless, a non-entity and non-human, according to federal law.

On a clear breezy day later that month, the packet ship, 'Victoria', departed New York harbor, bound for Le Havre.

Marcus Aurelius Coffin and Tilly Washburn stood in the stern, watching the land of their birth fade from view, first the gray, squared structures of the city, then the spire of Trinity Church. Then, slowly, the gray-green lands of North America sank below the horizon.

It was the last they would ever see of the nation that had denied them their humanity.

Epilogue

According to the scant records of these events, Marcus and Tilly arrived in Paris and set up housekeeping in the Rue du Bac flat. Marcus hired a private tutor to teach Tilly French, and once she was proficient in the language, she began voice lessons with the famous voice teacher, Pay Platt, at the school of the Paris Opera. They married in a state ceremony six months later and settled into a quiet life.

Marcus kept up his correspondence with Mr. Coffin, on both business and personal matters, and the firm flourished in the new French economic conditions of the Second Empire. Tilly gained a reputation as the American contralto, performing *spirituels nègre* in concert halls, and later in history was cited as the precursor to French appreciation for American jazz.

A year and a half later, a letter from America arrived from Saint Mary's County, addressed in a different hand. Marcus, suspecting the worst, opened it. It was from Mr. Coffin's new assistant, informing him that Mr. Coffin had died in his sleep on Saturday night, April 25. He was not apparently sick and he had been out working in the garden that same day.

As expected, Mr. Coffin left Marcus a substantial inheritance, including access to a sizable trust fund.

France was enjoying a period of prosperity under reign of Louis-Philippe. But Paris itself was becoming increasingly noisy and busy with the massive urban renewal projects and the clearances of the old neighborhoods as a part of Haussmann's state-ordered renovations. So, using the money from his inheritance, Marcus bought a small villa in Rambouillet and settled there.

Tilly founded a voice lesson school for children and occasionally performed in Paris, and often held musicales at home for the friends and neighbors from Rambouillet and Versailles.

Marcus assumed the role of country gentleman and in his later years, became reflective and comforted himself with walks along the local lanes, and sojourns by the riverside.

He died in Rambouillet in 1902.

As far as we know, Amanda never realized her dream to escape to France.

Made in United States
North Haven, CT
14 July 2024

54786631R00180